the Baby Doctor

Fiona McArthur has worked as a midwife for thirty years. She is the clinical midwifery educator in her rural maternity unit, and teaches emergency obstetric strategies while working with midwives and doctors from remote and isolated areas.

Fiona has written more than thirty romances, which have sold over two million copies in twelve languages. She has been a midwifery expert for *Mother and Baby* magazine and is the author of *Aussie Midwives*. She has also written the novels *Red Sand Sunrise*, *The Homestead Girls* and *Heart of the Sky*. She lives on a farm in northern New South Wales.

FIONA McARTHUR

the Baby Doctor

MICHAEL JOSEPH
an imprint of
PENGUIN BOOKS

MICHAEL JOSEPH

UK | USA | Canada | Ireland | Australia
India | New Zealand | South Africa | China

Penguin Books is part of the Penguin Random House group of companies
whose addresses can be found at global.penguinrandomhouse.com.

Penguin
Random House
Australia

First published by Penguin Random House Australia Pty Ltd, 2017

10 9 8 7 6 5 4 3 2 1

Cover design by Louisa Maggio © Penguin Random House Australia Pty Ltd
Text design by Samantha Jayaweera © Penguin Random House Australia Pty Ltd
Cover photographs: Woman by Getty Images/Ada Summer; Mother and baby by
Getty Images/Jessica Peterson; horizon by Shutterstock/detchana wangkheeree;
boab tree Cockburn Ranges by Shutterstock/Leah Kennedy; Derby Mudflats at
Sunset Release by Shutterstock/MelBrackstone.
Typeset in Sabon by Midland Typesetters, Australia
Colour separation by Splitting Image Colour Studio, Clayton, Victoria
Printed and bound in Australia by Griffin Press, an accredited ISO AS/NZS 14001
Environmental Management Systems printer.

National Library of Australia
Cataloguing-in-Publication data:

McArthur, Fiona, author.
The baby doctor / Fiona McArthur.
9780143799849 (paperback)
Subjects: Medical fiction.
Obstetricians—Australia—Fiction.
Country life—Australia—Fiction.
Secrets—Fiction.

penguin.com.au

This book is dedicated to the traits of human kindness and gentleness. We can all make a difference.

Chapter One

Sienna

The last triplet was always tricky. The beam from the operating-room light followed the flash of tiny limbs in the uterus like the final dancer on the stage. This baby did not enjoy the limelight.

Dr Sienna Wilson blew breath up under her mask to shift the wisp of blonde hair that had dared to escape from under her floral theatre hat during the struggle. Scooping the squirming passenger from his mother's previously crowded womb, she admonished the tiny face, 'I'm sorry, young man. It's your time to shine.' The staff in the theatre exchanged glances with relief.

'Born 0310.' Everyone heard the excitement in the scout nurse's voice despite the early hour, and there were a few smiles.

'A very determined young man,' Sienna murmured, as she handed the baby on towards the final team of neonatal specialists. Her clenched belly relaxed with the delegation of the last baby's welfare and she stretched her neck to see over the screen to the parents. 'Congratulations. Number three is a boy. And he's strong.' No one could see the relief on Sienna's face under her mask, but it was there along with the thrill of the chase. Worrisome wee people, babies, when they came too early.

She refocused her full attention on the operating field. She needed to ease the huge three-lobed placenta away from where it had nestled and nurtured the triplets for the past eight months.

When she was done, Sienna pointed with a finger to draw the attention of her junior. 'Looks like we've got all the fragments and membranes, but we'll get the midwives to check straightaway.' Her voice stayed low, instructional, inaudible to the parents. 'This over-distended uterus probably feels as bone weary as we do – if uteruses had bones, that is.'

Cilla, her registrar, nodded. She was a serious little thing, seven years younger than Sienna and a whole lot shorter, hence the nick-names Sienna pretended she hadn't heard pairing them as Snow White and Doc, but her work ethic endeared her to Sienna, who went on in a normal tone, 'Why do you suppose babies decide to knock on the uterine door at three a.m.? Why not wait until everyone else is awake?'

'Childish contrariness. Like my two-year-old.' Dave, the anaes-thetist, rubbed his stubbled chin. 'He thinks sleep is over-rated.'

'Poor Dave.' Her lack of empathy made Dave roll his eyes, because everyone knew Sienna considered combining family and career a recipe for exhaustion. Sienna glanced across at the neo-natal teams working on the three resuscitation trolleys.

She acknowledged with a nod the thumbs up from the over-seeing paediatrician. 'Good job, people,' she called. She listened with satisfaction to the soft, petulant kitten cries that drifted towards the big round light Sienna worked under. In her periphery of sound, she could hear the steady *blip, blip, blip* of the mother's heart monitor and the hissing gurgle of the wound suction gob-bling fluids.

With this team, she was enjoying her work in Sydney even more than she had in Melbourne. Life didn't get any better than this.

Cilla began to suture the first layer under Sienna's approving eye. She glanced at her boss. 'You were calm. Watching you deliver them made me nervous. How many triplet births have you had?'

'None myself.'

Dave laughed. Cilla looked confused.

Sienna closed her eyes for a moment. Not everyone enjoyed her sense of humour, or her teaching style, but she was working on it. And Cilla was learning at incredible speed. 'Sorry. Seven sets for other women. I can remember them all. Four sets in Melbourne and three sets in the six months I've worked here.'

She gestured to the personnel busy around the room. 'You need a good theatre squad – Dave doing his job brilliantly despite his lack of sleep.' Dave bowed. 'People moving in and out to take babies,' she continued, flicking her gloved hand at the paediatric ensemble. 'Scrub sister anticipating my every request before I make it.' She waved grandly at the friendly theatre sister she tended to team up with.

'Thank you, doctor. I must be clairvoyant.' The amusement in the sister's voice made Sienna thankful that someone else had a sense of humour despite the ungodly hour.

She watched Cilla insert another suture, dabbing at a swell of blood, all the while scrutinising the edge of the uterus. She needed to keep a close but discreet watch over Cilla's movements. 'It's like a ballet.' Sienna's voice became somewhat dreamy. She glanced up again to acknowledge the people, the skills, the technology that encapsulated her world. The urgency, decision making and intricacies of obstetrics fascinated her, filled her days.

3

The scrub sister asked, 'Any fun plans for the weekend, doctor?'

Sienna's endorphin high from the birth slipped down a notch like a loop of umbilical cord in a prolapse. Though she disliked to admit it, there was a *but* here . . .

But . . . she didn't have a life. Or life balance.

Ha! She pushed that thought away. Balance was something you did with a scalpel before you cut, not something you lived.

She ignored the question. It was the second time it had been asked this week. Scrub sister knew exactly what Sienna would do. Work. Research. Supervise. And that's if she wasn't on call.

Again, careful to maintain the sterile field, Sienna craned her head over the top of the screen and spoke to the parents. John and Lulu, a Fijian couple with tightly curled hair, pressed their heads together like two exotic flowers. They looked up. Of course they were dying to see their babies. Babies, who, no doubt, would be curly-tops, too.

'Congratulations. They all look healthy, and not as small as we feared. We'll get your babies to you one at a time as soon as we can, maybe even while we stitch you up.' Sienna thought she sounded more like her midwife sister, Eve, every day. They'd have to call her touchy-feely Wilson when she had those skills honed. Not likely.

She pulled back to where she felt more comfortable and dabbed again at the open abdomen. She really wanted to do the repair herself, but teaching was good for her soul. Good for Cilla's proficiency if Sienna did take a day off. Cilla could carry a lot of the load if she let her, she just needed more experience at surgery, and a chance to be the senior. She blinked a few times to clear her tired vision. Like that would happen.

Cilla's eyes creased in concentration.

'Great tie, there,' Sienna murmured. 'That angle is always difficult.' She directed Cilla's hand with a wave. 'Try from that angle.' Cilla adjusted and Sienna retreated.

'Perfect. We should be out of here by four a.m. Might even get two hours' sleep before clinic at eight.'

A long Friday later Sienna stifled one more yawn as she sat in her office doing paperwork and reminded herself that she'd hungered to be Director of Obstetrics at a tertiary centre.

She glanced out the window, where the sunset was pinking Sydney Harbour's skyline, and watched the tiny puff of low-lying cumulus drift by. Douglas had raved about the different formations at Christmas and she humoured him by remembering cloud classifications.

Her phone buzzed. She did not have time for anything else if she wanted to get home before dark for the first time this week. She scanned the caller ID and her eyebrows shot up in surprise. What? Now she had telepathy? Was Douglas in Sydney?

Today had been busy with a hiatus of highs. And now this. As if she'd conjured him. A telephone conversation with her sexy outback law enforcer, a friend with benefits. No doubt the theatre sister would approve. For Sergeant McCabe, she could make lots of time for fun.

'Douglas? Always a pleasure.' She could hear the throaty purr in her voice, something she found a tad embarrassing, though she couldn't seem to help it where Douglas was concerned.

'How are you?' His voice reverberated in her ear, the tone

deep and divinely Douglas. That hint of sincere concern about her welfare.

'I'm well. But,' she paused and her mouth tilted, 'you could come and feel my forehead.' Apart from when she'd first met him last year, there'd been only those two toe-curling connections. Last Christmas had been her best present ever. The second was Valentine's Day, when she'd been recovering from the flu – he'd shown her how the sergeant could heal her soul. Beautifully. Tenderly. Sensually.

She heard him give a masculine laugh. 'I'd love to feel your forehead.'

She wriggled in the chair, her smile spreading. A night in Douglas's arms is just what the doctor ordered. The thought of his hot mouth close to the end of the phone intensified the whole colour of her late afternoon – to a sultry, shiraz-coloured sunset. It was a shame she couldn't survive in the places he chose to live. Or he in hers. Her blood pounded faster than it had all day. 'Are you in town?'

'No, sorry.' Regret was clear but not helpful if he was a thousand kilometres away.

Sienna forced herself to shrug it off. 'So why call?' She could hear the subtle crossness in her tone aimed towards the source of her disappointment.

'Busy night?' A pause. 'Mother okay? Baby?' She heard the gravelly sympathy enter his voice.

How did he know? 'Babies, not baby. Triplets. Yes, yes and yes.' She suppressed the pang that Douglas might be the only one who cared about her physical and emotional health. Apart from her siblings, of course, but she never saw them, either. 'What can

I do for you?' This came out short, snappy. More at her own weakness than anything he'd done.

'I think we have a medical mystery out here.' His concern vibrated down the line.

This wasn't about her, then. Of course. She was not disappointed. Definitely not. 'And?'

'I think you could help,' he said in that simple, direct way of his. Like the man himself. No fancy frills.

He was a long way away, she reminded herself, and glared at the phone. Time counted as her most precious commodity. He knew that. 'You might remember it's a tad difficult to just up and leave a fairly new seventy-hour-a-week job and the whole department I'm responsible for.'

For a moment there was silence. One of Douglas's silences that Sienna had learned not to fill. Outside the window another cloud drifted by along with the time.

Finally, he said, 'A third family in town has a baby with a problem. It's only a small town.'

'What sort of problem?' she said, despite herself. She couldn't help it – it wasn't in her to ignore a mother or baby with a problem.

'Apparently,' the words came slowly, as if they hurt him to say, 'it's called microcephaly.'

Sienna sat back in her seat. A baby born with a small head, which often reduced brain capacity. An irreversible condition. 'Coincidence or familial?'

'The mothers are no relation to each other.' His voice firmed. 'And I don't believe in coincidence.'

'Typical police officer.' Sienna mentally weighed the causes.

'Is there any way the father could be the same person? Naughty farmers playing swapsy?'

He'd hate her saying that. She could imagine his grimace. 'Not these ladies,' he said, the scowl evident in his voice.

'Don't be a prude.' A delicious memory trickled across her skin. He wasn't a prude when he was naked. She fanned her face. 'Sorry. I see that kind of promiscuity occasionally in my job.'

'We need you to come and find out why.'

She kicked off her new red stilettos; something about talking to Douglas needed the grounding of her feet. She was trying for sensible. 'Sorry. I'm booked solid for the next two months.'

'You could do some poking around in the medical records like you did in Red Sand. Talk to the families and doctors involved.' His tone was neutral. Sexy, but neutral, sounding neither disappointed nor anxious. 'Come out for a week or so and check it out.'

She waited for it. Almost hoped. Why couldn't he say he wanted her to go all that way for him as well? Regardless of her desire for him, the idea of returning to those distances made her shudder. Even to fly commercially meant hours on the road at the end.

Sienna out of the city was like a fish out of water. She felt awkward in the outback, though didn't hate it like she once had when she'd coupled it with the father who had abandoned them as children for it. She'd got over that one. Of course her city mother and outback father had nothing to do with her reluctance to consider Douglas as a long-term partner. She dragged her thoughts back at the sound of his voice.

'Could be a perfect excuse to have you visit.' Was that the best he could do? Then his voice dropped an octave. 'Come look at some clouds with me.'

Sienna felt herself soften. Almost. He'd had that fixation with weather formations since he was a kid. She kept meaning to ask why. Someday she'd have to remember to do just that. She skipped her thoughts back to his request. 'Sadly, it doesn't work like that. You know the time investigations can take. I'm not a half-baked person. Everything needs quality assessment. Specific data. Unshakeable evidence.'

He gave her a moment to add more as she thought it through. 'Especially in the resource-poor outback. Everything takes so long because of the ridiculous distances.' She tapped the phone impatiently. 'It would take days to drive there. Before I know it, I could spend weeks out there. A month.'

'Then fly,' he reasoned.

'Nope. Too unreliable. Even when driving things can happen.' She shuddered at the thought of the dust and dirt and heat, and back here, well . . . There would be people other than herself in her plush office chair. Unless she lent it to Cilla while she played investigator in the outback. Cilla would manage and she wasn't yet competition. But it had been only six months since Sienna had made the move from Melbourne to Sydney. She'd rather not interrupt the flow of all her new innovations in the hospital. 'Nope,' she said, resolute. 'Not happening.' She tried not to dwell on the other side of the equation – the babies. Not to mention Douglas and long, sticky, languid nights. She needed to put out that fire. 'Sorry. I'm snowed.'

'Blanche wants your help,' he said.

Sienna's heart bumped against her ribs. Blanche Mackay. The seventy-something Annie Oakley of Western Queensland. Blanche who owned a goodly slice of the state and a diamond mine in the Kimberleys.

'That's not funny.' She closed her eyes. 'Not again? She's already dragged me from Melbourne. I'd hoped she wouldn't find me in Sydney.' Blanche could be part-Rottweiler. To give the woman her due, she did champion outback families, but Sienna wished she'd find someone else to solve her remote medical mysteries. Last time it had been a rise in the rate of stillbirths in Blanche's shire. As fast as humanly possible, Sienna had done what she could to put measures in place to help the climbing stats return to the previous lower rate. Thank goodness for the bonus of meeting Douglas or she would have gone completely mad there until she could hightail it back to her own world.

She assumed her new hospital wouldn't be so arbitrary in seconding her to a mad woman – no matter the carrot offered. Her voice dropped. 'Don't tell me she has another cattle station where you are?'

'The original Spinifex Station the town was named after. Right outside the settlement.'

Sienna picked up a seashell left by a patient's child and enclosed it in her palm. Trapped it. Like she probably was. 'I suppose she's had a good year in the diamond mines and can afford to bribe my administrator?'

'All of her cattle stations are thriving.' His amused lilt caressed her ear and Sienna's hand opened to stroke the shell. She listened dreamily as he said in his deep, sexy voice, 'We've had rain.'

'I know. I saw that on the news. I've been paying attention.' Since Douglas, she had noticed breaking drought and smiling farmers. She heard a bell in the distance and the phone muffled. Was there someone at his door? She could imagine Douglas's big hand blocking his voice. He'd go. He lived his job, which was only fair, she supposed. She lived hers, after all.

'I need to go. Think about it,' he said. Then more softly, 'Please.'

She wasn't committing to anything. 'Bye, Douglas.'

Before she knew it, Sienna's mind had galloped ahead. Surely Blanche wouldn't search her out here and expect her to drop everything again, she thought. Knowing the woman as Sienna did, something like microcephaly would fire her off like a gun. And that bullet would land smack bang on Sienna's desk. And ricochet around her life, causing major disruption. 'Damn it,' she said to the empty office. 'Who told Blanche?'

A sudden misgiving drew her brows together. Was it Douglas? She didn't know how, but she suspected that that was the truth of it. He'd tell Blanche because he knew she'd make it her next crusade and bribe Sienna's hospital to send her. Did he have an ulterior motive? Of course he did. The babies. But was he also trying to show her she could survive in the outback?

As she sat frowning, an internal email popped up on her computer and diverted her thoughts from blame. Her eyes narrowed.

Damn. Now she had an emergency meeting scheduled with the administrator of the hospital before she left that evening. She could guess what that would be about. She'd learned from last time about Blanche's fiscal persuasive power. And Sienna's possible lack of choice about going. At least Douglas had given her enough warning to consider how she would create some benefit for her department from the donation.

But that didn't change the fact that the outback pushed her way outside her comfort zone.

Chapter Two

An hour later Sienna stood on the top floor of the hospital outside the administrator's office. The administrator was the man who wielded the financial operations of this tertiary health service with scalpel-sharp precision.

She'd used the stairs to reach the floor up from her office, her stilettos clacking, and she'd passed one of her junior residents, who'd glanced at her shoes. What's with the awe? Couldn't people walk in high heels any more? She didn't understand why. Sure, she didn't perform surgery in six-inch heels, but she made sure she slipped out of those perfunctory crocs as soon as she was back in the change room. She loved the sound the heels made on the hard floors. They made her feel feminine and fearless. Which she needed to be now.

The office of power held the same views over the harbour Sienna's did, only higher, and the man who sat behind the desk exuded authority in an aura that made him seem bigger than he was.

Dominic Dauntry rose as she entered and gestured for her to

sit in a chair opposite the huge expanse of his mahogany desk. He studied her like a specimen under his stare-worthy monobrow.

When she was seated he said, 'Thank you for coming. I've had a request that you carry out an investigation in a town called Spinifex.' Dominic waited for an incredulous response, some response, but Sienna deliberately took longer to show one. Fools rushed in and she was nobody's fool.

'I see.' She stared back. Found her mind wandering which so wasn't like her. Monobrows were just plain wrong. Surely the man had a wife who could pluck a small gap in the hairline above his nose. Seriously? The silence lengthened.

When she didn't answer he said, 'Apparently, you have been near there before and would understand why you've been asked to go?'

'No. I hadn't heard of the place.' She shrugged delicately. 'But, yes, last year I was seconded to an outback Queensland town called Red Sand. That was for an investigation of poor neonatal outcomes.' Her lips firmed in a line before she said, 'My hospital requested me to carry out an analysis of the rise in stillbirths and pinpoint the cause.'

'I see. Well,' he paused, 'We would like you to do something similar again in Spinifex.' Unlike her previous boss, Dominic didn't seem to savour the power of telling Sienna what to do, but she could see that the promise of such a large donation from an unexpected source had created more animation than she'd seen before in his expressionless face.

Sienna smiled dryly. She must be getting wiser because her blood didn't boil like it had last time. No, she wasn't angry that now her new hospital thought that picking her up from her clinics and projects and teaching commitments and dropping her in out-back Spinifex was no problem – she chose to be coldly calculating in response. Sienna was a fast learner. The odds were she'd end up going. Blanche would make sure of it. If she was honest, it wasn't quite so bad because she knew what to expect. And, Douglas would be there. Though she wasn't telling Dauntry that.

Dominic wasn't the only person who wanted something. She'd already decided what she'd bargain for.

He stood up and went to the window to study the harbour. She stood too so he didn't stand over her.

'How much has Blanche offered, Dominic?' No doubt he would have heard how her last boss had won a state award, for facilitating advances in cancer research, when he spent his money from Blanche.

She watched his index finger lift to scratch a small brown-edged lesion she could see on his bald scalp. What was it with bald heads and bosses? She wished she'd worn higher shoes; she could have had a better look to see if it resembled a melanoma. Once a doctor always a doctor.

Dominic turned to face her. 'Blanche Mackay, yes.' He peered up at her then turned away, walked a few paces to even out their heights. She knew what he was doing because her old boyfriend had done that.

She thought briefly of that relationship with Mark, a trendy up-and-coming obstetrician she'd left in Melbourne. She couldn't go back to that kind of fairweather man. Not enough substance and heaven forbid, not enough morals when she compared him with Douglas. But Mark had been easy.

Douglas wasn't easy.

Douglas had too many morals. Mark and his kind would be like sickly diet cordial instead of Douglas's smooth single malt whisky. There was no comparison, even if her new affiliation constituted a very off-again-on-again relationship.

Dominic steepled his fingers and the movement brought her back to the present. Her brain seemed less tenacious to topic lately. She needed to stop that and concentrate on the moment.

He smoothed the sleeve of his impeccable suit. 'We have been offered generous research funds from our possible benefactor. Two million for your expertise.' At least he didn't rub his hands. Her last boss would have. 'She wants you and only you on the job. For as long as it takes. And she has the support of Queensland Health.'

Sienna spared a thought for her sister Eve's husband. Lex was the managing director of Mackay Holdings and the person who had to balance the books after his mother carved out huge chunks for her pet philanthropy projects. 'And my brief?'

'Discover why three Spinifex babies in the last month have been born with microcephaly.'

Sienna stilled as she thought about those babies. And their families. The problem did deserve an escalation of urgency. If she didn't go who would?

Dominic went on, oblivious to Sienna's lack of movement. 'She wants you to follow the women through the documents of their pregnancy, see if there is anything suspicious. Find a causative factor. She believes these women need you more than we do for a short time.'

Time was the unwelcome side issue. 'How short?'

He shrugged and Sienna felt his lack of concern. It wasn't his backside sitting in the dust and heat. And his department was safe.

'A couple of weeks should suffice. I would cap it at a month and want weekly updates. The intellectual resources of this hospital will be at your disposal, as well as the local obstetric departments.'

What local obstetric departments? She'd checked the position on Google Maps before she'd come up here, and apart from the town health centre, and the low-risk midwifery-led unit four hours away in Longreach, she'd be on her own. And apparently, Sydney Central could carry on without her. Lucky she'd trained Cilla as much as she had.

Dominic knew Sienna had already fostered two new cutting-edge, research-based medical advances. Their hospital saved lives. Made breakthroughs. She did feel a little more appreciated here, but it rankled that they could still be bought to let her go.

Dominic went on. 'This Mackay woman believes you have a nose for anything suspicious.'

Sienna almost sniffed at that. She had indeed become excellent at suspicious. Especially in Melbourne. The jury was out on this chief.

She sighed. The important point remained that babies had been affected and maybe she could help.

More to herself than to him Sienna began thinking out loud. 'It could be anything. Cytomegalovirus or toxoplasmosis during pregnancy or exposure to drugs, alcohol, toxins. Even PKU.'

Dominic nodded. 'Your brief, not mine.'

She held his gaze. 'It seems it is my brief. But I'd like to ensure a portion of the donation for my department.'

Dominic blinked, brushed off the polite cloak he wore as though he'd walked through a spider web, and swept it away to expose the hardcore business man beneath. 'What might that be?'

Her gaze didn't shift. 'I want to mentor and add to my team two more obstetric consultants. One has left and we need to share the load, but we need people who understand the concept of dedication and constant improvements.' She didn't add, *not just answering to the money men*. 'It's tiring being the lone voice for innovation.'

When he didn't comment she went on. 'I have two candidates that I think should apply. I'll recommend my registrar,' she said, because Cilla would soon have the balls to take these guys on and be ready to stretch herself. 'If we don't make a position for her we'll lose a promising obstetrician.' And that would be stupid.

Dominic nodded.

'The other is an O&G oncologist I met at a fundraising dinner with innovative,' she didn't say *radical*, 'ideas that could do with some major funding. I make no apology that they're both women, both young. The hospital would benefit enormously from their appointments.' The three of them would make a formidable team.

Dominic nodded, his eyes keenly watching her. She'd surprised him. Good. 'Send me the proposal,' he said.

'It will be with you before I leave.'

Sienna let herself into her secure harbour-view penthouse and paused to gaze across at the sparkling lights of the city. She loved this multimillion-dollar view. One she'd worked damn hard for.

Twelve weeks ago Douglas had stood here sharing the vista, his hard, rangy body dominating the room. Even in caring mode he'd looked big and powerful and so damned sexy. She smiled at the memory and slid out of her suit jacket. Stood there holding it by the expensive collar, holding the thought of Douglas. And frowned at the implausibility of their arrangement.

Below, the tiny fairy lights of the ferries scooted across the dark water between Circular Quay and the northern beaches. Beside the semi-circle sweep of the bridge, a tall cruise ship glittered like a tiara waiting for the next journey. Sienna's next journey would be a long way from the five-star luxury of that ship.

She considered the next week or two. And sincerely prayed to the shoe gods that it would not be a month. She also considered the thousands of kilometres she needed to traverse, not to mention the inconvenience.

With a sinking heart she turned her thoughts to microcephaly. Three separate families. If that town had another baby diagnosed, they'd need a full-scale enquiry.

If there was an additional case, at least she'd have some help. The whole escapade stood resource poor and barely viable. There'd be a fly-in fly-out midwife, but hopefully the health centre would have a full-time nurse, from whom she could find out about the antenatal records at least, maybe an office worker she could borrow to arrange meetings with the mothers and source all she'd need. Sienna would check the similarities, gestational markers, correlating facts and local knowledge of possible causes.

In her office at Sydney Central, there'd be Cilla, who could take over her work, trial the extra responsibility a consultant carried, be the backup for the more junior residents and registrars in their team and cover Sienna's on-call roster. She'd also be the back-end researcher if Sienna needed resources she couldn't access from the freaking boondocks. In Spinifex. The name conjured the image of wizened bent-legged drovers watching tumbleweed blow past the pub verandah. Despite the bleak picture she smiled; she would have Douglas.

She was not yet sure how she was going to insinuate herself into his house, and please if the stars aligned, his bed. He'd proved so darned old-fashioned and conscious of what a small town might expect of their police officer last time, but that was one of the carrots for this trip. The skirmish with Douglas. Could she win that battle?

They'd have to have that tricky discussion before she left. While she still had some negotiating power. The policeman could be stubborn and she needed to be smarter if she wanted the upper hand. She smiled at the thought. It was not something she usually had to fight for with other men.

Now, getting there – well she couldn't fly directly to the town. She'd checked the flight timetables. She could fly to Mount Isa or Longreach and then hire a strange car to drive the rest of the way. That would still take hours and hours. Sienna disliked flying at the best of times because flights often were cancelled, planes broke down, and she had no control over any of it. Especially when it involved more than one flight. If she was going to do much more of this outback sleuthing, she'd have to get her pilot's licence.

At least if she drove she'd be in charge. And, of course, the plus side of driving was the Mustang. She'd bought herself the new car because she'd come back slightly shattered from that last outback trip and she'd needed the reassurance that she was in control of her perfect life.

So, all the indicators suggested another road trip. At least this time she was leaving from Sydney not Melbourne, but the drive would still take days.

She'd googled that, too, and it was almost twenty-three hours' driving time. Two thousand one hundred kilometres. Near Winton in Queensland. Apparently, Winton had dinosaurs. Goody. She'd feel like a dinosaur by the time she'd finished that trek.

It would take two long days if she did around twelve hours of driving. Just like her normal days at work. With an overnighter in Roma. She'd catch up with the Flying Obstetrician and Gynaecologist while she was there. See what the FOG thought of the cluster of affected babies.

Did her hospital have any idea where they were sending her? She supposed it didn't matter if they did or didn't. She was going and at least the drive would be in comfort.

Her new car had been part of the whole new life she'd made since coming to Sydney. Six months since the esteemed professor who'd recognised her potential early and been the wind beneath her skyrocketing career, had retired and suggested she should try creating a new team in a new hospital to reach her full potential. It had been a good move.

So she'd ordered her new car before she left. Made that extra statement. It secretly amused her that her pony represented something a lot of men lusted after and couldn't have. It had arrived in Sydney from the States at the same time as she'd arrived from Melbourne. And it was worth every last import-tax dollar.

Her baby. In Lightning Blue, with long legs that could eat up the ridiculous number of kilometres between here . . . and Douglas.

At least the new design would give her more clearance over the rutted roads than her last car. Not that she'd factored the ground clearance when she'd bought it. That decision had been based whimsically on that enchanting cut out of light that had shone on the ground when she'd opened the door, shaped like the legendary pony that matched the emblem on the front of the car, and once she'd seen that, well, they'd had her.

This time, though, she would hire a satellite phone of her own for the duration because last time she'd not enjoyed unsupported medical disasters and she wanted to be able to rely on emergency contact if she needed help. Phone coverage could let one down. She'd discovered things had a way of happening in those out-of-the-way places that disorientated her and she liked, no, needed, some illusion at least of control. She didn't care if she never used the sat phone. She would have it as backup.

She didn't dislike the outback – apart from the fact that her father had left them to return to it, and she hadn't been able to do anything about that except cut him out of her life.

No, she acknowledged an inbuilt wariness and insecurity exposed because the outback shimmered into the distance under those big skies, and she felt insignificant out there, like a speck of sand in a vast desert, and she didn't like being a speck. Douglas said she needed to become a part of it and not try to keep herself aloof – but that wasn't part of her psyche.

Another reason she and Douglas were not suited long term.

She picked up her phone and rang Eve. Time to tell her little sister about the unexpected pleasure coming her way. Eve would laugh.

'Diamond Lake Station.' In Far West Queensland Eve's voice sounded as though she sat in the next room, not nearly two thousand kilometres away as the crow flew, and Sienna felt her mouth curve at the warmth in her sister's voice. Both women were above-average height and blonde, but Eve always looked bigger, stronger,

FIONA McARTHUR

softer, kinder, and Sienna knew it. Eve always sounded warm and welcoming. Typical midwife.

'You not in bed yet?' Sienna teased and a laugh drifted down the line.

'Close. It's almost dark.'

She could imagine Eve turning off the lights and crawling into bed with her hunk before the moon rose. 'And you do get up with the birds.'

'We do. Lovely to hear from you, Sienna. Is everything alright?'

Her brows knitted. 'Just because I've rung you doesn't mean there's a problem.'

Eve gave a small huff of amusement. 'Seeing as it's not my birthday, clearly something has happened.'

That wasn't true. She frowned and wondered for a moment. Maybe Eve did initiate the calls most of the time. 'I'm driving out your way.'

'Just passing?' Something in Eve's voice suggested this wasn't the first she'd heard about it. Sienna grimaced into the phone. Eve knew. Her sister had always had been a terrible liar.

'I'm not actually visiting you. Your mother-in-law has been donating again,' she said drily. 'Did you know?' She listened carefully.

There was a small pause before Eve sighed. 'I'm not surprised. She mentioned the congenital birth issues over at Spinifex and I knew she'd think of you first.' Then, hurriedly, she added, 'I did not suggest you.'

Sienna knew it. But why hadn't Eve told her? 'Thank you,' she said instead. 'Did you know Douglas is currently enforcing the law in Spinifex?'

22

This time the surprise came through very clearly. 'Reeealllly?'

'I'm hoping he'll let me stay with him.'

Eve released a huff of disbelief. 'You think that will happen?'

'It could?' She could hear the doubt in her own voice. She wanted definite – not doubt.

Eve said gently, 'Don't tell me Douglas won't be conscious of public opinion. He must be above reproach. You know what small towns are like, Sienna. It's the same here.'

'For goodness sake. He's a police officer, not a priest.'

'There're more similarities between the two than you would think when you're as remote as Spinifex. It'd be detrimental to the respect the town has for him if you moved in.' Eve's voice remained quiet, reasonable, and so non-judgemental Sienna couldn't understand how anyone could be so nice yet lay down the law.

'It's a pain.'

She darn well heard the smile in Eve's voice this time. 'You just have to marry him, that's all.'

'Like that's going to happen. He'd get claustrophobia in Sydney and I'd go mad in the outback.'

'At least when you visited you could have conjugal rites.'

They both laughed. Eve being arch amused Sienna, but a sudden image of Douglas when she'd seen him last appeared, filling her doorway just before he left, his beautiful mouth tilted at one corner, that final lingering kiss. She sucked in a breath and focused on the phone in her hand. 'He rang me first so at least I had some warning before I was shafted.' Sienna could hear the accusation in her own voice.

There was the unmistakable sound of Eve stifling another laugh. 'Not shafted. Seconded. And I think you're the perfect person for the job.' Before Sienna could jump down her throat she said, 'Remember, I was not the person who suggested you to Blanche.'

Sensibly, Eve directed them away from the rest of that conversation, but Sienna knew she would revisit why her sister hadn't mentioned it when they were face to face. 'So when are you coming?'

'I'll leave first thing Tuesday morning and stay in Roma for an overnight break. So I should arrive in Spinifex before dark on Wednesday.'

'That's a lot of driving. Will you drop in on me or Callie?' Eve was ever the peacemaker. Sienna admired her sister – and her half-sister. It wasn't Callie's fault that their father had preferred Callie's mother to Sienna's.

'Of course.' She'd detour on the way back. 'I'm planning a flying visit to you both on the home run. I'll stay one night at yours.'

'I'm glad,' Eve said, sounding relieved. 'And you could always stay and spend another night with me.'

If she had to go to the outback, Sienna would get home as soon as she could. 'No. I need to be back here for interviews.' A tinge of persuasion slid into her voice. 'You could come and help me at Spinifex?'

There was a short pause. 'Lex wants me to stay home. Just until I get over this nausea.'

Sienna's ears pricked up. 'Nausea? Are you pregnant?'

'You're such an obstetrician.'

She felt the pang of another thing her sister hadn't told her. 'How many weeks?'

'Twelve.'

Wow. Almost a third of the way there. Eve would be an amazing parent. 'I can so see you as a mother.' *Unlike me*, Sienna thought.

'And you.' Eve said, as though she had read her thoughts. 'You would be fine. *Hard but fair.*'

They both laughed. Their mother's favourite saying. Sienna would be like their ma. She didn't have a maternal bone in her body. Sienna just wanted mothers and babies to have good births. She had no desire herself to take a kid home. 'While you will spoil your children with love.'

Eve sniffed. 'You can't be spoiled by love, Sienna.'

'Sure you can.' She shrugged, even though her sister couldn't see it. 'You could grow up expecting it everywhere. And we all know that isn't the way it works out there in the big, wide world.'

'Sienna —' Eve started, but she cut her off.

'I'll be able to show you the new car when I see you.'

'You've sold the sports car, haven't you? I think Lex's daughter had her eyes on that.'

'See? Spoiling. And yes. I'll show you the beast when I get there. See you in a couple of weeks if not before. Say hi to the hunk.' Then she disconnected.

Sienna was left feeling loved and strangely quiet. Eve's warmth and serenity seemed to have become even deeper, and her marriage to Lex seemed so perfect, Sienna tamped down an insidious envy.

She flicked the remote on the Bose sound system and the Rolling Stones crooned to her about the lack of satisfaction out there as she removed her shoes. By the end of the song, she grinned at herself in the hall mirror. She took after her mother. Stilettos and city living – and a love of Jagger.

She turned back to her kitchen and pulled out a container of yoghurt. Sprinkled berries on top and a dollop of nuts and then dug her spoon in. As she chewed thoughtfully, she glanced around the state-of-the-art kitchen she never used. This time she would take her coffee machine. It would fit in the mid-size new blue hard-shell case. Thank goodness for the big boot because at least she knew what to expect in the coffee department.

Still, beneath the superficial props of control, she knew that once she hit the wide, desolate distances between towns, there were a lot of things she'd have no power over.

Chapter Three

Maddy

Madison Locke took a deep breath and steadied her shaking hands on the kitchen sink. And saw the bitten nail beds. This wasn't her. She was twenty-one years old, not a child.

The real Madison had backpacked all over Europe, had managed to disentangle herself from some sticky situations, but here, back in the country of her birth if not the state, in this dusty outback town – she'd thought she'd found love.

If this was love, then why was she soooo sad lately? That voice in her head questioned her again.

Trying to cook with Jacob leaning against the kitchen wall, watching, arms folded, made the nausea crawl around inside her stomach and there wasn't any room for that.

His hard brown eyes, eyes that had made her smile a year ago, held that distant sneer he seemed to have permanently acquired since he'd had his accident and so badly broken his leg. At first, a year ago, this built and handsome truck driver with a swooning ability to sing country songs had made her feel sexy, almost pretty, something she'd never felt before, and he'd said he was falling in love with her.

But he hadn't sung anything lately. Not since the accident. When he'd moved to the outback town to recover six weeks ago, because he'd inherited a ramshackle house, she'd left her friends and gone with him. To help until he could manage on his own. But it hadn't turned out like she'd thought it would. When they'd first met, he'd been all over her, but since coming to Spinifex it seemed he couldn't stand the sight of her. Which turned out to be lucky.

She looked down at the pot and realised the scrambled eggs had begun to stick and then the whey began to separate.

She panicked, lifted the cheap pot that would be a devil to scour-clean later, and the smell of burning food made her head turn sharply. 'The toast.'

Jacob pushed past on his crutches and violently hit the toaster eject button. Two charcoal bread relics flew up and landed with a crackle on the bench amidst curls of smoke.

She put down the pot to grab them and he put out his hand and pushed her away from the bench. 'Leave it. You're useless. I'll do it myself. Just go to work early.'

'No. No. I'll do it.' She could feel the sting of tears. If he'd just left her alone to prepare their tea.

Instead, he leaned on his crutch and pushed her again, harder this time, and she lost balance and fell backwards against the wall, slammed her shoulder into the corner of a cupboard, and cried out.

His face darkened. 'Bloody hell, Maddy. Stop making me lose my temper.' He glared at her. Stepped closer to help her find her balance, and then losing control again he began to shake her until her teeth rattled. 'You drive me insane. You have to stop making me mad. Doing stupid things.'

His eyes looked different. More out of control. Scary. Her

sudden fear made her rethink her situation. As if, however briefly, the cloud of uncertainty had lifted to allow her to see plainly. Terror that she could have hit her stomach during the fall cleared some of the black stickiness she'd seemed to be sinking into like treacle. Made her reconsider. Should she be looking for a time to tell Jacob their news? Or looking for a way to stop him finding out? Really contemplate getting away before . . .

Though goodness knew where she'd run to from here.

Jacob looked at her and then turned away in disgust, and her soul shrank a little more. He scooped the pain medication from the window sill behind the sink and swung away into the lounge with the bottle jammed in his shirt pocket. 'Forget it. I'm not hungry. Throw it out and then go.'

Maddy squeezed her eyes shut and breathed in slowly. Quiet. If she just stayed quiet. Silently, she began to clean up the mess. In fifteen minutes the kitchen lay immaculate. The tea towel folded so. The bench gleaming like he wanted.

There was just the rubbish to deal with. Then the lid of the garbage bin in the kitchen clanged as she lifted out the heavy garbage bag and she sucked in a quick breath and froze.

'What the hell. I was almost asleep then!' Jacob's voice rose along with Maddy's pulse rate, the shout from the lounge lifting the hairs on the back of her neck. She nervously backed away from the noise she'd made and the voice from the other room. Edged towards the back door.

'Come here!'

Reluctantly, she changed direction and eased her head around the doorframe into the lounge. He'd stiffened in front of the television, his hard eyes wild, turned in her direction, long fingers gripping the edge of the lounge as if he was digging them into her arm.

The saving grace was the plaster-covered leg that was elevated on the scratched coffee table, which had stopped him from rising.

Tears trickled out the side of her eyes and she tried to wipe them away one-handed, but it was too late. He'd seen them.

'Crying again?' Jacob ground his teeth. 'Stop being depressed,' he growled. 'It's pathetic. Get over it.'

She was trying. But telling him that only made him angrier. And he said he loved her. Sometimes. Nobody had said that for a long time, and she wanted someone to love her.

Maddy pushed away the dark thoughts and lifted her head. Nervously checked that her long ponytail was secure.

'I'm sorry. I'm going now,' she whispered softly and pulled her head back, slipping away before he could call her. She escaped out of the house, closing the wooden door with exaggerated care. Then the screen. Jacob wouldn't like it if it made that loud squeaking sound. She kept meaning to borrow some lubricating spray from work to fix the squeal of dry metal and doorframe.

Bizarrely, when she stepped out, instead of causing discomfort the hot afternoon air seemed to protect her in its heavy dry cloak as it wrapped around her.

It was so much easier to breathe outside the house, despite the bouncing waves of heat reflecting off the big refuse bin as she quietly deposited her load and eased the lid down silently.

She stepped onto the concrete path towards work. How had she come to this point where she was creeping around to keep the peace?

With another moment of clarity, Maddy saw how far she'd

come down in the last three months, even before they'd come here, how on edge she'd grown whenever he was there, which, apart from her time at work, was all of the time since his accident. It had been so much better when Jacob had been driving the truck for a few days, and fun when he came home for the next couple.

She knew it must be frustrating, the constant setbacks, delays in healing under the plaster, and she had tried to make it easier for him as time dragged on, but the longer it took the less she could do right. Or do to help. She seemed to make everything worse.

Unconsciously, her hand slid protectively over her belly again and she cupped her secret.

There never seemed to be a good time to tell Jacob. She hoped he wouldn't be too angry. Hoped she said it right when the time came. She felt the self-blame and self-loathing trickle over her at the fragility of that hope.

And why hadn't she told Jacob that they were pregnant? Seriously pregnant. Like almost ready to have the baby pregnant. Maybe a week or two to go? And she couldn't tell anyone else until she told him.

So it wasn't just Jacob. She'd dug such a deep hole for herself in leaving it this long, she hadn't told anyone when she'd grasped how blind she'd been not to know. Just nodded, agreed with Jacob when he'd told her she was getting fat. Not that there was anyone else to tell, with the last of her family across in Perth, except maybe her new boss.

But she might lose her job if she told Alma. And she didn't want Alma to think badly of her as well.

In the last month, since she'd realised her stupidity about her pregnancy, her time at home had become steadily more fraught,

Jacob's temper rising more quickly every day, and now he bruised her when he held her. Shook her violently when he was angry. She felt like she'd go mad with the humiliation and confusion.

The confusion that hadn't been a part of her life before the accident. Before her happy world had turned into cloying suffocation that swirled and made the tears sting.

She brushed away the new tears. She'd never been a weeper. She quickened her pace. Work always made her feel better. Made her feel stronger. Safe. Which was funny considering she worked in a pub. A job Jacob didn't like her having, but someone had to bring home money.

Thank goodness for the Desert Rose Hotel.

Chapter Four

Sienna

Late Monday night, in her eyrie of an apartment after a twelve-hour day, Sienna had successfully rescheduled her commitments at the hospital into Cilla's hopefully capable hands.

She probably should have waited a day or two more and had less of a rush, but the faster she left the faster she'd be back. Or at least that was what she told everyone else. It had absolutely nothing to do with the man she was about to call.

Now for the tricky part. Funny how tackling Douglas had her behaving like a pubescent kid in a teen movie.

Her mind trekked to the most recent time he'd arrived at her apartment. Just after she'd come down with that revolting flu, and though recovering, she'd had that flat, miserable feeling of self-pity that could come after a particularly debilitating virus. He'd phoned. Asked her what she'd been doing for Valentine's Day. If she hadn't been so sick she would have laughed.

Douglas had been on the other side of the city for a conference, and later that night the hero had appeared at her door and proceeded to look after her like her own private nurse. With benefits.

He had also brought that most delightfully quirky metal emu for her. Emus were one of the few things that had endeared the outback to her. She looked across now to the white marble mantle and she smiled at the odd little figure perched jauntily on the cold marble.

Douglas had even scrambled her eggs, bubbled her bath, and ever so gently washed her hair. Then taken advantage of her very sweetly until she had decided that being sick wasn't so bad after all. Her mouth curved at the memory. Nobody had ever nurtured her like that. Then again, she'd never allowed anyone to.

Of course, after, he'd driven away and she'd returned to the maelstrom that was work with only the occasional reminiscent smile to the north.

That must have been just before Douglas started the new position, which she realised now would be the one at Spinifex. It must have been no simple drive for an outback policeman to travel from the extreme western edge of the city, navigating the one-way streets and entry and exit motorways, to care for her. For one night. But what a night. She fanned herself at the images flitting through her mind's eye.

Her chest tightened as she picked up the phone. Good things happened when Douglas came to her town. Hopefully she could do the same for him.

But Sienna in Douglas's town sat in a totally different universe and she knew it. She'd needed that Pinot Noir of Dutch courage and a big breath before she'd hit the 'call' button. Her stomach fluttered like a girl's as she waited for him to pick up.

'Spinifex Police Station. Sergeant McCabe.' The rough timbre of masculine certainty and steady reassurance came over the phone, and Sienna could remember clearly the depth of his compassion for those he helped. Oh my, she loved his voice. Those shoulders. The sexiness. The way he held her. And the way he cared for her.

'I'm looking for the Spinifex Brothel?' Her voice took on a low vibrancy she didn't know she had.

'I'm sorry, madam. You have the wrong number.' Douglas dashed her hopes, not missing a beat. 'And the wrong town.'

He knew it was her. Damn. She'd blown it. In her mind, it had seemed like an amusing way of introducing a tricky subject. The first night she'd had off call for a month and one glass of wine had wiped out her brain.

She abandoned a bad idea and set down her glass. 'Douglas. Please may I stay with you?'

'Sienna. No.'

She tried not to plead. 'We are old friends. Surely nobody could complain about that. We could have separate rooms.' Not that she would stay in hers.

'It wouldn't look right.' Calm and reasonable Douglas. 'People expect certain standards from me. And . . . It's not happening.' There was that note of implacability. Geez.

'You do realise I haven't slept with anyone since you were here.'

After a long, pointed silence, he said, 'I'm not sorry to hear that.' This was Douglas at his driest.

At least that made her smile. 'So can we get a chaperone?' A deaf one, preferably. 'I need to at least spend some time with you. It helps if I can talk about things with someone.' Now that was a straight-out lie.

'You are extremely self-sufficient.' She could hear the smile in his voice. Knew before he spoke that she'd crashed and burned. 'I don't believe that.'

Not fair. 'I can't believe that I am almost begging to sneak into your bed and you're knocking me back.'

'Neither can I.' This was said very quietly and Sienna's heart jumped. She mentally rubbed her hands together.

'Meet me in Roma or Charleville and we could stay the night together and drive back in convoy?'

She heard him sigh. Softly. 'I'm on duty. On call twenty-four hours, seven days a week and I cover sixty thousand square kilometres.'

Duty schmuty. The guy was too much. Back to his residence. 'So? A chaperone?'

'Who did you have in mind?' he said with extreme reluctance. 'One of your sisters?'

Nah, that wouldn't work. 'Eve's pregnant with morning sickness. And Callie can't.' Her half-sister had a stepson and a one-year-old daughter. 'What about a housekeeper?'

Douglas had recovered from his weakness. 'Stay at the Desert Rose. Alma will look after you.'

She felt like stamping her foot. 'No. I do not want to sleep in a smelly, noisy pub with a shared bathroom.'

'The Desert Rose Hotel is immaculate and if it gets too noisy I'll quieten them down,' he soothed, always the voice of reason.

'I want to stay with you.' Now she just sounded childish. Not something the brisk and efficient Dr Wilson was known for, but damn it, Douglas unbalanced her. She didn't know why and, usually, she was too busy to think about it.

'Can't do.' She heard the finality in his statement and her heart sank. 'We'll talk about other ideas. When do you arrive?'

She pulled the phone away from her ear and glared at it. Put it back. 'Wednesday afternoon.'

'It might be a little noisy at the pub.'

Was he giving her an in? 'Right. I can stay the first night with you. Excellent.'

She heard that smile in his voice and he should not be smiling. 'No. But I will see you after work.'

That's it, she was over it. 'You might see me, but I won't be talking to you.' Sienna disconnected the call and huffed. She glared at the red wine in the bottom of her glass. 'Whose dumb idea was that about the brothel?'

Late Wednesday afternoon, after a long day of driving from Roma, more hours of red dirt and bare horizons, Sienna slowed to read a sign on the way into the last outback town before her destination. One more to go.

'For the next 120 kms you are in the land of the Min Min. This unsolved mystery is a light that at times follows travellers for long distances – it has been approached but never identified.'

Sienna huffed in disbelief, ran her tongue over dry lips and took one hand off the wheel to pick up her water bottle. Those Min Min lights were probably floating around looking for water.

Or sex. That made her think about Douglas and his stupid scruples. Maybe the Min Min was a female ghost doomed to never sleep with her policeman lover. She huffed in disgust again but her mouth twitched.

An hour later she reached the turn that led to the town of Spinifex. Thank goodness because right now her concentration span hung by one of those strands of spiderweb she could see on the wire fences outside town. She drooped, almost too tired to drive safely, even though it was just on six p.m. Who would have thought two days of driving could be more tiring than twelve hours in a hospital delivering babies. And the fact that she hadn't slept well in Roma hadn't helped – too blinkin' quiet.

She slowed down to the speed limit. Imagine if she was caught speeding by you-know-who! She drove grumpily over the bridge of another dry and cracked watercourse. She had to admit the soaring gums were majestic, but it looked more like an orange clay road than the river the sign claimed.

She sighed at the 'Welcome to Spinifex' sign. Population three hundred. The town spread before her like an outlined noughts-and-crosses plot on the red-earth bareness.

Yes, well. At least there were some small gum trees on the street, and two strips of short straight tar roads at right angles, but the edges of the town disappeared into the brick-coloured distance.

Dotted houses squatted in the sun on red-dirt petticoats, and for those owners who didn't shirk intensive labour there was even the occasional tinge-of-green grass underskirt but mostly the roads petered out into more red dirt. Delightful. Not.

She followed the sign to the police station at the western edge of town and spotted the two tiny, neat buildings and blue sign with weary relief.

Her glance in the rear-view mirror reassured her as she touched up her lipstick. Okay, she looked tired, but at least her makeup had stayed in place. She climbed out of the car and stretched, tilting her head from side to side, and flexing her shoulders. A cold drink would not go astray and she hoped Douglas had one waiting for her. She looked up at the huge expanse of azure sky. Not a cloud to be seen. The sky lay empty, and like the building, silent. She sincerely hoped that wasn't an omen.

Across the road lay a park, bare-earthed and deserted like the one out of *Terminator*, a swing hanging limply. It lay there perfectly still. She looked back at the quiet building, and in front of the office a sign proclaimed, 'If the police station is unattended . . .' It better not be. She had no desire to phone Mount Isa communications as directed. Although, triple zero might be tempting. Surely he'd be here.

She pushed open the door to the police station, heard a bell ring in a back room, which must have been small because the whole building was the size of her car space at home, and waited in anticipation for some appreciation at her arrival.

'Hellloo?' There was no response.

Nothing. Sienna sighed and pushed her way out of the building again. She opened the gate to the matching, slightly larger house next door and walked up the cracked concrete front path. There was no grass, nor was there any attempt at a garden remaining. A white piece of paper hung limply, stuck on by a tack to a white board. '*Glad you arrived safely. Had to go on a call. See you at pub later. D.*'

Sienna rested her head on the door and swore softly under her breath.

Chapter Five

Maddy

Maddy paused on the footpath outside the police station residence for a few seconds. She watched the stranger rest her head on the policeman's door, but she couldn't stand there looking for too long. She needed to be at work in a few minutes.

The flash car jarred amidst the red dirt and straggly weeds at the side of the tar. The woman, blonde and elegantly tall, looked as if she'd stepped out of one of those fashion magazines Maddy had loved to find on seats in airports when she'd been backpacking.

That world seemed like a lifetime away. Unconsciously, Maddy smoothed her worn pair of loose trousers and shapeless, long-sleeved top. The one that hid the bruises and the belly. Her decent jeans hadn't fitted her for ages, but she wished she'd squeezed into them today. She must look like the bag lady Jacob said she did. Today's not-so-subtle jeer echoed in her ear, and her hand tightened on the satchel swinging on her arm.

Before she could drop her eyes in shame and move on, the woman at the door slumped in frustration and tapped her forehead on the door.

Sympathy rose in Maddy's chest. Poor thing. Her voice crossed the fading afternoon heat between them. 'You right there, Miss?'

The woman turned and Maddy saw the face. The startling blue of her eyes, her long, aristocratic nose. Shining blonde hair that had been straightened into a perfect fall to her shoulders. She also saw the arched brows and fresh lipstick and the valiant attempt to push an unsuccessful smile onto her face. Maddy recognised the facial twitch from her own mirror.

'I'm fine,' the woman said. 'Just tired from driving. I don't suppose you know when Sergeant McCabe might be back?'

Ahh. The Baby Doctor. 'He left this morning. Shouldn't be too long, now. Are you the doctor?'

Maddy saw the hesitation. Sensed the fleeting hint that the last thing this woman needed was a medical discussion of some ailment. Maddy would never do that in the street.

She said, 'Not a general practice doctor, I'm an obstetrician, so not much good with the other sort of illnesses. I'm here to do research, that's all.'

Research only. That wouldn't be any help to Maddy, then. She'd thought she might have been able to make an appointment, her being a baby doctor. That fleeting ray of hope shrivelled in the sun like any other hope she seemed to try to hold onto lately. 'Here to find out why the babies have small heads?'

'To try. Yes. News travels in small towns.' The woman nodded and Maddy saw the tiredness swamp her again. For a moment she thought she'd crumple onto the dusty path. 'I don't suppose you know where I'm staying?'

Maddy shifted out of the sightline to the woman's car. She should get out of the sun. Maddy was used to it and even she could feel the hot sting on her skin. 'At the Desert Rose. Alma's expect-ing you.' She pointed to the only two-storey building in town. 'It's cooler up there.'

'Thanks.' Sienna dug her keys out of her handbag. Looked up briefly and offered the fake smile again. 'Sorry. What was your name?'

'Maddy.' Maybe she should have said Madison?

'Thank you, Maddy. Sienna Wilson. Perhaps I'll see you around.'

Maddy smiled with the first drift of amusement she'd had all day. 'Most likely. I work at the pub.'

The woman called Sienna blinked. 'Oh.' Then she indicated her car. 'Did you want a lift?'

Maddy glanced down at her old joggers, well-coated in red dust, imagined sitting next to this perfect woman inside her perfect car. Smudging it.

'No, thanks. I'd rather walk. You should park around the back. At the edge of the parking area there's a small carport everyone fights over to keep their car out of the sun. First in best dressed.'

The smile the woman gave her felt like a big shiny present. 'Thanks.'

She watched her drive off slowly. Shook her head at the bulky muscle-car look of the vehicle and the red dust clinging to the shiny blue paint.

Then, as she took her first step, the baby kicked and moved. After that the tightness crept across her belly and her fingers slid down silently to where her skin lay rock hard under the baggy top she wore. The hardness would come and go for a while and then it would drift away.

Like yesterday and the day before.

She glanced at her cheap watch. She needed to get going. At least she had a job. Her work at the pub and Alma's appreciation seemed to be the only things keeping her normal. Her job gave her the chance to talk to someone other than Jacob, because he didn't like her going out when she wasn't at work.

In the past, Jacob had been a little rough, a few jerking grabs, a shake, more ungracious than her memories of her dad, but she'd put that down to Jacob being brought up the hard way. Alma had said his uncle had been a hard man. But Jacob had never been violent, except for that first time after the accident when he'd slapped her and she'd been so shocked.

Though after Tuesday it had improved slightly again, so maybe it would be okay. But she suspected that it wasn't going to get better and she couldn't pinpoint how she'd managed to get herself into this situation. It had all started so well. She really did need that plan to get away.

The tears sprang to her eyes again and she brushed them away impatiently. Sook. Her hand stole to cover her belly as she began to walk again towards the pub. She'd been glad the clock had turned to worktime.

And maybe, just maybe, in a couple of days when she knew her better, she might be able to talk to the doctor about her baby.

Chapter Six

Alma

Alma Toms had turned sixty-nine yesterday, but she hadn't told anyone. She glanced at the low-slung wood-framed mirror on the wall of the Desert Rose Hotel and adjusted her peaked sun visor. Her face was like one of those dry creek beds at the edge of town, all lines and cracks in ochre brown, with crow's feet at the corners of eyes that'd seen too damn much. White hair notwithstanding, she didn't look too bad for her age. But, she'd thought she was going to have a heart attack during that last race.

The four-thirty gallops on the telly had been so close – she'd only just missed out on that Big Six again. Hooley dooley, that number six at Doomben had been a ripper. She'd only lost by a nose. She'd jagged four long-odd wins today. More for her savings.

Once, a few years ago and not long after Shirl had died, she'd won that six-race haul by sticking to her system of the horses with the best names and longest odds. She had a tidy bundle stashed away in the bank as a result of it. She used to think she'd move into a big house on a beach somewhere and kick back with her feet up – imagine. Then she'd thought of the crowds of people in the city and shuddered. She couldn't afford an island of her own, so maybe she'd just stay here for a while longer. Though there was that nice young couple if she ever wanted to sell.

She straightened her apron. She wasn't going anywhere. This was her pub. Her home. Her life. She glanced at the magnificent stairway that cut the building in two. The bar was on one side, the dining area on the other. She'd fallen in love with that sweep of stepped carpet thirty years ago and she still loved to run her hand down the polished mahogany rail every morning when she came downstairs to start work. All the way from England in a ship, that wood had come.

The heat was a bitch, but she'd lived in the outback forever and this was a nice sensible town. And those occasional winnings were a tidy nest egg. Just in case.

Her drifting thoughts broke off when she saw the smooth arrival of the dusty blue car as it pulled into the yard. She watched it park under the far carport. Nice to see the awning used by a decent car for a change.

A tall blonde climbed slowly out of the driver's side and Alma's eyebrows lifted. She took another look at the vehicle and saw the class beneath the dust. One of her regulars was into muscle-car magazines. Had to be the baby doctor. There'd be some discussion around the bar over that beauty parked at the Spinifex Hotel. And the woman who'd arrived in it dressed in high heels and tight skirt for crikey's sake. Bet she had a matching jacket to go with it. Yep, the woman leaned in and retrieved one to sling over her pinstriped shirt. Alma snorted and couldn't remember the last time she'd seen someone in a jacket. Last funeral maybe?

Lips twitching, she moved from behind the bar. Better open the side door for her only guest. Blanche Mackay had paid her already to 'meet the needs of the doctor'. Alma just hoped the woman could help those poor mites.

She watched a pale hand lift a bag from the boot, a blue and shiny hard-shell case reflecting beams in the sunlight. Flash suitcase as well. Alma didn't judge people, their lives were their own, but she loved a gossip. There'd be plenty to gossip about for the next short while, Alma thought, mentally rubbing her hands.

The front door creaked behind her and she glanced back to see that Maddy had arrived for work.

Alma had hired many barmaids and backpackers over the years, but she'd never seen as much potential as she saw in young Madison. Medium height, an armful of plumpness that suited her pretty face, though her real weight was hard to tell with the dark baggy clothes she always wore, and hinted at the no-nonsense hard-working country stock from WA. Ruby-red ponytail and a dusting of pretty freckles suited the surprising sense of humour that appeared when you least expected it.

Though, Alma thought darkly, she had her doubts about that man of hers having any sense of humour. Sure, he was a looker, but he had no real wit aside from the occasional smart-arse remark after a few drinks. His uncle had been quick with his hands before he died. So Alma worried a bit about Maddy. If anybody could pick it, the publican could. Especially one who'd lived through what Alma had. But there was nothing she could do until Maddy asked for help.

She suspected why the girl wore long-sleeved shirts. Alma used to wear clothes that covered her arms and legs. Soon she'd ask a few pertinent questions, but so far Maddy had been reserved and Alma was being unusually patient as she waited for the right time. There was a right time for everyone and she wanted to make sure Maddy knew she was here for her when that time arrived.

'Early again?'

Maddy smiled shyly at her and Alma smiled back. 'Run up and switch the aircon on in room one, will you? I'll get the new guest to sign in.'

'Sure thing.' Maddy put down the satchel in her hand and scurried up the steps.

The new guest came in on a wave of hot air and almost palpable exhaustion. Alma's brows rose at the fragility of others. Poor, dehydrated flower. It wasn't like the doc had ridden a horse from Sydney – geez, she'd just sat in a car. Then, Alma caught herself. Don't judge. Maybe she'd been delivering babies till all hours. Who knew?

'Welcome to the Desert Rose Hotel,' Alma said. 'You look like you could do with a nice cold lemon squash.'

The woman sighed. 'That would be excellent.'

Nobody said 'excellent' around here, Alma thought. Except maybe Blanche Mackay.

'Thank you.' The doctor put down her case and pulled up the handles and glanced around.

Alma didn't understand why she hadn't done that before. If the case rolled, why the dickens would she carry it all the way across the carpark? 'Don't the wheels work?' she couldn't help asking.

'I didn't want to drag it across the dust.' She straightened as she said it. A fine-boned woman with straight-cut blonde hair and direct blue eyes that looked weary but fiercely intelligent, and when she did lift her head she stood a good three hands taller than Alma. Alma was used to looking up at others, but this one was tall for a woman.

'I can't wait to relax and take you up on that squash.'

Right, then. Alma pushed the big leather-bound guest book and a pen at the other woman to sign in and turned to grab a cold glass out of the fridge. 'Blanche Mackay has paid and all food and drink has been taken care of.'

'Has she,' she said with dry sarcasm.

Alma's mouth twitched again and she returned with the drink and a healthy curiosity by the time the woman had written Dr Sienna Wilson and a Victorian phone number. Not giving out the mobile, Alma noted with amusement. It wouldn't do her any good. There wasn't much service anyway. When her guest settled in, in a couple of days, Alma had some women in town who needed a Virginia doctor. They were the ones too shy to show the male RFDS doctors who flew in. But she'd hold that thought until she'd checked the lie of the land with this newcomer.

'Blanche likes to dot her i's. I'm to meet your needs,' Alma said, tongue-in-cheek. Maybe the doctor had been railroaded? Not an uncommon occurrence around the Mackay matriarch. 'There you go, love. And your room is at the top of the stairs, last room on the right.'

Maddy came down the stairs again and Alma pointed to the bag. 'You want Maddy to carry your bag up for you?'

The woman glanced at the girl and smiled as if she knew her. 'No. Thanks, Maddy. I'll manage.'

Now that was friendly, Alma thought and noted the smile Maddy gave the woman. 'You two met?'

It was the doctor who answered. 'Outside the police station. Maddy gave me directions.'

Alma snorted. 'There's only one direction around here. Straight up the street.'

The lemon squash disappeared and Sienna put the water-beaded glass down with another heartfelt sigh. 'That was good. And thanks to Maddy, I didn't get lost.' Then she picked up the case and turned towards the stairs.

Alma spoke to her back. 'One thing.'

Dr Sienna Wilson paused and turned at the bottom step.

'When you need food, just ask. Either Maddy or I will cook, and the times don't really matter long as it's not after ten p.m.'

The doctor nodded. 'That's very kind of you. Thank you. I'll know more when Sergeant McCabe returns.' Then she frowned. 'Do you have a nurse, or health clinic person in town?'

Alma screwed up her face and shook her head. 'Not now. Two days a week, Monday and Wednesday mornings and after lunch for a couple of hours. They haven't been able to replace the full-timer who left. But the RFDS doctor comes every second Monday and the baby health nurse comes alternate Mondays. She's the midwife, too. You have to make an appointment to see them. They get busy. Unless you're dying.' Alma decided to test the water. 'The dentist and the Virginia doctor come every two months.' Alma hoped for a sense of humour.

The city slicker fell right in. 'What's a Virginia doctor?'

Alma grinned. 'Thought that's what you were. Ones that look at a woman's Virginia.'

To Alma's delight the doctor laughed. 'I won't be looking at any Virginias while I'm here.'

'That's what they all say.'

The doctor didn't comment on that. She just gave her a slight smile. 'What about the office they use? Can I work from there?'

Alma lifted her sun visor and rubbed her sparse hair where it had stuck to her head, reminding herself that she needed a haircut. Then put the visor back on again. 'Should be able to. Or the police station. That has the best office.'

The doctor stilled as she studied the handle on her case. 'That might work. I need a base with decent internet and plenty of bench space. We'll see. What about a librarian?'

'The van comes once a fortnight with new books.'

The pretty face screwed up. 'Is there anyone who can sort and do filing for an hour once a day?'

Alma looked at the girl beside her. 'Didn't you say you did that while you were travelling?'

Maddy nodded. 'Yep. Maddy can do that,' Alma said, 'long as she's back here before the six-o'clock rush.'

Sienna glanced out the window at the deserted street and then around the abandoned bar. Raised her brows and her voice was as dry as an afternoon breeze. 'If you can spare her for an hour or two after your lunchtime mayhem that would be helpful. Say four p.m. Thank you.' She moved to the first step then paused again. 'I'll have a shower and unpack. Then we'll have a chat if that suits you, Maddy.'

'Yes, doctor.' The girl glanced at Alma for confirmation, who shrugged.

Then the woman said, 'You'd better call me Sienna, if we're working together.'

'Yes, doctor.'

Sienna smiled at Maddy and climbed the stairs. She carried the bag carefully.

Alma wanted to know what was in it that was so darn special.

Chapter Seven

Sienna

Sienna narrowed her eyes against the glare from the late-afternoon sun. From the second-storey window she saw the dust-covered police vehicle pull into the parking area of the pub underneath her. Seven o'clock. It was about time, seeing as she'd been cooling her heels for an hour after she'd sorted her things. She'd changed into cream linen trousers and a black sleeveless top in deference to the heat.

Of its own volition, her hand rose to rest in the centre of her chest as she waited, and unconsciously she pressed over her sternum with her fingers.

The driver's door opened and Douglas's thick dark curls appeared first, then his big rangy shoulders. She sighed as he stood. With fluid grace for such a big man, he leaned back in and collected his hat, then as if he felt her watching him, he turned and looked straight up at her window.

His hand, still holding his police Akubra, lifted in her direction, causing the blue shirt to stretch to its limit across his impressive chest. The slow curve of his mouth caused a reaction she'd decided he didn't deserve – her own mouth tilted in response.

The tiredness, muted by the just-adequate shower in the communal bathroom, magically faded into oblivion. She watched his finger lift in an I'll-be-with-you-shortly sign, and then he strode across the yard to the door she'd entered through.

She said softly, 'I don't know what it is, Douglas McCabe, because you're no picture postcard, but you really do turn me on.' The words hung in the air in front of her and she shook her head, then scrubbed the empty space as if it were a blackboard. Thankfully, she had that comment out of the way without him hearing her, which was a good thing considering he was just a fling – the man had too much power already.

His lifestyle and his love affair with the outback would never gel with her world. She knew that. Just like her city-journalist mother had fallen in ridiculous lust with her publican dad, the whole situation was doomed from the start. At least Douglas wasn't married. But the whole state of this strangely compelling relationship had no solution.

Sienna glanced one last time in the age-spotted but blindingly clean mirror. In fact, everything sparkled with elbow grease and tiny touches of very tasteful memorabilia, and she wondered fleetingly if Maddy did all the housekeeping or if Alma had OCD.

Then her thoughts returned to the much more riveting topic of Douglas and a little fillip of excitement bounced around inside her chest. This was so unlike her. Dr Sienna Wilson took what she needed to achieve her goals, and she suspected she'd given in way too easily to the idea of dropping everything to come out here. Even her boss hadn't expected her to leave this week.

Normally, she didn't moon over ruggedly sexy men with more morals than a minister, and she needed to get a grip now. Especially as she could hear the tread of masculine footsteps on the stairs. He was coming.

Her mouth twitched. She hadn't had butterflies in her stomach for twenty years. She wondered, not for the first time, if that was the inexplicable reason her mother had fallen in lust with her totally unsuitable, already married father. Pure animal attraction. Pheromones. Whatever. Look how that had ended. *Control yourself.* Be cool, business like.

Still, she jumped when the knock came. Two solid taps. Not too loud, not too soft. A demand for response and she was very happy to obey. Though, the idea of 'obey' made the furrows crease in her forehead. She would have none of this *obey* stuff. She crossed the room and opened the door. Looked at him and stoically kept her face neutral, but inside she glowed.

'Douglas.' He loomed over her. He did it very well. She savoured the fact that his top button sat parallel to her vision, and even as she lifted her eyes to his she admired a couple of tiny dark hairs curled in the sunburnt V of his chest. My, my, she loved that chest. That big rock wall she wanted to climb right onto. Such amazing handholds. Her heart squeezed. *Stop it.*

'Sienna. It's good to see you.' Deep, rumbling, freaking sexy voice. She wanted to fling herself into his arms.

She looked away from those inflexible blue eyes that were searching her face with a thorough intensity. In a moment of clarity, despite the pirouetting delight of her senses, she saw that Douglas had himself under rigid control, so she wasn't the only one holding it all in.

That helped. 'Oh, hello, Douglas,' she said, as if she'd seen him yesterday. 'Come in.' She waved a languid arm towards the room.

It was not easily accomplished, but she was mildly successful. 'I've not long arrived and haven't started my investigations yet.' Clever move. That made her invitation to join her so innocent and all about the reason she was here. The real reason. Nothing to do with sex.

He hesitated and she wanted to raise her brows and dare him to enter her lair, double-dare him, but she'd learned he couldn't be forced. She glanced away and looked pointedly at the pile of documents on her rickety desk. She would leave the decision up to him, she thought, and took a purposeful step that way herself. 'I'm not sure where to start.'

She heard him step inside and shut the door. He crossed the floor to where she stood with her back to him, flicking nonchalantly through the pile of reports.

'You,' he said to her back, with a long pause and a stream of warm breath against her neck that had those tiny hairs fluttering in hope, 'are incorrigible.'

Then, thank goodness, he put his hand on her shoulder and turned her slowly to face him. She dared a glance at his face, trying not to laugh with delight at her success at getting him in here and with the door shut.

'Who, me?' She tried for a haughty eyebrow raise but could feel her face dissolving into a secret sultry smile. He looked so damn good.

'You.' Then he pulled her against him with one strong arm and lifted her chin with his other hand. 'I've missed you.'

She didn't get to answer. His mouth came down and swallowed any response she might have made, and despite the initial tenderness she could sense the massive restraint, his iron control. So much emotion swirled between them. Her eyes stung with the impossibility of this incredible attraction lasting, because he touched her at a depth she still couldn't believe was possible. She had never felt anything like this with any man except Douglas. Then she wasn't thinking anything at all because he spun her away like a whirlwind, and she was lost.

After a most thorough kiss and another quick follow-up as if he couldn't quite stop, Douglas moved her very deliberately away from him and gave her the tiniest squeeze. 'You will be the death of me,' he said grimly as he loosened his delightful grip on her shoulders.

'But what a way to go,' she said cheekily and his stern face softened a millimetre and he smiled. A smile that warmed Sienna more than the heatwave outside warmed the interior of her car.

'Yes, well, that's the kicker,' he said and turned away to look out the window. 'Let's talk about the babies.' He walked to the door and opened it. Held it for her. 'But not here.'

'Douglas, you are such a spoil sport.'

His voice stayed very low. 'This won't end well and we both know it. I'm a boots-and-all guy and you're a grown woman playing with me.'

Bugger, thought Sienna, as she picked up her handbag and checked that her notepad rested inside. She hoped she was playing.

'You asked me to come. Not the other way around.' But down to business. 'I need an office,' Sienna said as she led the way to the stairs. 'A place I can gather all the information, a printer for my computer, somewhere I can sit, plus space for an office assistant for an hour a day for collation and typing forms. Preferably with air conditioning and no visitors.' Sienna reeled off the list over her shoulder, punctuating each need with the next descent, as she walked down the stairs to the tiny reception area beside the bar.

'Watch where you're going.' Douglas loomed behind her as if ready to steady her if she tripped. Sienna felt like flipping her hair. It was her sister who tripped over everything. Sienna knew exactly where she put her feet, but to tease him she slowed right down to draw him near, and accentuated the swing of her hips, though of course he backed off. Cornering Douglas felt as elusive as trying to catch a wisp of smoke in her fingertips.

Chapter Eight

Maddy

Maddy saw the couple descend the stairs as she stood at the edge of the dining room, feet planted wide, arms above her head, sweeping cobwebs from the corner of the wood-lined ceiling. Or at least that was what she'd been trying to achieve – she couldn't see any web-like filaments to remove. She watched the sway of the doctor's hips in those soft linen trousers, and the poised readiness of the policeman as he hovered, as though afraid she'd slip, and decided there had to be something going on between them.

She brought the broom down with relief and leaned on it. Glanced nervously at Sergeant McCabe and then away. His kind grey eyes always seemed to see more than she intended him to.

'Hello, Maddy. How are you?' He paused before saying, 'How's Jacob?'

'Hello, Sergeant,' her voice squeaked. Fear of police hadn't been her history, but she'd never lived the way she did now either. Jacob hated this man with a passion. Had never forgiven the way he'd backed Alma when she'd banned Jacob from the pub. Nor the way he had forcibly removed him from the premises. Too many people had seen it happen. Jacob didn't like looking bad in public. Shame it didn't bother him in private.

Maddy felt guilty that she didn't dislike the policeman at all, but how could she?

She avoided his eyes. 'Getting better.' *Liar*, an inner voice accused. Jacob's leg might be healing at last, but his moods had become much, much worse. The tension that surrounded her boyfriend rose like a black fog that pulled her in and then, too often, swung in to hurt her. Too many times she'd hoped that he meant it when he said he'd never hurt her again. Because he sounded so sorry. Said he loved her. And so she stayed.

Stayed so long she almost felt like she deserved his anger. Because of the crutches, if she remained careful, he couldn't hurt her a lot if she kept out of reach. With the broken leg and all. But the plaster might be off next week. Only she didn't want to think about that. She knew with an uneasy certainty that she should be gone by then.

'You tell him I asked after him.' The words were said kindly about Jacob, but she had the feeling he was directing them to her. She wondered if he'd ever had kids because he would make a good dad. Not like hers. Or Jacob's uncle. She tried to smile.

She wouldn't breathe a word to Jacob, but she suspected why the policeman had said that and her face flamed. Did he know? Did everyone know that Jacob was changing? Maddy felt the shame creep hotly over her skin like a brand that everyone could see.

Mercifully, the doctor's voice broke in. 'Maddy's going to be my office assistant.'

To her surprise the policeman said, 'That's good. Alma's not the only one who thinks Maddy is a smart cookie.'

Now Maddy could feel the heat rise in her face for a different reason. She wasn't used to compliments, not real ones anyway, and it felt like she'd lost the ability to handle something kind.

The doctor included her again. 'The sergeant and I are going to look around and decide on an office space. When I find a suitable location, I'll let you know where and when.'

Maddy nodded and winced at the roll of heat as they opened the side door towards the police vehicle. It was one of those days when the temperature seemed to climb late in the afternoon instead of cooling off. It had been silly-hot this week. She looked towards the doctor's dusty car under the shelter of the carport across the yard and bet they wished the police vehicle had been parked there.

The policeman opened the passenger door and put a hand out to prevent his companion from climbing in. To let the heat out, even though he'd left both windows down. After a minute the doctor was seated and he shut her door carefully.

Now there was a funny relationship, thought Maddy, but inside she could acknowledge some wistfulness for the obvious respect. Jacob had never opened or shut her door for her. Ever. More likely he'd start to drive off before she'd shut her own.

With that thought returned the cold reality she'd almost accepted over the last few days. She felt panic not for herself, but for her baby. The thought that Jacob would be able to hurt her baby by hurting her made her stop again and lean on the broom, panting a little at what this decision meant, because like a premonition, she could feel the coating of fear at the back of her throat. Of course it was terrifyingly clear that she couldn't let Jacob find out about the baby. Maybe ever. She couldn't let anyone in this town find out about the baby because then he would know.

She needed to make final plans today, now, before the day she went into labour, because if Jacob found out she'd better be prepared to run.

Chapter Nine

Sienna

Sienna sat in the stinking hot police truck waiting for Douglas to get in and thought about that kiss. About the moment Douglas had pulled her to him and transported her out of that dingy room into a place it seemed only Douglas could take her.

There was no doubt about it. This infatuation had escalated and she had no idea how this blurring of lines between a fun flirtatious fling had morphed into wanting more. It made her cross. And maybe a little scared – a feeling she wasn't accustomed to. She needed to solve this threat to babies, keep her peace of mind, and hightail it back to Sydney where she belonged, ASAP. She needed to leave this insanity behind.

She drew in a discreetly fortifying breath and made the conscious decision to get on with it. Again. 'So where would you recommend for an office?' It was time to be crisp and to the point.

Douglas glanced at her as he shut his own door. 'The health centre might work. Not a lot of bench space from memory, but we'll go there first. I have the key. It's not far and we could have walked, but I have to be near the truck in case I need to leave.'

She looked up ahead of them and saw that the health centre was at the edge of town on a cross street, with the building close to the road. He drove the two hundred metres to it and stopped. 'How are you going to do this?' he asked.

Down-to-business Douglas. That had been what she'd just decided. So why the sinking, spiral of disappointment that settled in her gut?

'Right.' She didn't look at him, but oddly she felt his glance. Maybe she did have a third eye in the back of her head where Douglas was concerned. She pretended she hadn't noticed and stared out at the desolate surroundings as they both looked at the grey building.

'I have the photocopied medical notes from the mothers and the neonatal reviews from the paediatricians in my room. I'll need to talk to the three women. Go through the congenital abnormality questions to see if we can identify any common toxins or genetic history.'

Douglas rubbed the back of his neck and drew her gaze. Why was he uncomfortable?

He said, 'None of the ladies have family history of anything like this and they all live on stations out of town. Annette is on Spinifex Station, her husband is manager for the Mackays.'

'At least she's here. Hopefully she can shed some light on the situation when I interview her. She'd the only one not in Brisbane with her baby at the moment.'

'You'll go out and see her? Or she'll come in to you?' His voice held a subtle reluctance. 'And will talking about it upset her?'

This time she looked at him. Understood what he was saying and felt the sting. *Thanks for the vote of confidence, big boy.* 'Do you mean will I upset her?'

'Yes,' said Douglas. The call-a-spade-a-spade man.

She closed her eyes. Breathed in the hot air and then let it out. Then she opened them and looked at him. 'No, Sergeant McCabe,' she said sweetly. 'Believe it or not I do have people skills when needed.'

'Good to know.' Maybe he'd been teasing her, half the time she didn't know, but she suspected that he hadn't been for part of that question. His slow smile started with an apologetic twitch at the corner of his mouth and spread like a warm wave of delicious promise until Sienna had to force her rigid spine to stay straight in the seat and not melt towards him. Her lips pressed together before she said in a tight voice, 'Now who's playing with whom?'

His black brows drew together and his face altered to serious. 'You're right.' He stared straight ahead. 'But I have missed you.'

'Well, I haven't missed feeling like this,' she said waspishly, and dug in her bag for a mint. She popped it into her mouth and chewed furiously as she opened her door. Anything to distract her from the conversation they weren't having, she thought as she climbed out.

The sign read 'Primary Health Centre' with lots of times and explanations under that. She'd read it later. It was too hot out here. Sienna gasped as the heat reflected up from the concrete path like someone had pointed a blowtorch at her. 'This place is like an oven.'

'Same temperatures, but it'll cool off soon,' Douglas said laconically. 'Stop fighting it. Accept it and move on.'

'Drop dead.'

He looked her up and down with that tilt to his sexy lips. 'Drop-dead gorgeous and cranky as hell. Come on, Dr Wilson. Once we shut the door it'll be cooler inside.'

Actually, it was. Quite pleasant really, with a little collection of chairs and a coffee table. She could imagine women sitting around talking. Obviously, the pulled blinds and closed doors helped it stay almost cool. Douglas made it even better by turning on the aircon and suddenly she didn't feel so hot and bothered. Or so cranky. Right. She could think. This town's outside temperature was ridiculous. She looked around.

The front reception, if you could call it that, had just enough room for the five wooden chairs, the coffee table and the water dispenser. It didn't look like they had a receptionist here because there wasn't a desk in the waiting room, but there was a kettle and a tiny fridge for patients to make tea and coffee. Nice touch.

She walked past the open wooden door with one of those round black doorhandles up high, circa 1950, and into a small room with a narrow, high examination couch and a small desk with a phone and a blood-pressure machine.

The stethoscope hung on the wall and a silver wheeled trolley held the sealed makings for an intravenous fluid line, she assumed for emergencies, syringes for taking blood and giving injections, and basic dressing apparatus. Plus a set of baby scales.

Little spare space showed on the packed shelves on the wall or the few flat surfaces. She'd practically have to remove everything before she'd have enough area to spread out her work. And reposition it all every Monday and Wednesday or whenever Alma said they came. Maddy could do that part, but what a pain.

'Too small and no, it won't work. Where else have we got?'

'With internet? There's your room in the pub, but I'm guessing you don't want to sleep with papers all around you for the next week or two and it's probably too small anyway.' Then, reluctantly, he said, 'There's the police station. I do have a back room and don't use it often, only for interviews, and if we don't have any crime then it's free.'

'So if you have to interview someone I have to pack all my gear up and move?'

'Yep. Plus the QGAP office is also run out of the police station. That's eight a.m. to three-thirty p.m. Tuesday and Wednesday. The office clerk drives in and stays overnight.'

She must have just missed that excitement when she arrived. 'What's a QGAP office?'

'The Queensland Government Agent Program. A one-stop shop providing government services and information referral to communities across the state. Basically, to make paying fines and fees as easy as possible where services aren't available.'

'Services?'

He shrugged. 'To register births, deaths or marriages, business names, give instructions for a will and have the forms for enduring power of attorney processed.'

'You sound like a commercial.'

He grimaced. 'I answer that question a lot.'

She winked. 'Won't work, then. Does the internet reach across to your house and do you have a spare room?'

'Yes and yes. Two, actually.' He looked at her, pretending to be totally serious, but she could see the glint in his eyes. It did things to her stomach. Then he said, 'But what about the sexual harassment?'

She shrugged and turned to leave the premises. 'You're a big boy. You can protect yourself.'

'I'm glad you think so. I'm not so sure.'

She paused, turned back to face him and smiled grimly. 'Thank God for that.'

Chapter Ten

Alma

The next morning, Alma's gaze followed the mysterious blue suitcase as the policeman carried it carefully down her beautiful carpeted staircase and out the door. She desperately wanted to ask what the heck was inside those shiny blue waterproof walls. Not knowing the contents was killing her.

There'd been two other cases, a smaller one and a bigger one, all matching, that stayed upstairs, but this was the one that the doctor had so carefully nurtured. Like a baby – though Alma was beginning to suspect that despite her profession the doctor didn't do maternal as a natural skill.

Maddy followed him out the door with a black briefcase and the doctor was last down the stairs with her handbag and a swish blue laptop case, wearing pale-blue linen trousers and a floaty white top. It felt like Hollywood had come to town.

Although, it looked like the circus was moving out. The doctor had been on the phone all morning, but as soon as the big copper came back into town this afternoon the exodus had started. 'You shifting in with the good sergeant, Dr Wilson?'

Something she couldn't read flashed across the woman's face before she replied calmly, 'No. Just setting up an office. I'll be working out of the police-residence spare room through the day.'

Alma glanced wistfully to where the sergeant had carefully placed that mysterious bag in the boot of the blue car. Looked back at Sienna. The worst thing the doctor could do was snub her and Alma had been snubbed by experts. 'Been wondering. What's in that blue suitcase that's so special?'

Sienna glanced out the door, then raised her brows. 'My coffee machine.'

Alma cackled. 'Should've guessed. City folk and their coffee.' She'd ordered tea this morning. Maybe she didn't she trust her to make good coffee.

Sienna blinked slowly as if saying, 'Are you quite finished?'

Alma let the smile fade, before leaning towards her. 'Tell you a secret. I have the flashiest, most expensive, desirable coffee machine this side of Brisbane. We call him Maestro. Bought it after a big win on the Melbourne Cup. You wait until tomorrow's breakfast. I'll make you a cup you won't be able to compare to what you get out of your fancy machine. Mark my words.'

A faint smile curved the ruby-red lips. 'Consider them marked.'

Alma watched the sergeant come back in and speak to the doctor at the door. Took note of the close heads, the woman's pause as he opened the door for her, and the quick smile.

Alma fanned her face. 'Warm in here now,' she murmured to herself with a sly grin.

Now what had the big man said when she'd asked him? They'd met at Red Sand, with another project for Blanche Mackay, so it could be shared experience. But . . . he hovered just a little too protectively and the doctor's pale cheeks looked pink to Alma. Talk about chalk and cheese, she thought with a tinge of regret. She just couldn't see a happy ending there.

The doctor turned back and asked, 'Can you remember anything unusual that happened around mid-July last year, Alma?'

How could she remember months ago? She had problems with yesterday. 'Like what?'

The doctor shrugged. 'Meteor shower. A crop duster crashed. Someone poisoned the waterhole?'

Alma wasn't sure if she was pulling her leg. 'Apart from the camel races, I can't think of anything in July.'

'Douglas?'

Alma's suspicions ramped up another notch and she had to bite back the cackle. The way she said his name, seriously, a dead giveaway. Ha!

The sergeant didn't seem to notice, but then you never could tell what he was thinking. Dead-set poker face.

Alma watched the doctor study him, and smiled sourly to herself. Oh yeah. You've got it bad.

Douglas said, 'Only been here three months. Nothing since then that jumps out at me.' He lifted his hand to Alma and opened the door again for the doctor. 'We'll go. Thanks,' he said and Alma smiled at him. She stood at the side door and watched until the police vehicle turned out of the carpark towards the police station. She hadn't seen this much of the sergeant since he'd arrived. The benefits of a handsome woman in town. Though to be fair – he'd had a hand in her coming.

Alma wouldn't like to cross him, but just having him walk into the bar on closing time had saved her bacon a few times in the short space he'd been here. He seemed to know the nights Alma would like to shut down and obliged with his presence. And then there'd been that business with the drugs.

Nasty lot, that city mob, here to cause havoc with the young blokes. Sergeant McCabe had made some enemies there when he'd bundled them out of town.

Old Sergeant Jeffs had never been on the ball like this one unless she'd yelled for help, but 'the big copper', as the locals called him, could subdue most blokes with a hard stare. Could quell the wild women, too, but she'd never heard of him being with one. Maybe the blonde doctor explained that? Alma liked a good intrigue, but she preferred a happy ending.

Alma turned away as a regular came in. She could people watch from the bar and someone had to work. 'Evening, Blue.'

She looked at the tall streak of misery who used to drive the mail truck – his orange hair finally fading with age. Retirement didn't suit him. He was still the fire captain, but they didn't have much to burn around here and he was bored stupid. Blue stood as one of the reasons Alma hadn't taken the plunge to stop work. He'd been the epitome of his name since he'd lost his daily routine. And even more miserable since his wife had started to feel a bit sickly. She meant to ask the doctor about that.

'Evening, Alma. Just the one, please,' Blue said. He said that every night. Then just one more. And then another. But at least Blue cheered up as he got tipsy and didn't turn when the percentage hit. Not like Maddy's man.

Thinking of Maddy, Alma frowned. She'd been looking more strained. Usually this meant that her man was being difficult. Prick.

Today, Alma's concern for Maddy had ramped up to worry. Something was going on. The girl seemed to have a lot of aches and pains, more than before, not that she complained, but sometimes she moved stiffly, and Alma wondered if it had anything to do with him. And she was stacking on the weight, so she was probably binge eating when she got depressed. If Alma had had to live with that Jacob she'd eat too. Next time she and Maddy had some privacy she'd broach the subject.

She could remember a time she hadn't told anyone about her hell on earth, had felt too ashamed to think about telling, and she didn't like the possibility that Maddy might be living like that.

Blue said, 'Just one more, Alma.' And she smiled at him and pulled another beer.

Chapter Eleven

Maddy

Maddy decided that setting up an office in the policeman's spare room made her new boss smile. And Sergeant McCabe scowl. She didn't like to think about what Jacob would say when she told him where she'd be working for an hour every day; the thought sent a frisson of unease down her back.

Since the epiphany of the last few days about her need to leave Jacob for her baby's safety, she'd had a whole lot more to worry about. She'd vaguely accepted that at some stage she would go into labour, although she hadn't thought about it too much, because, stupidly, she'd been so absorbed in surviving each day and looking for the right moment to share her news.

But the time for not thinking about the birth was past, because she shuddered more at the thought of a baby under Jacob's roof than the actual labour. She'd grown up on a farm and had watched the animals give birth. And she'd read about it a bit. Had even helped at a home birth in Sweden once. Not that she'd done much during that experience, except look after the mother's other children, and watch wide-eyed as events had unfolded, but that all had seemed very peaceful and serene.

Maddy knew about placentas and rubbing babies when they were born. It all held a surreal distance with a tinge of horror that she kept locked in the back of her mind. Now, coming in contact with a baby doctor had a serendipitous feel that eased her tension fractionally in that department anyway. In the next few days she would tell the doctor – just knowing she'd be there in case anything went wrong helped lift the new load of guilt that had begun to crush her. How could she have been so reckless with her baby's life, thinking she could get away before she needed medical advice? At least if something went wrong before she actually could get away the doctor was here. As soon as the doctor left, she'd go.

As for when the baby came, well, that would depend on what town she was in when it happened. That was all there was to it now.

When she'd first suspected the truth, she'd dreamed Alma might take her in, but Maddy had been there last month when the other backpacker with the baby had called. Alma had said there couldn't be any babies in a pub. Plus, it wouldn't work long term. It was too small a town, Jacob would find out, and he'd drag her home.

Sometimes, after hard times when she'd done something stupid and Jacob had been crazy angry, her head had ached with dark ideas and insidious thoughts of just walking out of town into the heat and lying down under a bush to die. Dying of thirst. They say your mind sees the water before you die. It didn't sound too bad. But then her baby would die too and she knew she couldn't do that to the innocent life within her. No. Her life with Jacob wasn't so bad that she would consider that again.

The doctor walked past her with another box and Maddy startled and shifted into action – which kicked off another of those achy back strains. She'd been standing there doing nothing, not that the doctor noticed, but that wasn't good enough. This bit of extra money would come in handy for her and her baby and she didn't want to blow the opportunity. She'd need it desperately as soon as she got on that bus.

Maddy hurried awkwardly out to the road to bring in another box from the blue car. She could almost ignore the twinges when she walked, and if she hugged the box to her belly it helped hide her stiffness.

After the last item had been moved to the new office, Maddy and the doctor stood back and surveyed the space she now called her office.

'Between us I think we've created an organised space,' the doctor said and Maddy felt the swell of pride in a job well done. It did look good.

'Maybe we could move that dresser and the small bookcase closer.' When Maddy went to shift it the doctor did something strange. She put up her hand and stopped her. 'I'll do that. Why don't you pop the jug on?'

Maddy looked at her. 'I can lift it.'

The doctor shook her head. 'I know. But I'm not sure where I want it yet.'

Maddy stepped back and tried to understand what had changed. A minute ago they were sharing the work and all of a sudden Maddy felt a bit awkward. 'Right. I'll do the jug.'

When she got back the doctor was smiling. 'Good job, Madison. We make an efficient team.'

That brought back memories. Her awkwardness fled and Maddy smiled too. 'My mother's favourite word. She used to say, "Don't dither. Be efficient."'

'Your mother sounds like mine. She was into no dithering. Is your mum around here?'

She wished. She would have hightailed it home if her mum had been alive. 'No. We lived in WA, but she passed more than three years ago.'

'Mine, too,' the doctor said quietly. 'I'm sorry. Your family?'

She thought of the family she'd never really fitted into since her mum had died. She'd been the change-of-life baby. 'I've got two brothers and a sister, all older than me, the ones I had to learn efficiency from. But they have their own lives now, and I went backpacking for two years . . .' Her voice trailed off and she shut her mouth. Stood up. 'It's late. I'd better get home so I can sort tea before I go back to work.'

The gnawing worry that Jacob would be waiting for her, with his wild mood swings, and the fear she had trouble calming, bubbled up like one of those hot springs she'd seen in Innot when Jacob had taken her in the truck one day.

The bubbles were sulphuric and splattered fear that was growing larger every day.

Chapter Twelve

Sienna

Sienna watched Maddy hurry away to fix dinner at home and worriedly wiped the trickle of sweat off the back of her neck with one finger. When she'd said she'd better go home, Maddy'd had that slightly harried expression Sienna had seen on her a couple of times. There was definitely something suspicious there. And that wasn't the only concern Sienna had.

Just before she'd asked Maddy to put on the kettle she'd made a disquieting discovery that she was almost sure was truth. She couldn't believe that she hadn't noticed right off yesterday.

Maddy's long-sleeved shirts and trousers that baffled in the heat gave Sienna sudden clarity that she might wear clothes to disguise her shape. Maddy certainly wasn't the first woman Sienna had known who'd done that. Women hid pregnancies for all sorts of reasons.

Sienna decided that her hunch relied more on the infinitesimal pauses mid-stride that Maddy made, and the unintentional cupping of her belly or finger-stretching support of her back than the shapeless tops she wore. The more she thought about it the more convinced Sienna became. She should have noticed earlier, but she'd had eyes for Douglas and not much else since she'd arrived.

Dangerous thing that.

If Maddy's secret was true, just how far along was she? She didn't look that big, but Sienna had seen bellies of all shapes and sizes and the outside didn't always correlate with what was happening within.

Which raised the issue that pregnant women were supposed to decamp to a maternity-service hospital in a larger town at least three weeks before their due date. Typical. Outback towns were out to get Sienna with their emergencies that were not meant to happen.

That was why she'd brought that extra box in her boot with gynaecological equipment. She'd learned at Red Sand that sometimes it could make the difference for a geographically remote woman doing something about a problem or just living with a secret. Alma had already hinted with her brazen talk of Virginias.

But Maddy? Even if she was pregnant, and Sienna decided she was now that she'd opened her obstetrician eyes instead of her bedroom ones, then surely Maddy couldn't be that far along? Hopefully not near term. She didn't look it. Obviously, the girl didn't want the gossips to have a field day with her. Had it taken her a long time to realise she was pregnant and that was why she wasn't saying? Though Sienna couldn't understand how a woman wouldn't know!

The last thing Sienna needed to do was start a juicy rumour, but, she decided thoughtfully, she'd watch that young lady more closely and would offer convenient openings Maddy could take up when she needed to.

She thought back to her arrival, and how other people had

reacted to the young woman. Now that she thought about it, she'd noticed Douglas watching the girl with a worried look. Douglas, who was kind and had that old-fashioned protective male persona. Although, in Maddy's case, he'd looked more puzzled, as if he sensed but couldn't put his finger on the issue.

The tiny publican, Alma, looked hard as nails, but she didn't look like a person who'd suggest a pregnant woman carried a suitcase up a staircase. So if Maddy was expecting a child, then the boss, and Douglas, didn't know either.

She consoled herself that Maddy knew Sienna's profession and she'd ask when she needed advice. And Sienna would have her seen as soon as possible. She could arrange that. Douglas could find someone to drive her to Longreach.

Dear delicious Douglas. Despite the fact that she'd invaded his home, he'd been a good help this afternoon. Although he'd left as soon as the heavy boxes were in. Had bolted like a skittish stallion to hide in his office away from her and then he'd gone out on another call.

She smiled sourly. As well he might. Douglas the drama queen. She laughed out loud at the silly thought, which distracted from her previous worry. Douglas might be a lot of things, but he wasn't a queen. Or intentionally dramatic.

He'd moved the single bed against the wall and brought in a decent desk and an extension cord for the phone in Sienna's new office. She moved from the room to admire the hallway – remarkably wide for such a small house – where they'd set Maddy up. There was enough room for the tiny desk and another small chest of drawers with the small laptop and mini-printer on it, and a chair for a waiting visitor in the hallway. Sienna brushed her hands and stood back further to peruse their work. Thought of Maddy again. Worried her lip with her teeth.

Earlier Sienna had seen the young woman ease down on the receptionist chair in front of the desk and glance around. Then she'd fiddled with the pens with a small smile on her face. She didn't know what it was about Maddy, but she liked the girl. Something about her pulled at a cord inside Sienna. And every now and then, unexpectedly, she'd say something dryly amusing that made Sienna laugh out loud. Which in itself was unusual. It usually took a lot for that to happen.

She glanced around and nodded. It had been a big day and she suddenly felt all the effort. She was probably still tired from the drive yesterday. There was nothing more to do here now. She'd better get back to the pub.

She'd left Douglas with some of his own areas free from invasion – his kitchen (except for her coffee machine), his own lounge area and of course . . . his bedroom. Sienna had checked it out when everyone had been absent. She had plans for that room.

Chapter Thirteen

Maddy

'Well, hello there,' Jacob said, leaning against the kitchen bench, his monster truck T-shirt stretched over his solid chest. One metal crutch leaned out to stop her scooting away as Maddy pushed open the back door.

She looked at his tall frame, which was slightly stockier since his activity had been curtailed by the accident. His smiling mouth tilted as he watched her and she bit back a sigh. She'd hoped he would be engrossed in front of the TV. At least until she'd had her shower.

'Hello.' She leaned over and kissed him. His lips lingered. They hadn't slept together since before he'd broken his leg. He'd tried once after the accident, but the damage to his veins caused a cramp he couldn't relieve with the plaster on and he'd cried with the pain. He'd pushed her away and said he'd sort himself. Thank goodness. She doubted she could have hidden the pregnancy now, otherwise.

Today, she mistrusted the look in his eyes despite the smile. She hadn't seen this smiling mood for a while.

'What's your hurry?'

She checked the kitchen clock. 'I'm looking forward to getting our dinner. But it's not important. Can I do something for you?'

He put his other crutch up to trap her between the two supports. 'I've missed you. What fascinating things have happened to you at the Desert Rose Hotel in beautiful downtown Spinifex?'

Playful Jacob. The man she'd fallen in love with before she could read the signs. She tried edging past the silver crutch, but he held it steady.

He turned his head and glanced at the kitchen clock himself. 'You're twenty minutes later than usual.'

She shrugged, even though she knew it annoyed him, and stopped edging. 'We have a guest staying at the hotel. Came last night.'

His brows snapped together and she went on hurriedly. Jacob didn't like it when men stayed over at the hotel. As if she'd sneak into their rooms – or they would try to inveigle her to theirs. She guessed it was nice that he cared – or even thought some other man would be interested in her considering she was so frumpy. But as it always did when she mentioned guests, now the air seemed to flicker with danger.

'*She*,' Maddy emphasised the word, 'is a doctor here to look into why the babies have been born with the small heads.'

The crutch lowered a centimetre. 'Posh from the city, then?'

Maddy shook her head. 'More classy than posh. She's nice. And I'm to spend an hour a day helping her which is why I'm late now. Alma said to.' She didn't say it would mean extra cash. The doctor had said she'd pay her an hourly rate on top. That secret was for the escape.

Jacob gave an incredulous snort. 'You? Work for a doctor?'

Maddy froze then slowly lifted her chin to look at him. His mocking disbelief bounced off for a change and something stirred in the cold of her stomach. Something like pride. Something she hadn't felt for a while. She lifted her chin higher.

He didn't like that either.

'I've done it before. Clerical work. I can type and file and answer phones. I'm smart.' Jacob wasn't smart, though he hid it well. He could repeat things even if he didn't always understand them.

'Clever little thing, are you? You've been holding out on me. Then, before you rush off you can give me a decent kiss.'

Jacob was a good kisser. The best, not that she'd kissed that many men. And it used to make her tummy go all warm and gooey. But he'd taken to brutally squeezing her upper arms while he did it now and that hurt. Especially if the bruises hadn't faded since last time. She searched her mind frantically as she tried to figure out what she'd done wrong and how she could fix it. She hadn't told him where she'd be working with the doctor yet. Mentioning the police station certainly wouldn't go down well. 'Is everything okay?'

'Why wouldn't it be?' he asked as he lowered the crutch and drew her closer until she was standing too close and she slid her arm down between them to keep him away from her belly.

He frowned and studied her. 'Are you feeling guilty for something I don't know about?' His good leg supported him and the one with the cast was balanced to the side, the weight taken by the crutch under his armpit.

Now, for the first time she really considered giving him a shove, then walking out and worrying later what the consequences would be. But she didn't. Wouldn't. It was as if she couldn't see past the buttons on his shirt as his face drew closer to hers. She really had loved him.

Please be nice, Jacob. Her eyes searched for a hint of the softness that had drawn her to him, but it wasn't there. He used to smile every time he looked at her. Not any more. His hands closed over her shoulders and bit in.

Maddy knew she would make it to the pub with one minute to spare. She liked to be there a little earlier, especially if she needed to pause in the gap between the pub and the old gas station and pull herself together like she did tonight. But Jacob had been deliberately delaying her until she became distressed that she'd be late. Then he'd laughed, slapped her backside, as if in fun but hard, and let her go. Hurting.

She needed to make those arrangements to leave. And after the last two strong pains she'd felt in her belly as she rushed past the police station, she knew she might have to. Might need to find an emergency place to hide if the worst happened and she went into labour before she could get away. If she hadn't got away by then that was when she'd be at her most vulnerable. Her baby was even more at risk if Jacob went crazy.

Panic surged and instinctively she glanced to her left to the disused service station that sat next to the pub and considered it as a last-resort bolt-hole. She'd check it out tonight on her way home when no one was around. The last thing she needed was inquisitive eyes to see her. Imagine if some drunk told Jacob they'd seen her poking around in there. If she disappeared he'd know where to look.

She quickened her pace and moved onto the path in front of the pub. She pushed open the door and the cool of the air conditioning welcomed her as though she were a lost child. Sometimes, especially lately, she felt like a lost child.

Then there was Alma's smiling face. Her hand waving in acknowledgement as she bent her head to finish the beer she was pulling.

Maddy said quietly, 'Sorry I'm late,' as she headed past to the kitchen.

'Not late. Exactly on time or as near as you get.' Alma gave her a searching glance. 'You look hot. Have a cool drink before you start. Another minute or two won't matter. Then you can tell me how you went with the doctor this afternoon.'

Maddy nodded shyly. A drink would be good, but she'd be careful what she shared about working with the doctor. Although Alma was a good person, Maddy knew how to be discreet.

Chapter Fourteen

Sienna

Sienna heard a quiet step and Douglas stood in the doorway before she could actually leave. Maybe it was something about men in uniform that made a girl go silly. He looked big and strong and totally unable to be scared by her. Yet he didn't come in.

She'd heard his police vehicle grind away about an hour ago and she wondered when she'd missed it coming back. Big bonus. When she looked at him with a question he said, 'Give me ten minutes and I'll buy you dinner at the pub.'

She glanced at the clock. Five-thirty. Excellent. 'Technically, you can't. Blanche has paid for all my meals.'

'Then I'll buy my own and sit with you.' He flashed that lop-sided grin and she turned into a brain-dead bimbo before she could stop herself. She hadn't been looking forward to a solitary meal in the pub with Douglas away.

'Then you can go to bed early,' he went on.

She raised her brows suggestively.

'Alone.' Though his gaze lingered.

It was worth a try. She pretended that was what she meant. 'Of course.' Flicked her hair.

He gave her a considering look. 'You do look exhausted.' Another more though examination as if she worried him.

That was heart-warming. Not. Especially if he thought she looked exhausted. 'Thanks for that.'

'You're welcome.' His brows lifted. 'You're not still cranky, are you?'

Why would a man say that? She raised her brows at him. 'That comment is guaranteed to make me wild.'

His slow smile made her own mouth twitch. 'I'll remember that. You finish up, I'll shower, then we'll see what's on at the pub.'

Sienna watched his back disappear into the bathroom and the door shut. She wondered if he'd locked it. She took a step to check and decided to give him another day to get used to her being here.

Half an hour later Douglas held the screen door for Sienna. One of those gentlemanly mannerisms she'd never cared about before but somehow felt special because Douglas did it. She'd noticed a few of those emotional spikes that squeezed her heart and growled at herself to cut it out.

Perhaps a bit of space would help. 'We could walk. It's just up the street,' she said as Douglas steered her towards the police vehicle.

He looked down at her. Gave her that grin that she decided was an unfair weapon against her. There were so many endearing qualities she felt swamped and unsettled. She decided the lopsided grin was one of the bigger guns in his arsenal. 'I take the vehicle everywhere in case my phone rings. And I don't really want you to walk.'

Sienna nodded. It was moments like this when he let her see how much he cared. And now she remembered. 'You said that earlier about access to your car. Sorry.' Her brain did not do heat well. Or Douglas watching. 'Happy to ride,' Sienna said as she slid into the vehicle, warm but not baking thanks to the small overhang they'd provided for the work truck at the side of the station.

He started the engine and the air conditioner came on automatically, blowing warm air against her skin, which seemed so much more sensitive than normal. On alert? Not that it did her skin any good to be receptive to sensation the way Douglas avoided her. At least her perspiration would be dry.

Before pulling out into the street he asked, 'Did Blanche ring you?'

She turned to face him and became distracted for a second by the heady scent of freshly showered male. A hint of the expensive aftershave she'd bought him for Christmas drifted across and teased her senses. She closed her eyes for a moment and breathed him in. She kept them closed as she said a little dreamily, 'Blanche comes tomorrow.' Then she snapped her eyes open and she sat up. *Stop it.* She cleared her throat. 'I said I'd ring her even if I had nothing to report, to leave it till next week, but she'll come anyway.'

She made herself look out the window. Not that there was anything to see. Several blank-faced houses probably with aircon on inside. She turned back to him. 'She has to be worried about Eve and Lex's baby. I understand that.'

Douglas nodded and glanced ahead to the pub, as if the reason for all this tragedy might jump out and wave at him. She wished.

Then he said slowly, 'They're six hours' drive away at Diamond Lake.'

She chewed her lip. 'That's not far enough for Blanche. Though to give her credit she'd be concerned even if Eve wasn't pregnant with the next heir to the Mackay kingdom.'

Douglas looked thoughtful as they drove slowly up the street. They were nearly there. 'Are you concerned about your sister's unborn child?'

Sienna frowned. 'I'll admit it crossed my mind for the first time today. I'd thought her far enough away before coming here. Talking on the phone to the mothers in Brisbane today has really made it hit home. I'm glad she isn't here. It made me want to rush out and scan her – which you'll be glad to know I have mastered the urge not to do.' Her brow creased as she thought about that. 'Although Eve might refuse a scan anyway. She's not a believer in pre-empting disaster.'

Perplexed he said, 'Meaning?'

'Like Callie, she's not convinced about the idea of searching for disabilities in pregnancies. Even if an ultrasound showed some congenital aspect of her baby to be concerned about, she'd believe all will be well until proved otherwise at birth. Or deal with it then. It's not a bad way to be,' she said, considering it reflectively.

They pulled up at the pub. He said slowly, 'I've never thought about that aspect for parents – the ramifications of having ultrasounds in pregnancy. Finding a suspicion of something unexpected and having to make a decision on life and death.' He switched off the engine and turned to face her. 'That's huge. How terrible for them.' He rubbed his chin. 'If your child had an abnormality picked up on a scan what would you do?'

She blinked at him. This was an out-of-the-blue big question she didn't want to think about. 'I don't know, Douglas. Though I've had many patients in that position and wouldn't like to be in their place. Thankfully, I never will be – because I'm not having children.'

They were parked, but he hadn't turned off the ignition fully and the aircon blew forceful cool air at her. Blew his astonishment her way too.

His brows rose. 'Never have children? Ever?' His eyes drifted to her cleavage and ridiculously she felt herself blush.

He smiled. Raised his hands in apology. 'Sorry. Your girls distracted me. I meant you have time. Seems a shame to let all that brain power go to waste.' He said 'brain power' but he was looking elsewhere. Her neck grew hot.

Very softly she said, 'Stop it.' Her brain was scrambled enough without throwing that red herring at her. She reached for the door handle. 'I can't believe we're having this conversation. I don't have time for a family.' Then she looked back at him pointedly. 'You should talk. You're older than me.'

He glanced around the parking area as he switched off the engine. 'True. But I'm doing my part to keep small communities small.'

Phew. He wasn't serious. In that case she could laugh it off. 'Good job, Sergeant. Now we can go help the local economy by spending Blanche's money.'

'You spend Blanche's money. I'll spend my own.'

The first thing Sienna saw was Alma leaning on the bar watching them. Sienna felt like a bug under a microscope. She hadn't met anyone like Alma before and she looked at the woman again.

Petite, maybe one and half metres tall, crinkled crepe-paper skin. Wise eyes that said she'd seen a lot, been scarred, but had risen from the ashes. Though she was more like a wrinkled emu than a phoenix. Sienna guessed she probably *had* seen a lot, running an outback pub and all.

Despite the thorough perusal all the publican said was, 'You two here for tea? Maddy's just arrived. It's fish and chips and salad tonight, you okay with that?'

They nodded and Alma turned from the bar to pour them both a lemon squash from the fridge.

'I don't even have to ask,' Douglas said to her and indicated the preparation of his drink.

'I know you won't have anything else, Sergeant, and the doctor likes a cold drink.' The publican pointed a finger at Sienna. 'If you wanted wine, well, I could probably take the silver bag out of the box and squeeze that last bit out of the cask?'

Sienna forced a smile. 'No, thanks. I don't often drink alcohol.'

Alma nodded as if not surprised. Sienna felt as if she'd let her down. She supposed the woman did own a pub which relied on drinkers. 'Have you always lived here, Alma?' It was not like Sienna to be curious, but Alma intrigued her, just like Maddy did. She needed to be careful with that or Alma would be asking favours.

'Nope.' She flung her hair like a bird in a bath after wetting its head. 'Old Shirl was the publican before me, I came from Wilcannia. She said she'd seen possibilities for me. First one who did.' She cackled out loud as if that was the biggest joke. 'That Shirl had a dry, black sense of humour that more than bordered on politically incorrect. We got on well.'

Sienna could imagine that but the thought drifted when Douglas asked, 'What happened to Shirl?'

Alma stared at the cloth on the bar and smoothed it with her work-worn fingers. 'When she got sick I bought the pub off her. We was close by the end, the sister I never had.' The old lady looked distantly tragic for a moment. Then she brightened and glanced at Douglas. 'Hooley dooley, we enjoyed listening to the races on the radio together.' She raised her finger instructionally. 'You gotta limit a flutter to a fifty-cent stake. That's the secret to enjoying a bet.' She winked at Douglas. 'Isn't that right, Sergeant.'

'Sounds very sensible to me,' Douglas said. 'I heard a few rumours that you do okay with your wagers, Alma?'

The finger travelled to her lips in a secretive sign. 'I've won a few good ones with small outlay. Two hundred to one still happens. Had a nice, tidy nest egg by the time Shirl was thinking about selling the pub.'

'So you bought this pub with winnings from fifty-cent bets?' Sienna didn't believe it.

'It's true. One really big win started it.' Alma turned thoughtful. 'Me and Shirl, we were determined to stay afloat. I paid her back by looking after her until the end. It was a privilege, and a lesson. Even for me, sometimes, the lady is there, but you can't rely on her luck.'

Chapter Fifteen

On Friday morning, as promised, Blanche Mackay strode up the path of the police residence at nine a.m. Before she'd hit mother-in-law status, Eve had called Blanche an avenging flagpole, but now they both thought of her more as an outback queen stampeding everywhere. Probably because she stood tall and thin with a splendid nose and looked magnificent on a horse. Though Sienna hoped her new niece or nephew wouldn't inherit their paternal grandmother's proboscis.

Opening the door to her visitor, Sienna supressed a sigh at being checked up on already. Blanche presented like an advertisement for RM Williams as she stood at the entrance to Douglas's modest residence. The house was way too small for her height and her personality.

'Ah. Sienna. Good. What have you discovered?' Blanche fired the question as she strode in with long, swift strides which brought her to the end of the hallway too quickly.

Sienna watched her as she turned around and strode back. She felt her lips twitch. 'It's early days yet,' she said drily. 'Not much has been achieved,' that she couldn't have done from her own office in Sydney. Then, pointedly, she said, 'Hello, Blanche.'

Blanche threw back her thick grey hair and Sienna chastised herself for likening the action to a horse tossing its mane. 'Oh. Sorry. Yes. How are you, Sienna?'

'Fine.' Tongue-in-cheek, she said, 'You?'

Blanche waved that away. 'Microcephaly. Those poor babies and their mothers. You need to find out why and stop it happening again.' She winced. 'Imagine if one of my grandchildren . . .' Her voice trailed off.

'By the way. Congratulations on your coming grandchild.' Sienna wondered how long Blanche had known about Eve's baby and she hadn't. Was she really that bothered by that? Of course not. But Eve's pregnancy would be a factor for Blanche to jump so quickly on this danger to the bloodline.

Though, yesterday, Sienna had come to the same conclusion. If she was honest, she didn't want her sister hanging around here either in her present vulnerable state, and the urgency of finding a cause had ramped up with startling intensity.

Sienna said, 'It could just be a coincidence.' Because it needed to be stated.

Blanche shook her head. 'I don't believe that. Not three babies in this small town.'

'It's unlikely. But not impossible,' Sienna demurred. 'It could be an infection. One that comes in cycles and struck while these ladies were at the same gestation. Or it could be exposure to a chemical or some toxic substance. But again that's usually exposure at a certain time during the pregnancy to cause that particular congenital change. Whatever caused these changes could be gone now.'

Blanche frowned. 'Like a pesticide overspray on a certain date?'

What would they spray? The place was hardly a fruit bowl. 'Something like that. I'm talking to the mothers. As you know they all live on stations a fair way from each other and two of the babies are still in Brisbane under care. Though, I've spoken to those mothers on the phone.'

Blanche glanced through the doorway at the small bedroom-cum-office. 'Why are you working out of here?'

Sienna observed her surroundings. 'Because we have air conditioning and internet. The health centre is too small and I'd have to shift everything every clinic day.'

Blanche frowned. 'I should have ordered you a mobile office. I could still get one.'

Sienna could almost hear the *thump, thump* of a chinook helicopter rotor. See the vision of an office on a rope swinging over the town. You had to admire Blanche's one-track mind. And she'd be out of Douglas's house quick smart. 'It's not worth it for a week or two, maximum,' she said quickly.

Blanche frowned, clearly frustrated by her inability to help. 'Is your accommodation satisfactory? The meals?'

Why? Would she fly in a celebrity chef? 'Meals are perfect. Thank you for arranging that as well.' Last night had been fine anyway. She thought of the communal shower and had already decided she might shower down here. Tempt Douglas. The idea appealed. 'Everything is short term.' *Including Douglas*, her inner voice added. She shied away from that one. 'I'm not here for long.' She glanced pointedly at her watch. 'But I'd better get started.'

'Do you need help?'

For a ghastly moment Sienna thought Blanche was offering her services. The last thing she needed was Blanche under her feet. Or herself under Blanche's tapping foot. 'Thank you. That's very kind of you.' They both knew Blanche didn't offer just to be kind. 'I'll manage what I need to do. Most I'll do on my own, but I've arranged a clerk.'

Blanche's gaze narrowed like a kingfisher on a fat worm. 'Let me know the cost and I'll pay her.'

Sienna nodded. 'Sure.' If she got around to it. Maddy's stipend would be small for that tiny time and Sienna could cover that.

Blanche quivered. Disappointment that Sienna hadn't solved the mystery yet caused her nostrils to flare, but apparently she fought it successfully because she straightened. 'I'll go, then. I'm on my way to Longreach. Do you need any extra equipment?'

She thought of the blue case and her coffee machine ensconced in Douglas's kitchen and smiled dryly. 'I've brought what I need with me.'

'Excellent. I'll leave you, then.' Blanche shot her one last intense stare. 'I'll be back Monday. Let's meet at the hotel for lunch at say twelve. See how you're progressing.'

'It may not be worth coming.' Sienna inclined her head non-committally. 'Why don't you make it Tuesday? I don't expect it will progress much over the weekend. That's why I thought I'd come early and get all set up for next week. It took me two days to drive here.'

Blanche frowned and finally nodded, then strode out, her long, moleskin-covered legs covering the ground fast as her riding boots hit the concrete path. Bizarrely, the sound of her feet chirped like cicadas. She held her head poised as she scanned the area, as if the answer would be on a sign somewhere. She was erect and determined and fierce in her need to solve the mystery and sort that unacceptable risk to the families in her jurisdiction.

Blanche was an inspirational person, like Eve said. She could ride like the wind, shoot from the saddle and manage a crew of stockmen with the lift of one hand. A tireless woman, Sienna thought, with a huge heart, like Phar Lap's. Then she wondered again how Eve could live with her, even on the part-time basis Blanche had promised and apparently stuck to.

Sienna pulled out the copies of the standard Australia-wide congenital abnormality questionnaires the three mothers had filled in. The forms would have been completed at their hospitals when their babies were born, and included the background to their pregnancies and family history.

She'd read the relevant file on each baby and done a rapid analysis of any clinical factors, but they were few. There was a baby born with Down's syndrome way back in Annette's maternal relatives, plus a sister who had been to a third-world country and could have brought home the zika virus – but that had been years ago.

Then there was an episode of having the parental house insect-sprayed at the end of Lucy's first trimester, which Sienna didn't think was sufficient to be the cause. And Bella couldn't think of anything. They all lived on stations, so perhaps chemicals of some form were used at that time of year for all of them, who knew? Sienna hoped she would very shortly. She would make sure that query was in the new questionnaires she was formulating.

Sienna wasn't buying any of those factors as the main cause. There had to be an external factor. A connection. She threw down the papers.

She'd get Maddy to type up another set for interviews. She would email them to the two women in Brisbane and would talk to them on the phone again if they didn't come home before she left. See if she could tease out a common factor or situation between them. She spent the next ten minutes adding other pencilled questions for Maddy to type.

She'd heard Blanche's helicopter take off. Alma would be back later with lunch and Maddy a few hours after that for typing until five p.m. Douglas had left to follow a lead on a drifter who had stolen a handbag from a tourist and then interview a man about a missing truck.

Sienna considered another shower. Showers helped her think, and despite the aircon she felt sticky and clogged up in her thought processes.

As she opened the bathroom door and eyed Douglas's space, she could almost feel his presence. Could inhale the subtle tingling scent of him. It would be marketable. She glanced with just a little possessiveness around at the small room and the big cast-iron tub. The tub didn't have claw feet, but it did have the capacity to provide a lion of a bath. She'd ask Douglas what the consensus was on using that much water – she thought it came from the bore, which meant, of course, it would probably smell like sulphur, like the shower in the pub did. It gave you lots of hot water, but the smell didn't make you want to linger.

It had been the same at Red Sand. Situated on the Great Artesian Basin, the bore water there came out about eighty-five degrees celsius so had to be cooled before it could be circulated into the town supply. The good news was, if allowed to stand to enable the gas to escape, and chilled, it tasted like the sweetest and cleanest water in the world. Maybe she could get one of those heating elements and reheat her cold bathwater so it didn't smell.

She shrugged and fiddled with her necklace. She should have taken it off before her shower this morning because the sulphur had tarnished it already. She'd get it cleaned when she went back to Sydney. These were all minor irritations she could live with. For now.

She glanced at the neat pile of precision-folded towels stacked on the bench. There was also a man's deodorant and that old-fashioned but classic man's aftershave – now her favourite secret scent since she'd met Douglas, although he had used the new one she'd bought him last night. She made a mental note to order more online for next Christmas. Maybe she could have Christmas with Douglas again. Perhaps he could stay with her through to New Year's Day. Or fly back to her later in the week. She hadn't done the whole spending New Year's Eve on Sydney Harbour thing, and the idea of watching fireworks and especially bringing in the new year with you-know-who at midnight took on a whole new attraction.

Then her thoughts veered towards an event being the connecting factor for the cluster of affected babies. What had happened when those babies had been conceived? Or what abnormal events had occurred during their mothers' pregnancies at a time that gave the same congenital problem?

Three babies born at roughly the same time having antenatal care in a town as tiny as this did seem like a strange coincidence. Alma had mentioned a camel race.

She spun on her heel and left the bathroom as she pulled her phone from her pocket and opened the calculator app on her screen. No matter where she worked it was far from unusual to have to sit with a woman and try to figure out when their baby could have been conceived. Her fingers flew as she typed in the birthdate of the second baby and came up with conception at the third weekend in July. The first and the third baby had also been born within a week of that date, and they'd all been assessed as term babies.

Which reminded her, it would be good to check the clinic records for any miscarriages in the three months after their conception dates. If something toxic had occurred in town or its outskirts then the timeline would be marked by miscarriages as well. She should, in fact, check all miscarriages in the last year. She made a note.

Sienna sat at her desk and opened her computer. She typed, 'Western Queensland events for month of July' into Google and tapped her finger as she waited for results to come up.

Bingo. In July she had a rock and gem festival, an outback film festival, a big red music festival and, of course, the camel races Alma had mentioned. Third weekend in July. Apparently the longest camel race in Australia.

She chewed her lip. A snatch of conversation came back to her from the previous year. Eve saying their father had been one of the main organisers for the outback camel races at Red Sand. Apparently, she'd been told that at his funeral.

That would be the funeral Sienna had refused to go to. She didn't regret not going, not exactly, but she now found it galling to think Eve might have been right to attend. It was bizarre to think she'd be even remotely connected to such an intrinsically outback event as a desert camel race. She who hailed from one of the largest cities in Australia.

She shook her head. So Spinifex was on the camel-racing circuit. Who would have thought? She couldn't help the smile. A year ago she might have sneered, but she'd come to see that these outback families worked hard and they played hard, too. Played like maniacs.

So, what did it mean? Maybe a lot of opportunities for revelry and making babies after all those hard times, which could explain letting your hair down and falling pregnant. Eve had said the drought had worsened before it broke, so post-drought relief? Hope for the future? That would be tragically ironic. She wasn't closer to pinpointing anything. Not like camels could give you microcephaly. Nor could too much beer. Or gemstones or music.

Plus, there were too many occasions going on to narrow anything down, though she would concentrate on the ones held in this area. And she could get Maddy to add the events to the questionnaire for when she interviewed the women. As well as the happenings when they were around fifteen weeks. It was a tiny possibility, but she had little hope of a breakthrough with that one.

That's why investigating took so long. There were so many permutations and possibilities. Sienna's mind sharpened. Maddy could also add if any of the mothers knew of any friends who had miscarried at the same time or near when they found out they were pregnant. To back up the records the clinic nurse had. She could feel herself warming to the chase.

Alma appeared just before lunchtime with an avocado-and-tomato salad and, of course, a bottle of lemon squash. Sienna held the door as Alma passed laden with food into the house, then let it fall closed as she reached her arms up and stretched her neck. She didn't have an answer, but her data lay organised and she knew at least where she needed to start.

'Blanche said I had to look after you,' Alma said.

'Thank you.' She glanced at the enticing array of healthy food. She had not expected that. 'Love your work,' she said appreciatively.

Alma cackled briefly. 'You don't look like a hamburger-and-chips woman, but I can do that, too. So, you solved it yet?'

Sienna raised one eyebrow – was she for real? She'd been at it three hours.

Alma cackled again.

The unexpected teasing struck home and Sienna paused and considered the gnome of a woman, her wrinkled face twisted in a smile, her bright-blue eyes sharp and focused, her head up and slightly tilted as she studied Sienna. Again, she seemed like a cheeky emu. Not at all overawed.

Alma nodded, apparently satisfied. 'Good to get a rise out of you. You take things a bit serious, don't you.'

Sienna had to laugh. 'That obvious, huh? I'll watch that.' Sienna had heard Alma telling the tourists about how she'd seen the Min Min twice so she had no doubt the woman had a good imagination, too.

'Why do you stay here, Alma?'

Alma gave a quick shake of the bookie's cap. 'Spinifex is a good place for me. Plenty of company at the pub and I like a good sunset.' Alma waggled her finger and there was definite mischief in her wise old eyes. 'You'll have to get the sergeant to take you up to the lookout on top of the jump-up.' She winked. 'It's not very high, but the sunsets are spectacular.'

Was she matchmaking? Sienna regarded the twinkle suspiciously. 'That's very kind of you.' She tried not to think about a picnic rug and the possibility of finding a suitably discreet place to try some of that sexual harassment Douglas thought her capable of.

Alma gave a snort. 'Looking very serious there, doc.'

Alma's gaze remained fixed and Sienna hoped those thoughts hadn't crossed her face. 'Sorry. I'll try to look more frivolous.'

Alma grinned. 'See that you do. Don't want you to get wrinkles on that pretty face before your wedding.'

Sienna blinked. 'What wedding would that be?'

'Who knows? Maybe yours. I'm not blind.'

Sienna raised her brows to stop the rot. 'Maybe, but you're not seeing straight. Don't they have an optometrist in town?'

Alma snorted again. 'Optometrist flies in every two months. Which reminds me. So are you a real Virginia doctor?'

What was this woman going to say next? 'Bona fide. Though more of an obstetrician than a gynaecologist in my practice.'

'Blue's wife is bleeding down below and she's too old for her monthlies.'

Knew it. 'Blue from the bar? She should see the flying doctor next Monday. Get a referral to a gynaecologist. It's important she does.'

Alma didn't take her eyes of her. It was unnerving. 'Flying doctor is a man. She won't.'

Sienna sighed. 'Tell her to come down at two o'clock. Before Maddy comes. I'll give her a referral.'

'And you'll have a look?'

Sienna had to smile. 'Yes, Alma. I'll have a look.'

'And I'll do something for you.' She nodded solemnly. 'I'll make you up a nice picnic basket for the lookout. You get that man to take you up there. He's a good one, but he's a stickler for the right thing. I'll say no more.'

'See that you don't.' *I'll believe that when I see it,* Sienna thought cynically. 'And see that you don't make any more gynaecological appointments.'

Alma crossed her arms across her bony chest. 'None that aren't needed. You scratch our backs, we'll scratch yours.'

Absently, she replied, 'Don't need my back scratched, thank you.' Though the sudden mental image of lying at some lookout with Douglas running his big hands down her spine caused a moment's distraction.

Alma started again. 'That lookout is a popular place with the young ones. Not that there's a lot of those except on Friday and Saturday nights when the young backpackers and stockmen come in from the stations. But most just come straight to the pub.'

It was Friday today. 'Gets rowdier at the pub than last night, does it?'

Alma looked away. 'Some.'

The thought made Sienna's heart sink. She'd never been a fan of loud. 'If it gets too noisy I'll have to go to my sister's for next weekend.' Blanche would be happy because then she could dissect the progress Sienna had made. 'It's only a few hours' drive.' Well, six hours actually, though she tried not to dwell on that fact. The distances out here were ridiculous. The only good thing about that was the drive was air-conditioned all the way and came with music.

Alma's eyes widened. 'Don't drive at night. You want to watch the times for driving. If you travel after dark, there are other things to worry about apart from the roos.'

'Oh yes? What would that be?' Sienna suspected what Alma was going to say and wasn't disappointed.

Very seriously she said, 'You might get followed by the Min Min's light.'

Sienna humoured her. Remembered the sign on her drive up here. She must think Sienna was already getting soft. It was that gynae appointment she'd agreed to. 'I'll watch out for it.'

Now it seemed Alma's turn to stay serious. 'See that you do. Both times I saw it something happened in town. Funny thing is it always seems like a real bad thing – but then it turns out good. Just don't go following that light. They say if you do you'll never be seen again.'

Like she'd follow some fictitiously eerie light into the bush like a moth. Like a bug zapper. *It's so beautiful.* Not likely. 'Promise I won't.'

'Good.' Alma cocked her wizened face and pursed her lips. 'I know you don't believe me – but you'll find out if you're meant to.' Alma cackled again then glanced at the lunch she'd brought. 'Just leave the plates. Maddy will bring them back later.'

'Thank you,' Sienna said dryly and watched the little woman leave with a shake of her head. Mad. The woman was mad. It must be the heat. She glanced at the plates on the table. But she could provide great food and suddenly Sienna could eat a horse. For some reason she thought of Blanche.

———

Douglas arrived not long after Alma left and Sienna tried not to think how domesticated it was of her to leave him half of her salad in the fridge. She pulled it back out and put it on the table when his big form filled the hallway.

Then she lifted her glass of lemon squash in his direction. 'Ahoy there. How did you go seeing a man about a truck?' Surprisingly, she was interested in his day.

His eyes creased at her greeting. 'Ahoy there to you, are you a sailor?'

'Ships in the desert and all that stuff,' she quipped, with no idea why she was being so ridiculous. 'The truck?'

His face cleared. 'His brother borrowed it. They have a long running battle and he wants him to stop.'

Sienna raised her brows. 'Family politics.'

Douglas crossed to the sink and washed his big hands. His shoulders stretched the fabric of his shirt. Sienna's food paused halfway to her mouth. Something about sinews and muscle play and groaning fabric mesmerised her.

Then he used the towel and turned back to her. Hastily, she popped the fork into her mouth. His brow raised. 'You starving?'

In a way, she thought, shaking herself. Seriously, her brain had been doing very strange things since she'd come here. Since Douglas had visited Sydney last time, to be truthful. She said quietly, 'Join me.'

He eased his large frame into the chair and it creaked. He wasn't overweight – just strong, sexy strong, with solid muscle all over, and the kitchen shrank accordingly. He said, 'Family politics are way better than army politics. Here it's simple.'

She remembered Douglas had been in special ops. 'Simple is

good in that case.' She gestured to the salad. 'Alma brought lunch and I couldn't eat it all, if you're hungry.'

He hesitated. 'I don't think Blanche means to feed me as well.'

Irritation rose. Douglas and his morals. 'I don't imagine it will break the bank, but throw it out if you want to.'

He looked at her. 'Issues?'

She raised her brows at him. 'Why would I have issues?'

The corner of his mouth twitched, a smile crept over his face, slow, like the sun over paddocks in the morning until it warmed her. All over. Okay. It didn't just warm her. It ignited her. She fanned her face.

So maybe she was being difficult, but she wasn't used to going slow. Her whole world ran on efficient time management from dawn to dark. She wasn't even using her brain here, let alone her skills. 'I'm frustrated.' In more ways than one, she thought, narrowing her eyes at him. Maybe she should take Alma up on the sunset idea.

'Because?'

'I've arrived at the wrong time of the week. I should have left earlier or later and arrived on a Monday. But, stupidly, I hoped you would cave and meet me somewhere.'

'Working.' The word floated down with his gaze as he concentrated on his plate, so she couldn't read his expression.

He didn't comment on her lead, and she felt her ears heat. A tad embarrassing.

So she changed the subject. 'I want to interview the women, but two are in Brisbane. I want to interview the midwife, but she doesn't come till Monday, either. The flying doctor came four days ago and won't be back for two weeks.'

'You could ask Blanche to fly you up to Brisbane for the mothers. Or Charleville for the flying doctor. Or go out to the station and save the mother a trip in.'

'I suppose. Even the clinic staff have left town. At least I'll talk to the nurse on Monday. See what other paperwork I can photocopy. Plus, hopefully the midwife on Monday is the same one who has been seeing them antenatally. She might have something to offer. But for the moment I can't move on.'

'You could pretend it's Friday afternoon and have the weekend off?' He spread his hands. Pursed his lips as if to say *imagine that*.

And do what? She rarely had weekends off. Babies didn't take weekends off and she wasn't one of those consultants who told registrars to do something over the phone without dropping in to see how it went. Most times she watched them do it. 'Do you have the weekend off?'

'Technically yes. I'm on call but my office is shut.' After frowning at the plate Alma had brought he began to create a large sandwich from the salad. 'Would you like to go for a drive this afternoon? I need to run out to a station to talk to a family. Not one of the ones you need, but we'd be back before dark.'

Her lack of direction found a path. Serendipity. She could get Maddy to bring down the picnic basket when she came. 'I'd like that. After two-thirty alright? I have someone coming at two.'

He nodded as he chewed with his firm lips pressed together. That made her stare at his jawline. She whipped her eyes away and looked out the kitchen door to the clear sky.

'Alma told me about the sunset up on some hill, jump-up, she called it, and I guess barring important police business you could take me there on the way home. She offered a basket of goodies.'

He studied her, his face unreadable.

'You can tell me about your clouds, though I haven't seen any since I've been here.'

'The clouds are out there.' He narrowed his eyes at her thoughtfully, warily, then glanced at his watch. 'We'll see how things go.'

Chapter Sixteen

The trip to the station took forty-five minutes of dusty, bumpy, red-earth driving, thankfully not into the afternoon sun, but the heat shimmered every way she looked. This time she had a chance to notice the landscape – it was always easier when not trying to avoid flattening the next roadkill – and Douglas's steady pace allowed her to dwell on the blurred lines of mirages and distant rocky outcrops, the rugged tumble of rocks exposed by the elements, and the shaggy growth of hardy scrub all basted in orange and brown and deep ruby red.

'The colours hit you – as long as you like red.'

He looked pointedly at her stylish shoes. 'I see you do.'

She looked down as well. Turned her foot with satisfaction. 'They make me smile.'

'You make me smile.'

She patted his thigh. 'I'm planning to,' but didn't say more as she turned again to watch the view flash past.

She was pretty sure she'd seen a crinkle of those eyes when she'd said that, but enough said for the moment.

They didn't pass another car, saw plenty of emus that reminded her of Alma, though these ones ran off into the shimmer of heat on their approach, which she doubted Alma would ever do, and they saw enough signs to remind her the wildlife could be stupid, too.

Sienna pushed away the tartan blanket that brushed her legs. She'd found it in Douglas's kitchen cupboard in a plastic bag and, opportunistically, had grabbed it for ground cover. But it was warm against her calf. She should have put it back in the bag after shaking it out.

'So tell me why we're going out here, again,' Sienna asked as the sparsely covered plain shimmered and danced and blurred past her window. The latest emu brought a smile to her face, one of the few delights she found in the outback. She turned to the other delight as she waited for him to answer.

'A concern from a neighbour. Station owner's son has grown a lead foot. New on his P plates with a V6 ute and a fistful of driving lights. I don't want to see him wrapped around one of your emus . . .' he paused, 'or anyone else.'

The man was dreaming if he thought he'd be heeded by a teen. 'So some seventeen-year-old is going to listen to you?'

He glanced at her with a slight smile. 'The neighbour who is concerned also has a daughter on her Ps and our lead-foot hero nearly ran her off the road.'

'More politics.' She wrinkled her brows. 'I thought people didn't have close neighbours around here?'

'The houses might be five kilometres apart, but they use the same road into town.' He spoke slowly and clearly, as if she were a child. Sienna felt her hackles rise. This was the Douglas she didn't enjoy. Doctor Truth. Meticulous. Always right.

He must have sensed he'd lost her. He said reasonably, 'If people speed I will catch them and they will slow down or choose not to drive until they mature.'

Sooo serious. 'Choose not to, huh?'

He glanced at her again and then away. Sighed. 'Your sister's adopted daughter, Lily. She'd be sixteen, yes? She'd have her learner's licence. She'd be at risk of idiots who put others in danger on the road because she doesn't have auto-response driving skills yet.'

Sienna thought about bubbly Lily, all bright colours and high intelligence, scuttled by a hothead on the road. Thought about the short space of time for something to go wrong at high speed and Lily just around that corner learning about the tasks involved with navigating a car. 'Okay. You should talk to him.'

Douglas just nodded. 'I will. And I'll talk to his father.'

Twenty minutes later Sienna found a new source of respect for Douglas. She'd been invited for a cup of tea by Tommy's mother while Tommy, on his own first, then with his father, Jack, went for a chat. They and Douglas had gone to the shed to inspect the vehicle in question.

'I'm that pleased the sergeant came out,' Tommy's mother said as she placed the teapot on the table. 'We've regretted buying him that car since the day it arrived. I wanted to buy another farm ute, you can't get much past the speed limit in those anyway,' she said dryly, 'but his father saw it and fell in love with it. A case of some-thing he needed more than his son did.'

Sienna laughed. 'You could always swap cars and make your husband drive it.'

Tommy's mum laughed as well. 'That's not so silly. I might

mention that to my man. Be a good bargaining tool. But then, so is the sergeant. He's a man Tommy respects.'

Sienna thought about the lack of respect for police where she came from. 'Seems strange for a young man to like a policeman.'

'Experience does it every time. He learned from his friends. A couple of months ago a small band of drifters tried to bring drugs into town, that horrible drug ice. Some of Tommy's friends were drawn in, and Sergeant McCabe was onto the drifters like a fly at a barbecue. He sorted them quick smart. Kicked 'em out of town. Tommy's mate had been very close to being involved and they both saw a nasty incident that could have had ramifications for years. It scared the living daylights out of them. Now the boys realise not much goes on that our sergeant doesn't know about. Lots of towns are not so lucky.'

Sienna sipped her tea. 'I can believe that.' She tried to ignore the knot of pride that swelled in her chest. Douglas could be excellent in an emergency.

Her throat scratched as past memories and flashes of what Douglas was beginning to mean to her came together, and she couldn't help the plunge of spirits at how hopeless it all seemed. She reached for her cup and plastered a bright smile on her face. 'Funny how hot tea helps the dryness and heat. It doesn't make sense, but I feel refreshed. Thank you.' She drained her cup as the men returned, her chest easing back to normal, though her eyes strayed to Douglas and stuck.

She noted that behind them a subdued Tommy had peeled away and taken a different route. A few minutes later she heard a motor start and then a quad bike drove sedately away across the paddock with two dogs following.

Not long after that, she and Douglas left, though he drove far too placidly for Sienna. The sunset edged towards the skyline, and shadows and shades of rock and earth glowed golden in the afternoon light. Sienna's impatience made it seem as if they were crawling along the road. 'You do set a good example, Douglas,' she told him, adding dryly, 'I've never seen you speed.' Paint would dry faster than he drove.

He glanced at her and then back at the road. 'I've sped. But not without good reason and due care.'

She laughed.

After another half an hour Sienna wondered if his safety would kill her. Though, she must have undergone some kind of change because she thought it with humour, not frustration. His hands looked so safe and sure on the wheel. They could be so powerful and so tender. She sighed. His hands.

She glanced out at the skyline again and hoped they'd make it before the sunset show had been and gone. Before she died of old age. She had to admit the colours out here with the set-ting sun could lift her spirits – or maybe that was the man beside her and her plans for him. She shifted on the seat. Couldn't be far now.

'How long until we get there?'

Douglas glanced at her and smiled. 'You sound like an impa-tient kid.'

She thought of the responsibility she carried at Sydney Central as the Director of Obstetrics – the triplets, the lives she held in her hands, the decisions she made. The way the medical students looked her way nervously when she arrived for grand rounds. She laughed. 'Haven't been called a kid for a while.'

'I feel a hundred years older than you,' Douglas murmured without looking at her.

She stared at his hard profile and past him through the window to the harsh land flashing by. Land that could kill you in hours if you walked out into it without care. She tried to lighten the mood. 'That's because you live out here and I live in the land of oceans and light.'

He made a huffing sound in his throat. 'You live in an aquarium of seething population and sharks.'

She stared at him and thought of some of the sharks she knew. What did Douglas know of the city? There was vehemence there. 'We really don't agree on this, do we?'

'Nope.'

The sound of the vehicle's indicator and the brakes being applied alerted her. 'So we're nearly there?'

'Yes, child, we are.'

Sienna stroked his thigh. Not a child. The firm muscle below her fingers bunched into rock and she smiled to herself as she rested her hand.

Douglas drove through the open gate and up a small hill to the flat area. At the entrance to the car park two huge boulders sat on either side of the gate, a testament to the volcanic history of the area that had weathered them away to the pillars they were now. At the end of the turning circle three scrubby trees bunched to give shade, almost like a thicket, Sienna mused.

She checked her mobile. No service. Douglas wouldn't be happy because that meant he couldn't be contacted. She hoped nobody needed him. Surreptitiously, she made sure the satellite phone in her bag was turned to mute. She wasn't answering the phone for anyone. Then she glanced at her watch and saw that it was well past knock-off time for him. That should help his guilt trip.

Not too surprisingly, the place lay deserted, and Douglas parked a few feet out from where the dirt ended in Sienna's thicket. Behind her to their right, across the red earth of the turning circle, a brown park bench with a tin awning gave some shade, perched as it was to look over the plains towards the sinking sun.

'Do you want the basket on the table or beside the shade of the car?'

Alma had sent Maddy down with the supplies. Some nibbles and a big bottle of lemon squash and plastic flutes. 'Basket on table,' Sienna said decisively, and opened her door to step out. A small space between the car and the thicket gave privacy from the rear and the angle of his parking had created a barrier to any late arrivals. Excellent!

The afternoon heat hit her, but it wasn't as fierce as it had been earlier and the shade helped. It was almost pleasant, she thought gleefully, then, discreetly, she floated the thick picnic blanket under her arm onto the ground between the car and the scrub.

Nonchalantly, she followed the taut uniformed backside as Douglas crossed to the lookout seat. His shoulders hinted at tension – they were very upright, rigid – which caused some concern. She hoped he wasn't going to be obstructive.

Then he put the basket on the table and turned to face her. He leaned his delicious backside against the table and said conversationally, 'So you have me here, alone and out of service.' She noted the way he barely glanced at the horizon. 'Out of phone service anyway,' he said with a quirk of his lips. 'And you're not looking at the sunset.'

She flicked the vista a glance, 'Nice,' and then concentrated her attention back on the man in front of her. 'The view is nice this way as well.'

So tall, so delightfully constructed of hard planes and curves of muscle. Her attention caught at his hands again – she had developed a Douglas hand fetish, it seemed – as they moved in a 'come here' wave. Her heart skipped as she stepped up to him and put her arms around his strong neck. She linked her fingers to capture him and leaned back with her face inches from his. Watched his blue eyes darken, and the long lashes come down as his lips parted.

'What sunset?' she asked softly and put her mouth to his. They rested their mouths together, quietly breathing in the essence of each other, the air still and silent around them, the heat a blanket of sensation in itself, and then, thank you, dear heaven, he pulled her to him.

'You make it so hard to resist,' he muttered, as his mouth opened under hers and pulled her closer. His hands were strong against her spine. They slid down to cup her buttocks, squeezed, and he groaned deep in his throat. A man pushed beyond endurance. Hungry for something he couldn't have yet here in front of him. His mouth lifted from hers and for a terrifying moment she thought he was going to push her away.

He growled, 'I've been watching and wanting you all day. And I so wasn't going to do this.' He shrugged. Glanced at his watch. 'I am off duty.'

Then his mouth came down on hers again and he lifted her as if she were a floating grass seed in the wind and spun her, clutching her to him. The kiss deepened. His arms tightened and her eyes filled with tears at his fiercely possessive expression as she wrapped her legs around his waist. Then the heat and the promise of privacy and the mutual desperation overwhelmed them and they were both lost to the explosion of a need, which, thank goodness again, neither of them could resist.

Douglas carried her gently to the blanket she hadn't thought he'd seen and began to undress her like a present.

Afterwards, Sienna lay in the crook of his arm with her head upon his massive chest and gently twirled the dark hairs that had tickled her.

'Hey, you,' she said. His eyes were closed and he opened them a crack to listen. 'No man should be this good at pleasuring a lady and be so hard to convince.'

'Hmmm,' he said and she could feel the vibration in her ear. Wished he would vibrate again.

Then he rumbled, 'You tempted me beyond reason. I'm not a reckless man, but you make me reckless.'

This wasn't all one-sided, buster, she thought. 'I'm not a reckless woman except when I'm with you. You were lucky I can't keep my hands off you.'

He gave a deep chuckle. 'I concede that. But it's getting dark. We need to move.'

She nodded her head vigorously. 'I think so, too. Recklessly. Will I climb on top?'

His chest bounced under her cheek as he laughed. Then his tone became serious. 'This can't happen again after tonight. Not in Spinifex. You know that, don't you?'

She sighed. Yes, it wasn't fair of her to do this to him. Douglas was his morals. Something an earlier Sienna, one before Douglas, would never have contemplated or understood. 'I suspected as much. Will you come and have Christmas with me in Sydney again? And new year? I might buy a Mrs Claus suit and have my wicked way with you. Does that sound terrible?'

'Horrible,' he said as his mouth brushed hers.

'Now will I move?'

Douglas reached over and slid her body up and over his. 'Yes, ma'am. Please.'

She loved it when he said please.

They didn't get back to Spinifex until well after dark. Luckily, no missed calls pinged in when he drove into town.

Douglas stopped the vehicle in the street, which held a deeper pool of blackness than the car park to the side of the pub, and he alighted to stride around to open her door. Sienna knew better than to pull the latch herself. He could have all the minor wins he wanted. She had the big guns. She hugged herself dreamily and almost missed the opening of the door. Douglas looked at her.

'Take that smug expression off your face.'

She grinned at him. 'Seriously? Not a hope. It will be there for days.'

He gave a reluctant laugh and mock bow to encourage her out of his car. 'Scoot, tormentor. I'll see you tomorrow. I can't sit across from you in the pub tonight.'

Her lids lowered as she sashayed past him. 'Why's that?'

'You know why.' He shut her door and abruptly walked back to the driver's seat. Back to Sergeant McCabe.

She sighed. Might be best not to push tonight, Sienna conceded, but the smile still stretched her cheeks. She opened the passenger door a crack and poked her head back into the cab and grabbed the still-loaded basket. 'Thank you for a lovely sunset.' She winked. 'Good night, Sergeant McCabe.'

'Sleep well, Sienna,' he said drily.

'Oh, I will.' She waggled her eyebrows at him and pulled back to shut the door. He drove away at his usual sedate pace. You had to admire his control. And lack of it when called upon.

The first person Sienna saw as she tried to sneak into the pub had to be Alma. Alma didn't say anything. Alma didn't need to. But she did put one finger across her mouth and wink. To her chagrin, Sienna blushed.

Chapter Seventeen

On Saturday morning Sienna stretched out in her creaky brass bed and thought about yesterday's sunset, which she didn't actually see, and dragging Douglas to a public place and having her way with him. That had been selfish. And stupid. And dangerous for Douglas's reputation, which was important to him.

It had also been a five-star, mind-blowing, physically and emotionally moving experience. Right at this moment she wished with a hollow ache that gnawed at her with tiny needled teeth, that Douglas lay beside her – but she wouldn't be so unfair to him again. Which was why she could not jump up and run down to his house even if she had the excuse of leaving her coffee machine there.

She stared up at the ancient wooden slats on the ceiling, something any trendy retro restaurant in Sydney would have killed for, and watched the sunlight dapple against the wall opposite the window.

What was this about the way her body reacted, the way her mind seemed to drift off subject, the awareness that almost strangled free thought when Douglas stood anywhere near? Whatever it was it sent arrows of warning to her peace of mind as if she were the big red dot on a target board in an archery range. But she could back away, avoid the missiles and let them fall harmlessly to the ground. And stop harassing Douglas. Couldn't she? Her heart tightened beneath her ribs. She hoped she could.

She could handle this. She would do what she came here for and go home. Resume her life where she had left off. Extreme emotions had a way of settling down. Not that she'd been a fan of extreme emotion before now, but surely it was a phase.

Maybe she was going into early menopause and having an anxiety attack – or falling into an obsession. Maybe she could start some progesterone cream or fish-oil tablets because her emotions were all over the shop. Poor Douglas. The whole situation bordered on the ridiculous, and from this moment forth she would concentrate on why she had come here – getting to the bottom of the problem and, if she could, preventing microcephaly in future pregnancies in Spinifex.

Of course, business-hours-wise, being the weekend in the armpit of the world wouldn't help the access she needed – unless she harassed Cilla by phone. Cilla could possibly source experts in their homes to help her explain away other possible causes she'd come up with. Now that sounded like an excellent idea for after breakfast.

Then she thought about Georgina Poles, Blue's wife, who at her consult that afternoon had said her husband was worth more than the painting. That thought made her smile. Though of course his name wasn't really Blue Poles, like the Pollock artwork, and Georgina, despite her good sense of humour, did have a suspicious-looking polyp on her cervix. Sienna had clipped that nasty specimen and put it in a yellow-topped container in Douglas's fridge until she could fly it out on the mail plane on Monday. She'd put the container in a brown paper bag and hoped he wouldn't find it. The idea made her smile despite her plan not to fixate on Douglas.

And she'd spoken to the referral specialist herself, so that Georgina didn't have to wait past Monday for an appointment with the O&G guy's partner, a woman Sienna had met in Roma a few days ago.

She threw back the covers – she had always been an early riser – and reached for her computer. She'd email a few people, you could do that at any hour of the day, and see if they'd get back to her on a weekend about risk factors and possibilities. Then, when it was a decent hour, she'd try Cilla.

Except when she did, at seven o'clock, Cilla had just gone into theatre, an emergency caesarean, and it would be an hour and a half at least before she could call back. Sienna wondered if she knew the patient, what had happened, why the caesarean, then switched it off. Nope. She couldn't do that either.

Frustration ate at her. What was Douglas doing? Would anyone in town notice if she sneaked into his kitchen? Or his bed?

She took herself to the communal shower, a tad rotten-egg-gas-like in all its sulphuric glory, but hot as Hades, until her muscles relaxed, and then down to find breakfast.

Despite crowing about her new coffee machine, Alma had told Sienna she wasn't a morning person until eight a.m., had shown her the kitchen, the cereals and the plates, and offered her free run of the continental breakfast fare. If she wanted something cooked, Alma, with prior warning, would appear after eight.

Sienna didn't do cooked breakfast so strolled down the deserted stairs to quite happily poke around in Alma's fridge. She'd order in some yoghurt and berries for next week, but this weekend she'd survive on muesli. The tricky bit remained when to visit Douglas if she wanted coffee from her appliance.

Alma's magnificent coffee machine – she searched her brain and came up with 'Maestro' – wasn't a morning person either. One look at that and even she could see Maestro the machine required an involved set of pre-warming instructions and an A380-aircraft licence. So no help there.

Tap. Tap. Tap.

Sienna turned to find Maddy knocking quietly at the side door to the kitchen and she crossed to unlock it with hope flickering in her chest.

'Can you work Alma's coffee machine?' Abrupt much? Did she sound like Blanche? 'I'm sorry. Good morning, Maddy.'

Maddy laughed. 'Good morning. And yes, I can work Maestro. Give me ten minutes to wake him up.'

Thank goodness. Sienna squeezed her hands together in prayerful gratitude. She'd found a kindred mornings-are-good person. Then she remembered it was Saturday as she watched Maddy do strange things to the machine. Did she need the money maybe?

'I thought you weren't working on the weekend?'

Maddy flicked her an embarrassed glance. 'I'm not working for Alma. Thought I'd just check to see if you wanted anything typed up. Jacob likes to sleep in and I could give you two hours if you needed anything.'

Sienna watched the girl's face. 'That would be great. I'll start your time from now because Maestro and I need you now. I also have some changes for the questionnaire I haven't had a chance to give you. They're all scribbled in the columns – just ask if you can't read it.' She noted the relief on Maddy's face because work was available. 'We haven't really talked about it, but I was thinking forty dollars an hour cash for secretarial, is that okay?'

Maddy looked at her shyly. 'That'd be great.' There was no doubt about the relief.

Sienna thought logistics if Maddy needed money fast. In case she had a secret problem. One she was hiding – like a pregnancy. Sienna was sure now, and if Maddy didn't mention it in the next day she would.

'How about I put the cash for each day's pay in an envelope and you can tick it off when you take it. That way you can leave it there to accumulate or take it when you need.'

The young woman appeared to be concentrating fiercely on Maestro as she said, 'That would be handy, thank you. I'm saving up. It's a surprise for Jacob.' The last bit didn't quite ring true.

Thought so. 'Excellent.' There was a burst of steam. A lot of water going backwards and forwards, and then finally the wonderful sound and aroma of coffee grinding.

Maddy caught Sienna's eyes glued to the grinder part of the machine and laughed. 'Two minutes.'

At eight o'clock Sienna stood with Maddy outside Douglas's door and waited for him to appear and start her day as it should. Douglas rose early, too. She knew that.

When the door opened, his magnificent shoulders appeared, shrugged into a blue open-necked uniform shirt with a shoulder rank and the police badge, and work trousers. So he was going some-where. His thick dark hair curled damp from his shower and she reined in the instant imaginings of Douglas naked under a cascade of water like that kayak commercial, all sinew and wet bulging muscle.

His eyes narrowed at Sienna, reserved, maybe even with a hint of warning as if she'd throw herself into his arms, but she didn't miss the flare of heat in his eyes despite his attempt to veil it.

'Good morning, Sienna,' he said, and then his gaze slipped past Sienna's to smile at Maddy. How come she got the smile? 'Morning, Maddy. You girls are early.'

Sienna's tongue seemed to have stuck to the roof of her mouth, and after a quick glance at her, Maddy came to the rescue. 'There's a bit of typing to do and now's a good time for me if that's okay?'

'Fine. I have to go out after breakfast on a call anyway so the house will be yours.' He stepped back to invite them in.

As they strode past him into the hall he touched Sienna's arm. 'I'm going out to Spinifex Station if you want to come?'

She stopped and turned, and Maddy went to her desk and sat down, a tiny innocent smile on her face. That girl didn't miss much.

He said, 'Annette rang to say it could be a good time for her if you wanted to talk? That drifter I've been watching decided to try a bit of break and enter and they might have an idea out on Spinifex Station where he's headed next. She mentioned seeing you now instead of Monday and asked if I could bring you out today if you were free. You could see her while I talk to her husband.'

Sienna didn't waste time trying to figure out how a woman on an outlying cattle station knew the policeman could bring her with him to visit. She'd learned that all kinds of information beamed all over the outback in mysterious ways. The prospect of earlier progress on her investigation enticed, as did another private road trip with Douglas. And, his reserve just now needed a little sorting anyway.

Sienna nodded, glanced to where Maddy had settled herself and opened the computer. Her typist didn't need her and she could start her first interview. Excellent.

'If you could wait to leave until Maddy types in the amendments on the questionnaire that would be great.' He nodded, looked as if he'd been going to say something but changed his mind, and turned away. She watched his back thoughtfully. Something was up.

He'd said he planned on leaving after breakfast so it wasn't an urgent run and she'd have time to sort the envelope business while she waited. Maddy could stash yesterday's pay if she needed to.

After she'd done that in her office, she waved the envelope and tapped it to show Maddy where to find her pay. Then she quickly called Cilla to start her on her quest of contacts before looking for her driver.

When she found Douglas in the kitchen he stood staring out the window, a mug of tea in one hand and a slice of toast in the other, but his shoulders had that uncompromising stiffness to them. She sighed. Was he going to be all dramatic about last night? It just didn't seem like him. A thought intruded. A radical one.

OMG. Maybe it wasn't about her. Maybe he had something else on his mind. Thinking of other people could be so tedious.

Sienna patted her coffee machine as she walked past and said to his back, 'Do I need to ring Annette and confirm?'

He turned. Frowned as if his thoughts had been miles way and he had to search for her topic. His face cleared. 'No.'

She could have nailed it. Maybe he wasn't regretting last night at all. It could be her imagination and she'd worked herself up for nothing. 'Are you okay, Douglas? Is something wrong?'

'I'm fine. How long until you're ready to leave?' There was that slight hint of . . . impatience? Was he sick of her? Had she burned her boats with last night's escapade? Damn. Or was it all for the best?

Now she was worried again. 'Maddy won't be long.'

They were on the road by nine, the heat necessitating air conditioning. The plains shimmered all the way from the horizon and the eagles were poking about, smorgasboarding at the edge of the road like daylight vampires on a mission.

On a less morbid note, a flock of pink galahs lifted en masse from a passing fence line where they'd been holding a morning confab. Their wings caught the sunlight as they rose in glittering flight away from the passing vehicle. She saw a shiny lizard as round and long as her arm dart into a crevice in the rocky landscape. It seemed everyone was awake out here, too.

Her driver remained silent. 'Are we okay, Douglas?'

He didn't look at her. 'Why wouldn't we be?'

She lifted her chin and continued to look at him. Despite the way he made her feel, she wasn't a teenager. 'Because I pushed you into something you didn't want to do.'

The car slowed, pulled over to the edge of the gravel road and stopped. That was unexpected.

The cloud of dust that had been tailing them floated past as if it had missed the change of plans, dimming the outside world and leaving them alone in the centre. Douglas turned to her, his face unreadable.

'Dr Wilson. If I hadn't wanted to make love with you I can assure you I wouldn't have. Don't for a minute think you can blame yourself for that event. It was a joint effort.' The comment should have been funny, but the lack of humour in it made her wince.

'I knew what would happen,' he continued, 'I'm not stupid, or completely oblivious to how amazing it turned out to be. My reserve is because I can't see a good resolution here. And I think we need to protect ourselves from getting in any deeper.'

There was nothing there that she hadn't told herself. No unexpected shock to knock the wind out of her, but his words did so anyway. Left her gasping though she tried to hide it. The dust continued to drift past them, like his words, and the harshness outside and in had to be accepted.

'I understand.'

After a long look at her, his hands tightened on the wheel and he turned to stare directly ahead. 'I doubt that.' Then he put on his indicator despite there being no other cars visible, pulled back out onto the road and drove five kilometres faster than normal towards their destination.

They drove up to the homestead in a cloud of dust that must have heralded their arrival for miles. Annette nursed her baby, and her cowboy-hatted husband, the manager of Spinifex Station, waited under the bull-nosed iron of the verandah to greet them. Their baby, Eugenie, except for the noticeably smaller head circumference, looked like any other baby. Big eyes, dark brows, long lashes and pink cheeks, cute in a pink Peter Rabbit pinafore.

After initial introductions, the men strode off towards the machinery sheds and Annette invited her inside the cool, uncluttered homestead, which was all polished floors, high wooden ceilings and welcoming hospitality. Annette, almost as tall as Sienna, had a calm, unhurried manner as she carried her baby daughter into the dining room. A heritage green tea set and homemade biscuits waited on the polished table.

When she offered Sienna a seat, her sun-browned brow remained clear and untroubled and Sienna marvelled at her composure. Yes, Eugenie's head size looked under proportion compared with the rest of her tiny body, but she turned to follow her mother's voice, and her eyes were bright and interested. The muscle tone of her limbs also appeared normal. All of these were small blessings, and whatever fate awaited this baby was in the hands of the future.

'Thank you for allowing me to come to see you both, Annette.'

Annette pushed her fringe off her forehead with one finger, and assessed Sienna with eyes that held a no-nonsense clarity. 'It's all good. And it's easier for me as I don't have to go to three places in town. Just the appointment with the clinic nurse on Monday now and some groceries.'

'I'm pleased.' Sienna smiled. 'And your baby is beautiful.'

'Yes, she is.' This was said firmly but not blindly. 'It's a good thing we live in the country where people know us and won't make a fuss.'

'I'm not a paediatrician, but I did speak to Eugenie's doctor and he said she's meeting her early milestones. He sent me her reports – with your permission, I believe.'

Annette lowered her head. 'I've two older children. Twins in Year Four in the school here. All children are different, but Eugenie doesn't seem to act any differently than they did at her age. The paediatrician said that may change as she grows, but he also said it may not.' She lifted her head in acceptance.

A small silence fell and then she said, 'One of my brothers had a fall from a quad bike and he's never been the same. Any normal child might not grow up as expected, so we'll just aim for the best and share the love.'

Sienna looked at the woman in awe. And unexpectedly felt like crying. What was with her hormones since she'd come here? How could this woman be so uncomplaining? Annette didn't deserve more heartache after her family history. Nobody did. 'I'm here to try to find out if there is a reason, or reasons, two other babies have smaller heads like Eugenie. I've brought along another question-naire to see if there are any similarities that could be suspicious.'

'Of course I'll do what I can. Do you have any ideas?'

Sienna shrugged sympathetically. 'Ideas. Not answers. Because three babies born around the same time have similar symptoms, it could suggest an exposure to something at a certain stage in preg-nancy. To cause microcephaly, the time would be between eight and say sixteen weeks of pregnancy and most likely around fifteen weeks. It could be an infection, a toxin, a pesticide, even to think outside the box, an event like a heavy meteor shower causing radiation.'

Annette spread her hands out in question. 'How are you sup-posed to find that out?'

Sienna shrugged. 'By doing this. Asking questions. Collecting stories, data, checking local events and news, family history, and comparing with similar events in other places.'

Annette leaned forward. 'Has this happened in other places?'

Sienna shook her head. 'Not that I can find in Australia. We've looked, but I am still researching. Some events have happened overseas, for example, the zika virus has been causing microcephaly. And in past history, Hiroshima recorded microcephaly.' She held out her hands. 'I'm wondering if you can remember any illnesses or events that happened to you in that eight- to sixteen-week period of your pregnancy?'

'Not right now, but I'll have to have a good rethink about it,' Annette said.

They talked for another twenty minutes until Sienna had covered all her questions, then she said, 'That's great.' Sienna tapped the questionnaire. 'Write them down, if you could. Everything. Minor, major, unusual or even plain weird. Even events outside that period, although that's where I'm concentrating. Then, if possible, send it back to me by email, or drop it off at the clinic on Monday if you finish it, and I'll collate all the information from the three mothers as soon as I can. I understand you know the other mothers, that they're friends of yours, too?' At Annette's nod, she continued, 'I'll be asking them the same things. I'll let you all know on Monday if there's anything I need more information on. Does that sound okay?'

'Sure. I'll ask my husband.' Annette smiled. 'And my mother. I talk to her on the phone every day. She may remember me saying something.'

'That's a great idea. Or anyone else you correspond with. Maybe go through your emails for the period. It always amazes me the slice of life we put into even the shortest emails we send.'

Sienna hadn't re-read her emails before, but that had changed when she'd started to correspond with Douglas. Just a line or two when something funny happened. His dry sense of humour and lack of drama over major incidents would come back to her and she'd smile. She read those ones a few times.

'I've never read my old emails.' Annette laughed. 'Don't have the time.'

'When you do, you might decide to write a book. You know what they say. If people enjoy your letters, then they'd enjoy your stories as a book.'

'Now that would be a book. *Down on the Farm in Spinifex.*'

'See, you have a title already,' she said, and they both laughed as Sienna stood to leave. She smiled at Eugenie and the little girl gazed up at her like a tiny owl. 'Bye, Eugenie.'

'Thanks for coming out to us. Unless I get it finished earlier I'll drop the questionnaire into the clinic or Douglas's place on Monday when I bring Eugenie in for her check.'

'That would be great, thanks,' Sienna said and smiled to herself that of course everyone knew she was working out of the police residence. Imagine if she had moved in. Maybe Douglas did have a case for separate lodgings after all.

The drive back to Spinifex held little conversation. Sadly, Sienna felt the rift between them widen like the cracks beside the road and she wanted to ask if she'd done anything else to alienate him.

'You don't have to have dinner with me tonight, Douglas, if you don't want to.'

He glanced at her with brows drawn. 'Have you got another date?'

'No.' She laughed and thought of just-another-one Blue. None that aren't more interested in their glass. 'I enjoy your company,' she told him, 'but just thought you might like a night off.'

Chapter Eighteen

Alma

Alma watched the doctor and the policeman enter the pub, and thought back to last night when Sienna had come in. Luckily, all the regulars had been watching young Snubby downing his birthday schooner in one go. After that initial inspection, she'd looked up to where the shapely rear end of Dr Sienna Wilson disappeared up the stairs and noted the languid trail of fingers on the banister with one hand and the basket in the other. Alma had grinned. You had to hand it to that girl. Tenacity had nothing on her. And it was nice to know the policeman was as good as he looked.

Alma sighed. It was a bit different tonight. Pair of moping Mollys.

Someone called out for a beer. She had far too much respect for both of them to bring attention to something that was their business only, but it was Saturday night. She'd cooked them a nice roast dinner, and even found a bottle of not-too-cheap Sav Blanc she'd forgotten about.

Something was up after yesterday's shenanigans.

She sat them in the corner of the Dining Room for tea so the rowdies didn't disturb them. Fake pot plant and all. It was quite a nice setting if she said so herself.

Her effort to create a romantic atmosphere looked doomed. She'd thought they might be all lovey-dovey after their adventure last night, but nooooo. They'd barely looked at each other and the doctor had waved away the bottle.

They ate quickly and then Douglas stood up and left after a curt goodnight.

Sienna trailed over to lean on the bar as she waited for Alma to make her another coffee. She looked prickly and frustrated and Alma searched for something to cheer her.

'I do up a big breakfast tomorrow. Men love food, and you can invite that man of yours.'

Sienna made a sound that was almost a snort. Except she was too much the lady to snort. 'He's not my man.'

Alma glared at her. Seriously? She could knock their heads together. 'So you think that's all his fault?'

The doctor straightened, lifted her chin. Good. At least she had a bit of fight left in her. Alma didn't have much time for pansies and the lovelorn type.

Sienna said crisply, 'Don't try your matchmaking, Alma.' There was a bit of a bite to her tone, Alma decided with an inward grin. 'It would never work,' she went on. 'We live in two different worlds thousands of kilometres apart.'

Well, true, that had been Alma's own sentiments at the beginning. But, after watching them that first evening – the shared jokes, the regard they had for each other – Alma didn't think that was enough reason not to try to work it out, now.

She pulled a face. 'Just shows me at least one of you is stupid.'

Sienna lifted one brow. She didn't look offended. Not that Alma worried about that. The doctor said, 'Or it could be we are both incredibly smart.'

'I guess.' Alma shrugged. Well, they were brainy people. Both of them. She frothed the milk. Set the cup on the bar. 'Doesn't mean you can't play while you're here,' she suggested.

Sienna lifted her chin. 'It's not my backyard and I'm not invited.'

They looked glumly at each other. 'Seems a shame,' Alma said, starting to feel dejected. Then she brightened. 'Never knew a man who could refuse bacon and eggs on a Sunday morning. You should ask him. One last chance before you dive back into work on Monday.'

Finally, as if to keep the peace, Sienna said, 'Sure. I'll text him.' Alma decided she looked a smidgen brighter than before.

Chapter Nineteen

Sienna

Sienna hid her surprise when Douglas appeared for breakfast. He strode in with his dark-blue jeans hugging his impressive thighs as he scanned the room for her. Then he turned back to listen to something Alma said, and Sienna's eyes drifted down to his backside. She shook her head. Not fair.

Then he was coming towards her, a small smile still on his lips as his presence eclipsed her corner of the room. And her.

'Good morning, Sienna.'

She pushed the bubbling nerves back down into their pocket and indicated the seat. 'Good morning, Douglas.'

'Alma says it's our day off and we have to leave town today and have fun.' He quirked a brow at her. 'How does that sit with you?'

It sat very well. 'Does she?' Sienna cast a slightly bemused glance at her unexpected ally.

He did seem less careworn this morning and Sienna could feel her own mood lift the way his beautiful mouth had just lifted.

'Would you like to leave town and have fun with me today, Sienna?'

There was something in his tone that hadn't been there yesterday and certainly hadn't been there last night. She studied him. What had changed? Had Alma been offering him hope where he hadn't seen any?

The clothes had changed. No uniform. He looked relaxed in a cream shirt with the sleeves rolled up past the powerful forearms. Maybe that was what it was. She didn't think he'd been this relaxed since she'd arrived.

She'd kill for relaxed. A tiny starling of hope spread its wings low in her belly and swooped upwards. Just for today they both could let go. She'd play along. There weren't a lot of places on offer, but the company was great. 'Sure. Where would you like to go?' She certainly couldn't think of anywhere.

'It's a nice drive to Winton. Dramatic landscape on the way and you seemed to enjoy the wildlife yesterday. We could drop in on the Age of Dinosaurs Museum when we get there?'

Dinosaurs? Old bones. Good grief. She searched for something complimentary to say. 'You certainly know how to show a girl a good time.'

The lines at the side of his eyes deepened. He knew what she thought and it amused him. She could handle that. 'The museum is impressive,' he drawled.

He was impressive. And she could do with getting out of Spinifex, even if it was just for the day. Then she could come back, focus on the task ahead and hopefully get home by the end of the week or the middle of the next. 'Douglas, I'd love to see the dinosaurs with you on a Sunday in forty-degree heat. How far is it?'

'About two and a half hours each way.'

Typical. 'Is that normally the time it takes or just the way you drive?'

He arched one brow at her. 'Unlike you, I stay within the speed limits. Probably two hours the way you drive, but I would have to remove your licence.'

She'd like to see him try. 'I'm looking forward to our adventure,' she told him, tongue-in-cheek.

He smiled. Glanced at Alma, who approached with two loaded plates. 'And I'm looking forward to breakfast.'

Seems Alma was right about men and food on a Sunday morning. Sienna smiled at the wonderful woman, who looked far too smug.

The road to Winton stretched red and dry with dusty gravel for ever, but the light changed constantly, and despite the lack of trees the colours had a stark desert beauty that even Sienna could see. And the company made it perfect. Douglas had been almost chatty and Sienna sat back and enjoyed the show. Who was this man?

She gestured with one French-polished finger. 'What road is this?'

Douglas threw her a look. 'The Kennedy Development Road, but some people call it the Min Min Byway.'

She sat up a bit straighter. 'Alma's seen the light from the Min Min,' Sienna quipped.

'Hmm. So I've heard.' Douglas sounded unconvinced. 'Seems the light has upped its social skills and is getting out more.'

'Has it?'

'Apparently. Because young Jacob saw it, too, a few months ago.' He looked thoughtful. 'That would be around the time you were looking for unusual events. That's Maddy's man.'

She doubted a fictitious light could cause microcephaly, and she'd have liked to have asked why the negative tone in his voice when he spoke of Jacob, but she didn't want to destroy his mood. Or think about microcephaly today.

Instead, she'd save those ones for later. 'Tell me about where we're going.'

He obliged. 'Winton is a nice town. Historic. It's where Qantas was originally registered as an airline.' After a brief dissertation on the birth of Qantas – it was a damn shame she couldn't fly in and out of there then – he told her that Winton also had artesian water. So it was smelly showers for everyone, Sienna thought.

Then Douglas began on the dinosaurs with definite enthusiasm in his voice.

She shifted in her seat. 'Hang on a minute. I've just realised. You must have been one of those dinosaur-obsessed pre-teens who took his plastic tyrannosaurs to school and knew the names of all the species.'

Douglas glanced across with a small smile on his too-darn-sexy mouth. 'I could have been.'

She sat back. 'Bet you were,' she said thoughtfully. 'Clouds and dinosaurs.' It made her feel just a wee bit protective of the younger Douglas. A dreamy lad she could barely see when she looked at the man. She studied his profile. Admired the strong planes, slashing brows, dark eyes and that mouth.

She thought about what they'd shared in brief windows over the last twelve months and the bare minimum she knew of his earlier life. Earlier than a year really. All she knew was that he'd lost his sister who'd been pregnant at the time and he felt guilty about that for some reason.

She knew he'd spent time in special ops in the army until his head became screwed completely. So, he'd retreated to the outback to ground himself, protecting small towns as a policeman. She had to admit, like those small towns, she always felt safe with Douglas around.

'Where did you grow up?'

The conversation screeched to a halt as a big red Ford utility swung around the bend and towards them in a blur of roaring music, spraying dirt, and speed, and Douglas had to swerve skilfully to avoid a collision. The thick cloud of dust rolled over them and the cacophony departed as wildly as it had come.

'Idiot,' Douglas muttered fiercely as their own vehicle hit the heavier gravel at the side of the road and skidded briefly until he brought it firmly back under control. 'He'll be a white cross on the road if he keeps driving like that. Hopefully he won't take anyone else with him before we rip up his licence.'

Sienna's heart rate had doubled at the near collision on such a deserted road, and she could feel the thump under her fingers as she pressed her chest. That had been too close, she'd actually seen the whites of the young man's eyes. Rolled inside a metal ball was not the way she wanted to solve her dilemmas.

She felt Douglas's concern as he looked her over. 'You okay?'

'Sure.' She said it quickly to reassure him, but it had made her rethink his driving skills and the fact that in his job Douglas did save lives by catching the stupid risk-takers. And now the lovely mood would be broken. She sighed at the loss. 'I guess there's nothing you can do? He's gone in a cloud of dust and we didn't get his number plate.'

'I have the first three letters.' To her surprise his mouth twisted in wry humour. 'At least it's appropriate. K.O.K.'

She grinned back at him. This was the Douglas she loved. No. Not loved. Enjoyed. She didn't love him. The Director of Obstetrics in Sydney Central Hospital could not afford to love him.

Douglas went on and she was glad of the diversion from her own circling dismay. She heard him distantly as she stared blindly out the window at the swirls of dust settling around them, along with the influx of dread for the state of her heart.

'One thing about the distances around here,' he said. 'When I get to Winton, I can call in to each of the three possible towns out of here with a description and he won't disappear off the radar. We'll get him in the next couple of hours.'

She couldn't miss the tinge of satisfaction in his voice. She had to admit she shared the sentiment, but she had other things to worry about.

She didn't love Douglas. And more to the point, he didn't love her. He fancied her, which was a very good thing, but he was way too smart to fall in love with a city doctor when a real relationship between them could never work.

And she was way too smart, too. Really.

'Tell me more about the dinosaur museum,' she said, and hoped he didn't hear the tinge of panic in her voice. She did not love Douglas.

He obliged though she barely heard him. 'They have a collection room, of course, the largest collection of dinosaur bones and fossils in Australia, where the bones are assembled and laid out, but I admit it's the laboratory part I'm drawn to.'

Sienna caught the shake of his head, a shake of admiration, and she struggled to stay focused. 'You can see them painstakingly brush dirt from the bones, finding the contours that are nearly a hundred million years old.' His big hands were firm and confident, running smoothly up and down the steering wheel like they'd run up and down her body, playing her like an instrument until he hit the top note.

'That blows me away,' he mused.

Her heart rate had settled from the second shock. His words sank in. What blows him away? She'd just been thinking about what blew her away. She played back the conversation until she understood.

'So we're going to the collection room.' She said 'morgue' in her head. She'd never been one for dead things. Her job aimed to keep everyone alive.

Douglas became more animated as he described the museum and she had to smile. Here was another facet she would never have guessed lay beneath the strict and serious Sergeant McCabe.

Douglas went on. 'A full tour takes ninety minutes in Winton. If we had more time I'd take you to the stampede.'

'They have a dinosaur stampede?' She probably should have known or read up on this stuff, but it stood a long way from what interested her. However, it intrigued her now with Douglas so enthusiastic. Sienna in a dinosaur factory – that would have her sister Eve rolling on the ground holding her stomach from laughing too hard. There was never a dull moment with Douglas.

The museum and the laboratory were both noteworthy and interesting, but for Sienna it was Douglas – watching that hit revelation status. Especially in the gift shop afterwards. She had to drag him in there – trivia and trinkets weren't his style – but he humoured her.

Sienna picked up the silver-coated necklace with dinosaur bones arranged into a skeletal T-Rex, one of many hanging from a rack. She nestled it against her cleavage. 'Would this look good on me?'

His eyes widened and she held his gaze. The room didn't quite fog up, but she found herself lifting her shirt away from her suddenly warm neck and putting the necklace back hastily.

'Anything looks good on you,' he said, his tone low and sincere. Then he turned away and picked up something. 'Although, I like this,' he said, holding up a florescent pink shower-rose shaped like a dinosaur's head. The shower water would pour from the mouth in a spray. 'I can imagine this in Alma's guest bathroom.'

Composure hastily restored, Sienna raised her brows. 'There's already one in there. Or at least one that's as old as that.'

Douglas laughed. A sexy, teasing laugh. She felt the hairs rise on her arms. Felt her gaze zoom to his mouth where it tilted, lopsided and luscious. 'Poor Sienna. Slumming it in a shared pub bathroom.'

'Don't mock. One morning you'll find me dripping wet and naked at your house – when it's all been too much.'

He cocked his head. Dark eyes studied her. And she could tell he was seeing the picture clearly. Heat flared low and smouldering in her belly. How could he do that with a look? He said quietly, 'I'd have to arrest you for break and enter.'

She held out her wrists. Paused for effect and said in a low, sultry voice, barely above a whisper, 'Cuff me, Officer.'

Douglas laughed out loud. 'My schoolboy fantasy.' He shook his head and picked up a green coffee cup, still smiling. 'What about a Tea Rex mug?'

She snatched it off him and held it to her chest gleefully. 'At last we've found it. Your Christmas present.'

He grinned and sauntered off to check the other trinkets and treasure as if it had been his idea to come in here. She had the notion that he was having as much fun as she was, and she knew she should run from this place as fast as she could because she was falling a little more in love every second and she couldn't afford to do that.

His voice called, 'Over here.' The thread of amusement was already curving her lips as she followed him. She'd never seen him so light-hearted, so playful, and she wanted to drag him outside to some dark corner and beg him to kiss her. She who never begged for anything.

'I've found your gift.'

'Really? You've decided amongst all these stellar choices?'

He nodded serenely. 'Yup.' He pointed to a stand where a pair of black pantyhose were modelled by two inflated ladies' legs. The black tights were opaque to ten centimetres above the knee and then they sheered to see-through, where an appliqued T-Rex chased a feminine-looking Brachiosaurus around both thighs. She burst out laughing.

He laughed with her and she realised it was the first time they'd ever really laughed together. 'Is that another boyhood fantasy?'

'It could be.'

She chose an unopened packet in her size. 'I'll get myself a pair for Christmas.'

'Now I have to come.'

———

Driving home late in the afternoon Sienna thought about dinosaurs. Not just the ones on the stockings. Dinosaurs were a little like the outback. They made you made you feel insignificant in the scheme of time, in the same way the outback made you feel in the scheme of place. Concepts Douglas had no problem with, but for her, they sat outside her comfort zone. Or had done.

She rested her hand on his thigh as he drove, her deep need to have that connection surprising her, but every now and then his hand drifted down and stroked her for the few seconds he'd allow it off the steering wheel. She let the peace of the tiny world they inhabited surround her. They drove in a bubble back to Spinifex and she realised that this cocoon of feeling was peculiar to being with Douglas.

She'd felt it before, a feeling of wholeness and serenity that she didn't know she had in her makeup, like the calm in the middle of a storm after Callie's accident, and in her home in Sydney after her rotten illness, when Douglas had cared for her. It was not so much the passionate immersion she felt when they made love, though those experiences were also not of her usual universe. This was different.

It was very strange to feel so content after a day looking at old bones and quirky, silly knick-knacks. Her hand lay relaxed against Douglas's leg and her gaze drifted out over the long golden plains ahead. It had been a good day.

Chapter Twenty

Eight-thirty Monday morning at the police residence, Sienna heard the flying doctor plane go over. The carport that usually held Douglas's vehicle stood empty. Good thing, too. She needed to shake herself out of this romantic fog she'd come home in last night and do what she had come to do. Easy. Solve the mystery. Return fast to Sydney. Leave the poor man alone.

But they did have a fun day yesterday and she still hadn't figured out what had brought about Douglas's change of attitude.

Maybe she should have asked Alma if she knew the reason, but it was just too out of character for Sienna to ask anyone for that sort of help. Last night when she'd come in, Alma had winked and said, 'See. I knew you'd have a good day.'

Sienna had looked at her and no smart comment had sprung to mind. Instead, again out of character, she'd said, 'Yes. It was a lovely day. I'm not sure what you did, but thank you, Alma.'

The little woman had blinked and narrowed her eyes. 'You're welcome.' Then with a mischievous nod of the head had said, 'I found one more young woman with Virginia problems. One of the women from the mission out of town. Any chance of you seeing her?'

Sienna had closed her eyes briefly before saying, 'Send her down at ten.' It hadn't been worth fighting.

So she had an hour and a half before Alma's next referral arrived. Ten minutes later she heard the plane take off again. So the midwife had been deposited and the Spinifex RN would also be back for today. The clinic started at nine and finished at twelve and Sienna had arranged to interview the midwife from twelve to twelve-thirty. Any new questions she had for the FOG had to be by phone because he wasn't returning until the next fortnight.

At midday Sienna stopped outside the health centre and read the sign she'd glanced at when she'd first seen the place with Douglas. Read it more slowly. Tried to see what Kyeesha, the woman Alma had sent to her, had objected to when'd she decided not to go there for a check-up.

Opening Hours (for non-urgent consultation)
Monday and Wednesday 9.00 a.m. – 12 noon,
2.00 p.m. – 4.00 p.m.
After Hours Emergencies: 000
After Hours Health Advice: 13 43 25 84
Routine health checks and resupply of prescribed medications
Monday and Wednesday ONLY
Outside these hours – Emergencies ONLY
Consultations by Appointment
RFDS Doctor – Every second Monday

Child Health Nurse – alternate Mondays with RFDS

Dentist (as advertised)

Ophthalmologist (as advertised)

Podiatrist, Dietician (as advertised)

Optometrist (as advertised)

Diabetes Educator (as advertised)

Women's Health Doctor (as advertised)

The last line caught her attention. She needed to talk to the health service administrators about that. About options to go to a female doctor or nurse like women had in the city. Maybe every couple of scheduled visits they could try harder to get a female consultant here. Her heart ached for the woman she'd seen this morning. She pushed open the screen door.

There were still three patients sitting in the tiny waiting room for the clinic nurse when Sienna arrived five minutes early for her interview appointment.

The elderly Aboriginal man didn't look up and the young boy sitting next to him flashed her such a mischievous white-toothed smile in his dark handsome face that Sienna couldn't help returning it. The third was a blonde-haired young man in his late twenties with a plaster cast on his leg and crutches. He nodded at her with a flashy smile. Sienna nodded back. Handsome bloke.

She smiled vaguely at them all and ducked back out again to cross the road and walk up to the pub for a cold squash. Alma leaned on the bar and her crinkle-cut face wrinkled into a smile of greeting.

She filled a glass of squash for Sienna. 'Did Kyeesha turn up?'

Sienna nodded and thankfully Alma didn't ask. Just occasionally she surprised Sienna with the boundaries she left intact.

'How's the detective work going?'

She'd re-studied all of the patient notes on Sunday night. Nothing had jumped out. Sienna took the glass with a sigh of relief. 'Slow progress.' The heat from outside hung around her like a too-heavy pashmina and she lifted the cool glass to her cheek before she took a sip. When she did, the liquid chill ran down her oesophagus with a trickle of pleasure. 'I don't like slow.' As if to make her point she gulped down the entire drink and put it down. 'I'm waiting for the clinic sister to finish her appointments.'

'Don't like slow, eh? Never would have guessed.' Alma looked around. 'Well, you've come to the right place if you want action. In Spinifex we don't do slow. No siree. This place is jumping.' Alma used one arm to sweep grandly around the empty bar and the other to fill the water-beaded glass as it sat empty on the polished wood. Small raindrops of condensation raced down the outside as Sienna picked it up again gratefully and felt her lowered mood lift.

'I'm getting used to the crowds.' Sienna raised her eyebrows and then looked down at her drink with anticipation. 'The squash is exciting.'

'Reckon you can make your own fun. You looked pretty happy with yourself last night.'

Sienna used her professional face. 'It did turn out to be a lovely Sunday.'

'Glad you enjoyed the metropolis of Winton.' Alma raised her own sparse brows suggestively.

'Oh yes. Beautiful.'

Alma cackled. 'Never heard it called that before.'

Sienna drank this glass at her leisure, savouring it. Then she licked her lips. 'Seriously. If squash wasn't so full of sugar I'd drink a gallon of the stuff.'

'A bit of sweet never hurt anyone.' Alma reached back into the fridge and brought out a fresh cold bottle of the lemon drink. She stacked three ten-ounce glasses inside each other from the rack and put them all on the bar. 'Take the bottle back across. The girls will have a drink and can take the rest out to the pilot when they go.'

Sienna stood up. 'Thanks, Alma. Nice idea.'

Alma nodded regally. 'Yep, that's me. Nice.' And she snorted and cackled and waved Sienna away.

This place was crazy. Sienna smiled as she walked, carrying the cold glasses and bottle back down the street. Crazy weather, crazy dust, crazy publican. At least Alma wasn't miserable.

Sienna had to step aside as the young man with the broken leg manoeuvred his crutches out the door. Must have had his turn, then. His big smile widened and his voice sounded friendly. 'You must be the doctor my Maddy's been working with.'

'Madison. Yes. And you must be Jacob.'

'That's me. Your sister married Lex Mackay, didn't she? The Mackays are treated like royalty around here. Can even get a big-city doctor to come to a place like this.' He paused as he drew level with Sienna, just a touch too close, and instinctively she drew back. Now she didn't see his good looks. She could see why Douglas hadn't been impressed. Little big man. Personal-space invader. Too pretty and knew it.

She shifted to the left. 'Yes, well, Maddy's a terrific worker.'

He shrugged as if he didn't quite believe Maddy worked hard.

Said instead of commenting on Maddy, 'A doctor staying and working out of a pub seems pretty strange.'

'I'm working down at the police station. In the residence, actually.' She noticed, oddly, that his eyes seemed to glitter at that, but his voice stayed friendly.

'She didn't say.' He paused. Stared off into the distance with a strange smile on his face. 'Fancy that. Well, hope you find what you're looking for.' And he swung away awkwardly with his crutches.

She watched him go with a tingle of foreboding and tried to unpick what she'd said that had caused the spike of emotion she'd seen sweep his face. She frowned over the slightly unpleasant encounter, but growing no wiser, she walked through the door.

The screen clanged shut behind her. The waiting room stood empty, with a faint tang of leftover perspiration, and she crossed to where the door to the examination room stood open.

An older lady, mid-fifties and jolly looking with a first-aid kit under her arm, waved and said as she passed, 'You must be Dr Wilson. I'm the clinic nurse. The midwife's in there. Sorry. The butcher cut himself. I need to see how bad. Back soon.' Then she disappeared. Sienna blinked then peered into the tiny exam room.

A young woman busied herself tidying the room and packing a bag. Sienna hadn't thought about how she expected the midwife to look, but eyebrow and nose studs hadn't been a part of it. There was nothing unusual about that in Sydney or Melbourne, but in Spinifex the ornamentation made her blink. The woman's blonde hair was worn in a ponytail to one side, and on the other side of her head the dark hair had been shaved to about a centimetre long. Different. And she looked too young to be flying out to be a medical resource person at remote outposts.

'Hi. I'm Chrissy Doolan,' the young woman said as she invited Sienna into the air-conditioned room. Her eyes skittered to the bottle of lemon squash though she tried to hide it, and Sienna appreciated the publican's sentiment.

She put her gifts down on the steel dressing trolley with a metallic clunk and waved her hands. 'Yours. Compliments of Alma.' She paused and thought about that as Chrissy cracked it and poured herself a glass. 'Though possibly, compliments of Blanche Mackay.'

Chrissy laughed and Sienna saw the flash of her tongue stud. She wondered what Douglas would say if Sienna suggested she should try a tongue stud. The thought made her smile.

'Mrs Mackay is one of our patrons,' Chrissy said.

Dear Blanche. 'Not surprised. She does have remote medical access on her agenda. But I'd better not slow you down. What time does your flight come to pick you up?'

'Anytime after one.'

'Fine. Just a few questions if that's okay?'

'Sure. The FOG said you'd be keen to talk to me.' They sat down on either side of the cluttered desk.

Sienna began. 'So you would have seen Annette today and baby Eugenie? Did they drop off the questionnaire for me?'

Chrissy spun in her swivel chair and picked up some folded papers. 'Yep, here.'

She handed them over and Sienna put them on the desk in front of her. She'd look later.

'Great, thanks. So, you're the Family and Child Health Nurse and you check the milestones for the babies as well as do the antenatal visits between the FOG days?'

'Yes, I am. I hadn't long started with the RFDS so I remember when Annette came in for the pregnancy test. I know all three of the women involved. It was pretty exciting to have three pregnant women from a small town like this.'

'We've considered the camel race festivities might have a hand in that population explosion.'

'Makes sense.' Chrissy grinned. 'I did hear it's a fun event.'

'I've learned they play hard around here.'

Chrissy nodded. 'It's a tough life. The remote stations breed amazing people.'

They both thought about that. 'So you continued to see all three of the women antenatally in between the FOG's visits?'

'Yep. The pregnancies were all normal, so apart from the two visits when they saw the FOG, everything was routine until they left at thirty-six weeks to wait for labour. Babies were moving normally, normal growth, normal everything.' She looked down sadly. 'Except it wasn't.'

Sienna nodded. 'It's tough for everyone. I'm hoping to find a cause and try to prevent something like this happening again. I've already received a copy of the ladies' antenatal records, I'm really looking for unusual things that could have happened towards the end of their first and beginning of second trimester. So between ten and fifteen weeks?'

Chrissy swivelled to look at the calendar on the wall, one with a camel on it. 'What month would that be?'

'July.'

Chrissy screwed up her face. 'I was here. Like what?'

'Toxins, a run of some viral illness, aerial spraying over a water source. That sort of thing.'

Chrissy tapped her fingers on the desk. 'Can't think of any-thing off hand, but I'm a diary keeper, so I could look it up when I get home. Especially in the early days when everything in this job seemed so new and different.'

'That would be excellent.' Sienna glanced around the tiny room. 'Is it still new and different?' She pictured the waiting room twenty minutes before. 'You must have a diverse patient load judg-ing by the last three I saw.'

Chrissy thought about that and reeled off, 'Yep, diabetes, otitis media and plaster check. Then there're the swabs and the immuni-sations and the pregnancy tests, though often the women are too busy to even notice they're pregnant for a while.'

'Can't imagine that.' Then she thought of Maddy and amended the statement. 'Depends on what else is going on, I suppose.'

'Denial isn't just a river in Egypt,' Chrissy said, and they both smiled.

Sienna thought of Sydney and, before that, trendy Melbourne. 'Well, not where I come from, anyway. Most women I know test within days and then about three times more before they're six weeks into the pregnancy.'

Chrissy nodded seriously and the intelligence and empathy in her eyes made Sienna rethink her initial reaction about the younger woman's age. 'I guess it's back to access. Access to doctors, to chemists. But even if the women out here know they're pregnant, it's such a long way to anyone they can talk to, the visits usually stick to less than the recommended ten visits for the first pregnancy and seven or less after that.'

Not like the city. 'We'd probably run twelve to fourteen visits for most women.' Sienna's thoughts turned to Maddy again.

'Do you have any pregnant women on your books for Spinifex at the moment?'

Chrissy screwed up her face as she thought then relaxed. 'Nope. Not a one, which is funny after having three. There's not that many young families around and after the flurry in the last month it's slowed again.'

Sienna pondered mentioning Maddy and decided not to. 'And when do they leave to wait for labour?'

'They go to Longreach for the midwives or Charleville, or a Brisbane hospital if they need obstetric care, at thirty-seven weeks at the latest.' She pulled a face. 'It must be hard leaving home to wait in a strange place, especially for the Indigenous women who have the extended family around them. Hard for anyone leaving the family while you're waiting for labour and feeling the most vulnerable. So not surprisingly, some women wait till the last minute. Unfortunately for them, leaving any later than thirty-seven weeks means they have to pay for their own accommodation.'

'I remember that, now. Too late to get to a hospital if you leave when you go into labour.' She remembered Eve's experience. 'They had a breech at the Red Sand centre last year.'

'I heard about that. Glad it wasn't me.' Chrissy's eyes widened at the thought. 'Luckily, most women are stoic and just go early. And for those who don't, well, all we can do is deal with what arrives to the best of our ability. If I worried about what could walk in at any of the clinics we run I wouldn't sleep at night. And the phone's there for moral and directional support until help can get here.'

'I imagine that's the frame of mind you'd need.' Sienna looked around the small room. There wasn't a lot of equipment backup. 'I think you do a great job.'

Chrissy sighed. 'I wish I could have done something to help Annette and the other ladies. Eugenie is beautiful and we'll just have to pray that her brain capacity isn't compromised by her small skull bones.' She drummed her fingers on the desk and then her face brightened. 'Is there anything at all I can pass onto my patients to cut down risks of this in the future?'

'It all depends on what the cause is when we find it,' Sienna said. She refused to say if. 'I've been reading a lot, and there's research about cytomegalovirus causing microcephaly, but the numbers are very small. Hence the reason for the extra blood tests I ordered for Annette and Eugenie. The other two mothers will have those tests as well. When I get back to Sydney I'll talk to someone in Health about upping the public awareness campaign,' Sienna added, 'but I've discovered they have handouts on it already. Do you have some here?'

Chrissy turned her head slowly to look around. 'Haven't seen any, but I'll get onto it and we'll order some for all our clinics. Is there an immunisation?'

'Nothing licensed. The paper I read called the only precaution the CMV knowledge vaccine. That simple precautions will hopefully do the trick. I'm thinking you could pass this onto any pregnant women or immunosuppressed people you have in your clinic.'

'That's what I'm looking for.'

'Pregnant women need to know CMV exists so they can be careful. Second, the recommended three simple precautions are based on the knowledge that toddlers and young children are "hot zones" for CMV.

'The three tips to reduce exposure to the most common sources of CMV involve,' Sienna ticked them off on her fingers. 'Not sharing food, drink, straws or eating utensils with young children; so playgroups and preschools are told about this. Not kissing young children on or around the mouth or lips; and washing hands well after changing nappies and wiping runny noses or mouth drool. The study I read talked about bringing the infections down from 46 per cent to 6 per cent in those who were educated about extra hygiene as opposed to the control group. And the group educated on CMV were keen to take up the advice.'

Chrissy nodded vehemently. 'I'd think any mother would. Why isn't this out there more?'

Sienna didn't have a good answer for that. 'I guess there's so much info for women to hear when they're pregnant it seems just another frightening possibility.'

'But they're such simple solutions. You've converted me. No more kissing my nieces on the lips.'

Sienna stood up and smiled. 'Me, too. Though I'm not planning to be pregnant.' Then she laughed. 'I'll catch up with your clinic nurse when she does her next clinic. I've thought of something I want to follow up.'

'No worries.' Chrissy glanced at the bottle of squash and the glasses. 'And thank Alma for the drink. The pilot will love her.'

'Will do.'

When Sienna returned to the police residence she rang her registrar, Cilla, and asked her to find the phone number of the Director of Nuclear Medicine in their Sydney hospital. She'd been going through the causes of microcephaly again and another idea had needed checking.

Radiation exposure felt like an obscure cause, but she wanted to talk to someone about the possibility. Cilla would get back to her.

Chapter Twenty-one

Maddy

'You've been keeping secrets again, Madison. You know I don't like that.' Jacob wagged his finger at her. He'd been waiting just inside the door.

Maddy felt the cold trickle of fear along with the chill of the metal crutch against her thigh. She squeezed her satchel against her stomach to form a barrier to protect her baby.

She'd spent an hour down with the doctor typing up new reports and she only had twenty minutes before she was due at the pub after she came home to make Jacob's dinner.

He leaned his weight on his good foot and his backside against the bench behind him. Then the other crutch came up behind her so she couldn't reverse out.

Her heart pounded in her chest and she sucked in her belly as much as she could. Had he discovered she was pregnant? Did he want to have sex? Her growing fears for the safety of her baby crystallised into a pure animal terror and she was trying to hide that, too.

She'd been so stupid to let it get to this point. What if she'd gone into labour and she couldn't run from him? Had she left it too late? Could he hurt her and the baby in one go? Would he?

Thoughts tumbled and twisted through her mind as she stood frozen, and when she didn't reply he tapped her none too gently with the crutch at her back. That woke her up.

He whispered, 'No escape from the truth,' in that mocking, hateful voice she'd grown to dread.

'I'm sorry,' she said, very quietly. 'But I don't know what you mean.' Warily navigating the tricky waters of his volatile emotions made her eyes dart around as she tried to work out how she could escape, aware again of how urgent it had become.

His mouth leaned towards her ear as he whispered, 'Not good enough. Why didn't you tell me you were working at the police station?'

For a second Maddy sagged. Thank goodness, she thought, this wasn't about the pregnancy, and she tried not to show the relief that flooded her and instead converted it into the semblance of guilt for a different wrongdoing. 'I'm . . .' her voice stuck in her throat, 'I'm sorry. I didn't know where we would be working when I said I'd do the job.'

He frowned at her. And she could tell he was sensing an undercurrent he didn't understand. His temper flared and he squeezed her between the two crutches, catching the skin as she braced. She winced at the sting. 'But you've worked there for days now, haven't you, and you know I hate McCabe.' He ground the name out like a dirty seed in his teeth. 'You know I don't like deception.'

She put her hand gently on the metal and tried to push past the crutch in front of her. When he didn't budge she looked at his face. Forced herself to smile up at him. 'I was wrong. I'm sorry. Let me put my bag down and we can talk about it. I don't want to upset you, Jacob.' She hated the trace of fear she could hear in her voice. But he loved it.

Jacob's fingers slid off the crutch to pinch her arm, slid down and did the same at the soft part of her inner thigh, and hot tears pricked with the pain as she tried not to cry out. She'd realised the more she'd cried out the harder he pinched. Cruel, painful pinches that would turn into black bruises all over her white skin.

He pushed her away. 'Don't lie to me again.'

'No, Jacob,' she lied.

'But you have upset me, Madison,' he said and let her go for the moment. 'We'll do more than talk about it when you come home tonight.'

She tried hard to stay out of his reach for the next twenty minutes, but by the time she left her sobs were hard to contain. This time she needed to hide in the gap between the buildings for more than a few minutes before she showed her face at work. She pushed open the door to the old service station and closed it behind her. Hopefully nobody had seen her come in here, today or yesterday when she'd left more supplies.

Maddy leaned panting against the wall and sniffed in the dim light. Then she stumbled further inside holding onto the grubby walls for support with one hand, the other over her mouth to quieten her sobs.

Thank goodness she could get away to a place she could disappear into unnoticed. A place between Jacob's house and the pub, a place nobody could hear her if she locked herself in the back room and closed the door. She hadn't thought she'd need it before she went into labour. She closed her eyes and tried to stop the sobs that racked her body. *Enough. This is the end.* She just needed one more night to get her things, tonight when she came home – *please God, let Jacob be asleep* – and she'd be gone.

Her hands found the nob and she pulled herself through the hallway arch and closed another door behind her with an echoey click. At the loudness of the noise she jumped and then scolded herself. This was a safe place. She had control. Not Jacob.

Darkness shrouded the corner of the room and somehow that helped, but the light seeped across the backyard and in a slash across the middle of the room through the curtains hanging over the cracked window. More dust motes reflected and danced in the dull triangle of light and the place smelled musty and sickly sweet.

She shuddered and hoped mice or rats hadn't burrowed into her little hidey hole, but she couldn't hear any scratches or see anything scuttle away. Hard to comprehend she'd considered having a baby in this deserted room. It would be good to be gone tomorrow. This was her emergency-only plan. Soon she wouldn't need this place as a backup, but knowing it was here was a good idea. Especially after today.

The birth itself had stayed nebulous. Of course she'd seen births on TV and they'd been pretty noisy, but she had a good tolerance for pain. She winced at the thought of what she'd put up with in the last few weeks. Her lip curled. Training for this. Lucky her.

The best thing she'd seen had been a documentary on YouTube about women in the fields in Brazil and the way they simply stopped their work, squatted to give birth, and then picked up their babies and walked on. That had given her hope. She wasn't stupid enough to think it would be that easy, but they'd been real women and real babies, so somewhere in between would do her fine. And there'd been that beautiful birth in Sweden.

Adjusting to the light, her eyes could make out where she'd prepared a tidy corner on the floor with a clean old rug and the thick newspapers she'd been collecting. The cordial bottle filled with water sat there, as did the washed scraps of old towels from the pub, and some white string she'd found wrapped around a pile of magazines.

Thanks to Dr Google she'd known to boil the string in the kettle with a pair of small scissors when she'd made Jacob's coffee, and hung the string discreetly on the line. Then, she'd carefully wrapped up everything in a piece of aluminium foil and brought it here with a little bottle of hand sanitiser, some baby wipes and a box of tissues.

'Just don't get frightened. Everything will be okay if you don't get scared.' Her low-pitched words seemed to swirl around her with the dust motes. 'Just like the animals on the farm when you were a kid. You can do this.'

Maddy leaned down and scrubbed her face with the baby wipes. Washed her hands and drew in several long, calming breaths. She finally lifted her head. She knew that time was getting away and she needed to go.

She glanced down one more time at the torch beside the papers – there so she had more light if she needed it. The nest was ready. *Please God*, she prayed she wouldn't need it.

Chapter Twenty-two

Sienna

At five p.m., alone in her hotel room, Sienna picked up the ringing phone. Dr Regan Tindel was the Director of Nuclear Medicine and also acted as the lead on the NSW EDM Squad, Emergency Disaster Management. He had been flown to Japan after the Fukushima Daiichi nuclear disaster as a consultant on radiation poisoning. Just the sort of knowledge bank she needed.

'Thank you for ringing me back, Dr Tindel.'

'No problem. What have you got, Dr Wilson?'

Straight to the point, then. 'I'm looking for possibilities, but I don't have much. A small cluster of microcephalic babies and no cause. I wanted to sound you out on how to exclude the possibility of a radioactive cause. A leak, an accident, a natural event. Maybe on how to arrange a measurement of the area perhaps? Is that possible?'

After a small pause, Regan said carefully, 'What makes you think your health problems could be from a radioactive source?'

'No reason at all except radiation is listed as one of the causes of birth defects such as these. At present, we have three babies conceived around the same time with similar medical issues. It could be a disease process, a chemical spill or I'm asking you if it could possibly be a radiological incident that wasn't notified.'

Regan enunciated carefully as he said, 'Nuclear incidents from lost or misplaced sources are rarely missed. You don't just lose something that's radioactive.'

As she'd thought, but it had been worth a shot. 'I imagine there'd be strong penalties for inadequate safeguards?'

Dryly and succinctly Regan said, 'Very.'

Something niggled and Sienna wasn't ready to give up. 'So it's not possible?'

Regan huffed. 'Anything is possible. Where exactly are you?'

'Spinifex. Central West Queensland. Pretty close, on the map anyway, to the Northern Territory and South Australian borders.'

There was a pause. 'You're a long way from home.'

Sienna grimaced at the phone. 'Tell me about it.'

'Just a moment, I'll pull out my maps and see what we have near you.'

Sienna sighed. She actually didn't want to find out she was standing in a town with a radioactive source nearby. At least she wasn't pregnant, but Eve was, and she glared at the mirror on the wall as she waited.

'Nothing I can see.' His voice held a hint of amusement directed at a lay person. 'You're a long way from Maralinga.'

'Very funny.' Nuclear physicists were so freakin' amusing.

'Okay. That went over like a lead balloon. Let's see. There's quite a few fracking expeditions. South Australia has a fracking group we've been told has lost an isotope down a sink hole, but that's a long way from you. I'll phone a friend to confirm they didn't just drop it off the back of a truck like those guys in America who lost their radioactive isotope for a week.'

Sienna's antenna went haywire like she imagined a Geiger counter would rattle in the movies. 'What? People actually dropped a radioactive source at the side of the road off the back of a truck?'

'Yep. These things can end up in scrap metal and cause quiet havoc.'

She did not want to hear this. Or maybe she did. 'How does a fracking group use the radioactive rod?'

'Well,' he paused and she hoped he was dumbing it down for her. 'The radioactive part of the rod is cased in a metal tube and they lower it into a bored hole and use it to find optimum areas for hydraulic fracturing, or "fracking". Or they lower the rods down into wells to find the best places to break up shale to release deep oil and gas deposits. The rods are small, about fifteen centimetres long, not much bigger than the new iPhone.' His voice became even drier. 'There are all sorts of safeguards so that they don't lose them.'

'Let's hope so.' Sienna knew there were different types of radiation but hadn't researched it. 'What sort of radiation would this be? Could it be harmful?'

'Most rods are americium-241/beryllium, or Am-241. It's classified as a "Category 3" source of radiation by the Nuclear Regulatory Commission. That means, if it's "not safely managed or securely protected, it could cause permanent injury to a person who handled them, or was otherwise in contact with them, for some hours." I've got what the American NRC said on that particular incident report in the US in front of me.'

'So it's not fatal.'

'Probably not.'

'But capable of causing genetic changes?'

There was another long pause. This guy did careful wordage to an art form. 'Let me quote them,' he said. 'Though Queensland would use the Rad Safety Regs. The Americans said, "It could possibly – although it is unlikely – be fatal to be close to this amount of unshielded radioactive material for a period of days to weeks." So it's unlikely to be fatal. The source itself is encased in that steel container, but it does pack something of a punch. The rod is "not something that produces radiation in an extremely dangerous form. But it's best for people to stay back, twenty or twenty-five feet."'

'Is it possible something like that could be lying around Spinifex unnoticed?'

'Highly unlikely. Corporations should not lose their radioactive material, but unfortunately it is remotely possible. I'll talk to a colleague closer to you and sound him out about a surveillance trip for a neutron source. Get out his BF3 detector.'

Well, at least she had his attention. Although now she wasn't so sure she wanted it. Then she thought of Eugenie. Yes, she did. 'Thank you. What about if it was say, parked here in a truck for a day. Are there any tests we can run that can confirm exposure to patients or the area?'

More enthusiasm leached into his voice. 'There's some great work being done by molecular geneticists looking at identifying genes that respond to radiation. They're examining effects of time from exposure, gender, age and additional genetic factors to predict the radiation dose.'

Sienna felt her heart leap. 'That would help.'

His voice became less enthusiastic. 'It's not available in Australia at present, I'm afraid.'

Sienna looked at her phone incredulously and tightened her grip. He did not just dangle a carrot and snatch it away! 'Well, why mention it?' Sienna wondered if he could hear the grinding of her teeth. She forced her hands to unclench on the phone.

His reply showed him oblivious to her ire. She could imagine his shrug. 'I find it fascinating.'

Instead of labouring that annoyance she said, 'So you'll set wheels in motion to send someone to rule out this cause for Spinifex?'

'I'll ask if the HSQ Radiation and Nuclear Sciences team can send someone out to do a radiation sweep. If they can't find it,' he paused, 'well, it doesn't mean it's not there. But I'll start with some questions of accountability and make sure everyone has all their equipment.'

He was useful after all. And she guessed it had been a pretty big ask to send someone when it had taken her so long to get here herself. She upped her appreciation. 'Thank you for responding with that. And for listening.'

His voice came down the line and this time she could hear the extreme interest and she knew he would take this seriously and see it through. 'I live for this stuff.'

'Lucky someone does.'

She just hoped they didn't find anything.

Chapter Twenty-three

Maddy

That night, as she was walking home at five minutes past ten, Madison's waters broke. The sudden unexpected pop between her legs, and the sensation that someone had poured a cup of warm tea down her inside thigh, tricked her at first. Her nose crinkled as she looked down in disbelief, disgusted she'd wet herself, and then realisation sank in. The puddle widened on the path below her legs and she remembered reading that the bag of waters around the baby would pop and it could be a little or a lot. Felt like a lot.

The sudden spike of fear ran in tentacles around her body until she reeled it in shakily like a first-time angler. *Stop it. This was okay.* It could have happened two minutes ago at work, or ten minutes ahead, when she got home to Jacob, who she feared had uncomfortable plans for tonight.

This could be the best place for it to happen, the best time, here in the dark, alone. Not that she could change it now anyway. So she must be lucky. Her heart pounded, and she glanced up at the sky overhead and drew in a long, quiet, shaky breath. *Give me strength.* Why couldn't it have waited until tomorrow?

It had been a relatively slow night behind the bar, and she'd had far too much time to imagine the punishment Jacob would have been cooking up all evening, so she'd tried to stay busy. The clean-up had been completed in record time, which was lucky because the gripey pains had been coming at least every fifteen minutes or so for a couple of hours now, and towards the end she'd had a hard time hiding them from Alma.

So stupid, of course. These pains had been warning her that things might happen, and now she needed to be out of sight.

She eyed the door of the old service station she'd passed several paces away. Paces she couldn't do right at this minute. Now, in the relative cool of the late evening, the whole idea of being in labour, all alone, made her falter. Suddenly, a vice-like grip squeezed stronger across her belly and back, lasting longer than any of the cramps had before. A tiny fear-filled voice whispered in the back of her head: *Just how strong did these contractions get?*

In the dark, she leaned on the telegraph pole, feeling the dry splintery wood beneath her fingers as she dug her nails in and kept breathing – when all she wanted to do was hold her breath and moan.

The cramp continued, like Jacob's fingers had before work this afternoon.

Well, she guessed she'd got used to not crying out, because here and now, instead of making any noise she sucked in a breath while the fluid trickled messily down her legs and pooled on the concrete.

She should go back to the hotel and wake Alma – or the doctor. For a moment she let that enticing thought – the idea of handing over control to others and being looked after – ease the tension in her shoulders, but she just couldn't. Tears stung. She didn't want to see the disappointment in their eyes. They both seemed to think she was something special, and look at her now.

She sniffed and lifted her head. Her mother's words came back to her. *You're a strong girl, Madison.*

When that first heavy-duty cramp eased, she dragged herself along the footpath to the dusty door of the deserted garage. 'Don't get frightened,' she ground out through gritted teeth.

Then the next pain came and the vice in her back and her lower belly hurt more than anything Jacob had done to her, and she grunted to stop calling out.

Finally, gradually, that cramp eased and she puffed short breaths through clamped teeth, the discomfort reduced enough to allowed her to creak open the door, edge through, and close it behind her. She crab-walked her way towards the inside room and the outside world receded. Now she stood truly alone.

The pain came again and she leaned against the wall and breathed in shallow gasps as she waited for it to pass. A minute later she was through the next doorway seeking out the darkest spot, where she eased herself down to rest on the small milking stool she'd found in the back shed when she'd been exploring. The pain came back and she moaned her way to kneeling, dragging the stool in front of her so her forearms could rest on it.

She sighed as the backache eased with her belly hanging forward, but then the pain in her belly began to escalate again. She gasped and unconsciously swung her pelvis left to right, right to left, in a slow beat in time to her breaths as she concentrated on the picture in her mind of a beautiful baby that stared at her.

Her beautiful baby, the baby she couldn't take home to Jacob. She hadn't thought of that. Of afterwards. She would have to leave her baby for others to keep safe because she couldn't even keep herself safe. The tears rolled down her cheeks and for the first time she wondered if she would die in here and nobody would find her.

An hour later the idea of death occurred to her again and she stamped it down. She'd live and no way was she ever doing this again. No fear!

She pushed herself off the wall she'd been stumbling along, around and around, circumnavigating the room like one of the videos had said, and put her hands low on the back of her hips and rocked her way around the room again. Telling herself each time as she moved to the next place on the wall to lean, that that was one less contraction. One closer to the end.

The cramps grew stronger, longer, and she began to feel the tiredness steal over her like a robber pilfering her strength. She didn't notice the shuffle of her feet, or the gasp of her breath, or the dimness of the room. The world contracted to the end of one long cramp and the beginning of the next, and weariness stole her thoughts until she moved like a zombie, plodding mindlessly around like an ox at the wheel.

After another hour the cramps changed tempo, upped the ante, dragging low moans from her, making her grunt and her eyes widen and dart around the room as if searching for somewhere to hide.

Again the cramps intensified, grew crazy enough to make her want to pant, crashed one upon the other until she crawled to her little stool and knelt before it as if pleading at an altar to make the cramps stop.

Her breath panted in short, irregular gasps no matter how hard she tried to keep it even, and she squeezed her eyes tight as the tears began to trickle again. She would die.

Then, inexplicably, the eye of the storm paused upon her, and there was stillness and quiet except for the harsh breathing she could hear from her own throat. Her breath eased as tentatively she rolled her shoulders, sipped from the bottle she had been gulping from during the brief moments before the next onslaught, and felt the strange insidious gathering of energy.

Maddy blinked, wiped her face with one grubby hand, and felt the weariness fall away like a dusty cloak until suddenly nausea swelled in her throat. She heaved, grabbed a fistful of tissues and gagged into them. She pushed the wad away with distaste, and wiped her hands with more tissues until she saw the gel. She reached for the pocket-sized bottle and pumped some of the cleansing gel onto her fingers, and the cool of it felt like the most glorious sensation in the sweat-filled world she inhabited.

Her throat ached with dryness and she reached again for her bottle of water, glanced with disorientation at the dim room she'd traipsed unendingly around over and over again – now able to pick out on the dusty floor where she'd walked.

She looked down at the stool under her fingers as she knelt before it, staring at her pale hands gripping it. She had sudden clarity of what she'd passed through. So she almost expected the first wave of the new surge, one that built powerfully and overwhelmingly, and the sudden downward pressure of an urge to push from within burst through her consciousness like a switch had been thrown.

Now she understood the rigidity of a kitten's stomach as it heaved or a litter of pups began in expulsions. She'd watched the shudder of the animal, and the quiet, relentless maternal effort. She tried not to think about the pouting of labia as a cow birthed.

Everything would be fine if she followed her instincts. Nobody discussed it with the cow.

These cramps grew more powerful, slowly building, and she breathed them downwards with a sudden swelling of determination to have it all finished. She lifted her chin and pushed her belly out with the breath like the midwife had told the mother in Sweden. They'd practised that for weeks before she'd had the baby and it all came back with the memory of what happened at the end.

And then the burning began. The sting and the heat and the pressure, and she gasped until the pain eased back but the pressure remained. It was overwhelming, intense, like an obstacle she couldn't push past. Except when the surge returned she did push past it. With the next explosion of power the intensity driving her glowed like a hot knife and suddenly, exhaustedly, in a rush of hot fluid and exquisite pain, she felt the release and it was done.

She dropped her head onto her hands on the stool and she sobbed with relief until, with a catch of her breath, she heard the tiny sound behind her.

She swung towards the noise, craning behind, because there on the rug, between her legs, lay a vision, a miracle, a dream, and a flexing wet bundle of tangled limbs, purple twists of cord, and blinking dark eyes beneath a downy head. Her baby.

Maddy gasped, shifted awkwardly, carefully, and reached with trembling fingers to pull and slide the hot tiny bundle between her legs to in front of her knees and stared at the thick cord that joined the two of them.

Then the baby blinked, gazed owlishly at her as if trying to focus, and screwed her face up to make a mewling cry as if to say, *Well?*

Maddy jumped, inhaled, and her heart thumped with fright and delight and dawning realisation that the baby she had planned around with all her organisation and pre-thought – was actually a living, breathing person! She hadn't thought of that. And one who could make noises so she'd better get on with tying the cord.

She followed the cord to her baby's belly, took in the fact that she had a daughter and winced at the ramifications of the knowledge. From nowhere a wall of heat suffused her. She swore that no man would hurt her baby as she had been hurt! But she needed this done and for some reason she had begun to shake and the spotty pool of blood underneath her grew bigger, and suddenly another pain gripped her and she closed her eyes on the urge to push again, for a horrible moment afraid another baby might pop out, but it wasn't that. Of course it wasn't that. The pain heightened and fell away as she listened to her body.

She grimaced at the meaty afterbirth and dropped her hand to her stomach. So empty. So hollow, after the birth. She tentatively pushed into her flaccid belly and felt the strange hard lump that was her uterus and noticed that the bleeding had stopped as well. Her baby whimpered and snapped her vague thoughts back to the present.

So much to do and so little time. The thick, purple, braided snake of cord looked otherworldly, bizarre, and she remembered the midwife in Sweden saying how clever the cord and placenta were. Maddy decided they both looked gross.

Instinctively, she stretched to gather up her baby, remembered the mantra that wet babies grew cold, that the mother's skin would heat it up, and looked about for the towel. She wiped the bluish skin tentatively with the bits of towel she'd saved for this purpose, then wiped the baby's wrinkled face and her chest and her wriggling limbs, which did seem to make her even more cross but made the pink replace the blue of her skin, until Maddy stopped wiping.

Maddy heaved her own work shirt off her torso, pulled at her cheap stretchy bra to expose all of her upper body skin, and lifted the baby against her.

It was a miracle as the whimpering stopped, and they knelt clasped together, baby and mother, skin against skin, for a long time.

Chapter Twenty-four

Alma

Alma wasn't a morning person – more of a midnight-to-two-am reader of gruesome female detective novels, as long as the female detective kicked the male baddy's arse. Sometimes, when the female detective was having a hard time pinning down the baddy, Alma couldn't sleep. Evil had to be punished and preferably by a woman. Alma didn't delve too deeply into why she needed the satisfaction those books gave her.

The phone shrilled again in the dark as she surfaced from a deep sleep. Groped for it. Alma swore softly, succinctly using most of the not-inconsiderable collection of words she'd overheard these last fifty years from men. At last she found the instrument and put it to her ear.

'Alma. It's Sergeant McCabe. Someone's left a newborn at the police station. I need the doctor.'

'What?' Her head snapped up.

'A baby. And it's crying. Screaming its lungs out. Get Sienna.'

She couldn't believe it. It seemed twice as disorientating to hear the sergeant's voice filled with an urgency she'd never heard before.

Alma dropped the receiver instead of returning it to the charger, stumbled, groped for the light, and stubbed her toe against the bedside table. Swore again. But she managed to turn on the light, so she pushed her feet into her slippers and grabbed her robe.

Imagine. Oh my Lord. And to think they actually had a baby doctor in town. Alma crossed the long hall from her private rooms until she reached the accommodation end, then pounded on Sienna's door so hard her knuckles hurt.

The door swung inwards before she could knock again. 'It better be urgent,' said the calm woman who opened the door.

Alma blinked. She'd expected the doctor to look a little like she'd seen of herself in the old hall mirror as she ran past. Tousled, spiking hair, creased pyjamas under flapping dressing gown. Instead, Dr Wilson was fully dressed, bright-eyed, and was standing calmly waiting as if she had people waking her early in the morning every day, and Alma stared for a minute before she could marshal her thoughts.

Then the drama of the moment returned. 'Sergeant McCabe needs you at the police station.' The words spilled out. This had to be the most exciting thing that had happened since the last time she'd seen the Min Min. 'Someone's left a baby on his doorstep.'

The perfect brows rose, then she nodded and turned back to the room to get her bag.

Alma blinked again. Most people would ask for all the juicy details, not that Alma had any, but geez, the doctor could have been more flabbergasted or horrified. She tried not to be disappointed at the lukewarm reaction, but damn.

'He said it was brand new,' Alma called after her as she waited. 'And crying.'

She just discerned muffled words from the room that Alma couldn't quite catch, but it could have been 'that's a good thing'. Then she was back with her big handbag and indicating for Alma to lead the way.

'Why didn't the good sergeant just bring the baby here?'

'He said he didn't have a baby seat.'

'Spare me. Imagine Douglas carrying a child without a restraint. Someone might tell the police,' she said. 'Let's not break the law.'

Alma looked at her. 'How would he drive and hold a baby?'

The doctor shut her door. 'You're right of course. And it would be too cold to walk with a brand-new baby.'

Alma followed her downstairs to open the door for her and lock up after. She really wanted to go with her and see what was happening, but she wasn't invited.

The doctor said, 'Any sign of the mother?'

'Not that he mentioned.'

Alma opened the door and the doctor stopped. 'What time is Maddy due for work today? I'll need a hand with the baby until community services can be notified.'

Alma looked at her, then frowned. 'She doesn't work today. But I could give her a ring?'

'Thanks. As soon as you can would be very good.' She slowed her voice as if Alma was stupid. 'Just ask her to come to the police as soon as possible. Maddy's help would be excellent.' Then she said, 'I'll take my car. My other doctor's bag is in there.'

'I'll bring your breakfast down to the police station,' Alma said, 'and one for the sergeant.' She paused for a breath. 'And for Maddy as well. That girl likes her food.'

The doctor nodded. 'Do you have anyone in town who had a baby recently? We'll need supplies.'

'The store will have supplies, but it's shut for the week.' Alma shrugged. 'Tourists run out of basics and Liz keeps it pretty stocked with a couple of everything. But she's away. Damn shame that.'

'Who has the key while she's away?'

Alma frowned and then her brow cleared. 'I do.'

Sienna opened her bag and then her wallet and removed a fifty-dollar bill. 'Newborn nappies, a bottle with a teat and some newborn baby formula. Maybe a packet of maternity pads if the mother turns up. And any clothes and baby blankets would be good. Perhaps someone has a bag of baby clothes put away?'

Alma's mood brightened and she took the money. 'I'll slip up to the shop now. She has a second-hand section there. I'll grab a few things then drop them down to you. Then I'll ring Maddy, but Jacob usually takes the phone off the hook at night.'

Chapter Twenty-five

Sienna

The angry wail of a very annoyed baby drifted out of the police residence and the knot of tension in Sienna's neck loosened as she walked up the path. She closed her eyes for a second in gratitude.

In view of her suspicions, she felt heavily responsible for not tackling Maddy. She should have followed up with her yesterday, but in her defence, she had no idea Maddy could have been full term. This baby certainly didn't seem premature by the sound of it.

She could fix this. It would all be sorted out. A sick baby would have complicated matters enormously. And luckily, she didn't have to worry about a neonatal resuscitation. That kid's lungs sounded positively lusty.

Douglas opened the door and for the first time since she'd met him he looked flustered. His black brows stood as downward slashes in his face and the helpless, harassed creases of the usually steadfast Douglas drew a smile she didn't think she had in her.

Because inside she fretted about the baby's mother.

When she looked down at the red-faced baby in his arms, it

looked a lot smaller than the sound coming out of its open mouth. Sienna stared. 'Good grief. It's tiny. I thought it would be at least four kilos it's so loud!'

Douglas thrust the baby at her. 'Take her. It's a she.' He paused, looked between Sienna and the baby. 'She's very demanding – of course,' he said over the infuriated wails. 'I was thinking of calling her Sienna.'

'Funny.' Sienna lifted the baby confidently from Douglas's awkward embrace and carried her through to the bathroom. She could still see the look of pure relief on Douglas's face and it brightened her day immeasurably. She might not be maternal, but she knew what to do with babies.

Sienna put the swaddled baby down on the bathroom bench and unwrapped her from the woollen blanket she'd obviously arrived in. Gave the pink, vigorously squirming infant a quick appraisal. Later, they could arrange a paediatrician, but she did confirm that the white string tying the cord had stayed tight. She shuddered at the thought of a baby slowly bleeding to death from an untied cord stump. She ran her hands rapidly over the top half of the slight body – no way was she touching the rest until it was clean – and confirmed that all looked normal. Her new little friend lay naked and pink from her exertions and covered from nipples to toes and up her back in sticky black meconium poo.

'Douglas?' she called over her shoulder.

'Yes,' he said. She hadn't realised he'd leaned his massive shoulder against the bathroom door and was watching her with something close to amazement.

Their eyes met. His were alight and warm with appreciation, and what passed between them felt way too complicated for this time of the morning. She looked away and back down at the fiercely annoyed baby.

'I need a towel and a sheet to wrap her in. And a couple of face washers for the mess, please.'

'Face washers? I'm a man. I don't keep face washers.'

'Well, as you're a man, you can cut some up from something,' she glanced at him, 'or tear it with your bare hands if you like! One half I'll use as a nappy until the supplies arrive and the other will give me two washers.'

He smiled. Looked at her with admiration, before shaking his head. 'So practical. Hidden talents.'

Did he think she was stupid? 'Now would be good.'

'You can use that hand towel to start the decontamination.' He screwed up his face at the tarry mess covering the baby. 'Then throw it out.'

Ten noisy minutes later they sat with a clean-bottomed, snuggly wrapped baby, one that sucked voraciously on Sienna's freshly washed pinkie finger while they waited for the formula to arrive – or Maddy. Sienna admitted to herself that her concern mounted the longer it took the girl to get here.

She'd imagined, if healthy enough, Maddy would be here like a shot as soon as Alma rang her. If she didn't arrive soon she'd have to tell Douglas her suspicions. Get him to bring her here so she could check her out – but she wasn't sure that wouldn't open a can of worms she'd be unable to shut.

As if he'd read her mind he said, 'I'm worried about the mother,' but then they heard a knock at the door and he rose to answer it. He returned with a bag of supplies. 'Alma said she's going to pick up Maddy because she can't get an answer on the house phone.'

Sienna wanted to chew her own finger just like the baby seemed to be enjoying. She tossed up telling Douglas now but restrained the thought because Alma would be just as quick.

Instead, she said, 'Later she's bringing breakfast.' Sienna looked down at the baby, big blue-black eyes frowning as she tried to find the secret to getting sustenance out of Sienna's fingertip. Sienna decided she had the look of the suspected mother. 'And I asked her to ring Maddy to lend a hand.'

'She said that. It's a good idea.'

'I'm full of good ideas. Is your finger clean? I need to make up a bottle.'

Douglas laughed once and stood up to wash his hands at the sink. 'Anyone would think you didn't want her to start crying again.'

'I'd say she's less than three kilos and I don't want her to drop her sugar level. Small babies do that. Then I can let you go to find her mother.'

When his hands were thoroughly scrubbed she gestured for him to sit, placed the well-wrapped baby firmly in the crook of his arm, and slipped her finger out of the baby's mouth. Douglas replaced the tip off his own pinkie finger, but the baby frowned, twisted her head and refused. Then she started to wail.

Douglas tried to thrust the baby back at Sienna. 'She doesn't like me.'

'She must be too young to notice your nice chest.' Sienna held up her hands. 'No. I need to do this and it's easier than explaining to you. Stroke her cheek with the tip of your finger until she turns her head that way.' Douglas did as she suggested. 'Now, when she opens her mouth keep your finger still.'

'It won't work. My finger's too big.'

'Well, it's that or you could take off your shirt and offer her your nipple,' Sienna said with a straight face.

Douglas froze and then, seeing with relief that she was joking, he murmured half to himself, 'How about you offer yours?' But he lifted his hand and gently stroked the baby's cheek as instructed and Sienna watched his surprise as the baby turned her head and suddenly was sucking away on his finger.

Sienna spun away to where the kettle sat on the bench top, her stomach twisting at the picture of big, hulking Douglas and the pint-size face attacking his finger. She'd already had Douglas scour a cereal bowl and quarter fill it with boiled water to cool while they waited for the supplies to arrive.

Now she began to tear open the cover from the feeding bottles, rinsed them and the teats with dishwashing detergent and water at the sink, before half filling a pot with boiling water and submerging them in there.

'This one won't wait for me to sterilise everything. You can boil them on the stove in the water for a few minutes to do that, but we can certainly make it all very clean.' She glanced at Douglas. 'I'll run you through it in case I get called away later.'

'Why would you get called away?'

She shrugged. 'Maybe the mother could need me urgently? Just listen, will you?'

Douglas narrowed his eyes at her and she knew she'd made him suspicious. Nothing she could do about that now.

'Wash your hands if you're preparing a bottle. Always put the water in the bottle first instead of pouring water on top of the powder. Always scrape off any excess milk powder to make the scoop level before you add it. Otherwise the ratios are wrong and baby can get constipation or chemical imbalances.'

He shook his head. 'Geez. I thought it was simple.'

She glanced at him, still holding the baby in that endearingly awkward way. 'It is simple. Just follow the rules. You're good with rules.'

He looked down at the tiny screwed face sucking fiercely on his finger and the snuffly angry noises that were growing louder. 'Better hurry.'

'Okay.' Sienna sighed and tipped out the soaking water, using the lid on the pot to keep the bottles clean, then set it down. She went to the fridge where the previously boiled water had cooled and brought it across. Filled the bottle to the thirty-mil line and added a levelled scoop of the formula. 'You shouldn't add formula to still boiling water. It needs to be cooled first.'

He watched her sit the freshly made bottle of formula in a cup of cold water to cool it more. 'How come you know all this?'

'I'm a doctor.' She sniffed. She shook the bottle and tried a few white drops on her wrist before dropping it back into the cool water for a few seconds longer. 'Actually, my midwife sister gave me a lecture when we were in Red Sand last year. Said I should know. I don't have an issue with remembering things.'

He almost smiled at that and she could see that some of his tension had eased as he leaned back slightly in the seat. 'Good to know one of us has some basic knowledge.' The crook of his elbow had softened from ramrod stiff, and his other hand had finally stopped gripping the blanket so hard. Poor Douglas. It really did hit her funny bone to see how uncomfortable he was. Then she felt mean.

'You're doing very well.'

'It was hell until you got here. I tried your mobile.'

She shrugged. 'I have to put it on silent at night. Too many calls from the ward I can't help them with while I'm away.' She checked the temperature of the milk again and handed him the bottle, which he reluctantly took but stood up.

'No,' he said. 'I do have to start looking for the mother. She could be ill after the birth.'

Chapter Twenty-six

Maddy

Maddy had managed to shower shakily, get rid of her stained clothes, and drink some badly needed tea before Jacob even knew she was home. She could still hear him snoring – so she had to move fast if she wanted to get away.

The house reeked of empty bottles and spilt beer, so she knew he'd have a hangover this morning when he woke and she did not want to be there then. Maybe he did regret when he was mean to her, but she was past worrying about that now. She glanced around the kitchen and sighed for all the dreams that had turned into a dark collection of cloudy and painful memories.

She never wanted to be in this house again.

She wanted her baby and couldn't stop thinking about that last look – a wrapped bundle in a cardboard box – before she'd knocked and stumbled away from the police-residence door. How hard it had been to run.

As she collected her few belongings, the early-morning silence of Jacob's house exploded with the sound of heavy knocking at the door and Maddy's heart pounded in fright as well.

Jacob roared from the bedroom as surly as a bull, and Maddy ran to the door to quieten the noise, flinging it open to see Alma still with her hand raised. Maddy could hear him stomping towards them. She shuddered and tried to shut the door so Alma wouldn't see.

Unexpectedly, Alma pushed past, stepped into the house and beside Maddy, just as Jacob burst into the hallway. He jerked to a halt.

He toned it down a fraction, slowed his pace and assessed the unforeseen intruder. 'What are you doing here?'

'I need Maddy,' Alma said and Maddy wilted at the startling championship.

Jacob sliced the air with his hand. 'No. She stays.'

Alma lifted her own chin. 'She has to come. The doctor needs her.'

Like a petulant child, Jacob folded his arms. Expecting to get his way. 'Not happening. She's needed here, too.'

Alma said, 'She's coming with me.'

Already on the edge of control, his face contorted. 'No!' The base of his fist hit the wall beside him and the whole house seemed to reverberate with his anger. 'No. She'll stay here or else!'

Maddy shrank instinctively away and she felt Alma glance at her before she stepped in front of her, looked up at Jacob with her rigid chin high in the air, and said fiercely, 'Or else what?'

Maddy held her breath. They all stood there like some frozen scene in a bad movie until Jacob sent Maddy a smouldering, threat-filled look that said *you watch out for later*, spun on his heel and stomped back into the bedroom and slammed the door.

She and Alma sagged a bit and she sent thanks for the fact she was already dressed and didn't have to go in the bedroom for clothes.

Maddy realised Alma had also solved the problem of how she would find out what was happening. Though what Alma would do when she discovered the truth remained a looming black-clouded mystery. Maddy pushed the thought away. She didn't care. It was not her immediate concern.

She cast one final glance at the closed bedroom door. Neither was Jacob.

When they arrived at the police residence Sienna met her at the front entrance. She waved them in. Maddy felt the searching look as if she'd been waiting for them to arrive, but Sienna just said brightly, 'Come in, you two. The baby is fine.'

Maddy felt like kissing the woman in front of her because her being here meant her baby was safe. And she'd said she was fine. Relief rushed through her in a surge of gratitude.

In fact, Maddy definitely felt like kissing Alma for getting her here and away from Jacob. And maybe a quick hug as well for the policeman, who was holding her precious bundle, though she couldn't quite see her little face.

Her heart swelled. Her bundle. She'd known her baby would be safe with the policeman and she'd prayed fiercely that the first person he called would be the doctor. But she hadn't expected to be able to get here herself so quickly. Not when she'd left her baby on the doorstep without explaining and when she'd had to escape from Jacob at the house.

None of that mattered. The most important thing remained the safety of her baby. That and Jacob not finding out whose child this baby was.

She stopped when she came to the doorway and saw a minute face, a minute face so different already from when she last saw it, less wrinkled, more rounded and sucking ferociously at the bottle the big policeman held. His face cleared when she came in.

The sergeant said, 'Maddy. How about you wash your hands and hold the baby while I start what I need to do.'

She glanced at the kitchen sink, nodded and hurried to do what he asked. She turned around to see the doctor speaking softly to Alma and her stomach sank.

Maddy lifted her head. Straightened her shoulders. No, what people thought and what happened to her didn't matter now. Her baby was being looked after. Was safe and wrapped and being fed, looked nothing like the sticky red-faced baby she'd wrapped up in the scratchy blanket.

To deflect the idea that she was about to be outed, she said, 'What's her name?'

Before he could answer, Alma and the doctor came in and Sienna said, 'Can I borrow you just for one minute please, Madison? Alma can get on with the feed.'

Maddy could feel the drop in her stomach, the need to hold her baby, the desire to run, but also the urge to try to explain why she would do something horrible like leave her own baby in a doorway.

She saw the policeman frown, and glanced with a question in his eyes at the doctor, who said very quietly, 'Hold that thought.'

What thought? Maddy wondered, trepidation growing, but

Alma had bustled in. 'I'd love to feed the wee darling, you just hand her over to me.'

In a daze, Maddy followed Sienna into the small bedroom she used as the office and the door shut.

'It's okay. Unless I have this wrong, she's yours, is that right, Madison?'

Maddy stood there stunned. All her planning had been useless. She nodded miserably.

The voice stayed gentle, reassuring, but determined to find the facts. 'What time was she born?'

The world slowed and she felt the words but had trouble getting them out. It seemed so long ago. Was it only a few hours? 'About three-thirty.'

Maddy had sat there with the wet baby against her belly until it had begun to squirm and whimper. She sat like a robot but with a sudden strange energy flooding her body about making her baby safe. She could remember hugging the baby close as she glanced around the desolate and disused back room. Safe meant giving this baby up to be with someone protective until she could get away. There wasn't anyone safer in this town than the policeman. Yet inside she still felt frozen with what she'd done.

'Are you alright? Have you bled much?'

Maddy blinked. Returned to the room and the woman in front of her with a thud. Blood? Yes, there had been blood, but not as much as she'd thought there would be. 'Except when that afterbirth came, not much more than a period.' She remembered wrapping the mess in the newspaper and dropping it into the hole she'd dug, covering it and pulling the rock over it. Like a criminal hiding evidence.

'You're a very lucky woman you didn't bleed. Your boyfriend wasn't with you?'

'No.' Her tense shoulders slumped. She didn't have the mental energy to talk about Jacob. 'He's not to know!'

Sienna nodded as if she'd expected that. 'We'll get to that later.'

Maddy had to make it clear. 'I didn't plan the baby. Didn't know she would come so soon.' She didn't want Sienna to judge her badly. 'I didn't know for a long time. Couldn't face it for a time after that either. But I'd put some things in the place I had her. I've seen a baby born.' She had to make Sienna understand. 'I never wanted to hurt my baby. I just wanted to keep her safe.'

'I think I understand. That must have been terrifying.'

'Now it is. But then I just thought it was something I had to go through.' She shrugged. 'I grew up on a farm. I knew how it worked. And the animals never seemed to be hurt afterwards by it. I just kept telling myself it would stop when the baby came.' That she wouldn't die.

Sienna turned and picked up a towel that lay on the dresser, then spread it out on the single bed. 'I'd like to feel your tummy if you'll let me. It's how we can tell that the uterus is contracted. Have you passed urine since the baby was born?'

Maddy could feel the heat in her cheeks as she lay down on the towel. 'Yes. There's a fair bit of blood when I go.'

'That's normal.' Maddy lifted her top and after Sienna rubbed her hands together to warm them she placed them on her belly and dug in a few centimetres. Then she nodded as if she'd found what she'd expected. Despite her embarrassment Maddy glanced down. It looked almost normal again now except the doctor's hand seemed to go in a long way and bounce out again.

Then the doctor took Maddy's hand and put it on her rounded curved stomach and pushed in through the stretched skin so Maddy could again feel the strange lump under there.

The doctor said, 'You can feel the hard uterus. Because it's hard, or contracted like a big lemon, it won't bleed. Sometimes, if there is a fragment of placenta left inside it silently fills up with blood and your bleeding gets heavier. If that happens it feels like a squashy grapefruit. You need to rub firmly to expel the clots and make the uterus in your belly hard like the lemon again.'

Maddy nodded.

'The bleeding will slow in the next day or two if all the placenta came in one piece. I don't suppose you still have it?'

'I buried it.'

Sienna nodded with a strange smile on her face. 'You are amazing, you know that?' Then she went on. 'We have some maternity pads. If you need to change them every hour that's too much bleeding. What about down below? Does it sting?'

Maddy ducked her head. 'No.'

'I'd feel better if I could be sure you haven't torn yourself down there. That sort of trickle bleeding can quietly cause trouble. But you can say no if you want to.'

Maddy shrugged and climbed off the bed to remove her underwear. A few moments later they were done. The doctor had looked – Maddy had 'grazes' that would heal and the bleeding was fine. It was embarrassing that the doctor had seen the bruises on her legs, but maybe she hadn't. She hadn't said anything.

Maddy climbed off the bed and dressed. Now she could go back and feed her baby.

'Do you want me to tell Sergeant Mackay that you are the baby's mother?'

Maddy nodded. 'Please. And I'll tell Alma. But we can't tell anyone else.'

Chapter Twenty-seven

Alma

Alma's fingers shook as she held the baby in the crook of her arm and she could do nothing but think of another baby thirty years ago. The ache in her chest glowed like an uncovered coal from one of those old wood stoves she had in her kitchen once upon a time.

A coal you could uncover, and poke, and it would burst into flame and start the pain all over again for a new day. When she looked at the little crumpled face, the heat in that glowing shaft of pain flew straight to her chest and for a second there she thought she might be having a heart attack. Then the pain settled as the facial features of the baby returned to those in the present day.

Yes, she'd held a baby like this before, felt the warm weight in her arms, the heat from the small body seeping into her like a hot water bottle on a winter's night. She soaked in the sensations, sniffed the distinctive smell of a new baby, a scent she would never forget and thought she'd never smell again, wanted to bury her nose in it. She watched with fascination the diminutive chest rise and fall under the scratchy blanket she realised came from her hotel, listened with awe to the grunty, gulpy, gorgeous noises as the baby drank and sucked and swallowed, and spread her wrinkled and age-spotted hands to savour the warmth and baby bulk of her. And sobbed inside.

Alma closed her eyes. Her baby had 'fallen' from the bed where she'd tucked her in. It was all too heartbreakingly late to regret her stupidity. To regret the sad, tragic, horrific accident that was her fault. She should never have left the baby with him.

She didn't judge this baby's mother. Since that day she'd tried hard not to judge anyone for their choices because she didn't know their story – just like they didn't know hers. She couldn't believe she'd been so blind not see the signs of Maddy's pregnancy. Or how hard it must have been to stay safe beside the man she lived with. Poor Maddy. Poor baby. She understood.

In painful hindsight, she should have left her baby at the door of the police station, too, until she'd got away. Her baby might have been alive still.

The door to the spare bedroom opened and Maddy and the doctor came out. Maddy looked sheepish, as well she might, thought Alma somewhat grimly, but she lifted the bottle from the baby's mouth and stood up for Maddy. Holding the baby out. 'You take her, Maddy.'

Then, with resolution for a temporary solution, and with the determination to find a more permanent one, she suggested gently, 'From today, and as long as you want, you can both move in with me.'

Maddy shyly smiled. Bereft of bottle, the baby opened her mouth and began to yell, truly indignant with the interruption to her food, and Maddy hastily gathered her up and replaced the teat.

Alma heard the doctor's sigh of relief. She cast her a furious look. As if she'd let these two go back to that man. Maddy and her baby needed her and Alma would not let them down.

'Okay if I take breakfast next door and bring back the rest?' Sienna said. Then to Maddy, 'Maybe we can talk about breastfeeding next time?'

'Absolutely. We're fine here.' Alma nodded vigorously. 'Maddy will eat when she's fed her baby.'

The door closed as Sienna left the house carrying the bulging bag, and Alma wouldn't have minded being a fly on the wall for that conversation. She had no doubt the doctor would sort her man out. Taking food was a good start. Alma turned back to Maddy.

'And you, young lady, how are you?'

'Sienna said I'm fine.'

Alma closed her eyes and tried to shut out the thought of Maddy alone in the night giving birth. 'Where . . .?'

'I made a place. In an empty building. Just in case. I really didn't think it would happen this soon.' Her eyes filled with tears. 'I'm sorry I didn't tell you. I didn't want you to think badly of me. I won't go home.' She stared at her daughter's face so close to hers. 'She'll never go back there.'

Chapter Twenty-eight

Maddy

Maddy hugged her baby and the tightness in her throat gradually eased as Alma patted her shoulder. She dared to settle mentally into a safer place along with the sound of sucking. She revelled in the weight and warmth of her daughter in her arms, the strange achy emptiness in her belly, and marvelled at how different her world was from where she'd dwelt yesterday. Pregnant. Petrified. In her own private hell.

She sent another prayer of thankfulness for her baby being alive and well. For being alive and well herself, though the concept of death from labour seemed ridiculous now from the distance of only a few hours and surrounded as she was by those who apparently cared. Like her mother would have cared.

Of course she was designed to give birth. But the whole experience made her think of her mum. What would her mother think? What would she recommend she do?

Maddy watched the tiny rosebud lips work furiously around the teat and admired the perfection of her daughter's dewy-skinned features. How could something so beautiful, so flawless as this angel with a tiny upturned nose, those rounded cheeks, and dark, dark eyes, be hers? With a frisson of distress she added silently, and be Jacob's baby as well?

No. Never Jacob's. She needed to trust in the support of these people she really didn't know well but would be forever grateful to. She didn't know where she would go from here because nearly everything she owned was at the house with Jacob, but she would make it work. Her daughter would grow up surrounded by love. A mother's love. Like her mother had loved her. That she could provide.

An hour and a half later Maddy felt her heart accelerate as they drew up at Jacob's house. She could feel Alma looking at her and she tried to stay calm. Unclench her hands. Tried not to look as the police van pulled up behind them.

Alma's voice floated softly, almost a whisper. 'It's not just the way he talks, is it?'

Maddy felt her cheeks heat up.

Alma said, 'He hurts you, doesn't he, Maddy?'

Maddy cleared her throat. Unstuck her tongue from the roof of her mouth where the trepidation had dried it. 'Sometimes I might do things that make him angry.' The silence between them lay like a wraith. 'It's okay, Alma. I know I can't bring my baby here. Or tell him about her. And I'm never coming back after today.'

'One day I'll tell you a story,' Alma said quietly.

They'd left the baby with the doctor, safe from Jacob finding out. Alma understood a lot without being told.

As they got out she said, 'Nobody has the right to hurt someone else. You know you don't ever deserve to be hurt. Let's get your things. Let him know you are never coming back.'

'He's not coming in, is he?' She inclined her head to the car behind.

Alma glanced at the man with a satisfied look. 'No. But Sergeant McCabe will come in if we need him to.'

So they went up the path and the door opened and Jacob stood there. Dressed in his monster truck shirt and his work shorts over his plaster. Looking normal. Looking like the man she'd first met. Looking confused and hurt as he stood on one leg with his crutches.

'What's all this about?' Jacob said.

Maddy lifted her chin, darted a glance at his face and then away. 'I've come for my things. I'm moving to the pub.'

His eyes shifted to Alma standing at the front door. He glanced past them to the big policeman sitting in the police vehicle. Sent a look of pure hate and malice Douglas's way. 'I don't understand,' he said.

But she knew he did.

Chapter Twenty-nine

Sienna

Around morning tea time, Douglas went out on a call so Sienna closed the door to his house and drove the short way back up to the pub. Alma had ensconced Maddy and her baby in the pub accommodation and Sienna had come back to change her clothes.

'How's Maddy?' she asked Alma.

The old lady didn't look at her as she polished the bar with her soft rag. 'Settled now. I'm glad I went with her to see that man of hers,' Alma said darkly. 'Nice as pie and all hurt by her leaving – but I recognise the type.'

Sienna had her doubts, too. 'I met him the other day. Blond guy with crutches. I gather he had some type of accident?'

Alma nodded. 'In his truck. Drunk at the time. Brought up by his uncle and inherited his business. The uncle wasn't a good drunk either, nice as pie on a good day, but I don't think young Jacob was spared the rod. Not the best upbringing and no woman around to soften it.'

Sienna worked out the dynamics. Maddy obviously worked and ran the household while Jacob was trapped, without work, and possibly in pain and frustrated to be disabled by his plaster. And drinking. Not a good mix. 'What does he do for a job when he isn't on crutches?'

'Jacob carts animal livestock. Goes where the load is. A better business in his uncle's day.'

Something niggled about trucks, but she was more focused on Maddy and the events of the morning. Sienna wasn't naive, not after the stories she'd heard – sometimes from the women themselves but mostly from the midwives. However, there was something confronting and personal about the Maddy she liked being bullied and hurt by her violent boyfriend. Being damaged!

Sienna remembered clearly the black bruises on Maddy's pale legs, which she hadn't mentioned to Alma but was tempted to talk to Douglas about.

She detected the note of angst in Alma's voice, a personal darkness, as she said, 'No wonder she didn't tell anyone about the baby.' Alma turned away though not before Sienna heard the bitter words. 'Smart, she is.'

Sienna's head lifted and she stared at the side of the woman's face as she looked out the window. Saw that Alma's usually erect shoulders had bowed with distress and that her hand lay across her mouth as if stopping the words.

'Alma? What is it?'

'Nothing.'

Sienna noted the rapid denial. Saw the thin shoulders straighten as her hand fell to her side. 'It's nothing,' she said again. 'I'll get on, then.'

Sienna watched her leave the bar and head towards the kitchen, but a feeling of disquiet stayed with her as she walked back upstairs to use her phone in private. Something else had happened there. Something personal to the tiny woman. The raw heartbreak she'd glimpsed twisted inside Sienna in a way it hadn't since that horrible day a year ago when they'd nearly lost her half-sister, Callie, in a car accident. What was Alma's tragedy?

Sienna wasn't so hard-boiled and hard-cased that she couldn't care for people. But she usually didn't allow it. Though, the idea of caring deeply for the publican was carrying it all to the point of ridiculous and she ran her hand through her hair as if to rid herself of the notion. Freaking outback towns did her head in.

She glanced out the window to the carpark. She had to find the answer to the babies with microcephaly so she could get the hell out of here and back to where she belonged.

And then, out of nowhere, the nausea hit her and she had to run for the hotel bathroom.

Five minutes later, she leaned her forehead against the cool glass of the bathroom mirror, the damp tissue she'd wiped with pressed against her mouth as she slowed her breathing. Strangely, she could smell the paper tissue, a cloggy, harsh scent of paper not normally offensive, but she pulled it away in disgust. What the heck? She glared down at the tissue. What had Alma put in that breakfast? She did not have time to contract hepatitis A.

Ten minutes later she was settled enough to ring Eve.

Her sister answered on the second ring. 'Diamond Lake Station.'

'How come you don't ring me?'

Eve laughed. 'Hello, Sienna. How are you? And I don't ring you because you are currently on a mission and would only wish to speak to me if I could help you.'

Darn. 'Sad when your sister knows you better than you know yourself.'

'I know. How's it all going?' And then archly, 'How's Douglas.'

Sienna had been about to answer the first question when the second question diverted her. She had no difficulty conjuring the man into her mind space. 'Douglas is Douglas. Impressive. Annoying.' She paused as she thought more. 'Delicious.' Then heard herself like a mooning cow. Good grief. Hastily she said, 'But that's not why I rang.'

'Okay, but you sound . . .' Eve hesitated, 'funny.'

More briskly, as if to disguise her previous silliness, Sienna said, 'I've just brought up my breakfast so feeling food poisoned by the publican, but the call's not about me. I have a young woman here who free-birthed last night and needs some breast-feeding direction with her new daughter. I wondered if you were up to a trip over this afternoon with the hulk in his helicopter. Just until the clinic nurse can fly in and give some suggestions for attachment. Breastfeeding isn't my forte if the baby doesn't instantly get it.'

Concern filtered down the line. 'Birthed on her own? How many weeks? And how old is the mum?'

'The baby is small but has most of the characteristics of a term baby, good cartilage in the ears, creases over both soles. So term, though I'm guessing it is less than three kilos. Nobody knew she was pregnant. And the mum's twenty-one. We're suspecting DV as the reason she was hiding it.'

Eve's voice held empathy. 'Sounds like you need a social worker as well.'

'Of course.' Sienna's brows drew together. Yes, yes, Maddy

would get to community services, but at this moment she needed a friend. Or a mother. And she had both in Alma.

'I think she has support now. But there's only one of the three women in town who've recently birthed living on her station and she's naturally busy with her microcephalic baby. I don't want to ask her for advice. And I'd like to get Maddy away before the nasty boyfriend finds out he has access to her for life.'

'I can understand that.' There was a pause before Eve said quietly, 'This baby is fine?'

The penny dropped. 'No small head if that's what you're thinking.'

She heard Eve's sigh of relief. 'That's a good thing, then.' Eve took a few moments to consider things. 'Lex isn't here, but when he returns I'll run it by him. Can I ring you back?'

Sienna had a sudden realisation of what she'd just asked her sister. Her pregnant sister. To come to a town with a high incidence of congenital abnormality at a dangerous time in her pregnancy.

'Sure. But you know what?' She ran through the logistics and shrugged. Had to be done. 'If you have enough room in your enormous homestead maybe it would be better if I drive over with her instead.'

She considered the option of Lex picking up Maddy and baby in the helicopter by himself and discarded it. 'We could stay the night. She'd have an obstetrician and a midwife in you and me. What more could she want.'

Eve laughed, though a tiny incredulous note crept into her voice. 'You'd do that?'

Sienna acknowledged that perhaps her willingness to be inconvenienced could seem out of character. She glanced at her watch.

It was early, but it was a hell of a drive. 'We could be there before dark.'

Eve suggested, 'Or Lex could fly in and pick her up when he gets home.'

It wasn't that big a chopper. For some reason Sienna didn't like it. Surely not because it meant she'd miss out on all the fun and couldn't go with them? 'She might not want to put her baby in a helicopter.'

Eve might have thought Sienna's reasoning slightly off centre. 'Helicopters are safe. She just had a baby without any help.'

This time Sienna heard herself defending Maddy. 'I don't think she expected it so soon. She worked right up until she had it.'

There was another of Eve's pauses. 'You sound like you admire her?' she asked without judgement.

Sienna thought about that. About herself becoming involved when any other time it would be the last thing she would think of. Must be that small-isolated-town syndrome, she knew she could get infected with it if she wasn't extra careful. She sighed. 'There's something about her that makes me appreciate her. Yes.'

'Then I can't wait to meet her,' Eve said, her warm voice reassuring. 'What's her name?'

'Maddy. Or Madison. I guess I'd better find her and ask if she wants to drive half the day with me to a strange woman's house and learn about breastfeeding.' Then she thought about the noise explosion on wheels if the baby yelled like it had this morning. 'Any chance the kid will sleep most of the way?'

'If you're lucky, she's new and they do. If she's fed once, she could well sleep for up to twelve hours, they often can after birth.

But you'll have to get here before she starts demanding to cluster feed after that.'

Cluster feeding sounded like hell on earth to Sienna. She'd make sure she could hand over to Eve before then.

Chapter Thirty

When Sienna left her room, two groups of tourists were parked at the bar, and she could hear laughter as she walked down the stairs. Alma looked up as she arrived at the bottom. The older lady pretended to tip her peaked cap at her and Sienna smiled. She looked like an old-fashioned ticket collector and the tourists seemed amused as she regaled them with one of her tall stories.

Sienna raised her brows and Alma stared for a minute and then nodded. 'Number four,' she said.

Sienna lifted her hand in acknowledgement and climbed back up the stairs as she heard the words 'Min Min' drift from the bar.

When she knocked quietly there was a shuffle from inside the room and then the heavy wooden door swung partially open. Maddy's pale face peered out from behind the protection offered. She sagged a little when she saw Sienna.

'Come in,' she said breathily, and stood back to make way.

Sienna frowned. 'You okay?'

'I thought it was Jacob.' Her voice shook. 'Come to find me.'

Sienna felt her heart contract. Nothing had officially been said. Technically, it was all supposition about the domestic violence. 'If you don't want him to find you, we can help, Madison. We can all help there.'

Maddy forced her shoulders up. 'You've helped enough already.'

'We'll see.' She glanced across the room at the sleeping baby. 'Has she tried the breast yet? Has she woken for the next feed?'

'Not since we gave her that bottle.'

'And you're okay? Not bleeding too much? Going to the toilet okay?'

Maddy blushed and looked down at the floor. 'Yes. All of those.'

Sienna smiled at the bent head. 'And just checking, no pressure, do you still want to breastfeed? Or are you happy with the bottle?'

Maddy lifted her head and more fiercely than she expected said, 'I always assumed I'd breastfeed if I had a baby.'

Sienna smiled. 'Okay, then. I have an idea. My sister is a pretty awesome midwife. She lives at Diamond Lake Station, about six hours from here, and she's offered to be your mothercraft nurse for a day or two. I was thinking of staying the night over there tonight and wondered if you'd like to come and maybe pick up a few hints from her about the feeding and baby stuff. You don't have to, but she's offered their hospitality. Could save you flying out with the RFDS.'

Maddy had a strange look on her face and Sienna stopped and raised her brows in question? 'No?'

Maddy seemed to shake herself. 'Sorry. I couldn't quite believe it. I've been sitting here worrying about how I could get away for a little while just to get my head sorted without having to worry that

Jacob was going to swing in here with his crutches at any moment.' A shy smile crossed her face. 'And you offer that!'

Sienna nodded. 'A six-hour trip in a car with a newborn sounds good?' They were both mad. But needs must. 'So, yes?'

Maddy nodded vehemently. 'Yes, please.'

'Next problem. We'll have to find a baby capsule or Douglas will pull me up and fine me.'

Maddy laughed a touch hysterically, and Sienna couldn't blame her. But she sobered fast. 'Alma mentioned there's a second-hand one for sale in the shop.'

'God bless Alma.'

'Amen,' said Maddy cheekily, and they grinned at each other. Then on a less exuberant note Maddy said forlornly, 'At least my bag is packed.'

Sienna glanced at her but didn't comment. That would be a discussion for the car. 'I'd better go pack one of mine.' She turned back as she headed for the door. 'I'll ask Alma to come up for a minute and you can sort logistics with her.'

Thirty minutes into the drive with the sun at their backs Sienna decided it was time to out the elephant in the car. She sorted the variation of standard domestic violence screening questions in her head and came up with a shortened version. 'It sounds like sometimes you could be frightened of Jacob?'

Sienna kept her eyes on the road yet she felt the girl's shock. She didn't say anything else. Just waited. It was Maddy's choice to disclose if she needed to.

Finally, she said, 'Sometimes.'

'Was that a factor when you didn't tell anyone about your pregnancy?'

'Yes,' she replied in a smaller voice.

Sienna let that sit for a minute. Then in a matter-of-fact tone she said, 'My car's a safe place, Maddy.' She looked at the girl. 'We're speeding away from Spinifex and not even Douglas could catch us. Let alone a bloke with crutches.'

Maddy's shoulders did relax a smidge, and mindful of the precious cargo in the back Sienna remembered to reduce her speed from just over to just under the speed limit.

'I'm not going to judge you. I'm not even going to judge Jacob because I don't know enough. But you need to feel safe in speaking to me. If it helps I can tell you that I do have patients from difficult home lives and I want to help.'

Still no comment. Sienna tried again. 'When I knocked on your room in the pub today,' she paused and looked quickly at the girl and then back to the road, 'I had the impression you still didn't feel safe, even though Alma was downstairs.'

There was a long drawn-out sigh and at last Maddy began talking. 'It's been worse since the accident. His temper. But in some ways, it's better. He's changed so much and been getting more short-tempered lately. Since I got the job with Alma, actually. But at least with the plaster it's easier to stay out of his reach.'

Sienna digested the information for a few seconds. 'How did you two meet?'

'I met him in Boulia. The next town. My girlfriend and I came out for the camel race circuit. They call it voluntourism. I've done some in other countries so decided to try it now that I was back in Australia. I was only working casual for a cleaning company so I could come and go when opportunities came up.' She sighed. 'We met Jacob at the bar and the two of us hit it off.' Sienna caught the wince at the unfortunate wording.

Maddy went on. 'My girlfriend thought him handsome, too. He called me up next time he came through Brisbane and we had a nice time then, as well. I must have already been pregnant. I was on the pill . . .' her voice trailed off. Then she shook her head. Winced. 'I must have missed a pill. Anyway, he drove a truck that he inherited from his uncle, picking up cattle so he was away a lot. It was nice to have a boyfriend, even part-time. It was good at the beginning.'

Sienna remembered what Alma had said and it all tied in. But she didn't mention she already knew that. Sienna slowed in case the emu they were passing changed her mind about direction. 'Voluntourism? Never heard of that.'

'It's where you do unpaid work on a festival or sporting event for free entry and accommodation. The camel races sounded like fun, and we came on the bus from Brisbane just for the weekend.'

'So was it fun?'

'A blast. I've never laughed so much. Jacob swept me off my feet and I rushed in. Couldn't believe my luck. I guess I don't know how I ended up with Jacob controlling my life over the last few months. It was a gradual thing. While he'd been driving his truck between the towns, I had a life. Though, looking back now, he did manage to push my girlfriends away. The one I lived with rubbed him the wrong way and moved out. I spent half the time defending him to her and the other half defending her to him. But it was fun when it was just him there. I thought I was so lucky.'

Sienna minded her tongue. Isolation was the first sign, if she remembered the signs for DV. Not that they'd named it yet. 'Sounds tricky.'

'Sometimes it was. Between trips he moved in with me, but started to ring at odd hours to check if I was home. Made me feel disloyal if I was having a good time and he was working so I stopped going out. Unless I was with him. When he had the accident and couldn't manage the three flights of stairs he suggested he'd be better in his uncle's empty house out west in Spinifex. So, of course, I came to look after him. I'd been to Boulia so I knew what to expect. Or thought I did.'

She slid into silence and Sienna let it lie. After Maddy had turned and checked her baby she sat back and eventually began again. Her voice was quieter this time and Sienna strained to hear. 'When I got to Spinifex I figured out I was pregnant, not getting fat, but I wouldn't have been able to work if I told anyone.' Her voice became a whisper. 'There never seemed a right time to tell Jacob. I guess he didn't notice because we weren't sleeping together.'

Sienna still thought he was pretty blind. Or blinded by his jump into bullying. 'How did you manage that?'

'He just stopped making advances. Before the accident I think he might have been taking drugs to stay awake on the road. His moods were changing but I just thought he was tired.'

'So when you moved to Spinifex did you like it?'

'I like the town. And the people. Especially when I got the job at the pub. I think I love Alma. She'd been very kind to me.'

Sienna laughed. 'I think she's fond of you, too. They say the right people turn up in your life at the right time if you let them.'

She heard the words and closed her lips. Whose freaking mouth had that come out of? Sienna stared through the windshield, driving automatically as she considered the ridiculous statement she'd just spouted and how it was the reverse with her. 'I'm not sure I believe that, but . . .' Douglas and Blanche Mackay were the last people she needed right now. She brought herself back to the conversation. 'I think Alma is a good person, too.'

She slowed the car and looked at Maddy. 'Has it been bad long?'

'Since I started working for Alma really because I have to be out of his sight. He doesn't like the idea of me talking to other men in a pub.'

Sienna's brows rose. 'So why didn't he hop his way down to the pub and sit there and watch you?'

Maddy almost laughed. 'He did a couple of times, but Alma chipped him on the way he spoke to me and he told her to stick her pub.'

Sienna smiled grimly. 'Can't see Alma tolerating that.'

Maddy looked at her. 'I think she'd been trying for a rise out of him because then she said he was banned.'

Sienna laughed. Then sobered. Then her blood ran cold. She slowed the car and glanced at Maddy. 'How was that night when you went home?'

Maddy looked out the window. 'I don't want to talk about it.'

Sienna remembered the bruises. 'I understand that.' Softened her voice. 'But I saw the marks on your legs when I examined you earlier. I think Jacob did that to you.'

Then Maddy said something that broke Sienna's heart. And made her want to strangle Jacob. 'Please don't tell anyone about the marks. I feel so ashamed of my life.'

———

An hour later Maddy had fallen asleep, exhausted after revealing the stress, isolation and the escalating violence she'd suffered. Sienna felt exhausted herself. She'd always known of the black cloud some women lived under, but in her busy, treatment-orientated world, she'd immediately referred those women to the appropriate services and the connection had been fleeting and distant.

She felt uncomfortably mortified she hadn't connected more with the reality of their lives, and had to acknowledge how extremely fortunate she was that she'd never had any personal experience of violence.

It put her own childhood baggage into perspective – she'd been a lucky child and not a victim. When she thought about the bitterness she'd harboured since she was very young about her father leaving her mother – she'd had no idea what real hardship was.

Maddy's story had shocked her to the core. Perhaps because it was so real and so close. It had been happening to Maddy while Sienna had been teasing Douglas, complaining about the heat, letting herself get frustrated by petty delays. Maddy had suffered over in Jacob's house. And she hadn't known.

Though, apparently, everyone had a bad feeling about Jacob. Douglas and Alma said they had been keeping a protective eye on her while they waited for her to ask for help. Holding back – probably guilty about that now – because they hadn't wanted to interfere without Maddy's permission. No one had known for sure. But that wasn't good enough.

Well, she'd asked now and it was out.

Sienna glanced in the rear-view mirror at the sleeping newborn, an occasional baby snuffle making her mother's eyelids flicker, and then she glanced back at the young woman's face, softened from care in sleep, and felt a wave of unexpected empathy steal over her. Every woman and child, and, she thought of a very young Jacob's life in the school of hard knocks, every boy and man, too, deserved to feel safe. All she could do was be more aware. And she would change in the future.

But for today they'd concentrate on Maddy.

They arrived at Diamond Lake Station just as the sun tipped the crater that surrounded the station with dark slashes of golden brown. Soaring flocks of pink Major Mitchell's Cockatoos circled in for the sunset. Sienna remembered that Lex's daughter, Lily, liked to feed the birds and they had quite a crowd.

'Nearly there, Maddy,' Sienna said quietly and the girl beside her stirred and then sat bolt upright and spun her head to confirm her baby was safe. Then her shoulders sagged and she glanced apologetically at Sienna. 'Sorry. My nerves are shot.'

'You're allowed,' Sienna said, trying to keep the twinge of horrified sympathy out of her voice. Some of Maddy's disclosures still had her reeling. 'It will take time.'

Maddy bent her head and Sienna cursed herself for making a comment at all. To change the subject she said, 'I am very pleased to say your baby slept all the way.'

'I slept too,' Maddy murmured the obvious as she twisted her head again to check her baby, and then her hand fell to find the control at the side of the seat to adjust the angle. The soft whirr of the seat lifting coincided with their arrival at the entrance gate.

'You might just have earned that rest.' Sienna thought briefly of Maddy's last twenty-four hours, let alone the fact that she'd worked in a bar until ten the night before. Now that made her own usual work days look paltry. She smiled. 'You've had a labour and birth and been busy riding a wave of adrenaline since your baby arrived. You can't be in a constant state of readiness to run without exhausting yourself. You needed to sleep.'

'How long?'

'Three hours. It's a start. Eve will mother you into more rest and be there for the first few feeds in case you have questions.'

'Feeds? If she ever wakes up. What was in that bottle? I heard they sleep for one long time after birth, but this is ridiculous.'

Sienna laughed. 'Eve said she might and the movement of the car helps. Apparently, when she wakes you're going to have a cluster of demand feeds. Bet she goes off like a bomb when we stop.'

Maddy chewed her fingernail and then, realising, pulled her hand away from her mouth as if Sienna would scold her. 'I'm being a terrible nuisance.'

Sienna turned between the two large gum trees on the driveway. 'You were sensible enough to take help when it was offered. I'm happy with an excuse to see my sister.'

'Well,' Maddy looked at her sceptically, 'I do know how fortunate I am. Thank you.'

Sienna shrugged. 'I'm stuck on leads for my investigation so it'll give me a chance to bounce ideas off Eve.' Sienna realised that Blanche would probably be there and that she should mention her.

As they rounded the small hill and saw the homestead bathed in sunlight, Maddy seemed to shrink in her seat.

Sienna tried to think of something helpful and non-threatening for a young woman about to stay with people she didn't know. 'As far as I know, there's my sister Eve, her husband, Lex, and his daughter, Lily, living in the homestead. Lily's sixteen and her mother died last year. Then possibly Lex's mother, Blanche, will be there.'

'I can remember those names.'

'That's a good start. The house is surrounded by shady gardens. And there're a few nice places to walk with your baby.' She pointed. 'To the left is a view to the lake the station's named after.'

Maddy whistled when she saw it. 'It's huge.'

'I find that amount of water out here surprising,' Sienna agreed. 'There're lots of places to be by yourself. But if you go walking, wear a pair of gumboots. The snakes around here can be ridiculous.' She thought of her own personal viper in paradise. 'Have you met Blanche Mackay?' That was amusing but harsh and she mentally apologised to Blanche.

Maddy shook her head. 'Only seen her in the bar talking to Alma.'

'She's the bane of my life.' Sienna glanced at her passenger and softened the statement with a smile. Oops. That had sounded non-reassuring and stark. 'Only because she's concerned for the health of the women out here. And keeps uprooting me from my hospital like I'm her personal medical PI. Just warning you she might seem intimidating but her heart's in the right place.'

Maddy lifted her chin. 'Most people who live out here look after each other. I've noticed that.'

'Good. Then you won't stress. Eve is very keen to meet you and has missed playing midwife. Just let things unfold without thinking too much. Okay?'

'I'll try.'

They arrived. Thank goodness. Sienna could switch off the

engine for the day and pop the boot in the dusty circular drive out-side the front steps.

Eve hurried down and Sienna hoped she wouldn't trip. Her sister didn't do graceful – just wholehearted. That was Eve.

'Sienna, you look like you've just stepped out of a fashion magazine!' Then she engulfed her in a hug.

Sienna stepped back to examine her sister, feeling crumpled from the drive. 'I think you're reading the wrong magazines.' She glanced over the pale face but sparkling eyes of her next of kin. 'You look washed out but very happy.'

Eve shot a mischievous glance at the tall, extremely well-built man at the top of the steps and grinned. 'I am,' she said, meeting Sienna's gaze. 'It's so good to see you.'

A young girl bounced down the steps in denim shorts and a lime-green crop top, almost bumping into Eve. 'Can I carry something?'

Sienna blinked and looked at Eve. The last time she'd seen Lex's daughter, not long after she'd lost her mother and met her father for the first time, she'd been as quiet as a mouse. That's what living with Eve did to you.

'You remember Lily?' Eve asked.

'I do. Nice to see you again, Lily.'

'You, too.' The girl flashed her a grin. Then looked at Maddy. 'Hello, Maddy. Welcome. We've so been looking forward to you coming.' Then to Sienna she asked, 'What would you like me to carry?'

'Just the blue one in the boot. Thanks.'

Lily nodded and bounced away.

'Your luggage matches your car?' Eve teased as her husband arrived beside her.

'The little things in life.'

Lex shook her hand, and his head. Then smiled laconically at his wife and drawled, 'Your sister has been like a lizard on a hot rock all day.'

'Visitors.' Eve clapped her hands and shooed them all up the stairs. 'Come have a cool drink. Relax. It's so good to see you. I'm so excited!'

Chapter Thirty-one

Maddy

Maddy watched Sienna cross to her sister and hug her. Eve Mackay looked as tall as the doctor, but rounder and softer. Less abrasive than Sienna though Maddy had to admit that Sienna had turned into one of her favourite people.

As she listened to Sienna inquire about her sister's nausea, and Eve's assurance that it had disappeared, she wondered briefly if maybe she should think about heading across Australia to her family in WA and look for a sisterly rapport, not that she'd had the sort these two seemed to have. Last time she'd visited after her mum had died she'd felt in the way. Her sister and brothers had families of their own.

She heard Sienna say, 'You're always excited.' Saw the tilt of her head as she studied Eve. 'And you have less colour in your face.'

'Thank you, doctor.' Eve turned from Sienna to the car, and standing there Maddy could feel her face heat. Before she could totally regret coming here, Eve stepped forward and gently enfolded her into an embrace. Looked at her as if she were a present and then hugged her again.

'Welcome, Maddy, I'm so pleased you decided to come and I can't wait to meet your baby.'

Maddy felt the tears well up and could only nod her thanks. Her baby, who at that precise moment realised the car had stopped, saved her by letting out a blood-curdling bellow that made the cockatoos lift from the fence in a startled cloud. Then the tiny passenger totally lost it and nearly lifted the roof of the car with her wailing.

Eve laughed out loud. 'Now that's an outback Queensland voice. She'll have no problem calling in the dogs.'

Maddy didn't know why, but that funny statement had her dropping her shoulders and almost falling against the car with relief. She smiled at Eve and then Sienna and knew that for the moment it would all be okay. 'Maybe I should call her Clarion, or Clarry for short,' she joked.

Eve looked at her and then Sienna. 'She hasn't got a name yet? What fun!' She smiled reassuringly at Maddy. 'A name has to fit. It'll come.'

Maddy felt guilty about keeping her thoughts to name her baby Bridget, after her mum, to herself but she still wasn't sure.

'Hope you find one soon or I'll have Trumpet stuck in my head,' Sienna said loudly and put her hand over her ears.

Maddy giggled as she and Eve hurried to unstrap their fist-waving passenger.

Chapter Thirty-two

Sienna

Sienna allowed herself to be herded up the stairs. Glancing across at the tops of the shrubs below, she had to admit that her sister's home welcomed in a way her own didn't. The lake shimmered to the left and a mountain range formed a natural amphitheatre with the homestead in the middle. Cattle dotted the sparse paddocks.

'Blanche will be here soon. She wouldn't miss you,' Lex said as he waved her to be seated on the spacious verandah, where Eve had already set a table. Eve and Maddy had disappeared into the house with the baby.

'Hmm. I look forward to seeing her, too,' Sienna said darkly and Lex grinned without commenting. Then he said, 'Eve tells me Sergeant McCabe is stationed at Spinifex?'

Sienna pretended to frown. 'Eve tells you a lot.'

'One of the joys,' he said and smiled in the direction his wife had disappeared with a little too much love for Sienna's nausea levels. Get a room.

Lily must have had enough of her father's devotedness, too because she took the opportunity to say, 'I love your car,' to Sienna.

Now there sat a girl with good taste. 'Remind me to show you the light that shines on the ground when you open the door. It's shaped like a horse.'

Lily's eyes sparkled. 'Really?'

Sienna nodded her head enthusiastically. 'Yep.'

Lily bit her lip. 'Have you still got your red sports car?' She looked hopeful. 'I've got my Ls.'

It had been a cute car. 'No. Sorry, Lily. I traded that in when this one arrived.'

Lily nodded as if not surprised. 'That's okay. This one has better clearance.'

Lex glanced in the direction of a car horn that sounded from the drive. 'I'm off. See you later at tea.' He picked up his hat before striding away and down the stairs two at a time.

They watched him go. 'Still larger than life,' she said.

'I know,' Lily said.

Sienna sat on Eve's verandah and sipped another cup of tea. Eve and Maddy had gone off to Maddy's room again, where Eve had moved in a recliner rocker for feeding.

Sitting opposite Sienna on the wide airy deck, Blanche Mackay confidently expounded on her theories of what could possibly have created a cluster of microcephalic babies in her territory.

'I was reading about radiation poisoning affecting pregnancies. What about something from space, like a large meteor. I couldn't see where that had happened in the last year, but perhaps no one noticed.'

Lily joined them with a plate of biscuits. 'Or something radio-active dropped by one of those satellites that I see at night.'

Blanche smiled fondly at her granddaughter. 'Satellites don't drop radioactive "things" like something drops out of your handbag.'

'Okay. So maybe something bounced out of a truck,' Lily agreed easily and Sienna wondered if coming here had been an omen. Regan's words floated back.

'Apparently that happened in America.' Sienna took a biscuit thoughtfully. 'It's a possibility we're looking at, but there are so many regulations and safety issues in place in Australia when it comes to radioactive material.' Sienna frowned. 'I've spoken to the Director of Medical Physics at my hospital and he's contacted a physicist to rule that out. I'm hoping he might have some more ideas about what type of accident could cause something like this. He'll also run a scan to measure if there is any residual radiation coming from Spinifex. Though if radiation was a factor it would be an ongoing source, so you would think other people would be exhibiting symptoms.'

'Like what?' Lily asked and Blanche sat forward.

Sienna ticked them off on her fingers. 'Severe tiredness, hair loss, nausea and vomiting.' She looked up. 'I haven't seen any of that in Spinifex.'

'What about a short-term exposure? An accident that was cleaned up. Something in a rubbish bin that had been found, not recognised and thrown away,' Blanche said, warming to her theme.

Sienna nodded. 'Of course that's possible. Something short-lived is what we want to rule out.'

'If it's gone how do we find it, then?' Blanche's excited shoulders drooped.

Sienna sipped her tea. It tasted good like it did in Spinifex. Better than tea in the city. 'I have several people combing for events. The mums. Their families. The FOG. The flying doctor clinic nurse has a diary and she'll get back to me next week.' She lifted her cup. 'Or it could be cytomegalovirus running rampant in a playgroup. Or a coincidence. Or something we haven't thought of. But I'll address all of them and put strategies in place to help reduce the risks for the future.'

Blanche's questioning subsided and she turned her head to gaze out into the paddocks, her face sad. Sienna appreciated her concern for the families already affected. Although she didn't say there was nothing they could do for those babies already affected, because they were both thinking it.

The phone rang and Lily jumped up enthusiastically and dashed inside to answer it.

Blanche said, 'That girl is like sunshine and I have another grandchild coming, which I can tell you I'm thrilled about. So, you'll understand why I'm feeling the urgency to clear this up, Sienna.'

They both glanced towards the door where Eve had disappeared half an hour ago with Maddy.

'I know. The good news is Maddy's baby is fine and Maddy's been living there for a couple of months. And I've been there for a week and I haven't fallen ill at all.'

Lily appeared at the door. 'It's for you, Gran.'

'Excuse me, Sienna.' Blanche stood up and followed her granddaughter inside and Sienna suddenly realised what she'd said wasn't strictly true. She remembered the nausea earlier that day, and come to think of it, even the tiredness. It was something she'd noticed since she'd been there. Unconsciously, her hand went to her hair and she tried to think if her brush had accumulated more hair than normal. Actually it had. She'd noticed it yesterday. Good grief. Was she being exposed to radiation and she hadn't known it?

Her skin abruptly cooled, went clammy, and her pulse rate accelerated. With the rush of adrenaline her thoughts created, another urgent bout of nausea gripped her, and she almost knocked her teacup over in the need to make it out of the chair and into the house. Luckily, the bathroom was in the opposite direction to Blanche and she hastily shut the door.

Five minutes later, as she splashed her face at the sink and stared at her pale reflection, she tried to remember all of the side effects of radiation poisoning. Then she thought of Douglas. And Alma. And every other person residing in Spinifex. She needed the number of that physicist ASAP.

Someone knocked gently on the door. 'Are you okay, Sienna?' Eve spoke through the door, her concern clear as her muffled voice penetrated the thick wood.

Sienna let out a long sigh. She opened the door. 'I think I might have radiation sickness.' She lifted her eyes to her sister's face.

Eve tilted her head. 'Before you decide you're dying, are your breasts tender?'

Sienna frowned. 'No,' and automatically lifted her hands to pat her chest. 'Maybe.'

'Well, that's unexpected.' Eve tried to hide her dawning smile and remain sympathetic.

Sienna stared at her. 'What?'

Eve's smile lit the room and her hand came up to cover her mouth. 'I thought of it this morning when you said you'd been food poisoned. You and Callie both. Seriously? The GP and now the obstetrician? At least I knew.'

Sienna forced away a sudden unwelcome thought. Not possible. 'What's in your head? Don't be silly.'

'You wouldn't be the first medical person in the family to miss the signs of early pregnancy,' Eve teased.

'I'm not pregnant,' Sienna hissed forcefully, but deep, buried under the horror, she knew that the situation was perhaps possible. If it was true, well, it damn sure wouldn't be for long.

She glanced around urgently, realising the implications of this being overheard. 'Shhh. I'm not. And if I was I'm not having it. So, don't blab everywhere.'

Eve raised her eyebrows. 'Of course,' she said soothingly, as though Sienna was a child. 'But I don't believe you,' she declared, a soft smile on her face. 'I know you. And you don't give up on anything because it's hard. This has happened for a reason.'

'Great. What reason? So I can throw a brilliant career away? So I can have a microcephalic baby and spend the rest of my life being a carer? Oh, great idea, sis. No freaking way.'

'It's Douglas's, isn't it?'

'I only had sex at Christmas,' she hissed. But as she said it she realised it wasn't true. Twelve weeks ago she'd been knocked over by a virus. Alone in her flat, miserable until Douglas had come. He'd nurtured her, fed her broth, and made exquisite love to her before he left. Damn him! And her stupid contraceptive pills mustn't have been absorbed. She told others that all the time. Beware of illness and contraception. Not covered! Surely, this wasn't true. Couldn't be true. She raised her eyes to Eve's and Eve held out her arms.

'Things happen for a reason. It's meant to be.'

As she leaned her head against her sister's chest Sienna

whimpered, 'I can't do this. I'll be a terrible mother. You know I will. I'll be just like her.'

Eve stroked her back comfortingly. 'You'll be an incredible mother. And Douglas will be an incredible father.'

Sienna drew a shuddering breath and straightened. Enough of the pathetic whining. 'It won't work. It will never work.'

Eve smiled. 'It will work.'

'No, it won't. We're too different. We have no common ground.'

Eve glanced down at Sienna's flat stomach. 'You've got some common ground. And you're both strong, wonderful people. Stop thinking and just feel. It's a miracle, Sienna. Unplanned. Determined. Meant to be.'

Sienna sank against the wall and put her head in her hands. 'I don't believe this.'

Chapter Thirty-three

Maddy

Maddy stood with Eve on the verandah and waved as Sienna's blue car disappeared down the driveway. She couldn't believe she was still here in this oasis of warmth and support and not hiding from Jacob behind a thick wooden door in a room at the pub. For this time, she could allow herself to feel safe until she decided where she would go.

Still, she couldn't help wondering what Jacob would say when he realised she'd left town. She prayed he wouldn't find out about Bridget Clarice, who she'd named after her mum and the baby's loud voice. Already, though, they were calling her Bee, and Bee was the most important player in this tragedy that wasn't going to be a tragedy.

Then she glanced shyly at the woman beside her, who had been so gently supportive of her and Bee. Somehow, Eve had ensured that Maddy totally cared for her baby herself. She had been there but always as a bystander, with encouragement, and it felt good. Felt right. Felt wonderful that Maddy knew she could meet her baby's needs herself. She could almost feel the weight of her baby just thinking about her.

Alma had rung last night. She said she had a plan with help from a friend. It all sounded very cryptic, but both Alma and Eve had said to just concentrate on her baby for a few days and they'd talk about the future then. She'd been secretly pleased to not think. Not plan. Just be. Be with Bee.

Since her introduction to breastfeeding – something she could admit she'd found a little trickier than expected at first, perhaps because Bee had demanded the same fast feed she'd had from the bottle – it had become easier every feed. In fact, it had turned into an incredible experience, starting from when Eve had undressed Bee and placed her naked squirming body against Maddy's skin, until Bee had found her own way to the breast and at last settled by feeding.

The solid sleep of the first twelve hours of her baby's life had changed since she'd woken in Sienna's car. Now she was demanding to eat almost every second hour, but Maddy didn't mind. And Eve had reassured her that it was Mother Nature's way of making her milk come in. Who knew these things? After that first feed Bee had settled, slept and then woken again to feed.

Eve had made a small crib next to Maddy's bed and said to just lie there and get to know her baby. To feed as many times as the baby wanted in the next twenty-four hours, and gradually she'd find a pattern. Already it seemed to be working.

She heard a strident cry, met Eve's eyes with a smile and turned away to comfort her baby.

Chapter Thirty-four

Sienna

Sienna left after lunch, much later than intended, and hoped, gloomily, she'd make it back before nightfall. She doubted she would.

As she drove away from her sister's homestead, Maddy's problems were leapfrogged by her own dilemma. She'd sworn Eve to secrecy, though the idea of her sister keeping anything from Lex was ludicrous. She'd accepted that. No choice there – but Lex wouldn't share her news with anyone.

At least no one else at Diamond Lake Station knew of her horrendous discovery – though even she knew the word 'horrendous' sounded inappropriate. They'd managed to avoid Blanche finding out about the episode in the bathroom and the revelations soon after, and Lily and Maddy had been in their own worlds – bless the tiny vegemite for that.

The baby had taken the focus off Sienna. Even Blanche had been captivated and highly amused when the cute bundle roared and almost brought the roof down every time her mother had changed her nappy.

Strangely, this morning Maddy had looked rested despite the demands of the noise machine. In fact, the young mother had positively glowed in the nurturing environment of Sienna's saintly sister, and had even come up with a name. Sienna approved of naming the baby after Maddy's mother if that was what she wanted. Though they wouldn't be naming Sienna's baby after Sienna's mother, she thought grimly.

She could not in any way see herself being domestic or googly-eyed over some squirming demand-feeder at ungodly hours all through the night. Though she guessed night-hour motherhood wasn't so different from being on call for someone else's birth.

Her brain began that negative 'not now, how did this happen' chanting again, and she gripped the steering wheel hard until her fingers blanched. This could not be true.

Only it was true. The moment Eve had mentioned it she'd known in her bones. And Eve had supplied her with a pregnancy test that had confirmed it.

What the hell was she going to do? When should she tell Douglas? How could she tell Douglas that she, the expert, had stuffed up? Maybe she could just quietly go home and not mention it in case . . . But even thinking about that made her queasy.

This was all Eve's fault. Her and her bloody words, her sentiment about it being 'meant to be', 'a precious opportunity', 'destined'. All of which insidiously voted for Sienna to accept the inevitable. But she had a career. A life. A world that would change forever if she added a family into the mix.

And what of the other half of the new equation? What of Douglas? What would he think, feel, say? She eased her hold on the wheel to release the cramp in her fingers. He had his own world, too. In the outback. He was set in his life. Saving the world in his own way. What would Douglas say? She didn't know what he would say, but he certainly had the right to say it.

Twelve weeks. These were dangerous times for a pregnancy. When Mother Nature had the right to take a hand and orchestrate a loss. A huge proportion of foetuses miscarried before twelve weeks. And her eggs weren't young. Maybe she would be one of those mothers? More destiny? Though why she should feel hollow at the thought drove her crazy. This whole thing would drive her crazy. Her being a mother epitomised crazy.

Her own mother should never have had children. And she hadn't planned to until she'd fallen in lust with their father. After he'd left she'd told Sienna time and again that it had been a mistake.

She thought of Eve. Calm, capable, caring Eve, a woman who would without a doubt be a wonderful mother. Was already a wonderful mother to Lily. Eve was a product of their mother, so maybe there was hope for Sienna, too. Callie was a fabulous mother, and she shared half her genes with Sienna.

Nooo. Whyyyyyyy me! She pressed a hand to her brow and then her finger drifted down to press play on the stereo to drown out the voices in her head and try to listen to Mick Jagger. After three minutes of 'As Tears Go By' she switched it off. Looked at the wide open plains surrounding her. Tried to breathe in the stillness for her frantic brain. Noted the sun moving down behind the low hills in the distance, and hoped she didn't hit one of the foraging kangaroos that loved to jump out at dusk and play kamikaze.

Ten miles out of Spinifex Sienna needed to stop. And it had only been an hour and a half since the last stop. She needed to stretch her legs, pee. Or at least walk around the car. But she'd noticed the lights from a car coming her way, and she waited for it to pass before she pulled over. Except it didn't. Pass that is. *Weird.* The headlights had merged into one light and the undulations in the road made it dance left to right on the horizon.

Sienna yawned and decided she'd become more tired than she'd thought, and wished the vehicle would hurry up and approach so she could put her own lights back on high beam.

Annoyingly, the vehicle seemed to slow. 'Come on,' she said out loud, but it still took its sweet time to get to her. Later she couldn't remember when she realised the light had arrived as she drew level and saw it wasn't connected to a car at all. Just a light.

The light, glowing like a big white football of brightness, hovered at the side of the road and danced a jig. What the hell?

Sienna checked her rear-view mirror, expecting to see a car behind her with a spotlight, maybe shining on the trees, or perhaps moonlight off some hidden water puddle reflecting. No other car.

She slowed, confused, trying to work it out. The fuzzy light danced and shifted of its own accord, like a mischievous firefly on steroids, and her trickle of disquiet morphed into full-blown fright as she realised it wasn't anything she could explain.

Not freaking Alma's Min Min?

Her foot stamped hard on the accelerator and all the dozing horses under the bonnet picked up on her demand as the car hurled itself forward in a stampede of torque and power and eight pumping cylinders.

Sienna's hands clutched the steering wheel in a death grip and her heart pounded in her ears as the Mustang roared up the road and sped away from the light. Her heart punched like one of the pistons under the bonnet as the distance widened between her and the strange light, and unconsciously her hand drifted down to protect her stomach.

Flicking her gaze down, she realised what she'd done, and at the same time she eased her foot on the pedal and slowed the bolt for Spinifex to a safer speed. So, she'd discovered one thing – she'd rather grapple with an unexpected pregnancy than be lured to some spaceship or supernatural realm by a freaking watermelon-sized glow. She wasn't sure she'd be telling Alma or she'd never hear the end of it. She rolled her eyes, already thinking she'd imagined it. Had she really seen that?

And if she had, what would Alma say?

Half an hour later, parked under the pub carport at the edge of the yard, Sienna's hands had stopped shaking enough to get her key out of the ignition. Evidently, the locals had decided the shed belonged to Sienna, or maybe they just liked to park closer to the door of the pub, and she didn't disabuse that concept, very happy to take advantage. It almost felt like home after the fright on the road.

Alma looked up as she entered and handed the cloth she'd been using to wipe the bar to a very attractive blonde woman Sienna hadn't seen before. Maddy's replacement?

'This is Heidi. She's my new barmaid. From the Netherlands.' Alma frowned. 'You look pale.'

'Exciting times,' Sienna quipped.

'Tell me about it,' Alma said with a nod towards the bar. 'Maddy's Jacob is in there drowning his sorrows and I wasn't quite game to kick him out. I told him she was gone, but he doesn't believe me. I might have to ring that man of yours to move him along soon.'

Sienna glanced around. She didn't have the mental energy to correct Alma. Douglas wasn't her man. He might be her secret squeeze. The father of her child. But not her man. That would never work.

The last half hour must have muffled the urgency to sort out Douglas's paternity. It had almost drowned all that out. Though she still wasn't sure she should admit to the hallucination, she found herself telling Alma before she could stop herself, 'Think I might have seen your Min Min.' She kept her voice low, self-conscious in case anyone else heard.

Alma stilled. Searched Sienna's face and said, 'I'll get you a brandy.'

'I could do with . . .' She'd been going to say a double before she thought of her secret disaster and stopped. 'A cup of tea instead,' she said with a heavy sigh. Damn it. Brandy would have been good. 'I'll make it in my room.'

Alma glanced around the noisy bar. 'No. You go up.' She searched her face again with a frown. 'You okay?'

Sienna wondered how this tiny, tough publican could be so perceptive when she barely knew her. 'Of course. Just didn't expect to meet a travelling companion on the way home.'

'We never do,' Alma said with a hint of worry. 'I wonder what's going to happen?'

It was such a ridiculous thing to say that Sienna could feel the jangling of her nerves settle. As if the light from the Min Min always hopped about waving to cars on the way to Spinifex foretelling disasters. Right now her legs felt like lead and she wondered if she'd be able to climb the stairs under the weight of all the things on her mind.

Alma patted her arm. 'You look like a ghost. Go and put your feet up. I'll bring you a cuppa on a tray.'

Sienna nodded, like a docile, pregnant cow, she thought with disgust at herself, and turned to plod up the stairs. It must be the aftermath of that surge of adrenaline, she realised, and used her hands on the banister as much as her feet on the stairs to pull her tired body up to her room.

Within minutes she'd been followed upstairs by Alma, who apparently had come up with some plan to get Maddy away. After she'd made sure Sienna had her feet up in the armchair beside the bed, she placed the tray next to her. 'Have you eaten?'

'I had lunch at Diamond Lake.'

'Tsk.' Alma grumbled. 'That's hours ago. I'll get you a toasted sandwich.'

'Tell me about Jacob.'

Concern crinkled Alma's face even more than usual. 'He's in a filthy mood. Threatening revenge. That he'll make me pay, make Douglas pay. I tried to tell him Maddy had left town on the bus. He asked where you were. Said Maddy had changed and it was all your fault. Yours and mine, and that man of yours.' She looked more worried than Sienna had expected. 'He's down in the bar questioning people now.'

That didn't sound pleasant. And Sienna had no energy for a confrontation with a bully. 'Might be worth phoning Douglas. I'll do that in a minute, to let him know I'm back.'

Alma wanted to know what Sienna thought if she took Maddy and her baby to start a pub somewhere else. Would it be the best thing? Sienna agreed. She tried to look enthusiastic, but really, whatever. She had her own problems. But leaving town? Yes. Great idea. Everybody should do it.

She couldn't wait to shake the red dust from her shoes and get the heck out of Spinifex. The faster the better. Though she'd be leaving in daylight and avoiding flying watermelons. Eventually, Alma went back downstairs. Sienna glanced at her phone and called Douglas . . . her baby's father. She kept it brief. After the call, she closed her eyes and rested back in the chair. The feeling of foreboding wouldn't leave.

Chapter Thirty-five

Ten minutes later a knock at the door dragged Sienna out of her chair. She had been starting to feel marginally better until she opened the door to Douglas. Her phone rang at the same time. Terrible timing for a call. Or was it? She didn't know whether to hug Douglas or run away. She was glad for the excuse to turn her back to him after lifting her hand in greeting.

The caller ID said Regan again, no doubt with an update on the radioactive investigation team, so she had to take it. It was fortunate really, as she didn't know how to look into Douglas's face with what she knew. She could feel his presence behind her shoulder, as Regan expounded on whom he'd notified.

Douglas remained outside the door, despite her gesturing for him to come in, but of course he wouldn't risk entry. He hadn't been across the threshold of her room since that first day.

She glanced over her shoulder at him. Drilled him with her eyes. *Too late to be safe now, buster, I'm already pregnant!* She held her phone clutched like a shield between them. His eyes narrowed, as if sensing something he didn't understand until, with a shrug, he turned and left.

The desolation as that blue-shirted figure disappeared down the hall stung like a whiplash across her cheek and she lifted her other hand to her face. At least he'd chosen to go and she hadn't sent him packing by saying something stupid in her current state of mind. How the hell could she tell him? How could she not? But she wasn't ready for that. Nowhere near processed with her thoughts. And still the phone call twittered on.

Poor Regan explained how unlikely someone losing a source of radiation was, but he had set things in motion for an investigation. All with no attention from Sienna. Sienna pondered the *what ifs*. What if Douglas swooped on the idea and wanted to play happy families and she knew she couldn't? Sienna felt the scratch of emotion in her throat and tried to concentrate on Regan and his long explanation.

'Are you there?' she heard Regan ask.

'Yes, I'm here,' her voice sounded croaky and weak, even to her own ears, like she'd been crying or soon would be. That was probably the pregnancy, too. It made sense now when she thought of how emotional she'd been. How moody. Scatterbrained. She put the phone away from her at arm's length and drew a long, silent breath. 'Service is coming in and out here, Regan, can you repeat that please.' Her voice was steadier now. Crisp. She was back in control. She'd have to watch that.

She looked out the window and down on the street to where a young man on crutches was being escorted across the carpark by Douglas. Jacob threw his head around wildly, obviously abusive, and by the set of those erect shoulders Douglas was even grimmer. Once off the hotel grounds, Jacob moved down the street towards his house, the crutches swinging furiously. Sienna acknowledged with relief she wouldn't meet him downstairs when she went for dinner.

Regan's voice came clearly now. As if he'd moved to a better reception point. He began describing different scenarios that had occurred overseas and Sienna listened intently. It did sound sickeningly possible.

'Of course a common factor with such clusters is a great level of anxiety in the public and non-radiation staff, especially if it includes confirmed or possible pregnant women. I don't know how a clearly marked radioactive source would end up in Spinifex, but now I'm afraid it's not impossible although still highly unlikely.'

In her periphery, Sienna saw Jacob, sneaking back across the carpark but there was no plaster on his pale leg. And he didn't carry crutches. Then he was out of sight. How could that be? She'd have to tell Douglas right away.

Regan said, 'Searching for a lost source in a regional town would also be quite challenging and would definitely generate quite a lot of anxiety – and anger – if it became public knowledge. So keep it low key when the physicist assigned to this case arrives tomorrow.'

The smoke tendril drifted past her window as she listened to Regan. She froze, sniffing deeply to make sure it was smoke. It smelled acrid. Her eyes widened. Then a second later she couldn't see through the window, as the column of smoke thickened and obscured the view. She could hear the crackle and roar of flames now and it began to sink in that she was standing on the second floor of a hotel that would burn like a seasoned stack of best kindling.

Then the smoke alarm went off and all hell broke loose.

Forgetting the man on the other end of the phone, Sienna jammed the phone into her bag and was frantically glancing around the room to decide what to take when Douglas burst through the doorway, snatched her arm and dragged her out the door.

She pulled back. 'My things!'

'Will burn. Just like you. Now *move*.' There wasn't a skerrick of choice in his voice or his grip and instinctively Sienna obeyed. They hurried down the stairs which were already swirling with wisps of smoke though there was no fire to be seen, and they dashed across the overhung verandah and into the street and across the road.

Outside, those newly evicted from the bar gathered and milled in shock, which turned to horrified awe as the tall wooden building whistled like a sudden wind storm and the fire overwhelmed the left side and swallowed it in smoke and flames. It took less than a minute and half the building was engulfed. The new barmaid stood sadly in the shadows across the road, perhaps mourning her new-found job, a job that was burning in front of her. Old Seamus, their most loyal patron, stood next to her and chewed on his pipe, and spat on the ground in front of him every few seconds in disgust.

Sienna glanced around. 'Where's Alma?'

Douglas scanned the crowd, strode to the barmaid and then spun back to the hotel before Sienna heard what was said. To her horror, he jogged back up the steps and dived towards the kitchen – the hotel was not yet alight on that side but filled with smoke.

His tall outline disappeared like a terrifying magic trick into the thick cloud. Swallowed by the monster that breathed fire and poisonous fumes and took no prisoners.

No!

Her breath seized. She couldn't believe her eyes. Couldn't believe he'd done that. Couldn't believe he'd stepped into the inferno away from her – possibly forever. Her hand moved instinctively to her chest as she tried to process the shocking reality, the ramifications of her invincible Douglas being swallowed and consumed irrevocably by a hotel fire.

Her head swam as she forgot to breathe. Her eyes stung as she willed him to emerge. Willed his big, solid Douglas form to appear at the door like a mirage. To jog down the steps towards her. But he didn't. The scream began building in her throat, her lungs aching from holding her breath.

Chapter Thirty-six

Maddy

Madison watched the sunset over the volcanic crater with sixteen-year-old Lily by her side.

'I'll get us a cold drink,' Lily offered, her sunny smile infectious as she basked in the company of someone closer to her own age.

'Thank you.' Maddy smiled back, a touch flabbergasted that these people were making such a gentle fuss of her and treating her like a valued guest.

It had been a long time since she'd felt anything but a harried, clumsy servant to Jacob, and she'd always felt so lucky to have the pub job with Alma she would never have presumed to be waited on. Here, she felt bizarrely like an exotic princess, which was certainly a new experience. She tried not to expect the bubble to burst too quickly.

She glanced across at the tops of the shrubs below and decided that Eve's home glowed like an oasis. Red-brown paddocks stretched away to the lake. The lack of strain in her surroundings seeped into her like a soft mist and she could feel the memory of the last few months being pushed into the back of her mind, which was a much better place for it to be, at least for the next few days.

She'd never met anyone like Eve, someone so tranquil she impacted her surroundings with such a feeling of peace and gentle happiness that Maddy found herself humming without even realising she'd begun.

Lily bounced back and set down the drink without spilling any.

'Thank you.' Maddy turned to her. 'What about you, Lily? Any thoughts on what you'd like to do when you finish school?' It was nearly May so she only had another eighteen months to go. Lily had the world in front of her. Loved as she was.

'Sienna's pretty cool. I like the idea of medicine.' Lily glanced back at the house where Eve was making dinner. 'Or midwifery like Eve.' She paused, gazing out over the long, dry paddocks. 'Or maybe even ag school and animal husbandry like my dad.'

Maddy laughed. 'Well, I guess they all deal with life.'

Lily turned thoughtfully. 'What did you do when you left school, Maddy?'

Maddy hadn't had a young friend for a long time, especially one she felt decades older than, though there was less than five years between them, and she savoured the girlish conversations with an inner smile.

'Like yours, my mum died unexpectedly, and I'd just finished school. Unless I moved in with my older brothers or my sister and their families I didn't have a home. So I went straight overseas backpacking with a few of the girls from school. I didn't want to stay home without Mum.' She compressed her lips as the sudden longing for her mother swamped her for a minute.

Lily nodded. 'When my mum died, Lex came and picked me up. My mum always told me he was dead. So it was a bit of a shock when he turned up.' She looked back at the kitchen again.

'I miss Mum heaps, but Eve is the best. Blanche is good, too. I'm pretty lucky to have another family who love me.'

Maddy totally agreed. Nobody had come to pick her up. Her father had already died. But she was okay. These people were kind to her and maybe she did have dear Alma as her friend. 'Eve is wonderful. And so is Sienna.'

She thought about how the busy doctor had dropped everything to bring her here. Six hours of driving each way. She still couldn't believe it. 'Sienna's so smart and sophisticated. I can't believe all that she's done for Bee and me. And Eve, too, of course. So kind.'

'My dad thinks the sun shines out of Eve.'

Maddy smiled. 'I think maybe the sun does.' Lily's dad, the larger-than-life Lex Mackay, had taken Blanche in the helicopter to Charleville for the evening, to return in the morning. Even that created peace and a feeling of relief. Eve had said she, Lily and Maddy would have an early night so they could all sleep between feeds. Bee did have a loud voice.

'You are so good with your baby,' Lily blurted. 'As if you've done it before. I'd be terrified.'

'Maybe I should be a children's nurse. I always fancied nursing.' Maddy smiled and thought briefly about her own future before coming back to her daughter. A rush of love surged up and pushed away the feeling of isolation. 'We're moving forward on this mothercraft gig. I was an au pair for three months when I lived in Sweden.' The gentle art of child care had drifted easily back to her hands. This respite from the real world felt too good to be true.

A strident roar lifted a parakeet on the fence and she turned from the rail at the sound of her daughter's call.

'Well, that's the end of the sunset for me.'

Chapter Thirty-seven

Sienna

In Spinifex, Douglas still hadn't appeared from the smoke. Sienna swayed, her vision blurring, as the sound of the crackling wood was superseded by the freight-train roar of the fire beast. The first piece of tin roof tumbled two storeys to the ground with an almighty crash on the opposite side to where Douglas had disappeared.

The fire brigade arrived with their truck siren blaring, and Blue jumped from the passenger side, but everyone knew there was nothing they could do except try to contain the blaze from spreading to the next building.

'Move back, everybody! There's gas in that place.' The onlookers surged backwards, Seamus pulling a frozen Sienna gently with him.

The fire chief wanted information. Sienna supposed they should be grateful this had happened before Blue started his afternoon session at the pub. Her thoughts were scrambled and not making sense as if to protect herself from the horror to come. 'Anybody in there?' he asked.

Sienna snapped her head around at his voice but Seamus beat her. 'Big Copper went in after Alma. Towards the kitchen.'

Blue's eyes widened. 'Get those hoses pointed at the kitchen!'

he bellowed at the older men who'd hopped down more slowly. Blue scurried to the side of the truck and began yanking the fire-hose from the reel.

Too late. Fear chanted in her head. She knew it. Too late. It would be too late. Fire was fast, hot, dark and deadly. And Douglas had dived into it. The kitchen would be filled with black smoke and the heat would be building at an incredible rate as the flames crossed to the other wing. *Nobody could survive in that toxic smoke*, the words whispered like black devils in her head. He hadn't even wrapped a cloth around his face!

Then something moved at the far right. Was that him? After the longest breath of her life, a lone, swaying figure stumbled through the screen of smoke and heat around the side of the pub, between the two buildings. He must have come from the side kitchen door. Sienna sucked in a lungful of acrid air and a huge, retching sob escaped into the hand over her mouth. Douglas.

Alma's white head drooped from Douglas's strong arm, her body slack against his chest, a small shape, so tiny and helpless, convulsing.

Douglas staggered onto the road and across to them. People rushed forward to escort him to safety. He coughed as he lowered his precious bundle to the ground and then, kneeling, he dropped his head to suck in great gulps of air. The middle section of the roof gave way and now the whole right side of the building exploded as the gas in the kitchen caught fire.

Douglas coughed and gulped, and wiped his streaming eyes. 'She was trying to grab the till money.' He coughed again. 'Crawling the wrong way in the smoke.' More coughing. 'Nearly didn't see her against the bench.'

'Alma,' Sienna smoothed the white hair stuck to the older woman's forehead. 'Alma?' she repeated, but inside she was seething at what he'd done. At Alma for caring about money when lives were at stake.

Alma coughed without opening her eyes. And Sienna couldn't stop herself any longer. Her eyes filled with tears as she felt the fury of fear swell inside her until it took over just as the fire had devoured the building. 'Are you crazy?' She hissed at Douglas. 'You were seriously lucky. If I'd had to come in there and find you both you were in big trouble.'

Then one of the young members of fire brigade arrived with an oxygen bottle and Sienna called him over, breathing deeply to calm herself. She never exploded. 'Here,' she instructed, 'both of them.'

The young man scanned the crowd for the voice, saw Sienna and Douglas and then Alma on the ground and hurried over.

Douglas whispered hoarsely, 'How did it start?'

Old Seamus shuffled over and offered his two cents' worth. 'Seems to have been on the outside wall nearest the car park. Young Jacob was acting crazy. Wondered about drugs myself. After you escorted him out. Thought he might have ended up in the clink with the threats he was making.' Seamus nodded his head sagely. 'He could've done something foolish.' Then the old man looked around. 'Where's young Maddy? She wasn't in there, was she?'

Sienna heard him distantly as she listened to Alma's chest with the young man's stethoscope, pushing aside the oxygen tubing that hung from the mask on Alma's face. 'No,' she said without thinking. 'She's safe at my sister's at Diamond Lake.' Douglas probably needed oxygen, too. She wanted to check Douglas. Her heart still palpitated with the near loss of him. She wanted to hug him to her and not being able to publicly throw herself on his chest tore at her.

Two weeks ago her thoughts might have been focused on the fact that she'd lost everything she'd brought here that wasn't in Douglas's house. Maybe even her beautiful car. Now her thoughts focused on the man crouched down beside them. The incredibly brave, incredibly stupid father of her child. She leaned out and touched his shoulder. Felt the solid warmth of his body beneath her shaking fingers. Just a small reassurance that he was flesh and blood and she hadn't imagined him here beside her.

He turned his head and looked at her, his red-rimmed eyes apologising for her distress. Mercifully, his coughing had slowed.

'I don't care how long you can hold your breath,' she said grimly. 'As your doctor, I need to tell you that smoking is bad for your health.'

She saw the admiration flare in his face and she felt like crying. *Oh, Douglas.* 'Don't you ever do anything like that again,' she whispered, and scanned him for any signs of injuries.

His eyes still streamed, and his shirt lay plastered against his heaving chest, smudged with black, but he was okay and he'd saved Alma, and now that she thought about it, he'd also saved her.

Thank goodness he'd stopped her from dithering to collect her belongings. If she'd remained any longer in her room maybe he'd have been too late for Alma. She didn't want to think about what Douglas would have done if he hadn't been able to find Alma in there. He was safe. They both were. That was all that mattered.

She looked across at him and said very softly, 'Thank you.' She inclined her head towards Alma. 'And thank you for saving Alma.' Then she said, 'I saw Jacob cross the yard before I saw the smoke. He's cut off his plaster. I don't know where he went.'

He nodded and sighed heavily.

Chapter Thirty-eight

Alma

Alma opened her eyes to a world gone mad. There seemed to be a lot of noise and shouting and it felt like some big oaf was sitting on her chest. No one actually was – it was just hard to breathe. She did struggle against one of the younger fire-brigade blokes pushing an oxygen mask onto her face and sucked in a raspy inhalation before she tried to push him away. So much noise? Was that a train coming?

She struggled to sit up and found herself half lying on the far side of the road outside her pub when she realised there was no train. That horrific noise was her majestic Desert Rose Hotel roaring into oblivion in a mass of flames and falling timber.

She blinked her raw, stinging eyes and tried to make sense of it. A fire. Then, the last few events she remembered began to filter back. Her stomach plummeted. Ah, yes, the smoke.

A lot of the other noise was the fire brigade shouting to each other and hosing things down. Keeping people back. Keeping people back from her pub. Her verandahs. Her beautiful staircase. Being destroyed. All her years of polishing and love and dedication to restoring the grandeur of the lady. Even Maestro the coffee machine from the Melbourne Cup. All those hours of buffing and shining. Gone.

She sucked in another cold stream of oxygen to quieten the surge of grief and distress that welled up in her throat and threatened to embarrass her here in the maelstrom. But the loss. The loss of the only thing she'd had the right to love. The loss of her future taken away behind a wall of horrific heat and rolling smoke. Crumbling into ash.

'My pub,' she croaked and coughed. Her throat hurt and her chest tightened like a vice again.

A window exploded around the side and she winced, before pushing the mask away. 'How'd I get here?'

'You put that mask back on, Alma,' the fire-brigade boy bossed and Alma glared at his pubescent face.

'I've seen you in nappies. Don't you tell me what to do. I'll take it off if I want.'

'Woken up, have you, Alma.' Douglas looked at her with a glint in his eye. He nodded suggestively at the plastic face cover, and grumblingly, she put it back on.

She remembered being in the kitchen when the fire started. Didn't remember leaving it. She said in a muffled voice through the mask, 'So who carried me out?' Then she lifted it up slightly to say, 'Shoulda left me.'

'Sorry. I did.' Douglas waved at the mask. 'Keep it on.'

'And you both nearly died.' The sharpness in Sienna's voice penetrated Alma's distress. It was a note Alma had never heard from the calm doctor, and she closed her eyes. Thought about it. Opened them again and looked at the white-faced woman. 'Close, was it?'

'Too close,' Sienna said very quietly and she saw Douglas touch Sienna's shoulder. Saw the look of deep distress that still lingered in Sienna's eyes. Must've been close. Too bloody courageous for his own good, that man. Guess she was glad he had carried her out. Or would hopefully get to that stage of thought sometime in the next year or two.

'I'm sorry about your hotel, Alma,' Douglas said. 'She was a grand old lady and a part of you.'

Alma felt the tears prickle and she glared at him. Great. Now he was gonna give her sympathy and make her cry for the first time in Spinifex history. No bloody way was that happening. She dragged herself back under control and forced the lump in her throat down by sheer willpower.

'It's just a pub.' The words came out harsh. But Douglas was right, her pub had been a part of her. A big part of what she'd done with the rest of her life after Pearl. And that investment of blood, sweat and fear of failure was well on the way to gone now.

That building had been a part of Shirl, too. She guessed it was good Shirl wasn't here to see this. It was like losing a part of Shirl also, all over again. Why did life have to suck so hard so often?

Alma coughed. Turned her eyes away resolutely from the past, though she doubted she'd forget the picture she could still see of the crumbling wreckage in her mind's eye. 'Anybody hurt?'

Douglas's big hand came down gently on her shoulder in unobtrusive support. 'You're the worst. Unless you had some sleepover guests we didn't know about?'

That would be a real tragedy, she reminded herself, if she'd toasted some unsuspecting people. 'Nope.' She blinked her sting-ing eyes. 'Just the doctor and the regulars in the bar.' She sucked in a few more drags of oxygen until she could talk again. 'Main thing is nobody died.' She glared at Douglas. 'Except nearly me.' She had to rest to get her breath back. 'Not so sure I'm glad you pulled me free,' she managed once she could talk again. She glared at the young fireman. 'Would've given me peace from folk pushing things on me I don't want. Shouldn't you be somewhere else?' She growled at the poor young man, waving him away with her hand. 'Go and help your father.'

Chapter Thirty-nine

Maddy

Lying in bed in the early hours of the next morning, Madison tried to fall back to sleep, the tiny snuffles from Bee in her cot beside her bed making her smile.

Unexpected light danced across her ceiling and caught her eye, then the sound of a vehicle's approach lifted her head. The lights disappeared as the sound died into the silent night. A trickle of foreboding crinkled her forehead as she eased back the covers.

As she rose she told herself of course there were other staff quarters somewhere she hadn't seen on the drive in, but the unease made her glance at the clock and register the time. Four am?

Bee had woken three times since they'd all gone to bed and Maddy had just finished feeding her. At least she was sleeping now and swaddled in an extra wrap, because trying to keep her quiet as she moved around the room would have woken the dead, let alone Eve and Lily.

But now, slipping out to the verandah as she peered into the night, she had the sensation of eyes watching her, and unconsciously she tightened her grip on the torch Eve had given her.

A twig snapped loudly in the stillness beneath the verandah steps and Maddy spun and stared into the darkness towards the sound, and then the dogs, tied up for the night, began to bark in an explosion of ferocious growls and snarls.

Maddy's heart thumped uneasily in her chest and a sense of dread made her back away from the edge until she heard the screen door open behind her and Eve's voice.

'Come inside, Madison,' Eve said, calm and firm. 'We'll lock the door.'

Maddy hurried after Eve. 'Do you think there's someone out there?' she whispered.

The steps creaked. 'It could be an animal, but we'll lock up just in case.' Eve's voice remained serene as she shot home the bolt on the door. Then she flipped on a row of lights and outside the house and the garden were bathed in yellow illumination. They looked out the kitchen window and suddenly a man's head appeared. Both of them gasped.

'Jacob!' Maddy whispered and the nausea flooded her throat. He'd found her.

Then his body emerged as he climbed the last few steps until the full limping height of him stood on the verandah. She registered with shock that his plaster was gone. He must have cut it off himself.

'Ha!' he said, triumph in his voice. 'Don't hide. I knew you'd be here. Heard her say that was where she'd taken you. Come out, Madison. I saw you!' The voice shook with exhilaration at his find. 'You shouldn't run away from me. You're mine.'

Maddy turned to Eve. 'I'm so sorry.' Tears of fear and embarrassment and inevitability ran down Maddy's cheek. She lifted her streaked face and squared her shoulders. 'You keep Bee safe. I have to go out. I'll go with him. I'll make him go away.'

Eve shook her head firmly and there was no hesitation in her voice. 'You're not going anywhere with that man. I won't let you.' It was an order from an unexpectedly authoritative Eve, giving her no chance of disobeying.

Jacob's voice cracked as his temper flared. 'Come out!'

The women stayed silent.

He limped heavily across the verandah, trying to see into the dark interior with the external lights shining in his eyes.

'If you don't come out I'll burn it!' His voice cracked. 'Burn this house down with you in it. Just like I burned that witch's pub in Spinifex.'

Horror rose in Maddy's throat and she lifted her hand to hold it in. He'd destroyed Alma's beautiful pub. Had threatened Eve's home. 'I have to stop him,' she pleaded.

Eve's whisper penetrated her horror. 'No. You can replace property. Not lives. Your baby needs you. Come on, Maddy. I'll get Lily. You get Bee. We'll go downstairs and out through the laundry. I'll let the dogs go and they'll chase him off before he can do any-thing.' They began to quietly back away.

They heard the crack of something thrown against the glass of one of the windows and Maddy gasped. Hurriedly, she scooped up Bee then followed Eve to Lily's room, but the girl was standing in the hallway with huge frightened eyes as Eve quietly explained the plan.

The three women crept down the central staircase to the large open area under the building that housed the laundry. Easing open the door to the outside, Maddy watched Eve slip past and edge across the yard to the barking dogs, which was difficult to do without being seen now that all the outside lights were on. She made it across to the dogs and unclipped their collars and they bounded growling and snarling towards the verandah before Jacob saw her.

Maddy felt the first stirrings of relief.

There was a shout from Jacob and snarls from the dogs, then the sound of bumps and yells and Eve whispered, 'Come on. We'll move towards the lake, near the gazebo, until we hear his car drive off.'

Then Eve stumbled, muffled a cry, and inexplicably froze. Maddy bumped into her, and Lily into Maddy, and Eve threw a hand out. 'Stop! A snake.'

Maddy looked down, trying to spot movement in the lines of shadow and light, and that's when she saw the fat striped body and inhaled sharply. She spun around with her baby in her arms to follow the snake's path with her gaze. The tail disappeared into a cane basket of flowers. Brown stripes undulating. Jacob's threat faded a long way into second place.

Lily said, 'Did it bite you?'

'Yes.' Eve's voice was faint. 'I think it's a tiger.' Her voice shook.

'Yes, it is,' Maddy confirmed from the glimpse she'd had of the snake. She'd dealt with this in Western Australia when Tom, one of her older brothers, had been bitten. It was the reason she had learned first aid. A sudden surreal calmness settled over Maddy.

Lily had frozen in shock and looked about to faint. 'Lily. Take Bee. I have to help Eve.' Maddy pushed Bee into the young girl's arms. Then she bent down to confirm the two marks showing red on Eve's ankle. 'How many times did it bite you?'

Eve's voice came faltering and faint. 'Once I think. Struck and bolted.'

'Probably because it was going to be trodden on rather than because it was attacking. Hopefully there's less poison that way.' Strangely, as if in a vacuum, Maddy felt so calm that had Jacob appeared she would have told him to wait with such force even he would have stopped. She glanced around until she saw a heavy wooden chair.

She squeezed Eve's shoulder once, grabbed the chair with a surge of superhuman strength and dropped it in the dirt beside Eve. 'Sit. Don't move. Where are your compression bandages?' Anyone on the land would have bandages for snake bite somewhere for just such an occasion.

'Upstairs. Behind the fruit bowl. We keep them there.'

Maddy flew back inside and up the stairs, not sparing a glance for the verandah or the man on it, if he was there, and found the fruit basin. She vaguely heard the dogs barking and growling, and Jacob swearing as his voice retreated. Locating the bandages, and spotting the cordless phone on the wall beside the sink, she grabbed them both and hurried down to Eve. If someone had asked her she would not have been able to say if the dogs had caught Jacob. Stuff Jacob.

'Hold this and talk.' Maddy thrust the phone at Eve and briefly glanced at her baby crooked in Lily's frozen arms. 'I'll bandage. I've done this before.'

She checked Lily briefly again to see that Bee was fine, and waved once more at the phone, which had the emergency number taped to the front. She watched Eve's shaking fingers begin to press the flying doctor's number and listened for confirmation that it had connected.

Steadily, with her own fingers shaking, Maddy wadded her handkerchief against the faint scratch, and then began to bandage the foot from the toes to the thigh. Firmly. Evenly. Not too tight. Rolling the bandage out in a smooth upward spiral. A car started up in the distance and she barely heard it. Barely cared. This was more important. Eve could die.

Eve had begun to tremble and Maddy took hold of the phone and changed it to loudspeaker in case she needed to talk. Gave it back to Eve and returned to the bandages. Now she could hear the tinny voice from the handset. 'Dr Kent. Charleville Base Flying Doctor. How can I help you?'

Maddy heard the effort to be calm as Eve sucked in a breath. 'It's Eve Mackay at Diamond Lake Station. I've been bitten by a tiger snake on the foot. I'm fourteen weeks,' her voice wobbled, on the verge of tears, 'pregnant.' And Maddy knew where Eve's main concern lay. Maddy glanced at Bee and fought the sudden surge of panic she didn't have time for now. Damn Jacob to hell for attacking these beautiful people.

Eve drew a shuddering breath as she listened to the voice on the other end. Maddy couldn't hear the response properly as it was back jammed against Eve's head. 'Yes. She's binding it now. Yes, I'm sitting. I'll stay as still as I can. We're under the house by the laundry. There was an intruder upstairs and the dogs are out. I think he's gone.' She released a quivering sigh and held the phone away from her head so Maddy could hear, too.

The doctor's voice repeated, 'I'll just confirm. Diamond Lake Station. There was an intruder. One of our team will call the police. Tiger snake bite on foot. Fourteen weeks pregnant. You have some-one binding your foot.'

'Yes. Pressure on site and toes to thigh. Firm not occlusive,' Eve said.

Maddy nodded as she worked.

'And the airstrip is functional?'

'Yes. The cattle gates are shut because my husband will fly in this morning and we do have night lights. Maddy will turn them on in a minute.'

'Excellent. Sit tight. There's an aircraft not far from you with room on board for one more, and we'll divert them your way. We'll have the police find your husband, Mrs Mackay.'

Eve sucked in a calming breath. 'Thank you. He'll be at the Emperial.' But Maddy could see the strain on Eve's face and she suspected the pain had begun to escalate in her leg. She looked at her baby in Lily's arms and glanced around, scanning for something in the laundry they could use for a splint and found it. 'I'll use the cricket bat to strap your leg and we'll prop it up on this drum.'

'Should we move it at all?'

Maddy had already retrieved the bat. Had unwrapped another bandage. 'Hanging down it will swell. They'll raise it in the plane so that you can lie flat. I'll keep it well below your heart level.'

She carefully lifted Eve's leg onto the bat and began to secure it.

Eve said, 'How do you know all this?'

'Western Australia has lots of snakes. My brother was bitten.' She hurried to say, 'And he's good.' She looked at Eve. The words tumbled out in a rush. 'I read last week that a pregnant woman in Brisbane was bitten recently by a tiger snake. They gave her antivenom and she and her baby are fine.'

A tear spilled over and ran down Eve's pale cheek, but a faint, brave smile lifted the corners of her mouth. 'Nice piece of trivia you've stored there, Maddy. Thank you for that. Though they were probably a lot closer to the hospital.'

Maddy glanced up at a noise as she bandaged the elevated leg onto the flat side of the bat. 'I can hear a plane. Is that too soon?'

'Yes. It's probably an airliner. You hear them in the mornings. Would be kilometres high. But the runway light switch is above the phone in the kitchen.'

Maddy nodded, glanced once more at Lily, who still stood frozen with a sleeping Bee jammed against her chest, and ran up the stairs again. Best to do this part now in case Eve became unconscious. She found the spot and pulled the heavy switch down with a satisfying click.

When she returned to Eve the older woman had begun to shake and fine beads of sweat lined her face.

Lily held Bee, quaking with fright as well, and Maddy eased the phone from Eve's deathlike grip, in case she dropped it. The last thing she needed was a broken telephone.

Maddy inhaled softly and calmed her voice, emulating Eve from earlier. 'Try to relax. It'll be fine. They're coming and they'll help you and your baby.' *Please God let that be true.* Maddy was way more scared for Eve than she had ever been for herself during Bee's birth. 'You need to slow your pulse rate.'

This was all her fault. Maddy looked down at the woman who had only offered kindness to her. 'I'm so sorry I caused all this.'

Maddy watched Eve's shoulders drop as she fought for a semblance of calm, as if reminding herself that Maddy was right. 'I'm the midwife, I should know that.' Then, almost normally, as if glad to not think of the snake bite, she said, 'You didn't cause it. He did. Did you find the lights?'

It *was* all her fault. She knew that. 'Yes. It's a big switch. I've turned them on. How do you feel?'

'A little sick, but I don't want to think about it.' Eve said almost conversationally, 'Blanche had the lights installed when Lex went away. Said I needed them especially with Lily here. I've been dying to use them.'

Maddy half laughed and half sobbed. 'Not happy with your choice of words.'

Eve grimaced. 'I keep telling myself I'd feel worse if the snake had dumped a big load of venom.'

They heard a plane in the distance and all three women glanced up and then deflated because it was a far-off drone not coming any nearer and they were underneath the building so couldn't see it.

'We'll take the work truck out to meet them when they fly over the house. That way we'll know it's them,' Eve said.

Maddy squeezed the phone in her hand. 'I can't drive a manual car. I've never got my licence.'

'I can,' Lily said eagerly, visibly relieved to be able to do something to help apart from babysitting. She handed Bee back to Maddy. 'Take her. I'll back the ute up to here and as soon as they come we'll slide you across the back seat with your leg still on the bat.'

The next hour as they waited for the plane to arrive was the worst in Maddy's life, and she'd had some bad times. Eve remained conscious, though the pain in her leg seemed to be increasing, along with Eve's terror for her baby.

When they finally heard the miraculous sound of a plane flying low over the house, they moved Eve awkwardly into the utility. Lily steered the big truck across the paddock with barely a shudder of gear changes as she avoided pot holes to save Eve from bumping up and down.

Once at the airstrip – a long paddock with ground lights every fifty feet – they watched the lights of the plane blink reassurance at them and the now discernible bulk of the aircraft in the pre-dawn light grew larger as it came in over the far fence.

It landed with a small bump and as it sped towards them the sound of the engines grew so loud they couldn't hear each other over the noise without shouting. At last it stopped beside them, the roar of the propellers shutting down, and after what seemed hours but was probably less than a minute or two, the hatch opened.

The nurse glided down the steps not seeming to hurry, but strangely, she arrived beside them in a very short space of time.

'Hello, lovelies. What a morning you've all had.' She smiled briefly at them all but her attention encircled Eve like a protective shell. 'Great bandage. Let's do some observations before we lift you inside and I'll pop a cannula in before we leave.'

Ten very efficient minutes later the nurse was satisfied, the pilot came out and helped Eve to be loaded onto the plane, and after one last fierce hug, all goodbyes were said. The aircraft door shut. The engines started up again like banshees and the noise made the girls put their hands over Bee's ears.

The girls huddled together in the early-morning light with Bee between them, eyes glued to the retreating aircraft. Lily sniffed and Maddy felt like joining. Bee snuffled against her mother's chest, almost ready for her next feed, and Maddy hugged her tight.

She and Lily watched the aircraft take off until just a flashing light hung in the pre-dawn sky and grew smaller.

They climbed wearily into the work truck and Lily started it up and drove them less smoothly back to the empty house.

'The nurse seemed to think she'll be fine,' Maddy said, looking for reassurance herself from the words.

Lily nodded, still stricken, and tried to share the reassurance. 'Eve said everything would be fine. And the nurse said it, too. When she's been properly assessed.'

Eve had made Maddy ring the staff quarters and one of the male jackaroos had come up to the house and was patrolling the grounds as they drove up. The police had phoned to say an officer was coming out and the man would stay on guard with the girls until Blanche or Lex came home.

As they entered the house through the bottom stairs the phone was ringing and Lily hurried to answer it. Maddy heard her say, 'Dad!' and begin to cry.

Maddy's shoulders sagged and the guilt rolled over her like a tsunami at the beach until she was gasping with tears herself. She hugged Bee and took her into her room.

Ten minutes later Lily came and sat on the floor next to her bed. Maddy was on the chair feeding Bee again.

Lily's hand reached across and she stroked Bee's foot as it waved in the air. Her fingers shook. She sniffed again. 'Dad's meeting Eve at the hospital. Gran is being flown in to stay with us.' Then her face crumpled. 'I'm so scared for Eve, Maddy. Will she be alright?'

Maddy could feel her own tears far too close again, but she couldn't break down in front of Lily. Eve would want her to be strong. 'I know she will be. She did everything right. And they have her now.'

'But what about her baby?'

Maddy drew a deep breath and repeated convincingly what she'd read last week about the other lady who'd been bitten. Lily needed something to take her mind off the morning's events. Then she said, 'Do you think you could make a cup of tea while I finish Bee's feed? That would be so good. It's been a horrible morning and Eve would want us to make the beds and tidy up before your grandmother arrives.'

Chapter Forty

Sienna

Early the next morning, Sienna looked up from where she'd just placed a cup of tea for Alma instead of the other way around. Seeing as how Alma was now staying with her in Douglas's house, it was the least she could do. The older lady had been coughing through the night, but she seemed almost back to her old self this morning.

Douglas hesitated at the entry to the room and Sienna patted Alma's arm as she straightened. 'Drink your tea and have a rest in bed, madam. About time you chilled after all your adventures.' She left the room to accompany Douglas into the hallway.

'Is she okay?'

'Yes. Tough as old boots, she said.' Sienna couldn't interpret the look he was giving her. She should tell him. But couldn't. Didn't know how. She looked away. Seemed to spend a lot of time looking away. Said the first thing that came into her head that wasn't about the pregnancy. 'I heard you coughing on the settee last night.' Of course Douglas had given her his bed and slept in the lounge room.

'I'm fine.' He was looking at her. She could feel it.

She stared towards the master bedroom. 'You should have let me sleep on the lounge.' Had to turn back eventually. Still she avoided his eyes.

'I'm not fighting with you again.' His hand came up to catch her chin. 'Sienna?'

'I'll make another cup of tea.'

His fingers stilled her movement. 'I don't want one. I want to know why you can't look at me?'

She turned her chin free. 'I might want one.' She didn't.

'What is going on here?'

'Later.'

'Now.'

The phone rang and Douglas swore under his breath, something she'd never heard him do, and turned away to answer it. Sienna bolted for the kitchen.

The adage *be careful what you wish for* drifted sardonically through her mind as she stirred her unwanted tea. Well, she had asked to be ensconced in the policeman's house and she had requested a chaperone. Shame the pub had had to burn down to get her and Alma here. It was not her fault.

Five minutes later she couldn't miss the furrowed brow that marred Douglas's face as he stood at the door. Her stomach sank. Now what? Douglas put his hand on her arm and she placed her own hand over his fingers, suddenly afraid of what he was going to say.

'Eve's been airlifted to Brisbane. A tiger snake bite.'

Sienna sucked in a breath as pure cold fear seeped into her, and she swayed until Douglas slipped his arm around her. He drew her head onto his chest and she buried her face for a moment, before lifting it again. 'How bad?' Then another thought crashed in. 'Her pregnancy!' Eve would be devastated if anything happened to her unborn baby. They all would.

Guilt brushed sticky fingers over her skin, leaving a residue of shame amidst the shock. Here was her sister naturally terrified about losing her life and her baby and Sienna was in her own little world ruing and fixated on the horror of being pregnant.

Douglas's voice broke into her tormented thoughts. 'She's stable. They think the dose of venom was small.' The gentle pressure of Douglas's fingers grounded her as he stroked her stiff back. 'They think the snake could have recently envenomed something else, a rat or bandicoot, or was more startled than angry when she trod on it, so it didn't inject.'

Her shoulders sagged as sweet relief swept over her. Then, poor Eve. What a shock. 'My sister the disaster zone,' she said, frowning. 'Where was the snake? Not in the house? Are Maddy and the baby okay?'

He paused. Drew a slow sigh and the foreboding she'd felt before crept back. Was there more?

'The snake was outside under the house near the cars.' He stepped back so their eyes could meet. His brow was furrowed again and her neck prickled.

'Jacob turned up and they were hiding from him. He threatened to burn Eve's homestead if Maddy didn't go with him.'

Sienna's hand covered her mouth. Horror trickling ice along her veins. She imagined them hiding from a deranged Jacob and shuddered. 'I should never have taken her there. This is all my fault. Where was Lex?'

'In Charleville with Blanche. And it is not your fault that Jacob went off the rails. Or that Lex was away. But it's unfortunate that only Eve, Maddy and Lily were home.'

Surely Maddy didn't go with him? Eve wouldn't have allowed that. The danger to Maddy scared the daylights out of her. 'She didn't go with him? Where's Jacob? What happened?'

Douglas pulled her against him. 'Stop upsetting yourself. She didn't go. Eve let the dogs off and he drove away. A constable from Charleville is on his way out there to interview Maddy today. He'll suggest she puts an AVO on him. We'll find him,' he said grimly.

'If Lex doesn't find him first.' She could imagine her brother-in-law scouring the earth in his helicopter. He'd kill him.

'Lex is with Eve.'

That was a good thing. Jacob had ruined enough lives. 'I can't believe he threatened to burn Diamond Lake homestead.' Her bumbling attempts to help Maddy showed her ignorance of the situation. 'I should never have taken Maddy there. I caused more trouble than I helped.' It was hard to meet Douglas's eyes. 'This really is all my fault.'

'You couldn't have known he'd follow her there. It's a long way. Even here we had no idea he'd burn the pub, let alone drive hours to cause more havoc.'

Ignorance wasn't an excuse. She needed to stop interfering in things she didn't understand and get back to where she knew the way things ran. Where she was in control. She needed to phone Eve. But it would be too soon. How much longer would she have to be here? She wanted to just get in her car and go. Now. Right now. Run. She glanced at the door, as if assessing if she could actually do that.

'What is it?' he said, and there was a touch of impatience she wasn't used to. 'You're hiding something from me.'

She looked away. Pulled out of his arms. 'There's nothing.' *Just our pregnancy*, but she didn't have the headspace for that at this moment. She had to get away. At least after today she could rule out radiation when the physicist came. She didn't care what Blanche Mackay offered her future employers – she was never returning to the outback.

The phone rang again and Douglas sent her one dark look before he turned away to answer it.

An hour later, Sienna watched the physicist climb out of the non-descript car and stifled her vague disappointment. Well, what had she expected? An all-terrain vehicle with a nuclear symbol emblazoned on the bonnet like the *Ghostbusters* sign?

The young man who walked up the path did look like a mad scientist, though. Frizzy hair, wire-framed glasses, incredibly long, thin legs and intense expression.

'Dr Wilson?'

'Sienna. Yes. Mr Stein?'

He grinned sheepishly. 'Professor Stein. Art.'

Sienna laughed. 'I'm honoured, Professor Stein – Art. Thank you for coming. Come in.' She watched him stoop to enter the police residence. Not even Douglas stooped to do that. 'Where's your Geiger counter?'

He blinked. 'I keep forgetting that's what people expect. Some of the equipment is embedded in the car. For opportunistic scanning. It's surprising what you pick up. Nothing registered as I came into town, by the way, despite a quick drive around the block before I stopped here. But I have more sensitive equipment for specific areas in my kit.'

'So you could scan somewhere like a waiting room, for example, and tell if something had contaminated it? Scan a truck or a house?'

'Easily. Did you want this house examined?'

Why? She glanced around the residence and grimaced, thinking of her secret. 'Absolutely.'

He laughed.

'So if the area had been contaminated strongly then there should be some residual markers left?'

'Of course that's dependant on the strength of the radiation emitted, but radioactive residue will embed if the source is reasonably highly radioactive. And it will last for an extended half-life. Although if a source is sealed it will not leave residue. But I don't see how something highly radioactive could get all the way out here.'

She said, 'Hopefully it didn't.' He followed her through to her office. 'So can you refresh my radiation base knowledge? I remember ionising radiation is what atoms release when they have too much energy or mass.'

'Ionising radiation causes apoptotic damage to DNA to cause genetic mutation or even sterility. However, most cell types do not manifest evidence of damage until mitosis occurs, and several divisions may ensue before actual cell death.'

Sienna looked at him. Blinked as she assimilated. At least he hadn't gone into the DNA.

'Although some radiation can travel large distances, it can be stopped by a barrier. Like starlight can be stopped by a piece of paper. And like light, ionising radiation travels in straight lines until absorbed or deflected. Which is why we use different absorbing methods for different radiations.'

Sienna asked the real question, 'So is it possible some form of radiation has been transported here, accidentally?'

'Our record is pristine,' he said carefully. 'There's been no transport incident in the movement of ANSTO's materials with significant radiological consequences.'

Sienna raised a sardonic brow. 'That's a mouthful. Did you practise that?' He just looked at her. 'So a rare chance?' she prompted him.

He conceded and began to, she suspected, recite, 'ANSTO sends around two thousand packages per month of radioisotopes for medical and industrial uses to destinations around Australia and overseas. Strict international regulations govern the transport of radioactive material to ensure the safety of the public and the environment. The transport of radioactive materials gains significant media and public attention. We maintain robust safety methods.'

And that was all she was going to get from that. But she understood. It was a bit like talking to her ex-boss: CYA was important. Cover Your A.

Sienna shrugged. 'Well, let's get started. My main area of suspicion is the health centre here, it's back up the road past the hotel.' Then she remembered. 'You won't be able to check the pub because that burned down yesterday.'

He frowned. 'Not a good year for the town.'

'I don't think it's sunk in yet. Were you booked to stay there? I'm not even sure if there's accommodation around for you. But I can check with Alma.'

'I'll probably do what I need this afternoon anyway and then I have to be up in Longreach to put the car back on the train for Brisbane tomorrow morning.'

'So you made a special trip out here?'

He nodded seriously. 'We listen when people think there might be an unsafe "source". Safe transport and accountability is our motto, even though toxic chemicals and explosives are transported way more and cause more damage.' He shrugged. 'Bad press-wise, it's radioactive matter that attracts the media and public attention. We try very hard to avoid giving anyone anything to complain about.'

He glanced around the house. 'Right, I'll get some equipment out of the car and have a quick scan of this house and the office next door then go up to the health centre.'

Five minutes later Sienna watched as Art ran the hand-sized gadget, again disappointing in its size and simplicity, over the house and next door at the police station. Douglas had left to join the hunt for Jacob, so she let Art roam the police station at will before he reappeared for directions to the clinic.

Sienna rang the hospital in Brisbane where Eve had been transferred and spoke to the consultant obstetrician looking after her. Dr Bentley, known to Sienna and the doctor she would have suggested Eve see, allowed her to feel confident that the care provided would be excellent. He explained about the toxicologist's opinion that both Eve and baby should have no lasting effects. The dose of venom had been traceable but small and the first aid excellent at the scene. Sienna had meant to ask about that.

Then she spoke to Eve in her private room.

'Hello? Eve here.'

Hearing her voice made Sienna appreciate how much she had been suppressing the concern. 'Eve. My god. How are you?'

'Sienna? I'm fine, everything's fine. And no, thank goodness, the baby hasn't shown any signs of distress.'

Her sister's voice held volumes of intense relief and Sienna felt the prickle of tears as she absorbed the fear and strain Eve had been under.

Poor Eve. This was so her fault. She blinked the scratchiness away and cleared her throat, heartily sick of turning into an emotional sot at the smallest thing, though having your sister bitten by the third-most venomous snake in the world, because you'd exposed her to a psycho stalker, wasn't small. But seriously, these pregnancy hormones could quite possibly drive her senseless.

'That's what your O&G said.' She put so much effort into hiding her distress her voice came out flat.

Eve gave a small, poignant laugh. 'I should have known you'd go straight to the top.'

Eve probably thought she'd sounded unconcerned when she was far from it. To hell with hiding that she felt bad. 'I'm so sorry, Eve. I should never have asked you to take Maddy.'

'Stop it.' Eve's exclamation sounded incredulous. 'It's not your fault. And Madison was an absolute champion. She knew exactly what to do and was as calm as a paramedic as she did all the right things. That girl is amazing. She should be a nurse.'

Relief seeped into her and she almost felt faint with it. 'I know. But it's been such a disaster. Blanche is having her flown back here today. With Jacob on the run we think it's safe to bring her back to Spinifex. Alma needs her and I think wants her input on a long-term solution involving them moving together some-where safe.'

Eve broke in. 'You keep saying Alma. Who's Alma? Have you got a friend there I didn't know about?'

'Alma is the publican. I told you about her.'

Eve made a strange huff of suppressed laughter. 'Oh. The pub-lican. Sorry, I forgot. Maddy mentioned her, too. I didn't realise you'd become friends.'

Sienna paused. Was she Alma's friend? She didn't have friends. It was too much to think about now. 'Maddy's boyfriend, Jacob, burned down her pub and I think she wants to start fresh some-where else and take Maddy and the baby with her.'

There was silence until Eve said, 'So he *would* have burned down the homestead. I'd hoped it was said just to scare us.'

Guilt tightened Sienna's throat. 'I'm so sorry, Eve.'

'It's just so unexpected. If I was still in Brisbane it would be a shock but not unheard of for some psycho to threaten others, but out at Diamond Lake?'

Sienna could imagine her sister shaking her head sadly at the fact that everything would change from now on. Would they ever find the same feeling of safety and permanence that had mantled the historic station? Sienna felt a fierce anger at Jacob for his arro-gant destruction of other people's peace of mind.

Then Eve went on and confirmed her worst suspicions. 'It's sad when someone like that comes along and ruins the rose-coloured glasses I've grown since I've been here.'

'That's not true.' She didn't want it to be true. Tried to con-vince herself as well as her sister. 'You've always had rose-coloured glasses and you always will. Lex will make adjustments and put in safeguards, and maybe something good will come out of the near miss. I'm just sorry I blithely went along thinking I could fix Madison's problems by sending her to my midwife sister.'

'Stop it.' Eve's voice had firmed. 'I will never regret meeting Maddy and Bridget. It's been too long since I could interact with new mums and babies and it was lovely. It's not Maddy's fault, or your fault that there was a bomb about to go off in the shape of Maddy's boyfriend.'

Eve sounded tired and Sienna needed to stop indulging herself by trying to offload her guilt. Eve had had an enormous shock. 'Yes, well. Been a wake-up call for me. I'll certainly take a bit more time when I find a woman with DV issues in my rooms next time.'

Eve's voice drifted gently down the line as if she could see the creases of concern across Sienna's face. 'I know.'

Sienna said quietly, 'I saw Maddy's bruises. Made me feel far too guilty for hating our father so much when the worst he did was go back to the woman he loved.'

'Who are you?' Eve didn't say anything else for a moment and the pretend shock in her voice made Sienna smile for the first time in a while. 'What have you done with my sister?'

She feigned a laugh past the thickness in her throat. 'Just don't tell that half-sister of ours. I'd hate to ruin my reputation. Anyway, I'm so relieved you and baby are okay. And thank you for what you did for Maddy.'

As Sienna ended the call she looked up at the sound of someone at the door. The physicist had returned. Now to switch off the stupid emotions and get back to being herself. She turned away from him for a moment and put her hand to her forehead and breathed in sharply. Right. She turned back and walked to the screen door to open it. 'Come in, Art. So, a wasted trip for you?'

'Not quite.' His face looked too serious for Sienna's peace of mind.

'I've just had a call.' He came in and consulted his notes. 'We think there's been a lost source. We also think Spinifex may have been exposed.' He looked around to make sure nobody else was listening. 'Among the less common materials used for bore-hole logging is Californium-252, which surprised me as a physicist, as it is really nasty stuff. It's produced in only two reactors in the world, in the USA and Russia, and is so intense as a neutron emitter it's used to initiate nuclear fission reactors. Cf-252 sources are used for bore-hole logging, soil moisture testing, gold/silver detection and metal crack imaging/testing like aircraft wings.' He paused. 'Regen just rang. He's been alerted to a possible source that has been located unshielded. Had been lost. There was a very fast check of the transporting log books. It appears the vehicle carrying it broke down in Spinifex and spent the night and next day here. On the twenty-seventh of October last year.'

Sienna knew that date. That was the date when Annette's baby was fifteen weeks' gestation. Her heart sank. 'Could that have caused the cluster?'

Art nodded grimly. 'According to nuclear data that we've cross-checked from several sources, a capsule with ten milligrams of Cf-252 would have a neutron dose equivalent rate of around two hundred and fifty mSv/hr from one metre. That's a really hazardous radiation level and you would have to store it in a very large shielded container when not used.'

He went on, 'For some reason it was out of the protective shield, and basically, pregnant women three to four metres away could also receive two to three hundred mSv over five to six hours from a source like this, and the likelihood of foetal damage would certainly be significant. They have no idea why it wasn't replaced in the shielded container after use. Or how it turned up in Spinifex. The only positive note I can give is to assure you it has gone now and the company will be heavily investigated and very expensively made to pay for their mistakes.'

Sienna's head was spinning. It really had been a radioactive contamination. A disastrous one. Her mind darted to the consequences. 'What about ongoing effects to the women exposed? Leukaemias, cancers, future pregnancies?'

'We don't think the problems will be ongoing. But they are sending out a consultant physician who specialises in such incidents. She's from the US, visiting and keen to fly in to the Spinifex zone. She'll be able to answer your questions. That's out of my specialised area. Is Sergeant McCabe around?'

'Oh?' Her pulse jumped. Spinifex had its own zone? Her hand went instinctively to her stomach. 'Is there still risk of radioactive exposure now?'

He shook his head decisively. 'No. Not dangerous now. The sergeant?'

Relief flooded her and she'd think about that later, too. She replayed his repeated question in her head. 'No. Sergeant McCabe. I'm sorry. I'm not sure when he'll be back. But I can give you his work mobile number.'

'I'd appreciate that. There are residual readings, so when it did pass through the area, the source caused contamination.'

'But you're sure the source is gone now?'

'I do. They've found it. The amount of residual radiation in the health centre is not enough to cause any problems at this point.' He scratched his neck and his concern was palpable. 'Until now it was supposition, because it's happened before overseas and usually in less developed countries, that some form of source became mixed up and lost.'

'You mean like the fracking rod Regan mentioned to me from the US?'

He nodded glumly. 'This is bigger than that. And it was "parked" for an extended time outside your health centre. Say twenty-four hours.' He lowered his voice. 'This is a first for us and the situation will be dealt with comprehensively. Families will be given full disclosure, be fully compensated, and every assistance given, but I must stress this needs to be handled carefully.'

'Of course.' She was glad for the families if their financial burden would be lifted, but shuddered at the thought of the possible headlines and hysteria. 'I can't imagine the press would be good.'

He glanced back at the street behind him. 'The town is safe now, so we're not delaying information on possible danger.' He sighed. 'Radiation breaches are extremely rare and the public leans towards panic.' A tinge of bitterness laced his voice. It surprised her, but she did understand his passion for his field.

He went on. 'The public wonder about the health of the truck driver if an explosive truck turns over, or even if toxic chemicals spill and damage the environment. Yet anything to do with radiation sends them into a frenzy. It's my job to make sure a speedy recovery and level approach to the facts are followed.'

The slightly nutty professor had disappeared. Instead, a man who knew his stuff stood before her, one who could be decisive and didn't fudge the hard questions, and Sienna found herself impressed. 'So enough radiation could have been leaked at the most dangerous gestation for the three women involved? Enough to cause a genetic deviation?'

He sighed again. 'Yes. But I will make sure someone with more expertise in that area discusses the ramifications with you. She should arrive tomorrow. Several people will arrive tomorrow. We run a very safe industry and we don't hide things, Dr Wilson. There will be a full-scale inquiry and you and the public will be privy to the results.' He glanced at his watch. 'I need to make more phone calls and would prefer a landline.'

'Use the phone in my office. I'll find Douglas's number for you.'

He nodded and followed the direction of her finger with his head but didn't move. 'I'll wait for the number.'

She raised her brows. 'I'll just get my phone,' she said, and left him to locate it. On the way, she found Alma in the kitchen checking out Douglas's fridge and cupboards for what she could cook.

'How are you, Alma?' she said and wondered how much the ex-publican had heard.

'I guess I have less worries than that young man out there.' She winked. 'Mum's the word.'

Sienna pretended to frown at her, but relief that the older lady was recovering made her smile. 'That was a terrible pun, Alma.'

She shrugged and finally settled for eggs. 'Can't help myself. Too long in an outback pub.'

'I'll be back,' Sienna said and carried her phone through to Art. She flicked through the address book until she had Douglas's police mobile number that she carried for emergencies, and gave it to the scientist, who wrote it down. He thanked her and disappeared into the office and shut the door.

It was not her usual situation, being on the outside of her office door. She stared at it with residual horror. Blanche was coming today with Maddy, so she could let her know about the radiation. Maybe she could wrap all this up tomorrow? The thought made her step lighten. This had been a very strange assignment and Blanche had better cough up the donation to Sydney Central, because Sienna's life had changed forever and the name Spinifex would mean more than a prickly bush forevermore. Someone else would take over for the families.

This town had been busily undermining her self-confidence dreadfully. She shrugged, vaguely surprised she could be calm, and went back to Alma and the sound of spluttering eggs.

'You don't have to cook for me here, Alma.'

'Need to.' Her wizened face grimaced. 'I'd go mad if I don't have something to do,' she said as if it were a known fact she had no control over.

Sienna noted the bent head. The sigh. 'I'm so sorry you lost your lovely hotel, Alma. Jacob must have been insane.'

Alma looked as though she were going to spit. 'Or just that kind of man. They're insane alright. Men who think they own women. Insane with a clarity of purpose. He probably thought I was hiding Maddy in there and wouldn't let him see her. That's how they think. If he burned the pub she'd have to come out and he'd be back in control. Probably hung around to see when she came out and when she didn't he snuck away.'

'So do you think he was still there somewhere, watching? While it burned to the ground?'

'Probably. To gloat. That's how they think. Like they own you.'

Sienna felt indignation even if Alma seemed to miss the connection. 'Well, you certainly were caught in the middle of it all. Lost everything.'

Alma gave a sad shrug as she buttered the toast. 'Today I'm a little more philosophical. Might be my destiny. My chance to help.' Strangely, no bitterness could be heard in her voice. Sienna felt infuriated for the woman. She'd lost everything except the clothes she stood in.

Which reminded her. 'People have been dropping off small gifts for you while you slept. I put them over there.' She pointed to a corner of the kitchen where a small suitcase sat with some brown paper bags on top. 'Sets of clothes. Shoes. Bathroom necessities. And that suitcase.'

'There you go. I'll be fine.'

Sienna swallowed the lump in her throat. A battler battles. The bookie's cap had resumed stance, found jammed into the pocket of the apron she'd been wearing when Douglas had rescued her. A faint tinge of embedded smoke drifted off it. Sienna reminded herself that Alma had barely escaped with her life. And she remembered her sister's words. Alma had become her friend and friends helped each other. Like sisters did. Something she'd only learned recently. She would be Alma's friend.

This last twenty-four hours had been a huge world-altering event for someone who wasn't young. 'What will you do, Alma?'

Chapter Forty-one

Alma

Alma squinted up at Sienna. Saw the concern and softened her tone because she could see that the doctor didn't understand. Bricks and mortar, and even beautiful staircases, were nothing. Not when your heart had been broken in the worst possible way by your own stupidity.

She sighed and blocked out the picture that had haunted her ten thousand times. 'I will rebuild the pub. Insurance will pay for that and the town needs a pub, I wouldn't leave them without it, but I'll get someone else to make the decisions on the building and once that's done, someone else can run it. I've had enough.'

'You'd leave?' Sienna even looked startled. Which was funny when Alma knew how much Sienna struggled to understand why Douglas wanted to live here. 'What will you do?'

What would she do? Did Sienna expect her to shrivel up and die without the pub? She knew what she wanted to do. What somebody needed to do. What could have helped her all those years ago. For the first time in years and years she had a real purpose, not just an occupation. If she had the good fortune, the chance, to follow that path she'd do a good job.

'I'm gonna find myself a nice beach, I've had enough of the dust and drought, and the heat. This new place will have all the mod cons, and I'll settle there. I've a decent nest egg. Had a couple of good wins on the GGs and I invested. If things go the way I hope, if she'll come, I'd like Maddy and the baby to live with me. Get her some education that she can use for work. Until she finds herself a real man. One who treats her like she should be treated. Or even if she wants to be a single mum.'

Alma's dream expanded as she thought more about it. 'Maybe she could do some study and I could mind the baby while she decided what to do with that brain of hers. Even if it's a correspondence course she wants to do at first. I can be the family support she hasn't had since her mother died. That girl needs a champion. Make something good out of something that happened to me that's been eating at me for years.'

Alma bowed her head and felt that deep well of sadness shrinking her soul again like it always did when she thought of her Pearl. But this time, maybe, she could change history if she could find a place of safety for young Maddy and her young'un; there lay a tiny glimmer of hope for the future. Clear as if it was yesterday, she remembered her own baby's sweet sunbeam smile.

Something touched her. She lifted her head from her hands and realised that Sienna had moved to stand beside her, had put her cool hand out to rest on her arm. Long white fingers against the brown of her own wrinkled skin. She could feel the empathy from someone she hadn't expected it from, not pity, thank God, she'd given herself enough of that over the years, but honest understanding from someone she hadn't predicted had it in her.

'Tell me what makes you so sad, Alma?'

Alma sniffed. 'It's a tragic story from too long ago. You don't need to hear it.'

She saw Sienna glance through into the hall, where the door stayed shut to her office. 'Who knows how long he'll be in there.' She pretended to shrug. 'I can't do anything else until I have my office back.'

'Kill the time with my tragedy, eh?' She tried to smile, to make it all seem as if it were nothing this woman needed to put her big brain to. But it didn't work. She saw a bit of the terrier Blanche Mackay had described in Sienna when she'd told Alma to look after her. The one who would find out why the babies had been born that way.

Sienna said, 'Not killing time. Just saying that you are the most important person to listen to at this moment.'

Alma heard the emphasis on the 'you' and couldn't remember the last time someone had said she was the important one.

Sienna went on, 'Everything else can wait. Tell me, Alma.'

Alma tried to speak, but someone had stolen her voice. Her thick throat just wouldn't let any words through.

Maybe the doctor understood because she said, 'I'm barred from my desk until Art the professor gets through his calls, so how about we have a cup of tea with those eggs and then you tell me.'

Alma swallowed and studied the bewildering kindness in the woman's eyes for a moment, and saw with surprise how much Sienna did want to know what lay in Alma's past that made her so sad. Maybe she could tell her. She was a doctor, wasn't she? Guess she heard lots of things behind those consulting-room doors.

For good measure Sienna said, 'Please.'

Humph. 'Out with the dirty laundry, you reckon,' she said almost under her breath, but the doctor heard and nodded. Maybe it was time. She'd stewed on it for thirty years. Had never even told her friend Shirl about Pearl. Just that she'd run away from a violent man.

'You make the tea, then,' Alma said and Sienna moved quickly to obey before Alma changed her mind. Fastest she'd ever seen her move. *Double Humph*.

After the eggs on toast, which tasted like some of those mine tailings you'd see outside a prospector's site because food soured when she thought of him, Alma tried to put off the moment. She poked at the eggs she didn't want, not knowing if she had the energy to tell her story as she set down her knife and fork and sat back.

Sienna poured her a strong tea, jiggling the pot up and down until it was black like the tar on the road. Just how Alma liked it. Funny, she hadn't realised Sienna had noticed that with the few times they'd shared a pot in the pub.

She'd always given Sienna hers first – city people usually liked it weak – but she hadn't realised that the doctor had cared enough to wonder how Alma liked hers. It was that tiny human acknowledgement that allowed her the decision to share. Though she didn't make a move to touch the cup.

She sighed. 'I married a man like young Maddy's man, once. A long time ago. Thought he was the ant's pants until I found out how wrong I was. The pretty ones seem to have a head start because you think you're so lucky to get them until it's too late. And living like that you never forget how it was.'

She shook her head. 'I used to wear long shirts and long trousers to hide the bruises. Maddy's never told me, but I was gonna ask soon.' Alma remembered the silent winces, the stiffness and pain. 'You never see it on the face with those smiling mean ones.'

'I've seen the bruises,' Sienna said very quietly, and Alma felt her anger rise like one of those hot springs did at the artesian bore pools. She knew it! Bubbling, hot, stinking with rage. She should have asked.

Alma shook her head again. 'I've been watching her. I think it's been getting worse. I've been waiting for her to tell me – so I could help. I waited too long, didn't I?' she said, looking up.

'She didn't ask,' Sienna said.

Comfort words. That's what they were. Alma knew. She'd waited too long. 'I shoulda asked. I know how hard it is to ask for help. How they twist your mind and kill your free thought. How useless and powerless and,' she paused and searched for the word, grimaced when she found it, 'guilty you feel that they have to punish you because you can't seem to get anything right.'

She saw the wince on Sienna's face and laughed bitterly. But that wasn't the worst. 'The worst,' she paused. Swallowed the lump that seemed to sit in her chest like a piece of that rubble from the hotel up the street she used to call home. 'Was I had a baby to him.'

'A baby? You have a son or daughter?' Sienna's voice drifted softly across the table, when Alma's breath hitched and she stopped talking.

Alma could see her baby in her dreams every night. Hear her if she listened real hard to the wind as she lay alone in her bed in the dark. Smell her baby scent every time she used that sunlight laundry soap. 'A daughter. Pearl.'

'Where is she now?' Sienna's voice was hesitant. As if she suspected what was coming. The cruellest thing was Alma knew what was coming and her throat creaked like a rusty hinge with the untold secrets from so many years ago. Nothing hurt as much as when you'd held the still warm yet lifeless body of your baby daughter in your arms.

'She was buried in a pauper's grave out west of Wilcannia.' The words lay on the table cold and congealed, like the remains of Alma's eggs. It was enough to make you want to puke. She glanced up at a sound. It looked like the doctor wanted to as well. She had her hand over her mouth and her pretty blue eyes were wide with distress.

Sienna drew in a breath. 'Oh Alma. I'm so sorry. What happened?'

Alma lifted her chin. Remembered. 'She was a beautiful baby.'

Sienna was nodding. 'I have no doubt. How did you lose her?'

Yes. She had lost her. Lost her to stupidity and cowardice. The memories were as stark and real as they had ever been. She could feel the heat from the afternoon. The dry furnace heat of a Wilcannia summer. His temper had been fraying all day with the heat. And the beer that he'd wanted and they couldn't afford. She'd fed Pearl again, to stop her fretting, him saying *Shut her up or I'll shut her up*, and that had been the first time Alma had thought of leaving.

Her voice came thin and distant. Like someone else's voice,

not her own. 'She'd gone to sleep, her angelic face pink with the temperature in the house.' She looked up at Sienna fiercely. 'I remember tucking that thin sheet around her, to stop her moving and waking herself in the cot, but no blanket on top so she wouldn't get too hot.'

Sienna nodded. Then she looked through Sienna to the pain beyond. 'I left her with him when I shouldn't have. Hung out the washing after tucking her into bed, and she "fell" onto her head so forcefully she died.'

Sienna's teacup clattered back onto the saucer and the noise made them both jump. Sienna put one hand on her throat and the other hand over the top of the cup to stop it rattling. 'Oh, Alma.'

Alma's voice seemed to drift from a long way away. So long ago, though it was as if it had happened yesterday, the remembered grief so raw and etched with the bitterness of her own stupidity. Alma blinked away the sting.

She lifted her head again, refocusing on the room for a moment. 'I waited so long to have a baby.' Her voice croaked and she cleared her throat. 'He always said wait. One day. I thought her birth would change him. Help our relationship. Make us a proper family.' She shrugged. 'Maybe he was afraid of what would happen.' She clenched her fists. 'I should have left him before the birth. Or hidden my baby like Maddy did.' Her face screwed up with that vicious bitterness against herself. Against her timidity. 'I was too much of a coward and it cost my child's life.'

This time Sienna's voice snapped with authority. 'You are not a coward. He was a monster. Did they charge him?'

Alma sighed. Charging him wouldn't bring back her Pearl. Her skin had been so beautiful. Like a pearl. That was why Alma had named her that. 'No. They never could prove he did it. He said I left her on the change table when I knew I'd tucked her into her crib. It was my word against his. But I always tucked her away from him. The town believed him. I never judged anyone else after that. People don't always get the truth right.'

Alma turned her wrinkled cheek to hide the tears and looked into the empty hallway, seeing another time. Another house in another place. A tragedy too long ago.

She drew in a shuddering breath. Lifted her chin. Sought Sienna's eyes until she could look right into them. 'Did you know women are most likely to be attacked in a domestic violence situation when they're pregnant?'

Sienna nodded. 'I've read that but I didn't "know" it until now.'

Alma took a shaky sip of her tea, almost spilling the contents of the cup. 'So you see, if I could help Maddy be free of that man, and she can keep her baby safe, my Pearl would not have died in vain.'

Chapter Forty-two

Sienna

Sienna sat back, the air knocked out of her by Alma's tale. Sienna had always prided herself on her intellect. Her ability to stand on her own feet and grow her career, achieve new goals and be the savvy, consultant obstetrician that hospitals vied for.

She'd had it easy and it tasted bitter in her mouth at this moment. She looked across at Alma and didn't see the tiny wizened firecracker she'd first seen. After today, she'd see a woman who had suffered, been beaten and the victim of the cruellest crime in the world, the malicious death of her infant daughter, and yet this woman had survived!

Sienna wasn't sure she would have survived all that. Hell, she'd bitched and moaned about her parents not living together, but at least they'd both loved her. And now Douglas. She'd complained about falling for a man who didn't want to live where she lived, and whined about an unexpected pregnancy. It was pathetic really.

Not only had Alma suffered the most devastating loss a mother could suffer, the man responsible had shifted the blame to her, had never been punished by the law, and she'd had to live with that.

Yet, she'd also lifted herself away from the tragedy, had started a new life, until she'd come from being reliant on a monster to owning her own hotel in an outback town.

Yesterday crashed back. Of course, now, it had all been taken away from her by another violent man and she'd almost lost her life at the same time. No wonder she'd said she almost wished Douglas hadn't saved her.

Yet, Sienna could see how now, Alma's focus sat firmly in helping Maddy. Cynically, Sienna could only wonder if Alma should run as fast as she could away from the chance of being associated with another violent man. Jacob might go to jail, but he'd get out someday and Alma could be embroiled in heartbreak all over again. That thought didn't bear thinking about.

She glanced at the clock. Art had still not appeared, and Sienna took a sip of her own tea to ease the ache of thick emotion in her throat as she swallowed. *Oh, Alma.* And to think that Maddy had been travelling down that same perilous road clutching her pregnant belly silently in fear.

And Eve, her good-to-everyone sister, praying her baby wouldn't be affected by the bloody snake bite. And the three mothers of the babies living for the rest of their lives with the effects of a misplaced source of radiation. So tragically unfair. All of it.

Sienna sat, aware of her own pregnancy, one she had lamented as it grew within her, and squirmed with shame that she hadn't cherished the gift she'd created with a man she finally admitted she loved, probably from the first moment.

Guess she'd have to figure out how to make her blessings work.

Chapter Forty-three

Maddy

The excitement of Madison's first flight in a helicopter from Diamond Lake to Spinifex plummeted as they flew over the ruins of the pub before they landed. Thin tendrils of blue smoke still drifted from the charred rubble and a hollow horror sat like a stone in Maddy's chest as they landed.

An hour later she walked with Alma to the site of the devastation and she wished she'd brought her daughter with her to hug instead of leaving her with Lily at the police residence. She could have done with the warmth of that small body and the comfort she gave. 'I'm so sorry about your hotel, Alma.'

They stood looking at the scorched remains, breathing in acrid residues of smoke and visual reality of the tangled wreckage, and the whole scene made Maddy's throat close. If Alma hadn't befriended her this would never have happened.

Alma sighed. 'It's done. Sad but true and not the end of the world. She was a great lady, but she's great piles of rubble now.' She stared at the burnt and buckled remnants of the once-grand stairway. 'I did love those stairs and that beautiful banister. Real shiny it was. Never did slide down it. I should have.'

There was no shine to what was left of the banister now. Through her sadness, Maddy felt the flicker of a smile rise fleetingly at the mental image of Alma flying down the sweep of mahogany with her peaked bookie's cap on.

'I'd have liked to see that. Maybe I could have tried it, too.'

Alma straightened her cap. 'Well. Next time we see one we'll just have to do it.'

'You're on,' Maddy said, and wanted to hug the old lady but wasn't sure if she could. She settled for a small sympathetic pat of Alma's arm.

They stared for another moment at the blackened wood that lay where once walls and the grand staircase has resided. A few hanging steps led to the gaping holes in the perilously balanced sections of remaining roof. There'd be no poking around in there until the roof had been demolished. It wouldn't even be possible for Alma to search for any of her smaller possessions, or have a final pat of Maestro.

'Let's get on.' Alma turned away first. 'Lucky I wasn't one of them women who kept her money under the mattress or I'd be broke as well.'

Maddy thought about that. About how she kept her small savings tucked in her backpack. She should open a bank account. She had a daughter now. Maybe save up for life insurance. There were so many things she had to think about.

'I really do appreciate you coming with me to the house,' Maddy said. But even with Alma's presence there was an awful tightness in her throat as Jacob's empty house came into view.

'You just pack the rest of your things and be shot of this place now that he's done a runner. He won't show his face back in Spinifex.'

As they drew closer, Maddy could feel her heart begin to thump in her chest. She really didn't want to show her face back in Spinifex either. She doubted she'd ever feel safe showing off her daughter around here. Hence the reason she'd left her with Lily and Sienna.

Alma stopped walking. 'You know I'm moving on. Gonna find a new place to live out my days. Thought I might go to the seaside.'

Maddy stopped as well and turned towards her. Alma seemed to be waiting for something. 'I think that sounds wonderful.'

'Good.' Alma nodded her head decisively. 'Want some company though and wondered if you and Bridget might like to come live with me for a while. Till you find your feet?'

It was a gruff offer. Almost an embarrassed one. Maddy couldn't believe Alma wanted her to join her. That this was a genuine offer of a new life.

Her throat prickled at the enormity of this woman's forgiveness. Maddy's association with Jacob had caused so much pain and loss for Alma. She couldn't grasp it. Dared not. 'Me? And Bee? Live with you?'

'Yeah, well. Just until you get a better offer.'

Maddy threw her arms around the old lady and hugged her fiercely, fighting back the tears. Alma would hate tears. 'If you're sure. I'm not sure why you would. But yes, please. We'd love to. Can't think of a better offer. Ever.'

Alma grunted, but Maddy could tell that she was pleased. 'Get your stuff and we'll work it out.'

Chapter Forty-four

Sienna

Sienna pulled out the typed timeline of the affected pregnancies. Looked across at Blanche, who had flown in with Maddy and her baby.

'The problem for the babies was radiation exposure. At fifteen weeks' gestation. That's the most likely cause of the microcephaly cluster in Spinifex. The company will be prosecuted and the women compensated.' Her voice came out quietly, but Sienna might have shouted it for the effect it had on Blanche. The older woman paled and put her hand on the desk to steady herself even though she was already seated.

Sienna sat with Blanche in her office and regretted the bald statements in view of the shocks she'd been exposed to in the last twenty-four hours. Of course Blanche was still upset by Eve's snake bite, rattled by Maddy's ex-boyfriend attacking her house and her daughter-in-law and granddaughter, and wanted an answer from Sienna now about something she thought she had some control over.

She gave the older woman a few seconds to recover and glanced out the window to the street. Maddy and Alma had gone to pick through the ruins of the grand old Desert Rose Hotel and then on to Jacob's empty house to start packing the rest of Maddy's things now that Jacob had been spotted briefly in Charleville. Douglas said the police were closing in.

Sienna hoped that Maddy would take up the offer she suspected Alma would be making soon. For both their sakes. Genuine affection and respect existed between the two. Something they both needed to help them heal. The obvious remaining task was to find a safe place where Jacob wouldn't locate them.

Blanche still didn't look ready to hear more despite her urgency earlier. The Mackay matriarch had chafed at the bit while the hellos, commiserations, explanations and description of events had been covered over a cup of tea, and Sienna had known she'd have to tell her the bad news. Unfortunately, it had come out too bluntly.

Blanche sat back and took a breath. 'Please explain that.'

Sienna proceeded. 'It's true. A radioactive isotope was accidentally transported in an unprotected state and unfortunately, the truck broke down outside the health centre. The mining company traced it and the log books confirm the dates as those when the women were around the fifteen-week mark of their pregnancies. It irradiated the women waiting in the medical centre before it was repaired and driven away again.'

Blanche shook her head in shock. 'How could this happen? Why wouldn't it be safely shielded? Why didn't they tell us if they parked the truck? Didn't anyone notice?'

'It doesn't look like much, apparently. It's a metal cylinder with the isotope encased, like a cigar and inside a truck. But it should have been inside a big safety cone.'

'You say they've tracked the truck and the radiation "source". You called it a "source"?'

'Inside a truck. The authorities are examining the truck now. The drivers were affected too, though they didn't know why they were sick at the time.'

'Why come through here?'

Sienna went on, reading from her notes. 'It had a mechanical problem and this was the nearest town. Then it broke down. An employee from the company came and removed the truck twenty-four hours later. Regrettably, distressingly, the radioactive source stayed with the truck, parked within ten feet of the waiting room of the health centre overnight and all of the next day while they waited for a part. The mechanical repair was carried out when the part arrived and the truck was driven away.'

It had been a perfect, horrible storm of circumstances.

'The fact that three women were pregnant at the same gestation in such an isolated town was unusual. Other pregnant women at different gestations had been allocated different antenatal clinic dates so they weren't affected.'

She looked up. She knew Blanche's empathy would be stirred again with the next information. 'Sadly, one other woman in early pregnancy was also exposed to the radiation and went on to miscarry two weeks later. Her medical records confirmed her presence in the clinic that day.'

'You have proof of all this?'

'Nobody can prove it all. Some is supposition. There's a specialist physician, one with interest in effects of radiation on reproduction, and I spoke to her this morning. She confirmed that would be the scenario for very early pregnancies. Such exposed foetuses would most likely spontaneously abort. And the ramifications of exposure at ten to fifteen weeks she also concurred with.'

Blanche winced. 'The lady who miscarried. Are you going to tell her, too?'

Sienna tapped the notes in front of her with one finger. 'Absolutely, yes. The specialist is coming tomorrow and we have appointments here for all four women between twelve and four p.m. so they can ask questions. They're committed to full explanation to all involved.'

Blanche screwed up her face in confusion. 'Why were the women sitting there for hours? Wouldn't they come and go as soon as they were seen?'

Sienna tapped another spot on her flow chart. 'That's another part of the picture. The day the women had been exposed, the flying doctor had been delayed on another call. There's a record in their log books. The affected women spent four hours sitting in the air-conditioned clinic having a lovely extended morning tea and lunch session.'

Blanche closed her eyes briefly. 'While, tragically, their unborn babies were exposed at the worst possible gestation for genetic mutation. What happens at that time in pregnancy?'

'Between twelve and fifteen weeks is when the soft cartilage in the skeletal system is becoming bone. So the skull was forming. Hence the microcephaly.'

Blanche shuddered, as if this couldn't be true. 'That's so upsetting for everybody.'

Sienna agreed. 'It is a horrible set of circumstances. But, I don't think it's a set of circumstances that will be repeated so that's at least one silver lining of recognising the cause. It's not like there's another reason we had the cluster. Though, I'm liaising with the flying doctor's antenatal and early childhood clinic to bump up the awareness campaign of cytomegalovirus and the incidence of microcephaly.'

Blanche looked punch drunk. 'I don't understand?'

'It's a long story, but cytomegalovirus, or CMV, is another rare cause of microcephaly in babies, a herpes-like virus that lies dormant in a human once it's been contracted. Now seems an opportune time to campaign while families have heightened sensitivity to preventable congenital problems in babies. So basically, extra-good hand hygiene for child-bearing women who are caring for children. I'll send you the handouts.'

'I'd like that. Do you need money for that?'

Sienna smiled at the woman. Blanche sincerely wanted to make sure families weren't at risk just because of lack of funding.

'This one will be paid for by the government,' Sienna said. 'The information is printed and already out there, we're just taking advantage of resources while we can. It's a simple, healthy precaution for decreasing exposure to the virus for pregnant women by encouraging handwashing after changing nappies or caring for children. There're studies that prove extra awareness is effective and I have support to get the info out there through RFDS.'

Blanche closed her eyes for a few seconds and then opened them. 'You've done an excellent job again, Sienna. Thank you.' She stood and glanced around. 'And I must apologise for the lack of resources you had.'

Sienna shrugged. 'I'm getting less picky in my old age.'

Blanche laughed. It was good to see.

Sienna said gently. 'Everyone I spoke to helped a lot. The families involved were very helpful. They really are the most amazing women and mothers, Blanche.'

'I know.' Blanche rung her hands. Sienna had never seen her show that much emotion before. But then Blanche had had a big day. Even she could be forgiven for being overwrought. 'It's just so heartbreaking that these babies have been affected for life.'

Sienna remembered Annette's incredibly brave comment that things happen. 'Can I share a thought with you, though it doesn't change anything, because it made me think when I heard it. One of the mothers told me life can hand you a challenge at any time, not just from birth, Blanche. Thanks to your funding, these women have found out why and they'll be well supported financially so that they can give their children the best opportunities without hardship, and further safeguards will be instituted against any company that doesn't follow stringent rules. Companies will be caught and penalised. We've identified another risk and prompted safety precautions for CMV. All because you paid to have this investigated. It's a very worthwhile thing that you've done. Thank you.'

Chapter Forty-five

Douglas phoned to say he'd return to Spinifex around four o'clock. Blanche and Lily flew away in the helicopter, and surprisingly it had been a very pleasant middle of the day as the three remaining women allowed themselves to take a breath.

Sienna observed Maddy feeding Bee, the young mum barely watching what she was doing she'd grown so confident, while she and Alma had a delightful conversation about prospective towns they could look into with a view to settle.

Sienna's mind wandered and she decided perhaps she would breastfeed, while she was on maternity leave anyway, and then she'd head back to work after six months, and reassured herself of course she'd be only too glad to have her body to herself again.

The stressful phantom in the room again was Jacob, who hadn't been sighted as expected, despite the police net spread to identify him or his car.

By ten to four, Maddy and Alma were resting in their shared room while the baby slept in the wooden crib Alma had found at the closed shop. Sienna waited nervously for the father of her child, who still didn't know her news, to arrive home.

For a man who liked to live alone, Douglas's small house brimmed to overflowing with women. Poor guy. A week ago she would have said it served him right for not letting her stay in the first place. Maybe she did need to marry him and just come for conjugal rights like Eve had laughingly suggested. This whole world out here had become even more outrageous every day and sometimes she didn't recognise herself. She could hardly remember the Sienna of a week ago. Just a week!

She thought of that night she'd phoned Douglas. Leaning back in her office chair, mistress of all she surveyed in her red shoes. Wickedly lusting after a man she realised now she was in love with. But she still had deep, unresolved doubts that their happy future together could easily work. She knew that. Douglas knew that. Unfortunately, the growing baby inside her didn't know that. So they would have to work on it.

But first, there was a lot to tell Douglas with all the official confirmation they'd had, though he'd been filled in somewhat by Art the professor. There'd been Blanche's visit, Maddy's return and Alma's disclosures. And she wanted to hear the latest on Jacob. There were so many other subjects to talk about without the important news she still had to tell him.

But it was there. Haunting her. Making her fade out in the middle of a conversation with others.

She heard his car pull up and her stomach dropped while her heart seemed to lift in her chest. She moved to the door to watch him stride up the path, tall and too observant and watching her with an investigative gleam in his eye, until she felt like one of his suspects. About to be found out. His scrutiny made her even more nervous.

'Douglas. You're back.'

He raised his brows. 'Is that a problem?'

She was so over this. 'Why would you say that?'

'You tell me?'

She turned away and led the way into the house. 'There's a lot to tell.'

'How did it go with Maddy? I heard Blanche brought her back.'

Maddy. Right. 'She was upset. Devastated really, but she'd had a rough twenty-four hours . . .' Sienna thought again of her own rough twenty-four hours and how she was going to tell Douglas. Her sentence trailed off.

When she snapped back Douglas was looking at her. She hurried into speech. 'How was your day? Any leads on Jacob?'

He was frowning at her. 'No. A dead end in Charleville. They think he's gone interstate.'

'Sorry? What did you say?'

The conversation proved so difficult to remain focused on. She saw that Douglas had crossed his arms and his mouth was firm. Dark-grey eyes narrowed on her.

'Are you okay?' His searching regard watched her with concern and she registered again how Douglas was one of the few people who really did see her, could stay unwaveringly on her frequency, find her true north like a compass needle.

She needed to tell Douglas.

She blinked. What did he say? She searched and came up with, was she alright? No. She wasn't. 'We have appointments with all the mothers concerned tomorrow, and the physician and I will finalise the report we need to submit.'

Douglas tilted his head. 'Not what I asked.'

She walked into the kitchen to put the kettle on and make a cup of tea. What she really wanted was a drink. A strong alcoholic one that she couldn't have. She also needed privacy. She needed to find a space where she could sit down without the fear of interruption. Sit and take his hand and look in his face without a whole town watching. Maybe she should ask him to take her out to the lookout again.

The idea grew. There were a few interesting clouds for Douglas and she had an agenda that she didn't know what she was going to do with. She seriously couldn't think when Alma or Maddy could walk in at any moment.

She could feel him behind her, could feel his gaze burning into her neck, which of course she must be imagining, but deep inside she wanted him to hold her, cradle her in his strong arms and tell her everything would be fine. She was pathetic.

'You've been different,' he said. 'You're weighed down with something big. I can feel it.'

She looked at him then. Looming over her protectively, those dark brows of his angled in concern, his jaw a strong, determined line to get to the bottom of what it was, his beautiful mouth, one that could firm into uncompromising but soften like satin when he tasted her. She'd dreamed about that mouth.

She tried to smile. 'How can you feel weight on my mind?'

He stepped forward and put his arms around her. Lifted her easily. Swung her so his nose rubbed against hers and put her down again. 'You do seem to weigh the same.' Then he kissed her and stroked the line on her brow with the tip of his finger. 'You're not sick, are you? You haven't got radiation poisoning?'

If someone had said to her a month ago she'd be trying to have this conversation she would have recommended anti-psychotics.

She swallowed a hysterical snort. 'Worse than that.'

She thought then that he knew, but his face didn't read that way. Not that she could read him most times. When he chose to block her out he could do it. She wasn't so sure she could do the same to him.

'What do you mean?' Concern laced his voice.

'You're right. There is something I need to talk to you about – but we can't do it here.'

He glanced at his watch and then jiggled his keys in his pocket. 'Where would you like to go?'

They sat together on the wooden sunset platform and stared at the vista in front of them stretching out like a moonscape under the streak of clouds.

'Cirrostratus,' Douglas said. 'Where a large region of warmer air pushes against colder air. The warmer air gently rises en masse over the colder air.'

'I wish the colder air would come down here,' Sienna said. The heat made it sticky, but there was a warm breeze that helped. Douglas had said it wouldn't storm and she believed him. She wished it would. It would make more sense to feel the way she did inside if a raging maelstrom surrounded her on the outside.

The silence lengthened until Douglas broke it. 'So it seems you've done what you came here for?'

'What do you mean?' She hadn't meant to get pregnant.

His brows creased. 'Found the answer again. Blanche must be pleased.' He turned his head to fully see her. 'What did you think I meant?'

'Nothing. Blanche. Yes. She is pretty horrified actually.'

He was still frowning at her. 'I can imagine. But the disaster task force seems to have everything in line for support for everyone involved. So now you're ready to go again?' He looked away. 'I'll miss you,' he said to the open plain. 'When do you leave?'

She stared at his profile, admitting it made her heart ache with sadness. 'Day after tomorrow. We'll finish too late to go tomorrow.' Then she said, half to herself, 'And I'm not driving in the dark in case I see that bloody light again.'

He sat up straighter. Turned to look at her with deep interest. 'What light?'

She shook her head. 'So much has happened. I can't believe I haven't told you. The Min Min.'

His eyes widened. He pulled his head back to focus. 'If anyone else had told me that I wouldn't believe them. So it's true.' He stared at her. 'There you go. When?'

'The day the pub burned down. Was it only yesterday? And Alma said something always happened soon after it was seen. Though I'm not sure how this can have a happy ending when her pub burned to the ground and she doesn't want to run it again.'

'What?' His brows notched together as he tried to make sense of her statements.

'Nothing. Alma's superstitions. But yes, I saw a strange light that I thought were headlights and it turned out to be some bizarre,' she shuddered, 'and I admit creepy, beam of light that I couldn't explain.'

He rubbed the back of his neck, perplexed. 'So what did you do?'

'I put pedal to the metal and left it behind.' She grimaced at that. It was so far down her list of concerns. *Maybe I imagined it.*

'Good choice.' But she suspected he could still see that whatever she had on her mind superseded something that should have been riveting.

He fixed his stern look on her. 'When are you going to tell me what's bothering you?'

'You really can tell?'

He gave a small, deep, mocking laugh, looking at her incredulously. 'You're joking, right?'

She frowned at him. 'I thought I was doing so well.'

He raised his brows, shaking his head slowly as if mystified as to how she could possibly have come to that conclusion. 'Um. No.' He took her fingers and wrapped them in his. Looked down at her small hand and squeezed gently. 'I'm a little worried actually. I'll ask you again. You're not sick, are you?'

She almost laughed, though it came out more of a wheeze. 'Sometimes, but it's rare. Your fault.'

'My fault?' He looked at her dubiously. 'I'm poisoning you?'

Her smile wobbled. 'Try again.'

His eyes questioned her, until, with dawning shock, he stared at her in confusion, then deep denial. His face was going through so many different emotions she would have laughed if there had been anything funny about it. There was NOTHING funny about this.

He sat back and her hand slid from his as his fingers loosened in shock. She felt bereft, but Douglas had paled and she heard him suck in a breath. Good grief, was he going to faint on her? The bigger they were the harder they fell.

She still couldn't believe she was having this conversation. 'My midwife sister guessed when I didn't. I thought I had radiation poisoning. I don't want to be pregnant. I'm not maternal.'

He puffed out his breath, squinting slightly at her. 'I get that. I don't agree, but I get it. Give me a minute.'

This wasn't panning out the way she'd thought it would. She'd thought Douglas would commiserate. Agree that it was a dilemma and be her sounding board about how she couldn't possibly have a child. She hadn't been sure where the conversation would go from there, but the outcome should never have been in any doubt. Had it?

He straightened slowly. Moistened his lips and she offered the water bottle she held. He took it and drank until a dusting of colour began to appear in his pale cheeks. 'How far?'

Succinct is us. "Just over twelve weeks. I've been here for almost a week now.'

From the look in his eyes, she could tell that he was seeing what they had been doing twelve weeks ago. Comprehension dawned. 'Because you were sick your contraception didn't work?'

She sighed. 'Or my brain.'

'Or mine?' he suggested quietly and took her hand back in his. Incredible how much better that made her feel, her hand in his. She sighed again and leaned against him. 'What are we going to do?'

He tilted his head towards her, raising his brows. 'What do you mean?'

'I can't have a baby!'

He winced and she played the words back. What?

'I'm not maternal,' she reminded him.

He sighed heavily. 'You?' He looked incredulous. 'I think you've told yourself you couldn't be a mother for far too long and now you believe it.'

She frowned at him. 'I won't cope.'

His eyes widened comically. 'In what way won't you cope?'

'In every way.' She could feel the frustration and anger with being trapped in this situation, with Douglas for not saying she couldn't be a mother, with herself for not being decisive when the answer wasn't rocket science. Or nuclear-powered. Sienna stood up and stamped her foot.

Douglas stood too. 'What? What won't you cope with? Being pregnant? You seem to be doing okay – now that I know what's wrong.' He went on. Ticking her doubts off on his fingers. 'Cope with a baby? You were brilliant with Bridget. You have so much more experience than a lot of new mothers with babies.'

She winced at the words 'new mother'. She'd be one of those nearly forty, 'elderly primiparas' her colleagues talked about, who seemed to get every risk factor, from gestational diabetes to pregnancy hypertension.

But Douglas hadn't finished. Not a man to leave a job half done. 'And of course you will cope with your career while being a mother. I can help.' His eyes had softened. Kept straying to her belly. 'I could do most of it if you let me.'

He stepped closer until she looked at him. 'If you include me. Because my biggest concern is that you think you won't cope with being tied to me by a child we made together?' He stared down at her. 'That particular concern of yours I don't have a way to help with if it's not what you want.'

Her wild eyes met his. 'All of those except the last one.'

She saw the brief flash of intense relief in his eyes. Then his gaze softened and he stroked her cheek. 'You know this whole thing between us could actually end well in that case. Together we would manage everything beautifully. What can I help you with?'

She brushed away those stupid tears. She was seriously going to scream if they didn't stop. 'By not blaming me if I can't do this.'

He looked at her, his eyes still soft. They both knew she'd already decided she would. 'You can do this, Sienna.'

She stamped her foot again and his mouth tilted up. 'No, I can't, Douglas. You're just like Eve.' She narrowed her gaze. 'Don't you go all gooey-eyed on me. This child will be a terror.'

'Of course it will. Can't wait. I never thought we'd get to this point. Never dreamed I would ever think of having a child. But your child? I can't think of anything I'd cherish more. I want to be a part of your life. Our child's life. Have a family with you.' Then he straightened his shoulders. 'But I want to marry you, Sienna. I'm not living as your partner.' His mouth thinned at the word. 'That's not how I roll.'

She'd known that was part of the deal. At least she understood that much of Douglas – not that she'd tell him that yet. She just avoided the question. 'It's not possible for me to survive out here. You know that.'

He threw a hand out. 'Of course I do. And I know that city hospitals need people like you to save patients. Find cures. Teach new clinicians. You're too valuable.'

She calmed a little. Looked at him. Her man in uniform. The one who made her knees weak. He'd come to the city for her? Maybe he could move to an outer city police station. They could meet halfway. They could both commute.

'You'd do that for me?'

He stared into her eyes and the love that shone back at her made everything seem possible. And not just possible but wonderful. 'I'd do a lot for you. As much as you'd let me.'

A car slowed out on the road and turned into the picnic area. Sienna glanced towards it, and wished they could have had longer to talk before they were interrupted. The car drove towards them, a dirty old four-wheel drive, and just as it began to steer away from them she looked up and saw the driver.

Douglas saw him, too. Lifted his big hand and shoved her down onto her knees, pushed himself in front of her and pulled out his gun, just as a rifle appeared from the window. As if in slow motion Douglas rocked back. The return fire from Douglas exploded at the same time.

Time slowed even more as Sienna struggled to comprehend. She saw Jacob slump over the steering wheel as the car sped, the engine high pitched as it picked up speed, then it veered out of control and headed straight for one of the two huge rocks at the exit, where it impacted with a loud sickly thump in a grinding concertina of metal. Shock filled her throat. There was no surviving that.

Douglas swayed, kept his eyes on the wreckage for a few seconds longer, until like a huge felled tree, he crumpled to his knees onto the ground beside her. Sienna gasped in horror as the reality sank in. Douglas had been shot.

Chapter Forty-six

Sienna's mouth opened and closed. One minute they were talking, almost to the stage of making plans, almost to coming to some idea of where to go, the next the world had exploded into noise, shock, horror and blood. Douglas's blood.

The hole high in his chest circled with a bright-red rosebud and then the stain began to grow, like a horrific crimson cauliflower, expanding in fast motion until his whole shirtfront was soaked with cherry-red blood. So much blood. Sienna gasped and leaned towards him.

She shook herself fiercely. She'd frozen once before and she wasn't doing it this time. Douglas's hands rose to the source of the confusion, where the bullet had left a gaping wound as it continued through his body. She touched his back and found the exit.

Then Sienna's hand came back over his, pushing it hard against the wound. Then she pushed him flat to the ground onto his back. Her brain clicked into gear. An exit wound was a good sign if the bullet hadn't hit any bones and broken up. The blood seeped faster between both their fingers. However, it didn't spurt. It was a vein not artery, then. She fumbled with her other hand, tipped out her satellite phone from her handbag onto the ground and dialled triple zero.

While she waited for the connection, she leaned against him and whispered, 'It's not your heart. It's your shoulder. Maybe one of the big veins has been nicked. Hopefully no lung. Hang in there, Douglas.'

'I'm not going anywhere,' he said, sounding clearer than she'd expected.

'See that you don't. Someone needs to look after the baby.'

He laughed, winced, coughed and the blood seeped more heavily. Sienna's level of adrenaline skyrocketed. 'Don't do that!'

The phone squarked at her. 'Emergency services. Which service do you want?'

'All three. Ambulance first. Policeman shot. Spinifex Lookout, Winton Road, Queensland. Caller Dr Sienna Wilson.' Douglas's eyes closed. 'I need to put the phone on loudspeaker and render first aid.' Which she did for what seemed like forever after she'd finished the call.

For fifteen minutes she watched Douglas's condition deteriorate. Watched the crimson flower take over his whole chest despite the pressure she applied, despite the cramps in her aching, red-soaked fingers, despite her muttered commands to stop.

It was the longest fifteen minutes of her life. She sat there as the sun cast deep, bronze shadows over the desolate plains and stratus clouds fragmented into strips of colour in the distance and it felt as though fragments of Sienna's heart broke off as well to float away and never return.

Douglas's heart rate climbed, became thready with the effort as his body tried to compensate for the loss of blood, his breathing grew more laboured, and beads of sweat appeared on his face and neck.

Oh, Douglas. To think I'm going lose you twice in two days, it's too much. Tears rolled down her face as she gently rocked his unconscious body against her breasts. She'd wasted it. Wasted the chance to wake beside Douglas for the rest of her life. Wasted the chance of sharing her world, her baby's world, with the one man who understood her.

The next hour passed in a blur of milestones. Help arrived when Douglas was only just gasping for breath. It was the firetruck, and Blue rushed out with oxygen and medical supplies. The men he'd brought lifted Douglas and finally Sienna had something to work with.

At one point, she registered Blue telling her there was nothing they could do for Jacob in the other vehicle. He'd gone through the windscreen and had probably died on impact. Then at last, there was the sound of the flying doctor aircraft overhead, along with the police helicopter landing across the carpark. Ordered mayhem followed. Paralysing fear overtook Sienna as she watched the aircraft take off with Douglas, a metallic cylinder disappearing into the evening sky. She glanced around at the milling people. The most important one had left. Spinifex and Sienna Wilson would never be the same again.

Chapter Forty-seven

For the next twenty-four hours, Sienna was glued to her satellite phone as she made her way to Brisbane, where Douglas was flown. It was the cruellest of waits, one she wasn't sure she would survive. Douglas was taken into surgery on arrival, the flying doctor having managed to keep him alive on the way. Eve rang her as soon as he was out of theatre, still in the same hospital being monitored after her snake bite. *He was okay. He was going to make it.* She kept telling herself this as she drove through the night, but none of it was any good until she could see him with her own two eyes.

When she finally arrived, she rushed across the hospital room . . . and Douglas appeared almost chirpy and she lowered herself carefully so that her forehead touched his. 'I thought I'd lost you.'

He pulled her to him, hugging her with his good arm. 'Again? You really have to give me more credit for survival.' Taking her fingers in his, he squeezed them gently. 'Thank you for driving all the way from Spinifex.'

'There is that.' So close to losing him. 'Oh, Douglas.'

He stroked her cheek. 'Everything will be fine. And, all the time I've had lying here waiting for you to arrive . . .' was that a small glare? '. . . has given me time to think. I have an idea.' Staring deeply into her eyes he said, 'Say yes, Douglas.'

'Yes, Douglas.' She'd say anything he wanted her to. So close.

'See how easy that was!' Then he kissed her and she allowed the feel of his mouth against hers to heal the edges of the fear in her heart. To allow her brain to comprehend that he was here with her, alive, and healing. And that everything will be okay when he was out of here.

A while later Douglas said, 'Look at the clouds outside.' He raised his free hand to indicate the thinning white puffs of cumulus cloud through the window to the world outside the tiny room.

'They're elongating as they pass – changing shape like every-thing has to in life. Like we will. To accommodate our lives together. I love a simple cumulus. A new shape every minute. Did I ever tell you why I love clouds?'

Sienna blinked, lifted her head from his unbandaged side and glanced up. 'No.' She hadn't asked. It had been one of those things she'd beaten herself with while she'd waited for news. How stupid she'd been telling herself all the reasons she couldn't have a permanent relationship with Douglas that she'd barely asked anything about him at all. Had been afraid to be drawn closer when she'd thought it wouldn't work between them. Good grief. He could have died and they shared genetic material and were creating a child. Yet she knew nothing about him. She needed to know more, she needed to know everything about him. 'Tell me,' she begged.

'I collect them, you know.'

Sienna blinked. He collected children?

'Clouds,' he said and shook his head. 'I admit I have never seen you scatterbrained before. It's quite amusing.'

'I'm not scatterbrained. Just multitasking. Doing everything I normally do while growing a baby.' She frowned at him. 'Anyway, you can't collect clouds.'

He laughed and winced at the discomfort. 'Sure I can. They don't require shelf space. My collection comes with me when I move.' He shrugged just one of those glorious shoulders, the other tightly bandaged, and Sienna thought of something she could collect. If he could collect clouds maybe she could collect mental images of him. She smiled to herself.

He went on. 'I have a book I record unusual clouds in and log them on the cloudcollectors.com website.'

She laughed. 'You're pulling my leg. And there's no such site.' He raised his brows, daring her to bet on it.

She faltered. 'Just in case you're not, tell me why you love clouds.'

This conversation was so far from near-fatal gunshot wounds, unexpected pregnancies, nuclear contamination, burning hotels, domestic violence and everything else they would eventually have to talk about. All things she could be very happy to be diverted from. Thank the stars for small mercies.

His voice lowered and she had to lean closer to hear. 'When we first met I told you my sister died. I didn't tell you it was on an island. The island I was born on.'

That made her eyes widen. She could feel her face stretching with astonishment. 'You, outback Jack, were born on an island?'

He nodded, amused by her disbelief. 'Lord Howe. Though they haven't had a baby born there for a few years.'

Her mind skittered around as she tried to remember where he was talking about. First she thought it somewhere in the Queensland tropics, but that was Thursday Island, it would be far too hot, and then she remembered. 'Lord Howe Island as in between Sydney and Norfolk Island? Left of New Zealand?'

He smiled. 'A lot closer to Sydney than New Zealand. A two-hour flight. It's part of the Sydney area. I grew up there.'

'On an island.' Douglas the beachcomber? She couldn't picture it.

He raised his brows at her. 'As a teen I went to boarding school in Tamworth, in the bush. I didn't fit into the school in the city. It was an agricultural school and I loved the farming community. The boys were from the stations all over New South Wales. Their parents were so down to earth and welcoming – I'm pretty sure that's why I love being out west.'

That she could believe. But how weird it was to think that Douglas wasn't born in the outback. It made her smile at the ridiculousness of it. Though two hours from Sydney sounded very promising.

'Then my sister died. Killed by a stupidly rich and careless businessman tourist in one of the few cars on the island. She died before an air ambulance could retrieve her. She and her unborn child.'

Her good mood plummeted. Of course. Lack of advanced medical facilities. She could imagine that. Pregnant women could hide how much internal blood loss they'd sustained until they tragically crashed and died. This was something she knew too well.

'You know how that can happen.' He winced in apology. 'Anyway, I've never been back since my sister . . .' Here he paused. 'Both our parents were gone, just my grandmother on the island. My sister's husband left and I went straight into the army and came away with even more desire to escape people.'

He studied the thin shreds of white cloud in the distance as if seeing a place he'd avoided for a very long time. One that suddenly looked like home. 'It's time to go back. My grandmother runs a guest house. I'm the fourth generation. Even though I don't visit I help with the expenses. There's loads of room in the main house. Despite the tourists she always says it feels empty.' He met her eyes. 'I could see a child there,' he said very quietly, 'our child. Maybe even our children.'

Two hours' flight from Sydney and no drive at the end. She could too. 'Maybe. With you.' But she couldn't see herself isolated on an island like some busty woman out of a Gaugin painting. 'I couldn't live there full time, though,' Sienna added carefully.

He patted her arm. 'You don't have to. But I will, our family will. It's a small town with three hundred and fifty residents. Tourists are capped at another four hundred. That combined population's only twice as many as Spinifex, except it has mountains and magical beaches. And the snorkelling there is as good as the barrier reef.' He smiled at her. 'And clouds. The most amazing clouds circling Mount Gower like space ships. It's a great place to bring up a child. Kids don't wear shoes to school. There are very few cars.' He looked grim. 'And I'd make sure they stayed on the speed limit. The main transport is a bicycle.'

She laughed out loud. Looked at him as if he were mad. 'I don't do bicycles.'

'You could walk everywhere, though not in your red shoes.' He grinned wickedly. 'Or I could buy you a golf cart. Paint it blue and have a light installed that shines a horse on the ground. I wonder if Ford make them? The locals would shake their heads.'

She laughed again. 'You are crazy.' But he was warming to it. She could tell.

'It's time to return, funny how things work out. Help my grand-mother at the guest house. I've been offered relief police work because I was born there. In fact, I've got a bit of a rep.'

'As a hellion?'

He looked at her. 'As a law enforcer.'

Silly her. Her moral man.

'It'll give the current bloke a chance to get away when I've recov-ered. That way I also get to make sure it's a safe place for my family.'

Another thought hit her and she frowned. 'You say they have babies there?'

'I said I was born there. Birth on the island isn't encouraged now. Help is dependent on the weather if something went wrong. So not for a few years. But it does have a lot of the small-town dif-ferences I prefer. And the weather is better than Sydney. Better than Melbourne. Better than Spinifex.'

Umm yes. 'Not hard,' she said and grimaced at the memory of molten heat shimmering across plains and vast dust-filled distances between the critically injured Douglas and help.

Lord Howe ran mostly without temperature extremes if she remembered rightly. But it was windy. 'One of my patients came from there. I seem to remember it has some ridiculous airstrip. They cancel flights all the time.'

'You could commute on most weekends. Fly out again on

324

Sunday nights. Fly-in fly-out is big now. Lots of FIFO families do it all over Australia. We could come to you on alternate weekends.'

Sienna said dryly, 'Usually, it's the man flying out to the mines, not the obstetrician.' She could imagine her boss. Her career would crash and burn. 'And if some crosswind blows up I just go to work later in the week, cancel all the appointments. Is that right?'

He shrugged lopsidedly and she couldn't help admiring his shoulders again. Another snapshot to add to her collection. What was wrong with her brain? She was besotted. She almost missed his words because she'd drifted off on a tangent.

Then he said, 'You're looking for problems.'

Her hand crept surreptitiously to her stomach and cupped the invisible mound. 'We have a problem.' He or she would expand exponentially.

He looked at her and there was that glimmer of hope again in his eyes. 'At least you've finally called it a "we" problem now.'

'It might be wee now, but it will grow.'

'I can't wait.'

'Far out, Douglas.'

He tipped her sideways until she sprawled on top of him again and took her in his arms with a new tenderness. 'I know. But together we can do this and do it well.'

'Eve said I should marry you in Spinifex and get conjugal rights when I visit.'

'Your sisters are both intelligent, caring women. As you are if you would only believe it.'

Sienna rested her head on his chest and breathed in the woodsy smell of Douglas. The only man she could possibly contemplate having a child with.

Douglas growing up on an isolated island explained a lot about his choice to work amidst remote communities. There wasn't much difference, she guessed, between isolation through empty desert or isolation across a vast ocean. Except this town had beaches and restaurants and was two hours from Sydney. It really wouldn't be a hardship to live there on her weekends off.

As if he read her thoughts he said, 'You would be unavailable for consultations. That means you have to get your weekends off. To laze on the beach and play with the children.'

Like that worked so well in Spinifex. Then she thought about his 'play with children' comment. Children? More? Good grief. Was he talking about her? 'Is there a hairdresser and a coffee shop?'

Chapter Forty-eight

One month later

Outside Sienna's bungalow on Lord Howe Island in the grey of early morning, the kentia palm leaves rustled against each other like wooden fingers in the thick tropical foliage. She was alone, of course. Freaking Douglas and his morals.

In the background, the staccato sound of the leaves melded with the thump of the surf against the reef and created soothing notes that calmed her. An island? So different to what she'd expected.

The impact of the sea infiltrated all over the island, its scent, its sound, reflecting off everything, the birds that it brought and the tides that carried flotsam. She'd discovered flotsam when she'd gone for a walk with Douglas last evening after the small commercial aircraft had swooped in over the craggy mountains, then along the white beach, to land on the tiny airstrip.

When she'd stepped out of the plane it couldn't have been more different to Spinifex. Sea birds wheeled overhead, daring her to look up, and she first heard the kentia palms clacking in the breeze. Douglas had been waiting at the white gate that led to the arrival building, his solid frame a safe harbour she couldn't wait to anchor in. His eyes met hers steadily, warm and patient, and slightly amused at the luggage she'd brought.

So, Douglas was an island man. She'd been reading about the island history at night before she went to sleep, since Douglas had gone home last month after being released from hospital. It explained so many things. And she'd learned the rest from Alma, who phoned once a week.

Douglas's sister and parents had been born and died on this island. Later Douglas would take her over to the little cemetery where all his family lay at the edge of the rain forest beneath the soaring fig trees.

She rolled over and stared at the tiny grey gecko above her bed, the pads of his toes stuck to the wall like suction caps, his bright eyes inquisitive as she thought about the coming day. She couldn't believe she was actually marrying Douglas. Or having a baby, though she had a bit more time to get used to that life-altering fact.

Her sisters had been overjoyed, on both counts, and she could hear them stirring in the bungalows on either side of her with their families. Children's voices rose, with Callie's calm tones shooshing them.

Sienna still couldn't believe that Alma and Maddy remained a part of their lives, having moved with them to the island. Such a promising part. Maddy would au pair for Douglas while studying, when Sienna went back to work after their baby was born, though she'd seen Eve and Callie smile secretly at each other when she'd said that.

What? Well, maybe she would go part-time. Of course she would. After some maternity leave.

Alma had caught her up on Spinifex news. The hotel had been demolished and the insurance company were covering the replacement. She'd contacted the young couple who were interested and the sale was being prepared so that Alma would be loaded with a retirement fund. Alma even knew about Kyeesha, the woman Sienna had seen. She'd had her surgery for ovarian cancer and would undergo a round of IV chemo every four weeks but allowed to fly home in between. And Blue's wife was so much better after her surgery.

On the island Alma had connected big time with Douglas's grandmother, Mirabelle McCabe, who couldn't believe her luck that Douglas had come home and she'd finally been inundated with family. Alma took to helping Mirabelle at the guesthouse with her usual enthusiasm, and while she couldn't buy a house on the island yet, she could work here and start to put down roots, and in a few years she could cement them. That year she'd make a tiny memorial grave for Pearl on the island and settle for ever.

The whole guesthouse shone with fresh paint and hard work. All the pretty cabins had rapidly been restored to their former glory for the wedding, apparently, by an army of helpers Douglas seemed to know intimately even though he hadn't been here for ten years. And with money she hadn't known he had.

And the church was waiting. Sienna had never thought she'd do the whole kit and caboodle of wedding dress and bridesmaids, wedding cake and eternal vows but there you go.

The lengths she'd go to so that she could officially move in with Douglas. She couldn't wait.

Epilogue

Twelve months later

It was Sienna's third weekend on call since she'd returned to work from maternity leave and it was all feeling wonderfully familiar. Tricky triplets again. Cilla's first set. Though this time they'd waited for the booked caesarean instead of jumping the gun. Sienna winced at the thought. She hated that word 'gun'.

The beam from the operating-room light followed the squirming newborn as Cilla handed the baby on towards the neonatal specialists. Sienna's clenched gut relaxed as the new consultant leaned over the screen to talk to the parents. 'Congratulations. Number three is a girl. And she's strong.'

Sienna knew Cilla's relief was hidden under her mask, and despite the fact that Sienna was only assisting, she didn't envy her that responsibility. Worrisome little things, triplets.

An hour later the repair had been completed. The babies were well, the mother wheeled out of the operating theatre on the gurney, and the father walked beside her as they moved through to recovery.

Sienna looked after them wistfully. Douglas had been there when Destiny had been born. Holding her hand. Looking at Eve for reassurance during the tumultuous birth. His eyes wide with wonder as their baby had entered the world. And they'd both been so besotted and bemused by the exquisiteness of their daughter.

She wondered if Destiny was awake on the island. Before her return, she usually had an afternoon sleep and Sienna had taken to lying down with her just because she could stare and admire her while she slept.

She pulled off her mask and gloves and unhitched the disposable gown, pulling on her high red shoes. Then she alcohol-rubbed her hands absently and followed Cilla through the theatre exit. Already Cilla was filling her ears with ideas of what they could do. Exciting times. She pulled on her high red shoes. So why was she feeling so flat?

She pushed open her office door and her secretary looked particularly pleased with herself. 'You have visitors in your office.'

Sienna's heart jumped and she quickened her pace. She was going to be disappointed if . . .

'Douglas!' She breathed his name as she closed the door softly behind her. Looked across at her magnificent husband, holding their world in his arms, the heat of his expression warming her from the toes up. Her family.

'We missed you. Thought we'd come and spend the week with you. Alma's got the home front covered.'

She stepped into his arms for a threesome hug. 'I missed you, too. Both of you. We may need to tweak this separation business. Maybe we could do alternate weeks.'

'That sounds like a plan.' And then his mouth met hers.

Acknowledgements

The Baby Doctor was always intended to be Sienna's story, but it fast became Maddy's, too, showing her battle to be strong while experiencing domestic violence. Then along came Alma's story as well, and suddenly I had these three amazing women characters.

I love these women: none perfect, all human, and all with great depth of character and resilience. I love their unlikely friendship and the way they see the unique qualities in one another, the way they are there for each other. Like strong women are.

Sienna played a minor role in *Red Sand Sunrise*, where she first conducted research for Blanche Mackay. So thank you, Sienna and Blanche, for teaming up again to solve another medical mystery.

Sienna, with her totally unsuitable attraction to outback policeman Douglas, is a delight to me (and garnered many reader letters asking for their resolution) and I had such fun helping the two of them solve their barriers to finding happiness together. I hope you enjoyed their story as much as I did.

The background idea for this book came from an Emergency Disaster Management course at my small rural hospital about managing natural and man-made disasters. The course increased my already huge respect for the emergency services in our country and the regulatory bodies who keep us safe, but the highlight for me was a fabulous presentation given by Dr Andrew Kovendy, Director of Medical Physics and Area Radiation Safety Officer. Andrew spoke about nuclear accidents, radioactive fallout and even an incident in Ciudad Juarez, Mexico where a Co-60 treatment unit was dumped in the local scrapyard, broken open, and the Co-60 pellets ended up being recycled in steel products that were shipped to the US (nearly 1000 tons in total). One truck loaded with contaminated steel mistakenly turned into the Los Alamos Scientific labs (where the first atomic bombs were developed) and set off alarms everywhere.

I realised an incident like this would be perfect in my book to direct Sienna back into Douglas's orbit. Before the day ended, I asked Dr Kovendy if I could contact him if I came up with a story that involved radiation poisoning or exposure, as I would need an expert's opinion on the viability of my currently vague ideas. To my delight he said yes, and so I want to thank Andrew for his input and enthusiasm, especially considering his own professional workload.

I imagined the setting between Red Sand and Winton, around the remote town of Boulia because I wanted to include the intriguing Min Min light, and the stark landscapes of the area suited my story. The dinosaur museum at Winton also fascinates me – though not Sienna, it seems. I enjoyed the fact that Douglas studied dinosaurs and clouds and wanted Sienna to love them too: it is amusing when a character just won't be enthused even though you want them to be.

The clouds came from a fabulous little book that I couldn't resist picking up called *The Cloud Collector's Handbook* by Gavin Pretor-Pinney, which is an official publication from The Cloud Appreciation Society. There really is a site called www.cloudcollectors.com. Since then I've been collecting clouds from home – especially around sunset – and enjoying the chase.

I would like to sincerely thank my publisher, Ali Watts, for her fabulous input that helped me order the chaos as all the ideas flowed in, and Amanda Martin, my awesome editor. Alex Nahlous, thanks again for copy-editing, and Laura Cook for proofreading.

Also, of course, Clare Forster, my wonderful, clever and classy agent who has been such a supporter in my career. Thank you, Clare.

I'd also like to thank my wonderful writer friends. This time I mention Elle Findlay, historical and contemporary writer, for being her supportive self and for introducing me to Margie Lawson. Thank you, Margie, for teaching me new self-editing skills that I love. Trish Morey for being the sounding board when I'm pulling my hair out, and for sharing a fab research trip to Lord Howe Island (for which Sienna was very grateful). The Maytoners, my far-flung writers group, because, even after ten years, you are all there in the background cheering the little wins and commiserating for the less-fun moments.

I'd like to thank my workmates – the midwives, doctors and midwifery students – for being excited for me, especially my midwifery manager, Gail, who allows me to be creative with my work roster as book deadlines approach. You are all champions and make me smile every single day.

As always, I thank my darling husband, Ian, the kindest and gentlest man I know, who in our fortieth year together has the least fun workload – me – as I push through in deadline mode several times a year. I promise no deadlines on our next holiday, darling. But I do need to write every day or I go a bit mad.

And finally, to you, my dear readers, for your lovely letters, the reviews that mean so much in the techy world of today, and for the fact that you buy my books, borrow my books and ask for my books. It is such a privilege to have you spend time in my imaginary world. Thank you, sincerely. Fiona.

Also by Fiona McArthur

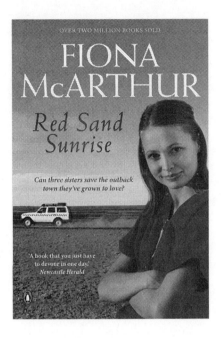

When the father she barely knew dies suddenly, midwife Eve Wilson decides she owes it to him to go to the funeral and meet her stepfamily in Red Sand. She doesn't expect to be so completely charmed by the beautiful remote township in far west Queensland – or by local station owner, Lex McKay.

After disappointment and heartbreak in Sydney, Dr Callie Wilson doesn't hesitate to move home and spend some time with her grieving mother. The chance to establish the area's first medical clinic seems a perfect opportunity, and Callie is keen to involve Eve, who she's just getting to know.

Melbourne-based obstetrician Sienna Wilson can't understand why anyone would want to bury themselves in the outback, but when her hospital sends her north to research the medical mystery affecting women in Red Sand, it seems fate is intent on bringing the three sisters together. And when disaster strikes, they must each decide if being true to themselves means being there for each other . . .

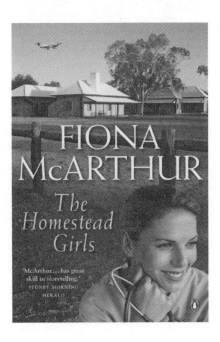

Moving to the outback to join the Flying Doctors
will change Billie's life forever.

After her teenage daughter Mia falls in with the wrong
crowd, Dr Billie Green decides it's time to return home to
far western NSW. When an opportunity to join the Flying
Doctor Service comes along, she jumps at the chance.
Flight nurse Daphne Prince and their handsome new boss,
Morgan Blake, instantly make her feel welcome.

Just out of town, grazier Soretta Byrnes has been struggling
to make ends meet and has opened her homestead to
boarders. Billie, Mia and Daphne decide to move in and are
soon joined by eccentric eighty-year-old Lorna Lamerton.

The unlikely housemates are soon offering each other
frank advice and staunch support as they tackle medical
emergencies, romantic adventures and the challenges of
growing up and getting older. But when one of their lives is
threatened, the strong friendship they have forged will face
the ultimate test . . .

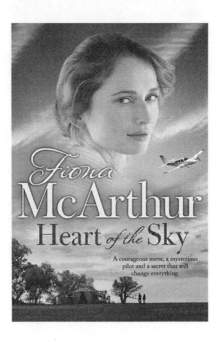

A year after a tragic accident changed her life forever, Tess Daley is in desperate need of a change. When she is offered a position with the Flying Doctor Service, she seizes the opportunity to make a fresh start. Yet once she arrives in remote Mica Ridge she feels like an outsider, unable to connect with her patients and unsure if she'll ever fit in with this outback community.

Station owner Soretta Byrnes has grown to love the company and chaos that comes with living in a house filled with boarders. So with tenants moving out and bills piling up, it's a welcome relief to have Tess and new pilot Charlie Fennes arriving in town and looking for somewhere to stay.

As they share life's triumphs and challenges, it isn't long before everyone at the station feels like family. But Charlie has yet to reveal his motive for coming to Mica Ridge and his secret will change the life of someone in the house forever . . .

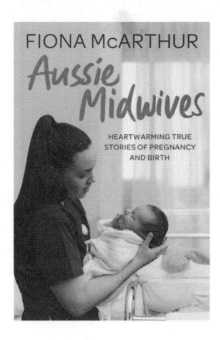

FIONA McARTHUR

Aussie Midwives

HEARTWARMING TRUE
STORIES OF PREGNANCY
AND BIRTH

'Being present as the midwife at a baby's birth is one of
life's glorious adventures.'

Nineteen Australian midwives share their incredible
stories with passionate midwife and bestselling author
Fiona McArthur.

Meet Annie, working on the tiny island of Saibai where
mothers arrive by dinghy; Kate, a clinical midwifery
consultant, who sees women with high-risk pregnancies;
Priscilla and Jillian who fly thousands of miles to get mothers
and babies to hospital safely with the Royal Flying Doctor
Service; and Louise, who gives impromptu consultations in
the aisles of the local supermarket.

Funny one minute and heartbreaking the next,
Aussie Midwives explores the joys, emotion and drama
of childbirth and the lasting effect it has on the people who
work in this extraordinary profession.

paint   Outwd

paint
milta man